The Last
ANASAZI

Written by
Shirley Welch

*Edited
and Cover Design
by James Van Treese*

Northwest Publishing Inc.
5949 South 350 West
Salt Lake City, Utah 84107
801–266–5900

*"Tis not the mentally superior who win at the last,
But the race that's nearest Nature sees
the weakness of the past"*

—*Benjamin Alfred Wetherwill
the Wetherwills of Mesa Verde*

Chapter 1

This was Anasazi country. Deep canyons, purple and tan-streaked sandstone cliffs. Blue sky with cotton-string clouds. Dry air, smelling of pinion. Heat radiating up from the earth. Hostile, vacant land. Sacred to some. Home to a few.

Eyes narrowed, a deep frown cutting a forehead, the Anasazi stood proudly, almost haughtily, at the pinnacle of the mesa. A hot breeze brushed against a young face.

Dark eyes scanned the horizon, pausing to stare. From the mesa the Indian could see miles and miles in every direction, but it was to the southwest that the figure faced. For two days the Indian had jogged along the mesa and anxiously watched the afternoon sky, looking, watching and waiting for the telltale signs of rain.

It was late July, the male rain season, when the air was hot and the rain—if it came—fell in torrential downpours, not like the gentle female rain of spring. The desert baked beneath a relentless sun. Huge white clouds had trailed behind cotton-string clouds, the forerunners gathering high in the sky in white, purple and black thunderheads. The wind picked up as

1

the heat from the earth collided with the moisture-laden clouds. Thunder rumbled as if the clouds were uncomfortable. Each day the puffs of clouds became bigger and whiter, some turning black and angry, some stretching to the heavens in great clay-shaped pillars, seemingly trying to reach the sun.

For two days now the clouds had put on their glorious display, then drifted away and it refused to rain. This day, at the horizon, the color of the clouds had changed from moonstone-white to deep dark blue and it made the Indian smile. It was a good sign—the color blue was synonymous with the Southwest, the direction in which the clouds formed. Nodding agreement with the gods, the Indian decided nature was in order—all was in harmony.

Alone on the mesa-top, the Indian scanned the land: flat terrain, miles and miles of treeless land, tan, gray and ochre-colored soil, land cut by deep arroyos. It was quiet.

Only the soft sound of whooshing as a soaring hawk cut the air, and the sound, which only an Anasazi could hear, of the sun touching the earth, made the Indian smile.

The moon of *Sho-wats* had long passed when the Indian had laboriously planted corn. So had *A-Clin* passed when the corn tassels were born. It was now the moon of *Hi-shin* when the ears of the corn began to ripen. The gods must send rain soon so the crops would come to fruition.

This day the Indian had trotted farther along the mesa-top, having left the shelter of the great cave. Inside the arched roof of the cave were houses made of stone which hung suspended in a cliff, well hidden from the view of enemies. The path across the top of the mesa to the edge was rough. No trail was visible and a heavy growth of cedar and pinion made the Indian constantly dodge and weave around obstacles. The trail wasn't flat, either. Quite the contrary; it was plagued with gulches to cross, sandstone to climb, the hillsides dotted with bothersome spruce and smaller patches of sagebrush, greasewood and rabbitbrush. No matter, the Indian jogged across scorched land, feet supple, lungs working hard, but not labored. Just the faintest aroma of the early summer flowers lingered in the air and made the day unusually impressive.

Woven yucca sandals covered the Anasazi's feet. A hand-woven cotton smock protected much of the Indian's body from the thorny vegetation common to the plateau country where the Indian called home. A necklace of sea shells adorned the Indian's neck. The shells had been traded for cotton and pinion nuts. The Anasazi had been told the shells came from a long way away, where water surrounded the earth.

Blinking, the Indian looked at the sun. The Indian was used to the July heat. The five-mile run had been only slightly strenuous for the Indian, although the heat of the earth radiated up exposed legs and felt like hot embers poking the Indian's legs. Perspiration covered the Indian in a shiny coat. Sunlight caught the moisture and the body glistened. The thought of a cooling, gentle rain did much to lighten the Indian's spirits.

Off in the far distance thunder rumbled. Smiling, the Indian nodded in agreement.

The clouds following the dying sun had grown larger and darker. The air held an ominous threat. Scanning the thunderheads, the Indian looked for streaks of white lightning.

Yes, there is one. The Indian nodded to the sky fire and waited for the answer of thunder.

Billowing thunderheads filled the sky to a dark angry shade. Wind whipped across the Indian's body. Small pebbles were kicked up and stung the Indian's legs. As the air turned heavy and depressing, crashes of thunder echoed constantly through the canyons and across the mesa. For a stagnant minute, the storm recoiled its arm. A deep silence covered the mesa.

Standing perfectly still, waiting patiently, the Indian faced the oncoming storm. No bolt of lightning caused the Indian to flinch, nor did the whips of wind cause the Indian to squint observant eyes. Although the male rains of summer evoked a terrible fury on the land, the Indian would not cower beneath the power of the storm.

Breathing deeply, as if to bring the oncoming storm into the body of the Indian, the Anasazi lifted callused palms to the sky in an offering. All was in harmony with nature, and it caused the Indian's lips to form a half-smile.

Far off in the distance lightning suddenly flashed.

The sharp resounding crack of thunder echoed off the walls of the salmon-colored buttes which protruded from the floor of the canyon like giant spears. To the Indian's right, the clouds were very dark and a wall of water fell from the heavens. The ground, voracious feeder of water, greedily gobbled up the falling rain.

The Indian stretched out both arms to the sky, speaking loudly:

"Embrace the Earth, oh mother of rain
Stretch out your fingers of water
Let all the crops be plentiful
Let all the hearts be glad."

As if answering the wail of a child, the sky responded with a dazzling bolt of lightning, followed by an earsplitting crack of thunder. The sweet smell of lightning striking the earth filled the Indian's flared nostrils. Seemingly, to appease the Indian who still stood with arms pointed to the gods and whose lips began to turn upward in a jubilant smile, the heavens opened and it rained. Drops of silver water patted on the Indian in random spots.

Soon she was drenched.

Thankful to the gods, the Anasazi woman stood in the rain, her arms pointed skyward, her heart full of joy. Her life, her world was in harmony. She talked to her gods and they answered. All around her was proof of a good life. Jubilation filled her heart as she slowly brought her arms down to her sides, allowing the rain to trickle down her fingertips where they dropped on the sandy soil and formed quicksilver spots at her feet. Rain hit her cheeks, her forehead, her thick lashes and ran over her mouth. Licking the water from her lips, she swallowed.

The gods had answered her. This was how it should be.

However, she had no idea her happiness would be short-lived. She knew not that her days of tranquillity were numbered. She was unaware of her great importance on earth. Pure and untouched by a modern world, she knew nothing of greed and selfishness. Her world was governed by the wind and rain and her gods. To this Anasazi woman, an angry July rain was an important happening in her life.

She knew nothing about the white man's ways.

She was the keeper of Willow Canyon. She was Ketl, the last Anasazi.

But soon she would learn that evil lurked in a world she didn't understand. It was coming soon, too, just like the suddenness of flashing lightning, booming thunder and torrential rainfall.

Perhaps it was a message the gods tried to give Ketl.

Perhaps it was simply destiny.

Whatever, it was coming and would change her life irrecoverably.

Chapter 2

Stiff-legged, shoulders slumped, Woody Hayes sat on the half-broken front step of the old ranch house. Where his gnarled fingers wrapped around the lip of the stair, he could feel weather-worn paint come off in his hands. For the last time, he watched the July lightning storm as it broke over the mesa in the far distance.

Brushing chips of paint off his faded work pants, he rubbed an arthritic hand over white stubble on his chin. He thought back to his younger days when he used to trek across the land he was viewing, sometimes for hours, even days at time, in wonder over nature, in awe of the ruins he found out there.

Now he was too old to do it. His knees creaked when he walked, his hips ached, and his fingers were so stiff it was difficult to button his shirt. His eyes were bad. Bright sunlight made them so sensitive he had to squint to see. If conditions were right, he could still drive, but his daughter and grandson refused to let him behind the wheel of a car ever since the danged Jeep left the road, jumped the shoulder and landed in the middle of a yucca bush. It took seven stitches to close the gap over his eye when he hit the steering wheel.

No matter how he argued, his daughter wouldn't believe the car did it all by itself. She refused to give him his keys to the Jeep or his truck. *Damn women*, Woody thought.

It wasn't so much not being able to drive that angered him, but the feeling of losing his independence which bothered him the most. The last bit of his self-reliance was going to be taken from him today; in back of him, just inside the door, were three cardboard boxes, packed with of his possessions. They were ready to be transferred to his daughter's house. Woody was moving there, too. They said he was too old to live alone, isolated from civilization at the ranch, removed from help if he needed it.

A man doesn't need very much, he thought and had adamantly argued—just a bible, a good hunting rifle and a woman who loved him. Woody possessed the bible and the rifle, but his wife of over forty years was buried beneath the sandy soil, over there by the spring, under the shade of the lone cottonwood tree.

Soon his grandson would be coming to take him away from this place. Sighing deeply, Woody looked over his shoulder at the house. He had been born inside there, so had his brothers and sisters. The house and property had belonged to his family for more than seventy-five years. Now it belonged to someone else.

Allied Oil. The company now owned Woody's home and the encompassing 2,360 acres which comprised the most ornery, dry, sandy country a man could imagine. It took thirty acres of land to raise one head of cattle from a yearling to adulthood, and the critter had better be fast stepping to find all it needed to sustain itself. Some years it didn't rain much and the cattle ended up scrawny-looking. Some years it rained so hard that the water carried away the topsoil and where grass grew that year, it didn't grow anymore. It grew someplace else. Fickle stuff, the grass, the water, the weather.

For an old man, a check for $2,000,000 didn't mean much, Woody reflected sadly. He was too old to enjoy it. Twenty years ago it would have meant something: a mobile home, a fancy fur for his wife, travel to all the parts of the country he hadn't seen and wanted to, a new home someplace where the land was a little friendlier. But now Woody felt like he was just marking time, waiting for the chariots to swoop him up and take him away from his boring, hellish life. There was no one who listened to him, no one who wanted him around, no one who would *want* to go traveling with an old coot like Woody.

Being old was worse than being young, Woody decided as he kicked at the red soil with the tip of a worn cowboy boot. An oldster was *expected* to know better about something, while a child was *taught* how to know something better. Growing old wasn't any fun, Woody knew. Yeah, his memory was poor. Yeah, he got a little grouchy now and then. Yeah, he was set in his ways. Sure, his driving wasn't the best. He just didn't want to be told how to spend the rest of his days, and it was exactly what his daughter was doing.

A plumb of dust rose from a long way away. It was all Woody could make out—the trail of dust, but he knew it was his grandson, Christopher, coming for him in his Ford Bronco.

This is it, old buddy, he said to himself, his tired eyes scanning the mesas, his heart racing. His active mind thought of all the years that had quickly passed, and he couldn't help wondering if there wasn't something out there on the mesas that he had missed. The country was so vast, so desolate: mesas, buttes, dry arroyos, land dotted with sage, cactus and pinion. Yet there had been people before Woody who had inhabited the area. All over the valley and cliffs surrounding it, Woody and his family had found evidence of ruined dwellings of ancient people. They had found fragments of oddly colored pieces of crockery with strange markings; chips of flint or obsidian; small and large arrow points; stone axes; yucca sandals.

It was well known that the Anasazi Indians roamed these parts hundreds of years ago, but it was even more intriguing to find remnants of them on the Hayes ranch. Chasing cattle out of arroyos was not a pleasurable job, but by doing it, Woody had discovered his first unexplored ruin and something even better than a ruin.

The ruin was tiny, just a one-room abode, but the thrill of discovery lasted him a lifetime. The ruin was up in a cliff which was easily reached by climbing the jagged rocks in front of it, although he found what was left of notched poles which indicated the Indians used those rather than the sheer rock. It was a small cave, the front of which had been sealed by the laying of rocks. A T-shaped door allowed access. Inside the house, Woody was amazed to find a huge mound of refuse in the back of the ruin and spent many days sifting through the rubble, trying to gain some insight into the people who had built a home in such an inhospitable place. He found a yucca sandal, corn kernels, dried beans, broken pottery and a lovely arrow with feathers on the end of it.

That was long ago. Years had passed. Other ruins had been found, some bigger, some already discovered by earlier wanderers of the Southwest who had removed whatever was loose. For Woody to come across such a ruin was most disheartening, because he felt he was getting closer to knowing something about the people who had lived there and then disappeared, but when a ruin was found empty, it gave him no further clues. Some ruins he found once and was never able to locate them again, the land being so ornery with its conditions.

Those days were long gone for Woody, and it left him feeling as though the desert was signaling to him, although he didn't know how to answer the call.

For a moment he looked directly into the sun and was blinded. He closed his eyes. The flashes of color behind his eyelids brought back memories of the summer when he had grown so fast he had developed stretch marks across his back. It was the summer when he saw the Indian. Woody had been 15. He would ride his mangy horse all over the ranch without a shirt so the sun could tan his skin and hide the stretch marks of which he was terribly embarrassed.

He'd gone way beyond the buttes, more than ten miles from the house. Following a deer trail, he let the horse wander close to the base of the mesa. A narrow opening had formed by the breaking away of a part of the immense cliff which left scattered rocks below the break and all but hid the opening from view.

He would have ignored the break in the cliff if it hadn't been for the water that flowed out of the canyon in a pretty little creek. Water was scarce in these parts, so the creek was portentous. It was a difficult job climbing around the scattered rocks below the break, and even harder leading his horse below the low outcropping of rock over his head, but Woody managed and he led his horse up the draw, back into the canyon.

At first the gorge was rocky-bottomed, then turned to sand where steep canyon walls of sandstone nearly touched and blocked out all of the sun. Beyond twists and turns of the steep walls, the canyon opened up, became wider, and along the creek bottom willows and cottonwoods grew. There the canyon sides dipped lower, not more than fifteen feet above Woody's head. The sun splashed over the cliffs and filtered through the cottonwoods.

Hot and tired, Woody slipped off his horse. Bending over the creek, he drank from his cupped hand and splashed water on his face.

Suddenly a shadow crossed his body. It happened only for

a split second, but it made Woody jump back and squint up at the sun, temporarily blinding him. The sun was about to slip behind the cliff, and rays of light shot off the cliff in fractured prisms. Something had come between him and the sun. Something was up there.

Quickly he moved to his horse and removed his Winchester from the saddle holster. Mountain lions thrived in the low desert, helping themselves to the numerous rabbits and prairie dogs. A large cat could take down a man without the man seeing or hearing it, and it made Woody's skin crawl to think about being on the ground with a two hundred-pound cat on top of him, the animal's foul breath being the last thing he would smell.

Scanning the cliff, he crept though the willows and slipped back and forth through the water. He didn't see any sign of cat—no tracks, no den, no dung. Pausing, he took in a lungful of air. No, he didn't smell cat dung.

Yet he felt something. Something strange. He had an eerie feeling that eyes were watching him. It made the hair on the back of his neck rise and his heart thud hard against the walls of his chest.

Then some premonition, some heavy feeling, some seventh sense, made him turn and glance to the opposite cliff. Nearly naked, facing the apricot sun, was an Indian. It was no flat-nosed Hopi Indian either. This was no drunken renegade off the reservation. This was a dark-skinned Indian with lustrous black hair, sinewy muscles, and stocky torso, who wore a loin cloth and leggings with feathers on the sides which fluttered in the late afternoon breeze.

It was his stance, however, which made Woody stand in awe; the Indian's back was rigid, his arms crossed over his chest, legs spread and cemented to the ground as if he were holding the cliff in place. A raw and powerful look covered his face. He stared straight ahead at the sun, then slowly turned and his look of steel fell on Woody, then went through him with a jolt.

Woody's jaw sagged open. The face was like no other face of an Indian Woody had ever seen; there was an inherent strength in his face as if he had lived many years and seen too many unhappy events, yet the Indian was young, perhaps only five years older then Woody. But his eyes, his eyes were the main thing that held Woody's attention. They weren't black like an Indian's eyes should be. No, the eyes staring at Woody were blue. Woody blinked, thinking he hadn't seen right.

Still staring at the Indian, who looked like he had walked out of the past, Woody watched, impaled to the ground by the hold the Indian had on him. Fascinated, unable to move, he watched as the Indian raised his left hand to the sky, let loose with a primal scream, turned and trotted away. Woody's knees shook. Although the Indian showed no hostile intentions, Woody found himself trembling and with a dry throat. He swallowed, still staring at the vacant cliff. When his heart had stopped jack hammering in his chest, Woody took a deep breath, tore his eyes off the cliff and scrambled on his horse. He kicked the horse hard, eager to leave the canyon.

That was the day it started, that festering need to search the desert, search and find whoever it was who had stood and looked down at him so defiantly, Woody reflected as he watched the tail of dust grow larger and closer. Being a fifteen year-old body who possessed an active imagination was one thing. Being raised out in the middle of nowhere was another thing. Seeing an Indian that Woody was sure must have been a leftover from Custer's Last Stand with Sitting Bull or, better yet, a son of the renegade Apache, Quanah Parker, was the best thing. It sparked a growing seed of inquisitiveness that lasted Woody the rest of his life.

At first, he thought it might have seen a figment of his imagination, seeing the Indian standing up on the cliff, standing so defiantly like he possessed magical power. Perhaps the hideous wail the Indian emitted was only something Woody had *wished* he had heard. He didn't want to believe the Indian could have come from one of the ruins he had found. That thought was much too scary.

When he told his mother about the Indian, she made him soak his head in the well and drink a whole glass of warm milk. She said he was daft, that by riding around under the sun without a shirt had poisoned his body.

His father said it was impossible, that any Indians around these parts were the Anasazi and they had turned their backs on the mesas close to 700 years ago.

"Maybe it was an Apache," Woody hopefully suggested.

"If an Apache were out on the mesa and he had you in his sights, he'd be swinging your scalp from his loin cloth right now," Nathaniel Hayes said to his son. "There ain't an Apache left alive who would tolerate a white man. I don't know what in the hell you saw, if anything, but it wasn't no Apache."

"It didn't look like a Hopi," Woody said, knowing too well how the Hopis looked with their flat noses and wide, black eyes.

"Weren't a Hopi, neither," Nat said firmly. "The Hopis don't move west or east of the three mesas."

Shaking off the effects of stomach-churning warm milk, Woody kicked his toe into the dusty soil. "Well," he drawled, "I seen somethin' out there and I'm gonna' find out what."

"You'll do nothing of the kind. You're getting strong enough to start helping me with more of the chores. Besides I don't need to go chasing after you when your horse goes lame. You put thoughts of the Indian out of your head. You hear me?"

Woody didn't answer, but decided his pa's words were just the challenge he needed. Tell a boy who's on the brink of manhood that he can't do something and see how fast he finds a way to do it.

All these years he had never stopped looking, yet he never again saw hide nor hair of an Indian with pale eyes and a regal stature out on the mesa. And the years had now mounted up to more than fifty. The most frustrating part of Woody's search was the fact that he never found the arroyo where he spotted the Indian.

One bend in the sandstone bluffs looked just like an other, one dry creek bed branched off into ten others, one box canyon had hundreds which could be called clones. The relentless wind changed the way the land looked; the grass grew in different places each year, depending on the wind and the rain. It was wide-open spaces out there, and try as he might he couldn't retrace his exact steps and wander into the lovely Eden-like canyon. Hours and hours were spent on horseback, on foot, camped beneath the stars with only coyote howls to keep him company.

To this day, Woody could remember the canyon. It was deep with cottonwoods and willows growing along the flat creek bottom where the soil looked extremely black and rich. Raspberries grew near the water and he remembered vividly that they were laden with fruit. Yucca and rabbitbrush grew in the dryer, higher sides of the canyon and the sandstone walls were decorated with beautiful, artistically painted water stains of black, grays and browns.

Over the years Woody did find numerous ancient Anasazi ruins. None were as magnificent as the cliff dwellings to the north in Mesa Verde or as mysterious and large as the cities in Chaco Canyon, but they were ruins, nonetheless—stone houses nesting in the shade of rock cliffs, pit houses of intricately laid stone, fragments of pottery, long ago abandoned gardens, signs of canals and reservoirs to catch the haphazard rain water. But there was no sign of present inhabitants: no Indians, no flourishing gardens of corn, beans and squash, no canyon with willows and cottonwoods growing in it.

It saddened Woody to think he would never know the answer to the mystery of *his* Indian. Staring off into the distance beyond the buttes to where the lightning had struck, he strained his eyes, as if perhaps today in these last minutes, an Indian would come toward him.

He watched as the clouds broke, and the late afternoon sun cast a path through the clouds, illuminating the moisture-rich air, creating a multicolored rainbow which arced across the entire western sky. The far-off buttes and the mesas farther beyond were framed in a band of multicolor while those same buttes came alive with pastel tints of salmon, rose and deep orange. The sight made Woody's heart light, but then his eyes became misty, his hands cold, and his shoulders sagged forward as he heard the sound of the Bronco as it pulled into the yard and the wheels crunched on the gravel. He knew he would never know his answer, nor would he again have the glorious experience of seeing the weather break over the desert.

Christopher Hayes extracted his long, lanky legs from the driver's seat of the Bronco. A tan Stetson shaded his handsome face, although clumps of blond hair refused to be dominated by the hat and poked over his ears this way and that. Rough looking cowboy boots kicked up dust as he walked over to his grandfather who was sitting like stone, staring off into the vast mesa country.

"You ready to go, Gramps?" Christopher asked as he tilted his hat back off his face.

Woody slowly looked up at his grandson. "I'll never be ready to leave this place," he replied, his stubborn streak speaking.

"Ma has your room all ready for you. She put a new recliner in the living room in front of the window just for you. She even had an air-conditioner installed."

Woody pushed himself off the step. He liked his front steps better than any recliner, and he hated air-conditioning. "She better not be gettin' ready to tell me how to go about my living," he said indignantly. "I didn't raise that child to be a bossy woman to her father."

"No one's going to boss you around, Gramps," Christopher replied, wondering how many times they had reassured Woody of that very thing.

"They better not. I'm not happy about moving into town."

"The ranch is not exactly town, Gramps."

"It's only sixty acres. You can *see* other houses. You know people are nosing around. It ain't the same."

"Nothing is ever the same. You don't own your house anymore. Allied Oil does. And you know you're getting too old to be living all by yourself. The doctor said so. Remember?"

"The doctor don't know nothin'. A man should be able to live and die where he wants. What's the difference if I drop dead tomorrow or the next day? I ain't got nothin' to keep me goin' anymore—"

"You're a rich man, Gramps. There's travel—"

"Hogwash! I can travel all I want out on the mesas and still never see it all." It wasn't exactly the whole truth. He'd love to travel, but not with Marybeth, his daughter, and Christopher wouldn't dream of going any place with his grandfather.

Rolling his fingers into tight balls, Christopher had to choke back a whole string of verbal lashings he wished he could spew out at his cantankerous grandfather, but his mother had made him promise to humor the old coot. Christopher was managing, but it was really grating on his nerves.

"Listen, Gramps, I'll be coming out here a lot. I've offered my services as guide to the geologist from the oil company. He has to survey the property lines. Besides, I'll be overseeing the cattle we have out on the mesa."

Woody's brows arched together as a frown split his brow. "Aren't you going to bring them in?"

Christopher had told him over and over exactly what the conditions of the sale of the land had entailed, but he would have to tell him once again. "No, we leased back grazing rights. Remember?" It seemed like that was all he said to his grandfather lately, *remember?* "We'll keep the stock. We'll go on raising cattle out there just as before. Oil and beef can manage together very nicely."

"Seems strange," Woody replied, but said no more, because it seemed even stranger that Christopher should be running things while Woody had nothing to do.

In a broken walk, made so by his joints being stiff and sore, Woody hobbled to the shade of the cottonwood tree where his wife was buried. For a laconic minute, he stood with his hands crossed, his head bent while memories of fifty years floated in and out of his mind. Then he turned and walked to the Bronco.

When Christopher had the motor humming and was backing away from the ramshackle house, Woody looked over his shoulder and then to his Grandson. "Remember, you said you'd bring me back out here anytime I wanted to come."

Smiling, his blues eyes lively, Christopher replied, "Anytime, Gramps."

"And don't call me *Gramps!*" Woody growled.

Christopher nodded, spun the wheel and fish-tailed out of the drive. From the mesa beyond the buttes, a wisp of dust could be seen springing up from the ground, following the vehicle, decorating the crystal clear air.

With one final look over his shoulder, Woody looked back, a spark going though his body, a thought that maybe someone out there still watched him.

Chapter 3

Woody Hayes new home was on the outskirts of Aguilar, New Mexico, some 30 miles west of Farmington. Lush meadows nourished the livestock. Ample water saw the animals through the long hot summer. There was electricity, indoor plumbing and a flock of grandchildren to entertain a grandfather. He had a freshly painted bedroom, a bathroom with brand new towels and a Sears recliner strategically placed in front of the living room window. An air-conditioner spewed cold air directly at the recliner.

While Woody poked at the recliner and grumbled about the blasted air-conditioner, some eleven hundred miles away on the western seacoast of San Francisco in an office on the eighteenth floor of the pyramid-shaped Bank America Building, Cameron January received news that made his prominent Adam's apple bob up and stay there.

"Cam," his boss, Andy Patk, said as the afternoon sun turned the bay into slivers of coppery-colored ribbons, "I hate to tell you this," which was a blatant lie, because Andy enjoyed telling the bad news to the unpardonably handsome younger geologist, "you're going to have to go to Aguilar and do the field work on the Hayes Ranch."

Nothing could have surprised Cameron more than Andy's words, and he closed his gray eyes which were haloed by long thick lashes most women would die to possess. "My whole day has been one disaster after another," he said with a long sigh. "The alternator on my BMW shut down on the Bayshore Highway in commuter traffic this morning. There I was surrounded by hundreds of angry commuters who honked at me and gave me the finger when they made it by my car. I couldn't do a damn thing about it." Cameron pointed to a plastic bag hanging in his closet. "The dry cleaner inadvertently laundered all my silk ties. They look like they went through a shredding machine. Federal Express lost the reports I sent yesterday to Dallas, and I received a polite rejection from *Oil Magazine* on that piece I did on the rebirth of wildcatters. Now this."

Andy suppressed a grin.

A wrinkled white shirt covered Cam's broad shoulders. Pushing himself up from his desk, Cam faced the floor-to-ceiling window which gave him a panoramic view of the San Francisco Bay plus a view in every direction of buildings, cement and steel. The view was partially blurred by all the cars and trucks which expelled poisonous exhaust fumes.

Cam ran his hand through his hair. "Andy, you have a way of ruining my life."

"Sorry, Cam, but a job is a job."

Cam turned, rubbed his temples with his fingers and asked, "Do you have any more enlightening information for me today? If so, I'm ordering two martinis and three Excedrins."

Inwardly Andy snickered. It wasn't that Andy was jealous of Cam. Well, perhaps a little—no, more than a little, a lot. He was everything Andy was not: handsome, single, young, virile, knowledgeable about women. Andy was gray at the temples, had a wife who had divorced him and three distant children. Andy couldn't seem to make it to first base with any woman he met, and it galled him to watch Cameron January motor down the freeway of pretty women like a well-oiled Lamborghini.

"No, that's it," Andy said, unable to hide a smile, knowing full well sending him to the desert would put a fender-wrenching crunch into his lifestyle.

Again Cam ran his fingers through thick, unruly brown hair. "Then how about telling me why I have to go? Hm? I thought Fred Davis had been assigned the field work on the Hayes ranch."

"Fred's wife just delivered a baby girl—"

"So? Can't she change diapers?"

Andy had been a family man, but he knew Cameron January was a diehard bachelor, a man who wouldn't know which end of a baby you diapered and which you fed, a man who thought of himself first, last, and forevermore. Of course the early birth hadn't been planned, but it changed the way things would be. "The baby was born two months early," he explained. "His wife hemorrhaged. He nearly lost her."

"Damn," Cam swore, flashing steely eyes at Andrew Patk. "Marriage and having kids are nothing but a pain in the ass. How do men get themselves into such irreparable situations?"

"I think it's a condition called love," Andy replied. "I would strongly recommend avoiding it."

"Yeah? Well, you can bet I will. I'm immune. It's a disease you won't find me catching."

Andy sincerely felt sorry for any woman who fell in love with Cameron, and he knew there had been quite a few. The women always did the falling in love where a man like Cameron was concerned. As he said, he was immune. He was hard as rock. His heart was made of stone. Granted, he was a fine geologist, but he had as much sensitivity as granite.

And Cam had no desire whatsoever to go to the Hayes Ranch. He'd done the work-ups on the place and knew it was a dry, semi-arid land of empty spaces. Below those spaces the chance of finding oil was very good, and it was on Cam's recommendation to Allied Oil that the land be purchased, but as Senior Geologist for Allied Oil, it shouldn't have to be Cam who did the tedious work under the broiling sun. No, it was supposed to be Fred Davis who was conveniently indisposed because of a wife and newborn daughter.

Cam pointed at Andy. "I'm allergic to sagebrush, you know."

"So take some antihistamine with you and don't sniff the sage."

"I hate the desert."

"Do you like your paycheck?"

A stagnant silence filled the room. "Yes," he admitted as he rubbed his temples again. "I just wonder why I have to go to New Mexico. Why couldn't it be the coast of Mexico for some offshore exploration? A place with sultry breezes, beaches and bikinis." He grinned, his teeth even and white contrasting sharply with his wan face. "Now, that I would *like*."

Andy had to smile, thinking of Cameron January out in the land of cloudless skies, cactus, ancient ruins and Hopi Indians.

Perhaps it will take some of the cockiness out of him, Andy thought. Then he headed for the door, turned and said, "I still don't see how you ended up being such a damn good geologist."

"When I was young, I liked rocks," Cam replied.

Probably because they were as hard as your head, Andy didn't say. "When did your hobby change to women?"

"When I found out that they were much better playthings."

Andy laughed. "If it's any help, why don't you invite your current 'plaything' to go along with you. I might make the job a little easier."

"Sharon?" Cam queried, his brows marching up his forehead. "You jest. She thinks dirt is malicious gossip, and perspiration an obscene word."

"Well, maybe you can find a squaw who has an empty hogan."

"Sure, and knowing my luck, she'll have a couple of *papooses* to go along with it."

"Knowing your luck, fellow, she'll have a spare cousin and a sister who both believe in the pleasure of your company."

"Yeah, that would be something wouldn't it?"

ް ް ް

Much Later, having argued with the mechanic at the garage about repairs on his car, after screaming his lungs out calling for a cab, after being wedged in a stale elevator with fifteen tired, ornery people, Cam lay with one arm dangling over the side of the bed, sweat encrusted and exhausted from gyrating on the bed with his long-legged girl friend. Sharon Frazier was not exhausted and ran her red nail up the naked flesh of Cameron's back, pausing and twining her fingers into the light brown curly hair at the nape of his neck. Bending over, as the white-white flesh of her small, torpedo-shaped breasts feather-touched his skin, she kissed his shoulder.

"Are you sure you have to go, darling?" she purred into his ear.

"Positive," he managed, wondering how she had the energy to talk when he was totally drained.

"But three weeks! I don't know how I'll exist without you."

He thought of telling her to get herself an oversized vibrator but thought he better not, because Sharon was very sensitive about what Cameron called her "overactive libido". She had been raised in the best private schools and polished off

her social schooling by attending the Atlanta-based finishing
school, *L'Ecole des Ingenues*, where she was dished-up instruction in fashion finesse, self-confidence, aesthetic aware-
ness, etiquette and the social graces. The erogenous zones of
the male body were not taught, nor were sexual techniques,
nor was there a class on "Staying Powers of Female Sexuality", but if there had been, Sharon would have been at the head
of the class.

He had to wonder if it only was the muscle between his
legs that she was going to miss when he went to New Mexico.

Rolling over onto his back, Cameron gazed up into the
beautiful face, and he chastised himself for the moment of
insanity when he came close to emitting a nasty remark to her.
Sharon, with her fiery blue eyes, high cheek bones, straight
nose with onionskin nostrils, heart shaped chin and full,
wonderful lips, would be the prize any man would dream
about. And there she was, plastered above Cam, ready, always
ready for more.

Brushing back long wisps of her reddish-blond hair, he
said, "The time will fly by, and the boss said you can come
down and visit me."

"To New Mexico? Aguilar? Are you crazy? Honey, I'm
not setting foot in a state that has more Indians than white
people."

"Who told you that?"

"Nobody. I just know."

Little Miss Bigot. He patted her naked, pink fanny. "There
may be Indian reservations, but beneath the ground there's oil.
Lots of it. It's going to make Allied Oil very rich, and it's going
to give me a big bonus and that means more money. A little
dirt, a little warmth, working with a few Indians, well, it'll be
worth coming back and spending it on you." He ran his hands
up her rib cage and cupped her small breasts. "I was thinking
of a new car, too."

"I'd rather you made less money and not have you gone for so long. You have everything you want, anyhow, and I have plenty of money."

Although Sharon was a model, she was more of a glorified coat rack. She was a thoroughbred woman with a lineage indecently long. Trust money piled up in accounts she used to pamper herself. Yes, she worked, did some modeling, but she didn't have to do it, not for the money, she did it just to have herself seen by leering eyes. She didn't understand about climbing the ladder of success. But Cameron January did.

"Believe me," he said he felt her arch against his hand. "I'd rather not go. I hate the desert. It's gonna' be hot, damn hot. I'll have to work out of a box-shaped four-wheel-drive vehicle and those things don't have good springs and it's going to be dusty. It's not going to be fun at all."

Sharon wiggled on top of Cameron January and felt his manhood begin to swell once again. "This is where the fun is, Cam, baby," she gushed and covered his mouth with a hot, fiery kiss.

Open-eyed, Cam groaned, glanced at his watch, then closed his eyes, willing his body to have the energy to satisfy her. Pulling extra strength from deep within him, Cam was able to oblige her quite nicely.

ﺀﺀ   ﺀﺀ   ﺀﺀ

Archaeologist Stanley Cahill gently brushed light dirty soil away from the half-exposed skeleton. Squatting in room 217 of Pueblo Bonito in the middle of Chaco Canyon, sweat dripped down his forehead, making a silvery bead in the dust. The armpits of his khaki shirt were drenched. Black, stringy hair plastered his brow while intense brown eyes riveted on the exposed fingers of the ancient remains.

The Anasazi were the most puzzling people he had ever studied: Where they came from was mysterious, why they left still a puzzle not completely answered, how they lived, how they prayed, their language, their beliefs. All remained an enigma. One of the biggest mysteries attributed to the Anasazi had to do with burial. Chaco Canyon had been inhabited for over 250 years with 1,000 people or more in residence, plus many, many more in the outlying areas, which extended up into Colorado, Utah and Arizona, including Mesa Verde. Take Pueblo Bonito, for example. Accounting for the time period the city was known to be inhabited, Pueblo Bonito should have contained the skeletal remains of close to 5,400 people, but those remains had never been found.

With each skeleton that Stanley Cahill unearthed, he became anxious, hoping he would learn something to lead him to the key to the mystery. Today was no different. He had been working in the room for more than a week. Although no ceiling arched over the rock structure, the quarters were cramped, especially for a man close to six-feet tall with gangly arms and legs. It was hot. The sun baked the rocks, absorbing the heat and throwing it back into Stanley's face. Yet his attention to detail, his absorption with interest in his work, kept him at his tedious task, merely brushing away the incessant drops of sweat which ran down his brow.

The skeleton had been found beneath several feet of dirt, buried with a water jug and some turquoise jewelry surrounding the head. It was typical of the traditional way the Anasazi buried their people. Nothing seemed out of the ordinary, and he wished something would tell him more about the people who disappeared from these parts more than 700 years ago.

With quick strokes of a nylon brush, he worked on exposing the left hand of the remains. A drop of sweat rolled down his cheek and landed in the dirt. Swallowing to ease his dry throat, Stanley wiped his brow, then attacked the bone with quick left to right strokes. More and more stark bone was exposed—white, dry, fragile bone. It was meticulous work, boring in fact, until the bone lay totally exposed.

Suddenly something flashed before his eyes. Bending closer, working feverishly, he flicked the paint brush back and forth, back and forth.

Then he clearly saw it. It shocked him, and he rocked back on his heels, the sweat now rolling down his temples and landing on his shirt. With shaking fingers, he raised the exposed fourth finger of the skeleton. Slowly, he slipped the golden ring off the finger. He took it to the T-shaped window and examined it carefully in the sunlight. The gold ring was scratched and worn. One side, where it obviously had met the palm of the hand, was almost flat. Squinting, holding the ring up high, Stanley turned it in his fingers. In mute shock, he stood absolutely still as his eyes followed the words inside the ring.

The words said, "To Maudie, from Bert. July 1, 1847."

Stanley trembled, thinking about the implication of the ring. This was no ancient Anasazi piece of jewelry. In fact, the remains were not even old, 140 years at most. White people wore wedding bands. White people had rings engraved. Maudie and Bert were names belonging to Caucasians. A ring belonging to a white woman was buried in the Anasazi ruins. Moving from the corner window built of stone, Stanley returned to the skeleton and stared down at it long and hard.

ɜ⪧   ɜ⪧   ɜ⪧

Out on the desert an Indian woman with a leathered face groaned and puffed as she climbed a steep sandstone cliff. It was an arduous climb, one which required all of her concentration and strength. When she had been young, this climb would have been more fun than challenge, but the years had sapped her strength and now each step was an effort. Her yucca sandals dug into the chiseled indentations and held. She was near the top of the sandstone arroyo, the sun burning into the rough cotton smock covering her back. A tightly woven grass flask was tied to her waist and swung against her body, the water in it sloshing back and forth.

Una was not happy. Her journey to the Hopi clan had been only halfway successful. It had taken many days to convince the members of the Pumpkin Clan that Ketl must have a husband. Yes, Una's turquoise had been abundant. Yes, her gift would make an impression on the young bucks. Yes, they all remembered Ketl's beauty and many eagerly stepped forward in anticipation of being the chosen one.

But there was a problem.

Qommatu, the Hopi chief, would not allow a member of his clan to reside in the ruins of Willow Canyon where the young Anasazi woman lived. Ketl was the last Anasazi. Qommatu argued with Una that Ketl should come to the Hopi mesa and begin a life with them. Ketl's present life in Willow Canyon held no purpose with no hope of marriage for children, of sharing the work, of surviving harsh winters, of having enough firewood, of growing enough food. No, the time had come for Ketl and Pavi and Una to come to the Hopi mesa, Qommatu argued.

It had been decided that Bright Eagle, a huge stalwart young man of twenty-one years, would be the chosen husband of Ketl. He was the son of the Antelope Chief, a very honorable position in the tribe. He was as strong as two men, ran with a lumbering gait, but could run for many miles without pausing, and Bright Eagle spoke highly of taking Ketl as his only wife. He was not especially pleasing to the eye, but his position in the tribe and his strength should make up for what was not outwardly favorable. Una should have been very happy with the choice of Bright Eagle.

However, Una didn't want to move to the Hopi mesa, nor did she want Ketl to merge with the Hopi nation. Just as Una was Anasazi, so was Ketl. In fact, Ketl was the last Anasazi and rightfully belonged in her home at Willow Canyon.

So she was making her way back to Pavi and Ketl with a

heavy heart, for she knew they would have to make a decision and, whichever it would be, it would not make the gods happy.

If they accepted Qommatu's request, then they must move to the Hopi mesa and spend the rest of their lives there, and if they decided not to go, then Ketl would have no husband. So Una was worried, her face strained with worry over the decision they must make and from walking under the midday sun in the stifling heat.

She had covered more than half of the 60 mile distance from the Hopi mesa to Willow Canyon. The July sun burned relentlessly, and Una had been smart and found shade during the day and walked most of the past three nights when it was cooler and the face in the moon smiled down upon her. She had eaten ground corn mixed with water and bits of deer jerky which Bright Eagle had graciously given to her.

However, this day had begun with the heavens cloaked in gray clouds and Una decided not to rest, but to press on, to walk on the roads built by her ancestors so she would arrive back at Willow Canyon to be joined with Pavi and Ketl by the morrow. This road she followed was a straight line. No obstacle lent her forefathers to swing right or left to make the road easier to build, or the way any easier for the one who must travel it. She knew the roads had been laid down in a straight line by the guidelines from one star in the heavens to another. The stars were the mileposts for the earthly beings, and the Anasazi regarded the roads as sacred messages from above.

This road, hardly visible to the human eye but well known to Una, cut across buttes, arroyos, mesas, both tops and deep bottoms. This section Una traveled was particularly hard. It dropped down a gentle incline into a deep arroyo, where at the bottom it was as hot as the center of the earth. The heat beat off rocks and continuously came at her in waves. The east side of the arroyo was not gentle, but steep, and she must climb with both hands and feet, feeling for the century old handholds her ancestors had dug out of the sandstone. Thorny bushes tore at her flesh. Paying them no heed, she pushed them aside with callused hands.

As her lungs labored to breathe in the stifling canyon, she looked up and saw the top of the arroyo. At last, when she crawled to the edge of the cliff, she sighed deeply. Nearly spent, she reached up. Her gnarled brown fingers trailed over the edge of the mesa and felt the flatness of the land.

All around her it was silent.

Her calf muscle tensed as she dug her toe into the sandstone and made the last concentrated effort to bring herself up and over the side of the cliff. Suddenly she heard a subtle rhythmic rattling sound which made her heart leap into her throat and her palms turn clammy cold. Years of living in mesa country had taught her what the sound was.

But it was too late. It all happened too fast. Already she was up and over the top, supporting herself on her extended arms and looking directly into the face of a coiled rattlesnake.

Like a rope unfurling, the large snake struck her in the eye. Its fangs buried deep in soft flesh. Then the snake recoiled. Flashing its tongue once, it slithered off to find shade.

The snake's strike felt like a bolt of lightning had struck Una's face. She twisted backward, her hands flying to her eye, her legs giving way, her body sailing through the air, hitting rock time and time again. She gained tremendous momentum. Her head hit a sharp rock with enough force to crush her skull. Still she went tumbling down the sheer cliff until she came to a deathly rest in a crumpled heap on the bottom of the arroyo.

Her body twitched once, then was still.

It was not long before the vultures began to circle above Una's broken body.

    ❧   ❧   ❧

The old Indian with soft gray eyes watched the young girl as she sprinted along the creek bed, sending up talons of water.

She was as beautiful as the morning mist, as lithe as a spring fawn, as bright as an afternoon rainbow. She was his flesh and blood, his granddaughter.

Watching her with his soft gray eyes, he thought of her mother, Una, remembering how she had scampered through the same creek when she was a young child and had used the spring water to wash away the first blood of womanhood. The sun had come up and gone down twelve times since Una had left them on her mission to the Hopi. She should have returned by now. She should have been here with news of Ketl's husband.

It had to be soon. Time was growing short. Pavi was old. His ancestors had made a way for him and soon it would be time for him to go. Already his bones ached to join his father and his father's father and the others on their journey to the gods, but Ketl, the flesh of his daughter's loins, must have a mate. She was the last Anasazi. She must have a husband and carry on the traditions of their people.

Pavi gazed to the West where the sun died every day. It was the direction Una had gone to reach the Hopi mesas. Covering great distances on foot was not foreign to Pavi, nor Una; for they were Anasazi. His ancestors had trekked up from old Mexico and all around the mesa country. A nomadic existence was commonplace to the Anasazi, because they followed where the gods directed them so they could find the center of the Earth; for once it was found, man and beast and rocks and soil and planets existed together in harmony.

Pavi's ancestors had chosen this mesa with the deep arroyo running though it, complete with fertile soil both on top of the mesa and down below in the dark earth next to the river. Certainly this must the Center of the Earth. Pavi believed it and Ketl believed it, but those who had left had begun to doubt.

If it were the Center of the Earth, they wondered, how could the gods not send rain? If it were the Center of the Earth, how could the children go hungry? If it was the Center of the Earth, why did the Tavasuhs come upon them with their atlatls and rock-clubs, killing and maiming those who had found The Center of the Earth? And the white man, who conquered all the other People, why didn't they come and claim these lands, if it was the Center of the Earth? Those were the questions the doubters had asked.

Pavi believed the answer to the last question rested with the fact that the white man was incapable of coexisting in harmony with nature. White men were destroyers, plunderers of what god had created. They could not exist in harmony with the Children of God, the Indian's of the Americas. No, the white man had killed their buffalo, infected them with disease, massacred them, herded those who where weak into reservations. Evil escaped their pores and Pavi steadfastly refused to move off the green mesa and onto the white man's chosen reservation for the last Native Americans.

In the cool depths of the kiva, Pavi and the other elders had discussed it a great length. The others argued that this land was not the Center of the Earth, because the land was barren, the trees grew so far away it took many moons to get to the wood supply, the rain did not always come and the people were hungry. Pavi told them the gods had given them the land, the sun, the moon, the stars and it was up to the Anasazi to do with it what they would. It was not up to the gods to give them an easy or perfect life. That must be proven. It must be worked for, and if what the gods had given them was held in great reverence, then they would be blessed with plenty.

Still they had doubted and left, following the ancient roads carved out of the mesas, trekking to the South, never to be seen again. Among those people who left were Pavi's mother and Una's husband. They had been the last to leave. The others had been gone for a long, long time.

Pavi, Una and Ketl, then just a child, had sadly watched

them go, although Pavi steadfastly believed he was right—he was not Hopi, Navajo or Apache. He was Anasazi. His forefathers had chosen this land. He would stay. He believed. So did Una. So did Ketl.

Now Ketl was the last.

Deep furrows cut into the already wrinkled brow of the old Indian. Ketl's mother had been gone too long. What bothered him was not the adverse trek, not the heat or the dryness, for Una was used to those dangers. No, what bothered him was the Hopi of the Third Mesa. Pavi, Una and Ketl had wintered there seven years ago, when Ketl had become a woman and the gods had been selfish with the rain, the crops had failed and there was no food.

Although reluctant to go, Pavi had taken the two women to the Hopi Mesa. Again two years ago they spent another winter with the Hopi clan. It was when Pavi's leg had broken like a twig when a rock slid out from under him and he fell down a steep sandstone ridge. He had developed a fever and moaned incessantly for days, writhing on the willow mats. Una did not know what to do for him, and fearful he would die, Una and Ketl had pulled him on a rig all the way to the Hopi village.

Although Pavi had hated the days spent with the Hopi, he knew Ketl had not. She was a bright and spirited young woman, and the young buck Indians had fawned over her, mesmerized by her Anasazi beauty and her rare green-gold eyes. There she met a young Hopi girl, Stella Red-Feather, who became a good friend of Ketl's and who enticed her to go to the Hopi school. Much to Pavi's disdain, she had learned some of the white man's English. In fact, she learned much more than Pavi was aware, because none of the bucks spoke her language and English was the only way to communicate with them.

It didn't take Ketl long to learn English, either, not with

Stella chattering away around her day in and day out. Pavi saw the encroaching white man's ways begin to invade the soul of his granddaughter. When his leg was able to hold his weight, Pavi took Una and Ketl home. Pavi forbid her to speak English now that they were back out on the mesa for fear the gods would turn against them, and Ketl never let on exactly how much she had learned.

It was not natural for Pavi to worry. As long as he obeyed the laws of moon and sun, paid homage to the land, then no harm could befall them, but Una had been gone too long. She should have been back by now, and yesterday as he gazed beyond the tall buttes to the south, he had seen a tail of dust climb to the sky and a feeling of foreboding washed over him. It was a heaviness in his heart, as though all was not in harmony, and he hated to think what would become of Ketl if Una didn't return before Pavi's spirit went to join his ancestors.

This weighed heavily on his heart as he watched Ketl play in the water. He knew he would have to go and find Una. He must go soon and Ketl must stay behind.

Chapter 4

Feeling like an upright pole, Cameron January walked off the airplane at the small airport at Farmington, New Mexico. His legs were stiff. They had been cramped under a seat on a commuter flight from Phoenix to Farmington. Rough material of new Levi's grated against his skin, and his heels hurt from calf-high Naconna boots.

Commuter planes were not designed for men more than six feet tall and who wore spanking new cowboy boots with two inch heels. Stiff as steel, hard as hell to pull on his feet, the boots made walking something he had to concentrate on.

The boots weren't his idea. Sharon had insisted he buy the boots and the hundred dollar tan Stetson which sat on his head, tilted slightly to the right side.

Sharon had insisted they go to a Western store in Mill Valley. There they found boots by the hundred, hats, colorful shirts, cowhide belts and assorted pieces of tack only a cowboy would know how to use. After picking out a large, tan Stetson for Cam, Sharon escorted him to the boot department that smelled of leather and oil.

Cam shook his head when Sharon picked up a black eel skin boot. "I don't know why you think I need this stuff—"

"Darling, the sun will fry you if you don't wear a wide-rimmed hat," she had scolded him with a wiry smile. "And you must have boots. Tall black boots. If a snake bites you, it'll hit the boot and not your leg."

"Don't mention snakes," Cam replied with a wince. "I hope never to see one."

Sharon waved a clerk to her side. "He'll try these. Size nine-and-a-half." When they clerk turned, Sharon poked Cam in the arm. "No snake could bite through leather as though as that. The boots will protect you."

"No they won't," Cam chided, "because I'll be flat on the ground. The snake could have my eyeballs for lunch."

Sharon chuckled and the accompanying grin created small indentations in her cheeks. "Wear the boots for me, sweet cakes, because I think they'll make you look like a mean stud."

"People will think I'm a cowboy," Cam responded.

"Nonsense," Sharon replied emphatically. "They'll know from your groomed fingernails, your white face and the way you walk in the boots that you couldn't possibly be a cowboy."

"Then they'll think I'm a fool."

"What do you care what other people think? I just want you back without a nasty snake bite and without the skin peeling off your nose. It's so tom-boyish." She wrinkled her nose in disgust. "You know what I mean?"

No, he didn't know what she meant, and he wondered where in her world of high fashion, teas and philanthropic work she had ever heard of snakes and boots and Stetsons. He meant to ask her, but never got around to it, and he didn't feel like arguing with her about the possibility of a sunburned nose and slithering snakes, so he bought the boots and the damned hat, but until he boarded the plane, he hadn't had the guts to put the wide-brimmed Stetson on his head.

On board the plane, squashed in a seat meant for a midget, he found no place to put the hat. It wouldn't fit under his seat, nor would it fit in the small overhead compartment, or if it had, it would have been flattened beyond all hopes of identification.

No wonder real cowboys don't take off their hats, he thought. *There isn't anyplace to put them.*

That was when Cameron January placed the Stetson on his head.

Christopher Hayes waited at the Farmington Airport to meet Cameron. When Cam walked into the airport toward Christopher, each man gave the other a cursory inspection. Cam decided Christopher Hayes could have starred in the *Marlboro* ad, although he would have been the son of Marlboro Man. Younger than Cam, Christopher had a round face, light hair, lopsided grin and youthful eyes. Still, he was consummately cowboy, dressed in faded jeans, scuffed boots, a white and blue striped western shirt complete with mother-of-pearl buttons, a silver belt buckle the size of a piece of toast, and a Stetson cocked on the side of head that looked well worn, not spanking new like Cameron's.

As Cameron assessed Christopher, Christopher did the same, deciding Cameron January looked ridiculous in his virgin Levi's, shiny boots and new Stetson. Nonetheless, both smiled at each other and shook hands.

Although Christopher was younger than Cam, his sun-bronzed skin already had lines at the corners of his eyes, telltale marks from too many days of work under the sun. His hands looked rough, too, like he was used to throwing ropes and wrestling steers to the ground. When Christopher ushered Cam to the luggage area, Cam noticed the swaggering gait and bowed legs of a man born and raised on the back of a horse.

After retrieving Cam's leather suitcase with his monogrammed letters on the openers, they headed outdoors.

A wall of heat hit Cam like an oven door opening in his face. Even breathing the hot air hurt his lungs. Immediately he felt his armpits begin to sweat as he followed Chris to his Ford Bronco.

"Some weather, you've got." Cam pointed at the car. "I hope the car has air-conditioning," Cam commented with a hint of question in his voice.

Christopher shook his head negatively. "Man," he said, "the only air-conditioning we have you get by sticking your head out the car window while breaking the speed limit. Otherwise, we have only one temperature, and it's called hot."

Cam sighed, took out his white handkerchief from his hip pocket and mopped his brow.

From the moment Andy Patk had told him the bad news about going to New Mexico, Cam was afraid he was going to hate Aguilar, have a passionate dislike for the Hayes Ranch, and knew that life in the desert was not designed for Cameron January. After two days, his beliefs were confirmed.

Aguilar, New Mexico was a one-dog-town, a no place sort of town, about thirty years behind times. At the busiest intersection, Main Street crossed First Street. There was no street light. At Ben Franklin Store Cam bought three scoops of ice cream for 49 cents—Cam could attest to it, because presently he stood with a dripping ice cream cone, waiting to pay his 49 cents. In front of him in the checkout lane stood a woman in polyester pants, plus a hive of pink foam curlers, perusing a *Family Circle Magazine.* When she threw Cam a cursory glance, he nodded, holding his purchase of a bag of butterballs in one hand and a dripping ice cream cone in the other.

Then she said, "Afternoon, Sonny."

Dumbfounded, Cam mumbled a reply, wondering when the last time was that he had been called Sonny.

The day was damn dry. Hot too. He hoped the hard candy

and cold cone would help his dry throat. However, they didn't. Farther down Main Street was a mom and pop market, which sported a meat department with a hardwood floor where a butcher stood behind an old refrigerated meat display, wearing a bloodstained white apron. You told the butcher what you wanted, and he hacked it off a slab of beef, weighed it and wrapped it in white butcher's paper. Then he handed it to you with a smile and a "thank you."

Across the street was a barber shop. Social hall was a better name for the place. Most of the day the chairs outside the shop were occupied by old men who didn't have any hair but had idle time on their hands. The men sat out in front of the shop under the shade of the roof valance, red suspenders growing out of dark green pants. A black dog slept next to one of the men, and as many times as Cam walked past the place, he never saw the dog raise its head or move from its spot. Cam wondered if the dog had learned the secret to the heat in the desert—don't move.

Cam heard the barber was called Butcher Bently. Cam didn't bother asking why, prudently deciding he would refrain from getting a haircut while in Aguilar.

The only redeeming value he saw from the place was the possibility of perhaps trying to do a small article on "the • America Lost in Time." He did like to dabble in creative writing, and he was sure he could find a lot of humor in a place like Aguilar, New Mexico. In fact, he couldn't help but laugh at the town, like it had been drawn up for a cartoon series which centered around life in the mid-thirties.

Cam was first put up in the We-Ask-You-Inn Motel. It had no air-conditioning and a solitary window with a screen over the window with one hole in it large enough for the Aguilar mosquitoes to enter. With the smothering heat, even a sheet was too heavy to sleep beneath, and it was the only motel in the world, Cam decided, where the lack of hot water didn't bother him in the least.

Meals were taken either at Rose's Cafe, which was across the street from the We-Ask-You-Inn, or at Hanrahan's Diner. At Hanrahan's, Cam found his fried eggs swimming in yellow cholesterol-laden butter, the toast limp and cold, the hash browns were lumpy and tasted like an alien form of grease. Dinner wasn't much better. The roast beef needed a surgical knife to slice a bite capable of fitting inside his mouth and the mashed potatoes were cold and flattened into a white lump which resembled a week-old pancake. However, at Hanrahan's, he could mask the taste and texture of the food with a cold beer.

While at Rose's the food was pretty damn good, not nouvelle cuisine, no fresh seafood and sourdough French bread, no expensive wines and good scotch, but a tasty steak, homemade rolls and French fries which were crisp and tasted like potatoes. On a whole the food was palatable.

There was only one problem. Cam didn't want to go back into Rose's Cafe because of a woman there whose hair was electric-blond, lips full and blood-red, hips wide, breasts the size of overripe cantaloupes. Cam first spied her when he was seated directly across the room from the kitchen entrance. She stood in the prep area, diligently working to push down her polyester yellow skirt which wanted to climb up her broad hips. She caught him staring at her.

Embarrassed, Cam looked away.

Interested in the handsome newcomer and more interested in the way he had been staring at her, Regina waddled over to his table. "Hello, cowboy," she drawled, cracking gum between words.

Cowboy! "I'm just visiting," he replied, then realized how stupid he sounded.

"Yeah? Where ya' from, cowboy?"

Looking up at a head haloed by dyed hair, a face layered in too much makeup, and a square jaw which was busily chewing gum, Cam cleared his throat and glanced down, his eyes now centered on the yellow buttons of her uniform which was straining over her breasts. "Texas," he uttered, lying, but not sure why or where the word came from.

"Yeah? I been there once."

She was not the type of woman Cameron would consider getting up for on a bus, much less involving himself with, and he wondered why in the hell he was staring at the gap in her dress the way he was. Perhaps, he mused, it was a matter of trusting his limits of uptightness, of trying to think that this *bimbo* waitress from Aguilar, New Mexico, who obviously had the IQ of a zebra, wasn't so bad after all.

"Texas is big," Cam said, pulling his eyes off her huge chest and smiling up at her.

"Yeah," she replied, darting a quick glance down at his lap. "So, cowboy, what can I get you?"

"A beer."

Regina placed a hand on her hip. "Sorry, cowboy, we don't have no booze in here. I got Pepsi, Iced Tea and milk. You want some milk?"

Nearly gagging, thinking of drinking milk in this heat to be terminally disgusting, he said, "No milk, thanks. Iced tea with lots of ice would be fine."

Regina nodded, scribbled on her pad as if she couldn't remember he ordered iced tea, bent over and whispered in his ear, "I got Gin over at my place. I get off in an hour."

With her cantaloupe breasts almost resting on his hand, Cam nodded, then swallowed, his throat painfully dry.

Sometime after midnight, Cam extracted himself from the mounds of Regina's body. He reeked of her cheap perfume. Naked, he stood and placed his hands on the wall to keep himself in a vertical position. His head spun, his temples pounding in unison to the blinking neon light coming in the window from the gas station sign across the street. A musty smell assailed his nostrils.

Easing himself off the wall, he pulled the sheet from the bed and wrapped the rough material around his torso. Looking up at the ceiling, he stared at the peeling flowery wallpaper. Huge peonies waved in circles around him. Blinking, he took his eyes off the wallpaper and glanced outside at the blinking neon light and wondered how in the hell he had ended up in this hovel in Aguilar, New Mexico.

He glanced down at Regina.

Damn! She'd been the equivalent of a sexual smorgasbord, and he felt as though he'd gone back for refills too many times. Even now he had trouble getting enough air to breath, remembering how her pendulous breasts had nearly suffocated him.

His stomach rocked and rolled from the straight gin, his head was full of oboe players, and he knew tomorrow was going to be a hung-over, purgatory of guilt, not because he'd banged the hell out of a woman, but because he had lowered himself to the dregs of a woman like Regina. He couldn't believe he had ended up in her bed, in her room, in this stinking nowhere sort of town like Aguilar. It was not like him. It was way beneath his meritorious way of life. Sneering in disgust at himself, Cam dressed quietly in the dark then tiptoed from her room.

That was why he couldn't go back to Rose's Cafe.

On Monday, when Christopher arrived to pick up Cam to take him out to the ranch, Christopher first had to listen to a long list of grievances about the hateful We-Ask-You-Inn, including the stifling heat, the lack of hot water and the solitary bare bulb hanging from the ceiling. He continued about the food situation, ending with his lack of judgment in finding solace in Regina's pendulous breasts.

"You can bunk out at the ranch, if you want," Christopher offered. "My grandpa lived out there all his life."

"Is he still there?" Cam asked.

"No," Christopher quickly replied.

"Good." Cam didn't want some old codger for a room-mate. "I'll move there." Solitude would be wonderful, he was thinking, and his own cooking couldn't be any worse than the food at Hanrahan's, and he'd shed his clothes, *all of them*, right down to his bikini briefs to bring some relief from the infernal heat.

"You'll be starting and ending from the ranch, anyhow," Christopher said. "That's where the horses are stabled—"

"Horses? I don't intend on getting on a horse—"

Christopher laughed. "You said you had to see every acre of the ranch, every nook crook and cranny, and I'm telling you, you can't do it by car…or by foot. No, only a sure-footed horse will take you from one end of the ranch to the other."

Things were going from bad to worse. "Andy told me I'd be using a Bronco. I *assumed* he meant a car…a Ford Bronco."

Christopher tipped his hat back off his brow and grinned at Cam. "You assumed wrong, my friend."

⸘ ⸘ ⸘

Ketl sat in the shade beneath one of the cottonwood trees which grew in the fertile soil next to the creek. Bare feet soaked in the water which ran clear and cool. The ravages of water had created a bottom land full of silt and her ancestors had taken rocks and formed damns across the spring-fed creek so that as it erupted from the ground and began its journey out of the canyon, it slowed and pooled, creating a long series of steppes.

When the gods were angry and it rained too hard, water cascaded over the canyon walls in hundreds of waterfalls, turning the creek into a boiling, brimming rampage of red water. In its aftermath, new silt collected in the creek. Although some of the damns had been damaged over the hundreds of years of occupation of Willow Canyon the damns had held and the layers of silt had built up and broadened, so a wide band of extremely rich, fertile soil, stepped down and out of the canyon.

From far away her grandfather's grandfather had brought the seeds of the cottonwood trees and planted them next to the creek. The trees had grown tall and sturdy. They gave shade. They offered protection to the homes of stone built beneath the great arc cave below the cliff. The trees were sacred and had been for more than a hundred years. No one was allowed to cut one to the ground, no matter how dire the need for firewood. Grass grew in the shade of the trees and some errant wild flowers scented the glen with a sweet fragrance.

Ketl would not have thought of removing the slightest shred of loose bark from one of the trees to help start a fire, and this day she was thankful for the shade the great tree offered her. Below the cliff her pit-house was dark and cool. She could go there to do her work, but she couldn't see the sky or smell the leaves of the trees, nor could she hear the laughter of the water as it fell over the red-rock damns.

She held a long, tough stalk of the broad-leafed yucca in her left hand. With her right hand, she deftly stripped away the outer hair-like fiber of the stalk. The fibers were long and tough and when woven together while still green, they dried into a tight mass. She would weave them into a pair of sandals for herself. The footwear was a necessity for living in her homeland; rocks and thorns were constantly a foe that only sturdy coverings for her feet could conquer. These sandals would be constructed from the shredded yucca leaves, woven crosswise with the fibers she now removed from the stalks. Her expertise at her job allowed her the ability to end with a sandal with buckskin fringe across the toe, secured at the heel by twine thongs.

A slight breeze ruffled the leaves of the trees above her. Craning her neck skyward, she looked up through the branches to the indigo sky. A silver airplane cut the sky, its vapor tail creating a line in the sky like a stroke of white chalk. Ketl stopped what she was doing and stared at the plane. A frown cut her forehead.

Pavi moved along a trail in the sand. He balanced a long pole over his shoulder to which yucca fiber ropes hung suspended, each attached to small round jugs. When he bent down and began to fill the jugs with water from the creek, he noticed Ketl staring at the airplane.

"The bird can draw pictures on the sky," she said.

"Birds can't draw, granddaughter," he replied.

"The silver birds can."

"They are the white man's machines," he said. "They aren't birds."

"But they fly."

"Yes, they fly."

"Then they must be birds," Ketl argued.

"Do they sing? Do they make nests and nurture their young ones?"

"I don't know. I've never seen one on the ground or in a tree, only high in the sky."

Roughly throwing his water-carrying pole back on his shoulder, Pavi stood and pointed a timeworn finger at his stubborn granddaughter. "You will never see one, either. They belong to the white man's world, not to yours."

His voice held a firm tone of reprisal, and Ketl knew not to argue with him, but she couldn't help wondering what one of the great birds would look like, and she was sure if she got close enough to the silver bird, she would hear it sing.

When her fingers grew tired from working on the sandals, Ketl climbed rock steps to the plaza and blew on the embers of the fire. She added sticks and soon smoke drifted up beyond the cliffs and the aroma of simmering sage hens filled the air. On her knees, Ketl ground corn on her *metate* with a stone *mano.* The corn she mixed with water and then ladled some onto a hot, flat rock which had had hundreds of corn cakes cooked on it and was smooth and shiny. To the serving baskets, besides the corn cakes and sage hens, Ketl added cooled cooked wild potatoes and a dollop of pinion butter which would be scooped up with the corn cakes. A special treat this evening was a separate basket of raspberries and thimble berries.

Ketl called to Pavi and the two of them sat cross-legged on the plaza stones. They ate their dinner while they overlooked the canyon below them and watched a soaring red-tailed hawk as it dipped and curled above them.

After the sun had slipped behind the sandstone cliffs, while Ketl prepared the fire for an overnight rest, Pavi sat in front of a wall of evenly balanced layer of red rocks, the rest of which continued on behind him in a series of one and two story rooms. The whole of their abode consisted of over forty-five rooms, some fifteen kivas and ten pit-houses. The rooms were small tucked as they were back under the cliff out of view from above, out of the way of snow and rain, out of sight from the mouth of the canyon because of the tall cottonwood trees. At one time, their village was on the mesa top and the rooms were much larger, but when the Tavasuh began to raid the villages, the People had taken refuge down in the arroyos and steep cliffs which dotted their homeland.

Pavi paced the plaza lost in thought. Suddenly, he stopped, sat down next to Ketl and held Ketl with hard eyes. Pavi made his announcement just as Ketl had covered the last of the fire with ashes, then sat beside him. "I will go tomorrow and find your mother," Pavi said.

Ketl's head shot up, her eyes wild with concern. "No, grandfather! You must not go!" She did not say he was too old, too fragile, too near his time of passing. It would have been rude for her to say such things to him, yet she held a very true concern for his well being. "Let me go—"

"No," he said sharply.

She tried another tactic. "Let me come with you," she said, going to him and placing her hand on his shoulder in a sign of respect.

He didn't look at her. "No, I must go alone. You must stay and care for your home." For the People, all belongings belonged to the woman. This was Ketl's home, Ketl's place, and she must not leave it. "I will go before the sun rises. The moon is just beginning to grow. I will be back before it is full."

Ketl sat at his side and rested her head on his bare leg. Tenderly, Pavi stroked her short black hair. "Don't worry, granddaughter. I will be all right. The gods have told me the path is paved with good fortune."

Weakly she smiled up at him, her chin trembling ever so slightly, her gold-green eyes beginning to brim with the mystery waters. She nodded, placed her cheek against his leg and remained there as the dusty rose sky turned inky black and the stars became a velvet blanket doted with silver chips.

  ❰❰❰

Pavi had walked many miles. He followed the ancient roads made by the People. He knew Una had traveled the same roads and would use them to return from the Hopi village. Somewhere the two would meet. He was sure of it.

Beneath the broiling sun, the trek was arduous. Pavi was tall for being one of the People. He had grown fast as a young man, soaring past the other boys his age. Some teased him, others were jealous of his height, sure the gods had singled him out for great deeds. Besides his height, his blue-gray eyes were held with great reverence, eyes as mysterious to the People as when the ground shook or the sun disappeared in the middle of the day.

Pavi could distinctly remember his grandmother. She was not one of the People, but had been taken in by his clan because women were in such short supply. He didn't like her much, he remembered. He thought her weak, because her spirit had been broken. She was a white woman. Her eyes were blue and her hair like dried grass. She'd lived with the Apaches for years before they traded her to his clan. Besides having a broken spirit, he had heard tales of her weakness when she delivered his father. They said there had been cries and screams, something no female member of his clan had ever done. After that, he was told, she had changed. She loved her son and became one of the People.

No matter, Pavi still considered her weak. He didn't miss her when she went away, although he was only a child by the time she was old and stooped and made the great walk to the South. However, he still remembered her white skin, and blue eyes, and he knew that part of her flesh coursed in his veins.

Instead of stout tree trunks for legs, Pavi felt as though he was supported by mere twigs. Long ago he had been considered one of the strongest among the People who had chosen to remain in Willow Canyon. Now he was no stronger than a baby, he chastised himself, praying the pain in his chest would go away, reminding himself of his dream where the path to the Hopi village was smooth and cool and successful.

Stooped, the sun beating down on his leathery back, he climbed a long, gentle rise and padded down the other side, sidestepping cacti and small, thorny shrubs.

He came to a sharp drop down to an old wash, climbed down the steep sandstone and grunted as he pulled himself up the other side, the pain in his chest becoming more intense as he strained to make the last few steps up the near-vertical wall. Telling the pain to go away, muttering to himself, he struggled along the mesa-top, not realizing his gait was broken.

High above him the sun left no shadow as it fell on the rocks and tall saguaro cactus whose arms pointed the direction he must go. The afternoon sun baked the sand which held the heat and Pavi could feel it though the sandals Ketl had made for him. To the south clouds gathered, but they seemed to hang there, non concordant with the earth, not moving like when they were chasing the gods. Pavi had counted on the clouds bringing him relief from the sun, but it didn't appear they would do what he had hoped.

Coming up a sandy rise in the mesa in front of him stood a giant frog. Stopping, Pavi stared at the frog. As his ears buzzed slightly and his vision became blurry, the frog moved forward and backward. The frog's wet body glistened under the sun, and it slowly turned its head toward Pavi. He blinked and the frog was gone. Hurrying on, sure it was a good sign, for just as nature dictated he should, the frog followed water, and now Pavi was sure that just ahead was either a spring or he would encounter clouds and rain.

Just up ahead, he told himself. *Soon. Ahead.*

Now each breath he drew was labored. His vision was shooting with dazzling bolts of lightning. He would feel a lot better if the frog would show itself again.

Perhaps it is just ahead a little farther on the road, Pavi thought. He hurried faster, sure he would find the frog, or if not the frog then a storm with welcome shade clouds and rain. Sweat dripped down his face, the color around his lips turned ash gray, and he grunted as he commanded one foot to move after the other.

Suddenly, he stopped.

With his jaw sagging open, his eyes turned upward, he spread his legs. A horrendous pain shot from the center of his chest up along his left arm and ran down to his fingers. His whole body shook violently. His right hand came up and clawed at his chest. Waving, his vision fading, Pavi struggled to make things right. He opened his mouth to speak, but no sound came out, then he tried to move his foot forward, but he couldn't command it to move. He willed the pain to ebb, for air to fill his lungs, but his power to talk to the spirits was weak.

Far off in the distance, rain fell to the earth and a rainbow arched across the sky. *It is so close,* he thought. The pain again shot through him and his knees gave way beneath him. Sagging to the ground, still open-eyed, he watched the return of life to earth.

All at once the pain stopped. He smiled up to the gods as a blinding light beckoned to him.

All is well. The gods have spoken. The path is of good fortune.

Suddenly the frog reappeared in his vision. Huge, with bulging eyes and green shiny skin, the frog stared at Pavi, then leaped into the air and was gone. Pavi smiled as he followed the path of the frog up into the heavens.

Then Pavi, the Grandfather of Ketl, fell forward and died.

Chapter 5

Cameron was settled as well as could be expected in the rough house, a house with a large kitchen where a wood burning stove sat idly in one corner. Against a wall was the modern convenience of a two-burner electric stove. A sink with a hand-pump brought water into the house. In the middle of the room a large table covered in tacky red-checkered vinyl was surrounded by four timeworn chairs.

A ratty looking metal frame sofa faced the sink and was logically the place where every person dumped their jackets upon entering the house. Cam found that sitting anyplace but dead-center of the sofa caused his body to list. However, if he stretched out on the sofa, the springs held his weight evenly and weren't too bad, especially since he could look through the screen door to desert and the buttes in the distance.

Two small bedrooms branched off the kitchen. Outside, about fifty feet downwind from the house, stood an outhouse. The outdoor opened on rusty hinges. Squeaking loudly, Cam shut the door behind him. This morning, he was an odd looking man, hardly the big city yuppie, nor the newborn cowboy. He wore only Playboy bikini briefs and his cowboy boots. He had learned quickly not to go barefoot to the outhouse—lizards and scorpions lived outside, besides other things Cameron didn't want to know about, those same things that Sharon said would not bite through tall cowboy boots. His legs were white as was his stomach, but his shoulders were hot pink, a testament to how quickly the sun could burn a man used to living in a city with fog.

This was the third day Cam had been at the ranch. He wasn't used to the quiet and solitude, so when he saw the dust coming from the road, he knew a car approached, and he hurried to the house. Inside he yanked a white T-shirt over his head and pulled on his Levi's.

In two strides he was on the front porch, watching Christopher stop the Ford Bronco in a cloud of dust. It was the same car for which Cam had developed a firm hatred; he and Chris had covered as much terrain as possible the past two days in that car: two days of bumps, dust, sand and intense heat inside the car so great that Cam was almost looking forward to being on the back of a horse instead of inside a car. As Cam squinted against the midmorning sun, he saw someone else in the car with Christopher.

An old man sat in the passenger seat, and from the looks of it, the old geezer didn't look happy. Maybe it was because Christopher was yelling at him.

Watching Christopher point a finger at the old man and scream so loudly that the chords on his neck stood out, Cam strolled to the car to find out what was going on. Leaning against the car, gazing though the window, Cam watched Christopher hit the steering wheel with an open palm.

"Damn-it all! I've explained it to you a hundred times!" Christopher said, his voice angry.

The old man looked out the front window. "Yeah, ya' have. And it still don't make sense. If someone else is staying here, then I'm stayin' too."

"This place don't belong to you anymore, Gramps," Christopher replied with a weary sigh.

The old man looked wounded. Slowly his head turned and his eyes landed on Cam and stayed there.

It was an eerie feeling, the way the old man could look right through Cam. It gave him the creeps. Cam shoved his hands in his pockets.

Woody's eyes narrowed to mere slits and glared at Cam as if he were an alien from outer space. "Hmmmp," he growled. Then he got out of the car, shuffled around the front of the Ford and pointed a shaky finger at Cam. "You're the one! You pup!"

Christopher pushed his door open and stepped in front of Woody. "He had nothing to do with you," Christopher said, trying to sound calm. Then he said to Cam, "This is my grandfather. I caught him trying to drive the ranch truck out here. He can't drive—"

"Hell, fire and damnation! I can too drive," Woody interrupted.

Christopher pointed a finger at his grandfather. "Just shut up! Hear me?"

Woody mumbled something unintelligible.

Christopher shook his head. "The truck is in a ditch about five miles back. Woody was lucky not to have been hurt." Removing his hat, Christopher ran his fingers through his hair, then sighed deeply as if unsure if he should continue or not. "He found out you're staying here and he wants to stay here too."

Woody moved around Christopher and faced Cam. His eyes were a deep blue, old eyes ringed with yellow, eyes that had squinted under the sun for too long. "My daughter says I can't stay out here alone. She don't know what she's talkin' about, but I gotta' humor her in my old age." He looked expectantly at Cam, as if Cam should know all about what it was like to be old, cankerous and ordered around. "Now, I says to myself, if someone is stayin' at *my* ranch, then there ain't no good reason why I can't be there too. I spent more than sixty years here, and I don't rightly know why I can't go on eatin', breathin' and sleepin' where I want." Limping, he awkwardly moved back to Christopher. "And I can too drive! I can see pretty good most days. The truck just leaped outta my grip. I think there must be somethin' wrong with the steerin' wheel."

Christopher shook his head and pushed his hat back off his face which was his manner when things were not going the way he wanted them to go. "The truck is *fine*, Gramps. It's you who have something wrong with it. You're too old to drive. You haven't even renewed your license since it expired last year." Christopher turned back to Cam with an apologetic look on his face. "I told him you didn't want company," Christopher said. "That was last night. He stole the truck this morning before daylight. It's a good thing he didn't run head on to someone else on the highway or kill himself when he plowed into the ditch."

Cam studied Woody. His face was rough with whiskers, his eyes yellow from age, his clothes wrinkled, but there was a spirit of independence that Cam admired. The way Christopher talked about his grandfather was close to being disdainfully rude. Perhaps what Christopher was saying was right, but couldn't he see the old guy had some pride left and didn't want to hear those things about himself?

Thinking back to the miserable attempts he had made on the electric stove that had two temperatures—warm and scorching hot, and the oven that seemed to have no control whatsoever, Cam crossed his arms and asked Woody, "Can you cook?"

"I ain't no maid," Woody replied, eyeing the city man with distaste.

"Neither am I," Cam shot back. "But I can wash dishes, I just can't cook."

A twinkle came to Woody's eyes and he seemed to soften. "I eat a lot of biscuits," he said, trying to stare down Cameron January.

"With strawberry jelly?" Cam asked, holding Woody's glare, not flinching or willing to give in to those blue eyes ringed with yellow.

Woody nodded. He released his locked stare and his mouth curved into an unconscious smile which exposed a set of surprisingly white teeth. "Boy, I think I'm gonna' like you," Woody said, then turned and limped off to his house.

Cam wasn't so sure things would work out that way, but he was willing to give it a try.

ⅎ   ⅎ   ⅎ

Christopher and Cam had made a grid on a map of the ranch. The roughest country was to the northwest, beyond the red buttes, miles from the ranch house. Christopher had studied seismic maps of the land so he had a general knowledge just what was on the Hayes Ranch. Besides limited grass, sagebrush, prickly cactus and weird sandstone formations, there wasn't much.

"There's nothing of interest beyond the valley floor," Christopher told Cam. "Here in the valley, we irrigate 'bout six hundred acres and the grass is nutritious. Beyond what you can see, there's nothing but desert."

Cam pointed beyond the buttes. "How about in that direction. My maps show a mesa."

Christopher shook his head. "Mean country beyond the buttes. Empty. Rattlesnake infested. Deep canyons and impassable cliffs. Even the cattle don't go in that direction."

"I guess that's where I'll have to go," Cam said, having decided to get the worst out of the way first. He was an exploration geologist; prospects for oil were evaluated on the basis of maps and potential reserves of hydrocarbon. Once likely beds of oil were pinpointed, it was his job to choose the sights where Wildcat wells would be drilled to test the potential reservoirs. If the prospect was determined to be economical, the field would be turned over to the production geologists for development.

Cam had studied the maps of the ranch. He knew where there *should* be oil. He also knew the boundaries of the ranch were somewhat questionable, what with acres of it going up blind gullies, across steep cliffs, down into desolate arroyos. Less than a third of all exploratory wells produced oil or gas, and only one out of every forty or fifty oil-producing wells became a commercial success, so it was Cam's job to recommend where the Wildcat holes would be drilled. It made no sense to drill in an impossible location, not at first, not with the amount of expense it took to sink the well. Cam would look at the entire ranch from end to end, make endless notes in a little book and go back to Andy Patk and tell him where the company should first sink an exploratory well.

All this he would do under the broiling sun, out in the middle of nowhere, while rooming with a crotchety old man, thinking it should be Fred Davis doing the work instead of Cameron January. He had mentally prepared himself to hate every minute of it, and so far he had been successful.

Christopher saddled a buckskin gelding for himself and gave Cam a roan mare which was as gentle as a puppy. It suited Cam just fine because the only riding he had done was at summer camp when he was a kid, and from that experience he knew that he and horses were not destined to be soul-partners. He looked the beast in the eye and did not like it at all when the horse threw him a sidelong glance that gleamed with the whites of its eyes.

"What do you know about the land out here?" Christopher inquired.

Cam was bouncing on the back of his horse and reached up to pull down his Stetson. "I know it's made up of tableland and dry river drainages, most of which are considered desert."

"It's mean land," Christopher said, while sticking a pinch of chew under his lip. "It ain't very friendly at all. The mesa land is almost totally impenetrable—all slickrock and cactus."

"I don't know about that, but I know from the Geological Survey that the mesa is mostly sandstone although heavy with iron. Under the sandstone comes a little shale and then a body of coal and also some fire clay. In some places iron with shale or slate and sandstone covers the entire distance from top to bottom of the canons. In different levels many plant and marine fossils can be found, although more fossil material is found on the valley floor. It's there that we'll sink the Wildcat wells."

Already Cam's mouth was dry from the heat and talking so much. He could go on, telling Christopher about the volcanic activity in the area, but he felt it was too much of an effort, and he wasn't so sure Christopher was even understanding what he was saying, so he shut up.

The horses split up around a dense clump of thorny cactus, then came together on a long strand of reddish sand. "Just what is it that you have to do?" Christopher asked, pausing to spit.

"I make the recommendations of where to drill for oil."

"How do you figure it?"

Talking in the heat was a real effort, so Cam made it short: "I look at the land and tell the drilling crews where to drill." He had simplified years of schooling into one sentence.

"Can you do it from maps?"

"Preliminary work is done from maps," he replied. "With computers and the like, the maps are pretty accurate, but they don't tell the whole story. I have to see the land, to see the difficulties of getting to the areas where we think the oil will be found. It costs thousands of dollars to sink a well and I recommend where we drill. I also have to make sure we are drilling on *our* property and not stepping outside the property lines just because it might be a little easier to drill in one spot rather than the other. That's why I have to see every acre—"

Riding easily in the saddle, Christopher laughed, interrupting Cam. "Mister, I've lived here all my life. I've chased down lost steers which were hotfooting it way back into the mesas, going into new and different dry gulches each time. I've been lost. I've seen canyons I couldn't find again if you paid me to, and you think you're gonna' see it all? Brother, you gotta have big eyes, tough feet and plenty of water."

"Aren't there any trails or roads out there?"

"Ha!" he laughed. "Only the 700 year-old roads built by the Anasazi—"

"The who?"

"Anasazi Indians. The Ancient Ones. They lived here a long time ago, then vanished."

Cam wiped his brow with a handkerchief, thinking anyone who would willingly choose to live in this godforsaken country was crazy. "What'd you call them?"

"Anasazi."

"Anasazi," Cam tried, finding the words made his tongue do odd things in his mouth. "I've never heard of them."

Christopher stared at Cam queerly.

&. &. &.

When they rode into the ranch in the evening, Cam stepped off his horse slowly. His behind felt anesthetized and the feeling reached down his thighs. His knees ached. His face was sunburned and his lips were cracked and dry. Taking a wobbly step, Cam slapped his thighs to make his circulation work.

Out of the corner of his eye, Cam watched Christopher slide gracefully off his mount, and he noticed Christopher was chuckling to himself. He knew Christopher was laughing at Cam. He didn't care. All he wanted was a cold shower, a cold beer and a soft seat.

Later when his needs were taken care of in that order, Cam collapsed on the sofa in the kitchen, stretching out with his feet up with one hand behind his head, a cold beer clasped in the other. Through the door, Cam watched a hawk making lazy circles in the sky.

Woody had something cooking on the stove. It smelled like chili. Whatever it was it smelled damn good, and Cam was forever thankful he wasn't doing the cooking. Woody sat out on the front step where he perched most of the time.

"Hey, city boy," Woody yelled.

"Yeah?" Cam replied.

"Come out here where I can talk at ya'."

Cam sipped his beer. He hated the thought of moving, but he liked Woody. The old guy had to be lonely, Cam thought. Groaning, Cam pushed himself to his feet and joined Woody on the step. It felt like it was a long way from the standing position to the sitting position, but once he got settled on the step, smelled the cooler twilight air and gazed off to the two buttes and the mesa beyond with the sun slowly sinking, he had to admit it was an admirable place to be.

"Beautiful sunset," Cam commented.

"Damn right," Woody mumbled.

"The clouds are different tonight."

Woody nodded. "Musta' rained like hell west of here. The clouds are all spent."

The clouds drifted along in long cotton-type strings. Soft clouds, not angry looking like the huge thunderheads. Still, they were pink and lavender and chalky white.

Woody pointed southwest. "Look." Like a curtain, a thick finger of purple rain went from the sky to the ground. "Every night it's different. My wife used to call it the twilight show."

Spears of fractured light radiated out from the sun which had slipped behind a huge thunderhead. "Good name," Cam commented, then sipped his beer.

"You married?" Woody asked.

"No way," Cam quickly replied.

Squinting, Woody took a better look at Cam. "What's the matter with you? You got somethin' wrong wi'cha?"

Cam laughed. Old age allowed a person to be blatantly direct. "There isn't anything wrong with me. I've just never fallen in love."

Woody snorted. "Hell, boy, if you ain't lovin', you ain't livin'."

Cam tried to brush off the comment with a grin, but Woody looked at him was as if he were handicapped. It was impossible not to be bothered by Woody's remark. He placed the bottle of beer to his lips, letting the cold liquid slide down his throat while he gazed out at the desert.

Cam thought of Sharon. "I've got a girl," he said, then realized he sounded defensive.

"She pretty?"

"Yeah."

"My wife was the prettiest thing this side of Mexico," Woody said nostalgically. "She taught me how to live."

Cam couldn't envision Sharon teaching him anything except how to apply makeup properly. "Sounds like you were a lucky fellow."

"I was. I don't know about young people today. They seem to be searching for somethin' that ain't there."

"Like what?"

"Instant happiness. Success without work. Taking and not giving. Livin' and not lovin'."

There was that phrase again, 'living and not loving'. It made Cam feel uncomfortable.

"I hadn't thought much on the subject before," he admitted

as he watched the huge orange sun escape the cloud and dip below the horizon.

"No, I suppose not, and that's why I say you young people have a problem." With that, Woody got up and shuffled into the house to stir his fire-hot chili.

ë&ª   ë&ª   ë&ª

Christopher rode with Cam for the first two days, then had to excuse himself because he was needed back at the main ranch, because new bulls were to be delivered and Christopher wanted to be there to inspect them. So Cam rode out alone, going farther than he had the two previous days, retracing the hoof marks of his horse, then making fresh ones.

Perhaps it was just his imagination, but it seemed that the sun came up earlier on the Hayes Ranch than it did back home. There was none of the gentle warming of the earth like when the dew ran down tall strands of grass or when the fog clung to the land as if shrouded in a vaporous blanket. There was none of that sort of thing in this godforsaken land, Cam was thinking as the sun beat down on his back.

It was only ten in the morning and already it was hot. Sweat dripped down his temples, down his back and even his hands were sweaty as he held onto the reins of the mare. By noon, when his mouth tasted like an old penny and his face was beet red from the heat, Cam found himself near the northwest corner of the ranch.

Behind him stood the two tall buttes which had been in front of him when he left the ranch that morning. He had crossed a large flat-bottomed drainage which ended abruptly at the beginning of the mesa edge. He passed scraggly pinion and cedar, some stunted bushes, strange shaped cactus, pointed yucca plants and the beginnings of sandstone cliffs poking out from the rise of the mesa. He saw no sign of animals or any indication that humans had ever been there before him. He saw no cattle, nor any sign cattle had been in the area.

He felt as though he were on an alien planet.

It was an eerie feeling.

For the next two hours he followed the mesa bottom to the north, stopping and marking the property lines and other things he felt important. He would have given anything to have remembered to have brought along his Sony Walkman. It was so vast a land, so empty the spaces, so devoid of life that he found he was talking to himself. Listening to Carly Simon would have improved things considerably.

Suddenly he heard the sound of running water. It was the same sort of thing as when he was awakened in the middle of the night by a dripping facet; immediately he knew what it was and it bothered him. Swallowing, he pulled the horse in quickly and listened. The sound was very faint, yet the sound was so odd, so out of place amidst the dryness that it seemed unpardonably loud. Then the mare smelled the water. The horse threw its head back and pulled anxiously at the bit. Curious, Cam relaxed his grip on the reins and let the horse take him to the water.

It ran in a deeply cut wash right next to sandstone cliffs which jutted up to the mesa top. The wash wasn't more than ten feet wide, but was half again as deep and cut through the land as far as Cam could see, then made a sharp turn to the right and was gone from sight. In front of him, the water emerged from the mouth of an arroyo. The cut in the sandstone cliff was sharp. The left side of the cliff bulged out abruptly, nearly touching the right side. Tall brush grew all around the mouth of the arroyo, so that if a person hadn't stumbled upon the creek and followed it to the opening, he never would have seen it.

Cam checked his typography map. The creek wasn't on it. Nor was the canyon.

For some unexplainable reason a rumble of excitement ran up his spine as he stared at the hole in the cliff. A flicker of exhilaration pulsed in his veins when he realized he might be discovering something new, something no other person had seen before, perhaps being the very first person to set their footsteps down where no other man had ever done.

Cameron January was not an adventurer. He liked roaming the perimeter of the pool in the courtyard of his apartment. He liked exploring the contours of different women's bodies, but he had never been a Boy Scout, a hunter or a person who excelled on the outdoor experience, so this increase in the tempo of his heart and the knowledge that he must see what was at the end of the canyon was very foreign to him.

All he knew was that he had to enter the arroyo, had to follow the creek, had to see what was at the end of it. Something compelled him to do it.

Because the sandstone cliffs were low, he dismounted his horse and led it beneath the ledge. With the creek flowing through the narrow opening, it was difficult to stay on dry land. He tried to keep out of the water, but the sandstone was slippery and more times than once he slipped and fell, landing on his behind in the water with his hands scrapped on the rough stone. Finally Cam gave up trying to keep his feet dry and walked up the middle of the creek. One time he stepped in a knee-high hole and his boots filled with cool water. After that, when he walked he made a squashing sound. The canyon leveled, widened and the creek broadened, becoming about ten feet wide, very shallow, the sides of the cliff steeply climbing skyward with tenacious shrubbery clinging to patches of soil. Scrub oak, juniper, pinion and young cottonwoods made his progress maddeningly slow.

The cliff walls reared up in front of him. Water stains decorated some portions while lighter hues of tan and gold rock took off in vertical directions. After zigzagging his way back up the canyon more than a mile, walking his horse so he wouldn't be knocked out of the saddle from a low lying branch, to his surprise, he found himself on a faint path. At first it was just the way a few limbs had been broken, the way the shrubs were pushed out of the way, but later it became a well-defined trail and Cam threw himself back in the saddle and let the horse find its way down the trail.

Probably a deer trail, Cam told himself, then glanced up at the sharp cliffs and wondered how in the hell a deer could climb rock.

He was now in and out of the shade of stands of cotton-woods and aspens. The white bark of the aspen trees was a sharp contrast to the green of the leaves and the red which totally surrounded him from the sandstone cliffs. Taking in a deep breath, he decided it smelled loamy, rich with just the lingering aroma of smoke.

Smoke?

What could be burning? With his curiosity increasing, he hurried along the path, glancing around him, an uneasy feeling that he was not alone, that eyes were watching him. Patting the horse's front flank to reassure the beast all was well, Cam's heart pounded errantly in his chest, his eyes darted right and left, up and down, to the top of the cliffs and back in front of him.

Swallowing, he took a deep breath. He wished his heart wouldn't beat so fast. He saw nothing unusual and tried to shrug off the unwelcome feeling.

The trail veered away from the creek and went up on the side of the cliffs where thousands of years of rain and snow and sun had left layers of loose sandstone. He came around a bend and suddenly stopped dead in his tracks. His jaw sagged open. Thinking his eyes were playing tricks on him, Cam leaned forward in the saddle and closed his eyes. Slowly, he reopened his eyes.

It was still there.

What Cameron January saw that July day in 1991 was as

stunning a vision then as it was to the first men who laid eyes on the great cave. Only now, instead of being a great, arched empty cave, Cam gazed at a city of rock beneath the protection of a curving palm of sandstone. Wind and rain and ice had formed the almost perfectly bowl-shaped cave. The ceiling of it had to be two hundred feet tall. But the ruins, and he *was* sure they were ruins, were what made him gasp in awe.

With his heart caught in his throat, he dismounted and walked forward toward the city of stone. His eyes never left the magnificent ruin for fear it would disappear and he would awaken from a more vivid dream. As he approached the cave, the walls of stone became more clearly delineated. He could make out many different rectangular shaped homes all joined, but some were higher then others, some with T-shaped windows, some with square windows, some with no windows, some rooms built right out of the back of the cave, some built in the middle out in the open but reaching more than three stories high.

He blinked hard again, sure this time he wasn't seeing what he thought he was seeing. A nearly invisible plumb of smoke drifted up from one of the rock houses.

No! He told himself. *It couldn't be smoke! It must be dust, made by some hastily retreating animal.* Perhaps bats roosted in the darkness and they had stirred up some guano. Perhaps rodents had taken over the place.

Then movement to his left made him jerk. Squinting, he looked hard. Disbelief covered his face and his jaw fell open. On the side of the vertical cliff was a series of steps made out of jagged pieces of sandstone. They looked like giant pillars marching up to the mesa top. Covering his eyes against the glare of the sun, he could see that the steps were connected by round poles, ladders actually. Near the top of the cliff, the poles had to be more than a hundred feet above the ground.

Crossing one of the ladders was a *human.* In awe, Cam sat

perfectly still and watched the person gracefully move across the ladder. One mistake would certainly result in a death plunge. Cam swallowed hard.

Just then the horse snorted, pawed the earth and sent out an earsplitting whinny. Cam watched the Indian stop. Placing its back to the red cliff, the Indian stood stiff-legged and looked down the canyon.

The Indian found Cam and their eyes locked for a fleeting second. Then the Indian turned away and ran up the ladder, crossing the open spaces between rock and wood with the grace and agility of a young deer. At the top of the mesa, the Indian didn't pause or look back but disappeared from sight as Cam watched.

Silence bombarded his ears. A shiver of unknown fear radiated up his spine. He looked around him and felt like an alien from an other planet. Nothing around him was familiar. Nothing was right. Fear of the unknown caused his heart to thud in his temples.

He started to turn the horse away from the ruin, but the wisp of smoke from the city of rocks made him pause and look again first at the smoke then crane his neck up to where he had watched the Indian disappear.

Cam overheard himself say to the horse: "Was that an Indian or just my imagination?"

His words echoed off the canyon walls and Cameron January thought he was going crazy—talking to horses, seeing Indians. He looked at the cave. When he glanced back at the cave, he knew he wasn't crazy, because he knew he couldn't imagine all that he saw—the rock city, windows, wooden ladders, smoke.

Curiosity took the place of fear. Cam tied the horse to a tree and went to take a closer inspection of the ruin.

Chapter 6

Ketl ran across the top of the mesa. Her heart thundered inside her chest. Frightened, lips pale, she was uncertain her knees would keep her on her feet. First she ran to her carefully tended garden of corn, beans, squash and cotton where she hid behind some of the tall corn stalks, her eyes wild with fear, her breath coming in great gulps. Peeking from behind the stalks, she glanced back at the edge of the cliff where the trail emerged from the canyon bottom.

The white man did not appear.

Still fearful, Ketl left the protection of the corn and ran along the rim of the canyon, some three hundred feet above her home. She ran fast. She prayed to the Creator, Tawa, to spare her from the white man. She prayed for the safe return of Pavi and Una, so she could tell them of the intruder who had found their canyon. Confusion and dread centered in her heart at the thought that she would have to defend her home all by herself, and she would do so, if need be, because as a woman the village in Willow Canyon belonged to her and her alone.

Running hard, Ketl reached the stone ramparts and tower

which overlooked the great valley to the south. Entering through a rectangular window on the bottom, she grunted as she rolled a large stone in place to cover the opening. Then she climbed to the top, pulling herself up by her fingers on the jutting stones inside the tower until she stood on a larger stone which had been purposely placed so that a watcher could stand comfortably on it and view the land in all directions for miles and miles.

First she hopefully looked north—the way Pavi and Una had gone. Nothing extraordinary was in sight, only familiar land and yarn-like streaks of clouds in the sky. Holding her breath, she looked south. A great sigh escaped her lips as she also saw only vacant land, cut in the middle by the two buttes.

She was afraid she might see a whole army of white men, marching to invade their canyon. The Apaches and Navajo hadn't found the canyon, nor had the Athabascans who came out of the North when her people were living in the Second World. This was the Fourth World, and Pavi continuously told her their only enemy was the white man.

Ketl didn't understand, because she had seen white-skinned men at the Hopi Mesas and they didn't appear warlike. However, Ketl remembered Pavi's words to her.

Sternly, Pavi had told Ketl: "The white man is your enemy because he does not understand the People and he never will. The white man has little regard for the land, America, which he has chosen as his home. His roots of life are shallow. They don't grow deep and embrace the roots of rock and soil." Pavi shook his head, his eyes steady, his voice soft, yet firm. "The white man goes forward, but he has no roads of antiquity to travel. His harmony is not with the land, not with each other. He has not accepted the kinship of all creatures, the unity of heavens and stars, nor has he found the true essence of civilization.

"If you accept the white man's beliefs, my granddaughter,

you will not remain a free spirit. You are of the Eagle Clan, and you must remain pure of heart and body, not tainted by contact with people who do not share your beliefs. Only then will you emerge from this life and go onto the next one, which is where all your ancestors are, and which is why we pray to Tawa and hold sacred all the beliefs taught to us by the People. The white man is the only one who can threaten our road of harmony, and that, Ketl, is why the white man is your enemy."

Ketl had nodded. She knew her own roots were deep, as were those of her people. She believed Pavi. Believing the white man to be as foreign as an alien from one of the stars, Ketl grew into womanhood with a festering fear of the dreaded White Man.

Now the enemy had invaded her home.

Dumbfounded, Cam stared around him. He had climbed a well-used trail which snaked its way to the ruins. Only when he stood on the plaza beneath the roof of the cave, he found they weren't ruins.

He had climbed a perfectly carved set of steps which were cut directly into the sandstone. There, he found himself with a commanding view of the valley below him. Looking up, he saw a natural sandstone roof, and below his feet lay an intricately laid pattern of stones. His first impression was that he was in the center of an active plaza. Signs of life were everywhere: the smoldering fire near the edge of the plaza, pots of water, pots of dried corn and beans, a small pile of firewood, a rock bowl with a grinding stone, unfinished fiber sandals, a rack with a freshly killed rabbit hanging from it, strange tools and stranger designs on pots which looked like they had been recently formed. Turkeys strutted to and fro, one casting an arrogant beady eye at him. A pile of cotton lay in a basket and another basket was filled with some odd-looking bulbs which resembled potatoes but weren't.

In front of him were three holes in the rock work, out of

which emerged smooth ladders made of pine poles. The rock work indicated that whatever was below had been constructed in the form of a circle. Tentatively, Cam peered down into one of the holes. It was dark inside. He couldn't see anything, so he climbed down the ladder into one of the dark pits.

When his eyes adjusted to the darkness, he could make out a stone bench lining the side of the circular pit, a dirt floor, a roof made of logs, brush and mud. Large pots sat near the fireplace which was backed by a vertical slab of rock. Curious about the rock, Cam looked behind it and found it was an air shield, for there was a ventilation hole just beyond it in the rocks. The floor was dirt but hard as rock and as clean as a cement floor. Between the ventilation hole and the fireplace was another hole. Bending down, he ran his finger around the perimeter of the hole and found it to be deep, but he felt no bottom and could discern no reason for the hole. He could tell it had some meaning to whoever lived here, because it was it was apparently kept open and free of debris. It was very strange.

Around the perimeter of the chamber ran an interior bench expertly crafted out of layers of rock. Six masonry pilasters sat on this bench and supported the large timbers of the cribbed roof. No windows nor doors gave light within, except from the hole he had descended, and it was very dark inside the room. On the floor were grass mats. On a shelf made of wooden branches, sat several fiber bowls, dry ears of corn, and a large pile of dried yucca leaves. Against the wall leaned a primitive looking bow. Next to it sat a leather quiver filled with arrows.

With shaking fingers, Cam extracted one of the arrows from the quiver. He took it to the light from the overhead hole and examined it.

Oh my god, he thought, *the arrow should be in a museum.* It was made from some sort of hard wood and obviously shaved of bark, because the wood was smooth, but darkened from handling. The tip of the arrow was of bone and lashed to the shaft with what Cam guessed was grass. At the opposite end the arrow was split and feathers had been wedged into the wood. Turning the arrow in his hand, Cam discovered dried blood on the shaft and a bit of leathery flesh on the point. Quickly, he put the arrow back, a shiver of unknown fear radiating down his spine.

Something wasn't right.

An ancient ruin doesn't have water in jugs, fires burning and blood on arrows!

Bolting up the ladder, Cam's breathing came in ragged gulps. His mind wouldn't focus. He felt in a daze. He couldn't decide what it was he had found.

And who was it that he saw climbing out of the canyon?

He didn't know, nor did he have any answers. A creepy feeling came over him, like maybe he didn't want to find out who lived here...or for how long. This place wasn't like the world he knew. He didn't belong there, and he felt like he was intruding on something very personal.

Suddenly, he felt an overwhelming desire to leave. His eyes flew through the cottonwood trees, to the trail he had followed into the canyon. In a run, he crossed the plaza. In his haste, he kicked over a black and white pot filled with dried beans. The pot broke and beans scattered helter-skelter. He swore, damning himself for his clumsiness. Cringing, he bent over and began to pick up the beans, but his fingers seemed numbed and he dropped more than he picked up. Frustrated, he gave up. When he stood, the emptiness of the place, the hugeness of it made his head unclear.

He felt as though he had been breaking and entering someone's home. Guilt washed over him. He'd like to apologize, but to whom? His mouth was dry, and he thought of his pocketful of butterballs. He wasn't sure why he did it, but he retrieved three of the candies and placed them in the middle of the spilled beans. Then he left.

ða   ða   ða

It was twilight when Cam returned to the Hayes ranch. Hot and dust-covered, Cam was ornery, but most of all he was bothered by what he had seen in the canyon. He wasn't sure if he should tell someone, and yet, he wasn't sure if he should keep silent. It was a puzzle which left him with a throbbing headache.

Woody noticed Cam's unusually sour disposition, plus a pale face and frown which was digging a trench across Cam's forehead. "You run into a ghost out there?" Woody asked while Cam washed at the kitchen sink.

"No," Cam replied quickly.

"You sick?"

Cam didn't reply, but answered the question with a question, "Are there Indians around here?"

Woody's eyes narrowed. "Son, we are surrounded by Indian reservations. The Ute are north of us, Navajo to the east and west and Hopi farther west."

"No, I mean Indians who aren't living on reservations, Indians who are still living like Indians."

Woody laughed. "No," he said sadly. "Ain't any more Indians out there. They all left these parts more than seven hundred years ago."

Cam smeared shaving cream on his face. "What were they called?"

"Anasazi."

Using a steel razor, Cam began a methodical removal of whiskers. "And they're gone?" he asked, pausing to flick shaving cream into the kitchen sink. "Where'd they go?"

"Nobody knows."

Cam glared at Woody over his shoulder. "Come on, Woody, they didn't vanish into thin air—"

"No, of course they didn't vanish. They left slowly, over

a course of hundreds of years. They weren't a very sophisti-
cated group of people and they left no written words of any
kind to explain why they left. Not like the Egyptians did. No,
sir, those Injuns built stone penthouses, farmed land impossible to farm, built hundreds of miles of roads, learned to make
exquisite pottery and baskets, then, poof, they were gone.
Even the wall paintings they made were mere stick figures, no
letter, words or scenes that might tell us something about
them."

"That's incredible," Cam commented.

Woody beamed, happy to have someone listening to him.
"Yeah, sure is. Why, those Injuns came to this territory long
before Christ was born. They tramped around the Southwest
like bunnies, popping up here and there in the most god-awful
places a man could imagine. First they built crude homes up
on the mesa tops. They dug pit houses and hauled rocks from
the cliffs to build rectangular rooms."

Cam placed his razor on the counter. "No wood was
used?" he asked incredulously as he began to splash water on
his face.

"Oh, they used wood, all right. But not from around these
parts." He pointed north. "They carted pine trees from fifty
miles away to be supports for the kiva roofs, which is what the
archeologists call the pit houses the Injuns dug into the
ground."

"Why from so far?"

City pup! "There weren't no wood on those mesa tops,
that's why!"

Now Cam faced Woody while drying his face which was
spanking clean, and which felt about ten pounds lighter what
with his whiskers gone and all the dust gone that he had
accumulated throughout the day. "How big were these trees
they used?"

Woody could see the look of disbelief written on Cam's

face. He had felt the same way when he first started reading about the Anasazi. "Big," he said. "Fifty feet or more. Amazing, huh? They must have weighed more than a couple-of-hundred pounds, yet they marched off, cut them and hauled them back without the help of horses or machinery. I always wondered if they did it in the middle of summer. The heat alone should have killed them. Besides hauling wood from miles away, they traveled great distances to trade goods. Some of the burials around here were found with sea shells and turquoise from god knows where. I can't go more'n a quarter mile in the desert without thinkin' I'm gonna' keel over.

"How those Indians did it is beyond me. In fact, I got to wondering if they were different from us, like maybe the heat didn't bother them so, but I talked to one of those archeologists, and he said 'no, the Anasazi weren't no different from you or me.'" Woody pointed to the front step. "It's hot in here. Let's go outside where we can breathe."

Cam nodded and followed Woody to the front steps. Woody groaned as his old bones lowered him to the step. Cam sat beside Woody and gazed out into the desert. Squinting, he pulled the Indian figure from the canyon back into his imagination. "What did they look like?" he asked Woody.

"Like people," Woody chided. "With legs. Arms. One head."

"Aha," Cam said dryly, knowing how Woody loved to tease. "I know you have more to say about them," he commented.

"Well, let's see. They weren't tall, either that or they could never stand up in their houses. They were good looking, though—not like the Apaches or Navajo. Not flat-nosed. Their hair wasn't totally black, some grew mops of red-brown or sorrel colored hair. I seen a book once. There were pictures of what the Anasazi must have looked like. The women all had short hair, while the men had long, flowing hair. They grew cotton, you know, and wove themselves material so they weren't dependent on stinkin' animal skins for clothes."

"How about the eyes?" Cam asked.

"Black," he said simply. "Black eyes."

Cam raised a black brow. "No variation on that?"

"No sir, same with all Injuns. You see an Injun with anything but black or dark brown eyes and he ain't hundred percent Injun."

"What does that make him?" Cam inquired.

"Abnormal," Woody replied.

Cam was silent for a minute. As if lost in thought, he raised his leg and pulled off one boot, then the other. Instantly, he felt a great relief. "What about the houses you said were built up in the cliffs. You just said the Anasazi built on the mesa tops."

"You're rushin' me, boy. I was coming to that." Woody ran his hand over his whiskered jaw. "Pretty soon the Athabascans, ancestors of the Navajo in case a city boy like you don't know, migrated down out of the North. Whereas the Anasazi were a peaceful people, those Athabascans liked nothing better than to smash in a few heads with clubs. They wanted the Anasazis' crops and their women, and they generally got what they wanted, so the Anasazi began to build their homes down in the cliffs so their enemies would have a difficult time reaching them. Even so, in the cliff cities, the archeologists have found the lower windows and doors sealed with mortar, as if the damned heathens found a way down the cliffs to the Anasazi homes."

What Woody related to Cam was astonishing. He wondered how he had gotten though school and not known such a fascinating people existed in America. "So they eventually left because they were driven out," he summarized out loud.

"Maybe, maybe not. Some say so. Some say it was that plus a long drought which made life impossible in the four corners area. Me? I say life was already impossible. I say there was some other reason those blasted Injuns disappeared. There were just too dang many canyons where they could have successfully hidden from the Athabascans. I say we don't know why they left. I say it's the greatest mystery of all."

Cam glanced out to the buttes and beyond, then back to Woody. "You know what I say? I say the greatest mystery of all is why in the hell they *came* to such a godforsaken land in the first place!"

Woody's jaw sagged open. He'd never thought on that side of it before, and it surprised him that the boy from the city would have the sensitivity to think of such a thing. He nodded at Cam and said, "I'll have to give it some thought."

Cam grew silent. Before his eyes came the vision of the great cave, the stone houses, and the Indian he had seen. Now he was sure that it was a female. A male wouldn't have moved as gracefully as the Indian he had seen.

He got up and went into the house with Woody on his heels. Although the old man had explained to him about the people who inhabited the area, Cam grew more troubled, knowing he had found something that shouldn't be there. He took off his sweat-stained shirt and wrapped a damp towel around his neck. The coolness immediately made him feel better. Joining Woody at the large table, he pulled a chair out and swung his leg over it, leaning his arms on the back of the chair.

"What would you say," Cam began in a low voice as if testing the words, "if I told you I saw a god-damned Indian today and an ancient ruin that wasn't a ruin?"

Woody paled. Forty years of his life passed before his eyes. He saw an Indian standing on a cliff and canyon which seemed to disappear from the face of the earth. "I'd say, boy, that you had too much sun."

꿈   꿈   꿈

That night Cam didn't sleep.

That night Woody didn't sleep.

And that night, lying on her yucca mat, staring up at the canopy of stars, savoring the strange taste of the yellow balls, Ketl didn't sleep, either.

        🐚   🐚   🐚

The next morning Cam was dressed and wrestling to saddle his horse while the horizon was pale lavender.

Woody appeared from the house, disheveled, still clad in his cotton pajama bottoms. "Where you goin' so early?" he said in a coarse, still-sleepy voice.

"I think you know," Cam replied.

Yes, Woody knew, and he cursed his bones for being so brittle, because he would give anything to be going, too. "Son, you remember, whatever it is you find out there," he paused as if contemplating what he wanted to say. Then he finished, saying: "You be respectful. Don't do anything stupid, you hear?"

"I'm not stupid, just curious," Cam said between gritted teeth.

Placing his once new, but now dusty, sweat-stained Stetson on his head, Cam struck his foot in the stirrup, mounted and kicked the horse hard, leading it northwest.

        🐚   🐚   🐚

Ketl had made up her mind. She must go and find Pavi and Una. The moon was not yet full, and she didn't expect Pavi to return for some time, but she couldn't wait for him to return, because she was more frightened than she had ever been in her entire life. Tawa had not answered her prayers. Yes, the white man had gone away, but he would come back, just as it had been prophesied by Mockingbird who had been created by Spider Woman. "When the white man enters your canyon, it will be the beginning of the end of the Fourth World," Mockingbird had stated.

And Ketl knew that only her people of good heart would

emerge from this world onto a new beginning in the Fifth World. It was like facing death. Her heart ached and the palms of her hands grew icy cold as she thought of the coming end. However, she didn't want to go alone on this journey; Pavi and Una must be with her, because they were all that was left of the Eagle Clan. They must go together. So she must find Pavi and her mother.

The way to the Hopi mesa was long and arduous. It crossed lands belonging to the Navajo who for centuries had been oppressors of the People. It was a dangerous walk. Just as she had feared for Una, she had feared for Pavi, and now a greater fear joined her spirit. Not only did she have to make the journey to the Hopi, but she would be bringing disastrous news of the coming of the White Man.

She prayed Mockingbird would guide her along the ancient roads laid down by her ancestors as the fulfilled their migrations. Although she had been to the Hopi Mesas twice before, the journey was very long. Before Pavi had led the way. He was old and wise. Mockingbird spoke to him and told him the way. It was the same for Una, but Ketl was not old or wise, and Mockingbird had not spoken to her. However, she was filled with naive determination and a desperate resolve to reach her family now that the white man had arrived.

First she must put things in order. She brought in the bowls of grain and stored them in the dark, windowless room far back against the cave wall where it was cool and dry. She put away the cotton and yucca fibers. With expert swiftness, she climbed out of the canyon along the treacherous ladders spanning the pillars of sandstone while balancing a pole from which hung two jugs filled with water. Quickly she went to the garden.

The water was not for the corn or beans. Rain must feed the garden now. No, the jugs of water were to refill the sacred vessel which was buried in the soil in the north corner of the garden. This vessel had been buried there as long as Ketl could remember, and it never was allowed to become dry. Her ancestors, the first who set foot in Willow Canyon, had carried the vessel from the last spot where they had constructed rock homes. Before that, the vessel had been carried to the west to the Great River where shells and seaweed had been especially chosen and placed in it. With great care, it had been brought back and buried in the soil; the vessel was the secret weapon of the People, for this vessel guaranteed rain. And it had not failed her people for hundreds of years.

So Ketl filled it to the top with water from the spring-fed creek which was born beneath the great cave. She left another jug of water next to it, hopefully to make the gods aware that she would be gone on a journey, yet that she was concerned about the water vessel.

Then she went back down to her home, tied on her traveling sandals and climbed down the ladder to the pit-house to gather her arrows. She placed a knife in the leather of her sandal, swung her quiver on her back and held onto the bow in one hand.

When she climbed the ladder from the kiva, she squinted against the brightness. Pushing herself up onto the plaza, she whirled around and came face-to-face with the white man.

Chapter 7

Feverishly Stanley worked to brush away dirt from the skeleton. The room was sweltering hot, the air smothering, but he refused to slacken his pace, because he knew the person who had been buried in room 217 beneath a pile of refuse was different from any of the other remains unearthed in Pueblo Bonito.

Anxious to extract the whole body of bones, Stanley wanted to move them to the laboratory and have carbon-14 testing done on them. Once an organism died, the amount of radiation emitted by carbon-14 diminished at a predictable rate. Therefore, by measuring the amount of radiation still present in an object, the approximate date of death could be determined. However, the carbon-dating, or newer amino-acid testing, couldn't be accomplished in the field and no more information could be gained from the skeleton while it remained entombed in soil.

Stanley wasn't sure what he had found when he unearthed the bony finger with the ring of gold on it. Most certainly the ring wasn't native to the Anasazi, nor did the Anasazi fashion it. It was definitely a product of a white man's construction. Who made it was not a question; what remained a puzzle was what it was doing on the finger of an Indian who had been buried in the refuse pile of a city of people who inhabited the place some 600 years ago.

Using the utmost care, flicking a medium-stiff nylon brush back and forth over the bones, Stanley gently freed the skeleton from the clay-like ground. The figure lay in a curled, near-fetal position with both arms crossed over the rib cage, legs lying straight, head facing once what had been a mud ceiling.

Except for the small water vessel and the trinket of turquoise, he found no other burial trinkets: no pottery, no jewelry, no vessels of food, no indication the Indian had been buried with solicitude for an easy journey to the 'afterlife' which was common to the Anasazi. This human had been buried in a refuse pile with shreds of pottery, bones of wild turkey and deer, discarded yucca fibers, hundred-year-old-corn husks, human waste and ashes. Stanley even wondered if the water vessel and turquoise had been buried with the body or casually tossed aside with the refuse after the body had been buried.

It was very puzzling.

Finally the backbreaking chore was finished. Now he jotted down his observations. He wrote fast and furiously, glancing from white bones to his note pad. When he was finished writing, he made his conclusion—the skeleton was female. Her bones were less robust than those of a male. The ridges which provide attachments for muscles and tendons were less prominent than those of a male, the pelvis wide. Stanley made measurements just to be sure. Yes, the difference in ratio between the lengths of the pubis and ischium confirmed the skeleton was definitely female. Her arms turned slightly outward, which was another indication of sexuality.

Carefully, Stanley had examined the small cranium and con-cluded, by the total fusing of the skull's sutures, that the woman had past her prime of life. All of this information Stanley knew simply by observation, but what he really wanted to know was how old the bones were, and only by carbon dating would he know for sure how long the bones had lain in the heap.

Standing and gazing down at the skeleton he had named "Goldie," Stanley mopped his brow and sighed with relief. The obsidian, vacant holes of eyes stared up at him, and her teeth, all except the missing bottom right lateral, mockingly grinned back at him. He had no doubt that the skeleton in room 217 of Pueblo Bonito was a woman. He further suspected the ring he found on her finger had not been placed there by accident or by some mischievous prank. There was an expla-nation for the ring and Stanley intended on finding out what it was.

With clear blue eyes, Stanley glared at her from the smooth cap of cranium to the end of bony toes. The skeleton appeared whole, all put together, like her bones were con-nected by invisible thread, so that he could grab her by bony shoulders and pull her into a sitting position or lift her and set her on her feet. She didn't look like a pile of disconnected bones which she was.

Of course even a pile of bones lent a wealth of information to a trained archeologist with Stanley's education. If the person had been buried deeply in the ground and no other living form had tampered with the grave, when the skeleton was uncovered, it should lay in exactly the same position as when it was buried. It would give the archeologist valuable information as to the rituals of burial, the importance of the person buried, and perhaps more—perhaps some unknown unexpected bit of information.

Stanley remembered finding an arrowhead embedded in

the fifteenth vertebrae of a young-adult, buried in a shallow grave in the foothills outside of Denver. At first the male adolescent was thought to be white, a victim of Indians dispatching white men who invaded their territory, but the carbon dating on the bones proved to be too early: circa 1713. The arrowhead was much older than that, perhaps by fifty years or more.

Further study of the arrowhead proved it came from slate only common to the mountains a hundred miles to the west which the Utes inhabited. The Utes considered the mountains personal property given to them by The Great Spirit, and if they ventured out onto the plains to hunt buffalo, they were fortunate to return to their camps alive.

Found beneath the skeleton was a perfectly preserved buffalo skin pouch which may have belonged to one of the plains tribes, Cheyenne or Arapaho. It was finally decided the skeleton was of Indian origin, Cheyenne most likely since they stayed close to the Big Thompson River. Because the Cheyenne were nomadic wanderers of the plains who possessed distinct territory taboos concerning venturing into the Ute's mountainous domain, the young Indian with the arrow in his back had been trespassing on ground that didn't belong to him. That's what made archeology so exiting. The bits and pieces that finally come together to form a whole. Stanley could vividly envision the raid by the Cheyenne Indians into the mountains in search of game. The Utes, fierce defenders of the mountains, must have greeted the Cheyenne with a barrage of arrows. The Cheyenne retreated. Still the Utes sent their arrows into the air—one found the back of a boy who would never reach adulthood.

Stanley hoped the same sort of information might come from the bones from room 217 of Pueblo Bonito, so after photographing the skeleton from three different angles, careful to photograph exactly the position of her finger bones and the way he had unearthed the ring, he painstakingly lifted each bone from the dirt and placed them in a sterile wooden box. When he was finished, he secured a lid on the box, put the box in his Jeep Wagoneer and drove down the dusty road leading away from Chaco Canyon.

& & &

"*Hakomi?*" Ketl asked in a shaky voice, using her native tongue.

Cam had no idea what she said. "What?" he said, his voice excited.

Ketl took his tone of voice as one of threat. Slowly dropping her hands, she hunched over slightly, ready to spring in any direction. Inching backwards from the white man, she never let her eyes leave him. She moved like a cat, all liquid movements, but primed, her muscles tight with a growing fear running up the center of her body. Her heart crashed inside her chest and her mouth felt dry, her throat constricted.

"*Hakomi?*" she repeated again.

He had no idea what she said. Curious, yet cautious of her hard stare, Cam tentatively stepped closer to her. "Who are you?" he asked.

It was the same question Ketl was asking him in her own language.

He was tall, his skin fair, his eyes like the sky, his hair not long—even shorter than her own. Sniffing, she smelled the sweet aroma of horse flesh and sweat. Running her fingers down her thigh to her calf, she felt for the razor-sharp elk-bone knife.

With her free hand, she pointed at Cam. "White man," she spat at him with hateful venom.

These words he understood and her words shocked him. Never had he seen such abhorrence conveyed by two words. *What in the hell have I done?* he thought. He straightened his back and glared down at a set of green eyes and a woman who was only half his size.

He wasn't about to let her frighten him and said, "Yes, I'm a white man, a damn friendly one, too, and who in the hell are you?" He pointed his finger at the tip of her nose.

The white man was angry. His finger was aimed at her face. "*Pinu'u*," she hissed, letting him know that she was who she was.

He didn't understand her, because she spoke in a strange dialect he didn't understand. Everything about her was strange, from her clothes to the fact that she seemed at home in the cave. In fact, he wasn't sure he was really seeing and talking to a real person. Perhaps she was a living fossil. He blinked, wondering if she was a vision. No, she was still there.

This can't be real, he thought. *This sort of shit only happens in adventure magazines. Maybe I'm hallucinating.* Reaching out, he attempted to touch her, to reassure himself that she consisted of flesh and blood. His fingers touched her cheek.

Frozen to the rock plaza, Ketl stood riveted to the spot. She felt his fingers run down her cheek. Shock and horror hit her like a blast of midday heat.

She was not a chosen woman and no man could touch her! In a blaze of motion, she pulled the knife from its sheath, sprang upward and sliced at the tall white man. Around the knife's handle Ketl had carefully placed five rings of flint which she had chipped into a circle. The flint gave the knife the right amount of weight, so when she threw the knife, it flew on a true course. She had aimed for his chest, but he jumped back when she moved, and the knife sliced the soft underside of his left arm.

Cam yelled, grabbing his arm. Immediately warm blood oozed from the deep cut and trickled between his fingers. He hollered curses at her as his anger became a scalding fury. "You bitch!" he screamed at her.

Crouched like an animal about to spring at its quarry, Ketl began to circle the white man. She eyed him warily, not sure how a white man would fight, but sure she must not give him a chance to catch her off guard. She was not the least concerned that he was a foot taller and heavier than she was. She felt no fear, because she was defending her home. It was her duty to defend what was rightfully hers, and she would die doing so if necessary, although she would much rather have the handsome white man spill *his* blood and die, freeing *his* spirit to find another world.

White heat pulsed in his arm. Cam grabbed the wound and pressed hard while his cold eyes sniped at her. Mumbling swear-words, his mind reeled with confusion.

This is the 20th Century, he thought. *The days of cowboys and Indians are long gone. I'm not even armed,* he thought with a laugh, because it sounded so archaic.

However, the woman in front of him was armed with a weapon that had opened a deep gash on his arm. Blood oozed between his fingers—no, it didn't ooze, blood pumped from his arm. *Damn, she cut me deep.*

The woman crouched in front of him, ready to spring at him again. When he heard her utter a low growl, he felt as though he faced a rabid wild cat. Glancing around him, he saw nothing he could grab to use to defend himself. Even that thought was stupid, he told himself. He didn't want to have to defend himself against the Indian woman. He only wanted to talk to her, only wanted her to understand he meant her no harm.

"Put the damn knife down," he told her.

Swaying to and fro, she watched him, her eyes holding him, every nerve in her body primed. She acted like a wild animal, Cam decided and his words had no effect on her. Damning himself for getting into this situation, Cam placed his hands in front of him and made ready for her next attack.

As Ketl circled, grinding her teeth together as terminal hate filled her veins, she watched fascinated as the tall man extended his hands, bent his knees, placed one foot in front of the other, centered his gaze on her, rolled his fingers into a half-fist and faced her as she circled him. Blood trailed down his arm. Lunging at him, thinking he looked like he was about to commence a tribal dance, she attempted to plunge the knife in his stomach.

Cam sidestepped.

Ketl groaned as her momentum caught her off-balance, and she fell to her knees. She jumped to her feet quickly, turning and facing the white man. His stature, the constant waving of his hands made her heart crash inside her chest. His eyes were like Pavi's, the color of the midday sky. He wore a strange hat on his head, yet she could see dank tendrils of hair curling down over his forehead. It was the way he carried himself, though, that made her brow pinch together with a frown; he bobbed and bounced, constantly moving, coming and going, his hands weaving, his eyes centered on her until she thought he had speared her with his look.

She had never seen anyone fight like this. He didn't charge her. He had no weapon, he had no club, spear, arrow or knife, yet he showed no fear and stood facing her, looking at her, looking down into her soul. She was sure he was possessed by an evil demon. Lunging again, this time going low for his thigh, Ketl flew through the air.

Cam sidestepped, spinning around. Reflexes took over. His foot kicked her in the arm, deflecting her next attack. He sprung around again, automatically sticking his leg out and lifting her off her feet.

Ketl went to the ground with a thud, her chin scraping the rocks. Her knees ground into stone. For a laconic second, she was stunned. A flash of bright lights flashed through her head, then disappeared to be replaced by dull fuzziness.

"Look," Cam said, letting his arms down to his side, "I don't want to hurt you. Put the knife away. I'll leave if you'll just put the knife away."

Ketl heard his words, but he spoke too fast; she didn't understand what he was saying. She couldn't believe he had gotten the best of her by simply sticking out his foot. It was humiliating. Her Grandfather would be ashamed of her.

Cam wasn't proud of himself. Most of his yuppie friends took karate at the fitness center in South San Francisco. It offered exercise and a certain training of mental powers. Most of the guys said they took it so they wouldn't be mugged down on Market Street some foggy night, but Cam knew differently. None of them had ever had to put the exercises to practice outside of the fitness center, and Cam never envisioned he would have the opportunity to do so. Learning karate was an ego-booster, a macho thing for the guys to do. No one ever said so, but that's why Cam did it, and he knew damn well it was why all the other guys did it too. Most of them secretly hoped the opportunity to use it would come along. It would be a great thing to talk about at the Foxfire Lounge where they all went for beer and red-hot burritos after working out.

Right now Cam wished this situation didn't include him. This wasn't the way he had envisioned using karate. He felt no wondrous sense of accomplishment by overpowering a slight woman by a swift kick. Granted she was armed with a lethal weapon, and the look in her eyes told him she intended to use it on him the best way she knew how, and there was no mistaking the blood which dripped from his arm, but there was something oddly strange about her. She seemed vulnerable, like a wild animal backed into a corner, like someone frightened beyond all reason. He had the sensation that she didn't understand he wouldn't hurt her, in fact, he wondered if she understood anything he said. He didn't know who in the hell she was, or why she was camping out in the middle of the desert, but he did know he didn't want to hurt her. He just wanted her to put the damn knife away.

But Ketl didn't put the knife away. Instead she pushed herself to her feet and turned to face her enemy. Her back faced the opening of the great cave, and the white man stood on the rock stones her ancestors had laboriously placed. *He* had invaded her territory. *He* had touched her. *He* was her mortal enemy and she would extinguish his life. With lightning speed, Ketl pulled back her arm and flung the knife at the white man.

Singing though the air, spinning, making a dizzy arc, the knife came straight for him. Cam's reactions were excellent and he jumped back, fell and watched as the knife clattered to the rocks behind him. Then his angry eyes filled with renewed fury.

Ketl turned on her heel and bolted from the plaza. Like a gazelle, she ran around stone houses, over baskets and along the carved set of stone stairs which led to the notched poles leading to the mesa top. She had done it thousands of times and knew each foothold, each step to take. Furious at herself because she had failed to kill him with her knife, her thin nostrils flared as her eyes darkened like angry thunderclouds.

🐚   🐚   🐚

She would lose him on the mesa, she decided. He would follow. Then she would become the hunter and he the hunted. It would be her territory, she would show him no mercy and this time he would not live. A renewed sense of hope spurred her on as she clambered up the rock trail to the top of the sheer cliff.

In an instant Cam was on her tail. Some crazy desire for revenge coursed through his veins. He wasn't going to let her stab him with a knife, try to kill them and then run away without an explanation. At least he expected an apology from her before he went back to the ranch—if not an apology, at least a sensible answer for her existence. Sane logic told him there had to be a good reason for her animosity, some reason she wanted to kill him, some rational reason she was out in the middle of nowhere with ancient weapons, dressed like a person from the middle ages and spoke in a language foreign to Cam.

There had to be a logical reason, he told himself as he started across the plaza after her.

Ketl grunted when she jumped onto the first pine ladder leading to the top of the mesa. She had traveled the path across the ladders and sandstone pillars hundreds of times. She knew each step. She knew where to put her hands to make the way easier. She was not afraid of the great distance below her, even as the route went higher up the cliff.

Behind her, Cam refused to look down. He didn't like heights, because they made him dizzy. He even hated the feeling of going up in an elevator just because he *knew* he was going *up.* But now he wasn't thinking of where he was going or what he was doing. Besides his male pride being wounded, his arm ached and blood trailed down his fingertips. Puffing hard, he ran after her, jumping over rock walls and up the first set of steps going to the trail that hung suspended on the edge of the cliff.

He concentrated on catching Ketl and his longer strides, and his fierce determination to stop her made him gain on her. "Stop!" he cried, puffing heavily. "Stop! I just want to talk to you!"

She didn't respond or slow down. She looked like a lithe bunny hopping from stone to ladder.

The ease in which she navigated the trail infuriated him further. "God-damnit, will you please stop!"

She didn't pause. Cam pushed himself harder. Groaning with the effort, he stepped onto a ladder and reached out for the woman's ankle.

Ketl jumped from the notched log ladder to a five-foot wide stone pillar. She was just about to place her foot on the next wooden ladder when she felt a hand grab her ankle. Lunging forward, she twisted off balance and landed on the outside pole of the ladder. Grunting as she fell, her body hit hard, momentarily taking her breath away. Her arms and head tipped downward into thin air and the rest of her body followed her momentum. As if in slow motion, she twisted and began to slip off the pole beam. Frantically she grasped the pole with both hands, but it was smooth from hundreds of years of hands holding onto it when the people of her clan climbed in and out of the canyon.

Panicked, she clawed at the pole. Her fingers wrapped around the hard wood until her fingertips touched. The ground below her waved back and forth. Praying to Mockingbird, she held onto the pole until her knuckles turned white.

Cam had a hold of her ankle when she tumbled off the ladder, but his hands where blood-covered and slippery. To his relief, he saw her fingers wrapped around the pole. He grunted and reached for her hand.

Twisting to avoid the white man's touch, Ketl's hands slipped off the pole.

"Damn!" Cam swore as he grabbed her ankle again.

She fell. A heart-piercing scream cut the air. Ketl closed her mouth and cut the scream off when she realized she wasn't going to hit the ground, but was being held by the white man. Yes, it was humiliating that he had caught her, and yes, he had no right to place his hands upon her, but if he didn't hold onto her, she would fall.

In her native tongue, she begged him not to drop her. Strange words poured from her mouth, and it confused Cam, because he couldn't understand her, but he could recognize the panic, the desperation in her voice. Yeah, there was no doubt she was begging him to save her life.

And he would, if he could.

He lay on his stomach, half on the rock outcropping which was part of the trail out of the canyon, while the upper part of his body splayed out over the wooden ladder. His face was plastered to the smooth wood, while his arms dangled over the side of the ladder, slippery with blood, her ankle precariously held in his hands. His face was ashen, his eyes glaring down at the drop to the ground.

He hated heights.

He hated flying, he hated tall buildings and most of all he hated where he was at that moment.

Grunting, Cam felt himself being dragged to the edge of the ladder by her weight. He sweated bullets. He damned her for cutting him and damned himself for bleeding, because the blood made her smooth skin slippery. His breathing came in labored grunts, not from the effort of holding onto her, but from the fear of where he was.

He heard her yell something at him. It wasn't a dialect he understood. "Damn it!" he growled. "Make sense if you're going to talk to me."

In her own tongue, Ketl told him that if he would pull her onto the ladder, she would spare him his life.

"I don't understand," Cam replied.

Ketl wiggled, trying to swing upwards and grab the pole.

"Stop!" Cam screamed. Her wiggling made his fingers slip on her ankle.

Seemingly, she understood him, because she stopped jerking and hung limply upside-down.

I'm not cut out for this kind of shit, Cam told himself.

Daring to recheck his position, he looked down. The drop had to be 30 feet to the ground, with red soil at the bottom sharply falling away from the edge of the cliff until it became dense with grass where it met the creek. The depth of the canyon made his heart leap into his throat while his vision became blurry.

What would McGuyver do in a situation like this? No answer came to him, although a gentle breeze hit his cheek as if to remind him he was higher than his level of comfort allowed. The fear settled in the pit of his stomach like a lead weight, and his palms grew icy cold. All he could manage was to grip her ankle tighter and brace his feet against the rock cliff. A tingling sensation, like champagne, began to grow in his arms at the edge of the ladder. Yeah, he knew her weight was cutting off his circulation. He wondered what would happen when he lost all feeling in his arm.

He could hear her moan and say something he couldn't understand.

Things were happening in slow motion. He felt numbed all over, and he knew if he could only draw his eyes off of the vast emptiness below him that he would be all right. But he couldn't; it was as if his eyes were glued to that which made him nauseous and incapable of moving.

Ketl knew she was going to die. *Wasn't it prophesied by Mockingbird that the white man would be the end of the People?*

🐦   🐦   🐦

Yes, she knew it was true. When she fell, she would land on her head. Never had she envisioned her death happening like this, and she knew it would break her grandfather's heart to return with her mother and find her bones scattered on the canyon floor. Wretchedly hating what she knew to be her fate, Ketl hung upside-down and cried a bloodcurdling scream to her gods to let them know she would join them soon.

The god-awful scream caused Cam's heart to stop for a split-second. Arm muscles jerked then went slack, and he felt her ankle slip through his fingers. Another scream bounced off the walls of the canyon, but this one was a pitiful wail and was silenced instantly.

The walls of the canyon pulsed in at him. The ground grew fuzzy, then turned black. Blinking, he tried to focus. Now colors returned to him—the streaks of red of the canyon walls, the cornflower blue sky, the green of cottonwoods and brush by the creek. And there, below him, a flesh-colored crumpled heap.

Her scream echoed in his ears. As the echo faded away, the scream was replaced by the tranquil silence of Willow Canyon.

Chapter 8

Outside on the front steps where he liked to park his old bones, Woody stared off into the sunset. The sun dipped low in the sky, hidden behind gigantic rearing cumulus clouds. He loved watching the weather form, and he knew it was putting on a particularly good show this afternoon. Sneaking up behind white thunderheads, a wall of heavy black clouds pushed inland. Laden with moisture, the clouds looked angry. Streaks of lightning split the sky, nudging the front-runner clouds higher and deeper into mesa country.

Blue eyes, the whites smeared with the yellow of age, kept a sharp eye to the Northwest. It was the direction Cameron January, the greenhorn, had taken the mare early that morning. Woody wasn't worried about Cam, not exactly. In his old age, he had learned the difference between worry and exhausting mental work. He worried about someone he loved or about someone who was doing the very best they knew how to do despite adverse conditions, whereas mental exercise was what happened when some dumb, incapable young upstart went gallivanting off into the desert alone and didn't come back when he should have.

Woody had always told his wife: "Me worry? No, I don't worry. Worry makes me sweat, sweat makes me stink, and I hate myself when I stink, so I don't worry."

So Woody wasn't worrying about Cam, he was merely in the throws of heavy mental exercise.

It would serve Cameron January right if his horse spooked at a snake, jumped left and right at the same time, and dumped him on the ground, leaving him grabbing at bunches of cactus instead of a mane of horse hair. The city slicker demonstrated gross naiveté when it came to riding or much else about the outdoors, for that matter.

From the start, Woody had suggested Christopher hobble Cam's leg to the stirrup so the city-slicker wouldn't fall off, but Christopher had thrown Woody a look which said, "He don't need no help. Let him find out for himself."

Woody had to wonder if Christopher wasn't jealous of the city boy with the styled hair cut and suave demeanor. A year didn't pass when Christopher didn't swear it was gonna' be his last on the ranch. He said he hated ranch work and the desert. He was a born complainer, Woody decided, wishing if the pup really thought that way about the ranch and the desert he'd get his hide gone.

Either put up or shut up or move out, Woody used to tell his own children. Christopher couldn't seem to make himself do either of those things.

After listening to Cameron talk about San Francisco with its tall buildings, bridges, parks, flowers, fancy restaurants, beautiful women, good wines, sleek cars, tailored suits and 100% cotton shirts that 'breathed', Woody could see the envy festering beneath Christopher's stiff wall of indifference. How many times, he wondered, had Woody told Christopher that monetary things didn't buy happiness, but Christopher thought he knew much more than Woody and repeatedly told

Woody he was going to find himself a rich woman and just see if those monetary things didn't bring happiness. Woody wanted to tell Christopher he wasn't going to find his rich woman a one-dog-town such as Aguilar, New Mexico, that he better get his ass in gear if he thought he could carry out those plans, but he didn't say so, feeling that old age gave him the right to speak when he damn well pleased and to be silent if the mood sparked him.

Christopher wasn't around today. If he had been, he would have told him to go look for Cam. Whether he would have gone after the city slicker is something Woody didn't know, but Woody wasn't going to work up a sweat about it, and he placed his whiskered-chin down on the cradle of his hands and watched as the weather played out its magical drama.

Far off in the distance, a bolt of lightning streaked across the sky. The bolt seemed to be pointing an angry finger at some far-off canyon, behind the buttes, way off so far that it was more than three minutes before Woody heard the rumble of the thunder. When the clouds clashed together, the bigger, blacker ones consumed the white puffy ones which seemed pure and innocent.

In the next few moments, a wall of water fell from the black sky beyond the buttes. The water came down in a straight sheet, starting and stopping at exact points. In front of the tenebrous rain, where rays of brilliant sun struck the earth, the rain and sun split the air, creating a magnificent rainbow that arched across the desert. A new spear of lightning escaped the sky and collided with earth. This time the resounding thunder came quickly and boomed, and for a split second, the repercussion felt like a giant vacuum. A hot breeze brushed Woody's face, then a dust devil danced in front of him, seemingly teasing him to get up and join it. The whirl of dust flitted away and was replaced by a stronger gust of air which picked up desert sand and blasted him.

Wiping sand from his eyes, he groaned, then pushed himself off the step and slowly lumbered into the house, shutting the screen door behind him. His body needed a nap. Ambling to the bed in the back room, he flopped down, stretched out on the bed, and decided he would push the mental exercise of thinking about Cam out of his mind and let sleep overtake him.

Besides, he thought to himself, *Cameron January is a grown man. He can take care of himself.*

ò   ò   ò

Cam didn't remember the climb down from the rock pillars and notched timbers. He wasn't sure, but he thought he might have been crying, because his eyes were blurry, his legs and knees shaking, his mind filled with remorse, a great sadness and guilt washing though him for what he had caused. Never in his wildest dreams did he consider his actions ending with the Indian being injured, and now due to his stupid ego and machismo she was lying in a heap at the bottom of the cliff.

He didn't remember the sick feeling in his stomach taking a firm hold of his senses, nor did he recall the total paralyzation of his limbs when he stared at the distance to the ground. He did remember holding something heavy in his hand and then not feeling the weight suspended from his fingers anymore. He did recall hearing the most pitiful, frightened scream which snapped him back from his numbed condition to a person with a body with feelings.

In horror, he had watched her fall. At first she didn't tumble but went straight down, head first. Fifteen feet below her a rock shelf jutted out from the cliff. She hit it hard—her shoulder and side taking most of the impact—then bounced off the rock and tumbled, ending up falling feet first.

With a muted thud, she landed squarely on her feet. For a moment, Cam was dumbfounded. She stood still, didn't cry out, didn't collapse, didn't jerk. It was as if the fall hadn't been anything—nothing more than a miss-step or a stub of her toe, in fact, he expected her to look up at him, laugh and then saunter way.

But she didn't. Nor did she look up at him. Instead her body trembled violently, and she collapsed like a limp doll.

"Shit," Cam swore.

Immediately, Cam started after her. Mountain Goat he wasn't; he was as sure footed as a whale. His feet felt huge, and they seemed not to want to do what his mind tried to tell them to do. Leaping wildly inside his chest, his heart was icy cold, but on a rampage which left his body shaking both from fear she was dead and from the greater fear of heights. One slip and he too would be lying in a crumpled heap at the bottom of the canyon.

He couldn't hurry, and he damned himself for his fallacious fear of heights. Going down was worse than going up, too, he realized as he carefully placed each foot on a solid foothold. A hawk swooped down from the cliff and screeched loudly.

"Shut up," Cam hissed at the bird.

Finally Cam jumped from a red rock and his feet touched ground. Immediately the dryness in his throat disappeared and the rubbery feeling in his legs went away. He ran along the red sandstone cliff, pushing aside sagebrush and rabbitbrush. Panting, he stopped over her body.

He wiped the back of his hand across his brow. "Oh, man," he mumbled and sighed wearily.

She looked dead. She lay on her side with one arm beneath her head, the other arm limply resting across her body. Her face had turned deathly white and was dirt-covered with a large bruise one her forehead with an accompanying goose egg the size of a golf ball. Blood oozed from the lump, trickling through her eye socket, across her straight nose, then trailing off her face where it formed a puddle in the dusty soil.

The sight of her blood left him nauseous, even though his own bloody arm didn't bother him one way or the other. Her left leg extended straight from her torso while her right leg was hitched beneath her, her knee almost touching her stomach. The right leg didn't look so hot, he decided. On her ankle was a bloody gash and beside the gash a lump the size of a baseball turned her ankle into a misshapen shape.

"Shit," he swore.

He didn't know what the hell to do with her. He didn't know anything about First Aide. The only thing drilled into Cam since he was a kid was to dial 911 in case of trouble. Palms open, he shrugged, then glanced from side to side, feeling totally helpless and incompetent. He couldn't leave her, he reasoned. She needed medical care. Bending down, he gently placed his arms beneath her. As he lifted her, she groaned a throaty sound, causing more guilt to wash though him.

Walking slowly with her gathered in his arms, he back-tracked to the village beneath the great cave. Climbing the carved stairs, he felt like he had stepped back to some other time and dimension. His cowboy boots tapped up the stone steps, echoing in his ears. His footsteps were only sounds he heard in the eerie surroundings, and the silence seemed to be compressing in on him from all sides. Darting a look right and left, he felt as though unseen eyes were watching him, wondering what alien had invaded their sanctuary.

Compassionately he laid her down in the shade on the stone plaza, and after stepping back and looking down at her, he hated himself for placing her there. He would have liked to have placed her on a mat or a bed—a hospital bed would have been his first choice. Placing her on cold, hard stones seemed criminal, but he had no other choice. So he left her there while he went in search of water.

He darted into and out of many of the small rock rooms.

Each, he noticed, displayed a different range of masonry: good, bad, rough, jagged stone, to finely finished stone eight to ten inches square. Inside one room, which was flooded with direct sunlight, he noticed the cracks between the stones were filled with sticks to keep the mud mortar from washing or crumbling away. In some places mud plaster covered the rocks, while in other places they were left barren. In some rooms the plaster had been covered with paint—one room was deep pink, another a soft tan. One had geometric designs painted on the walls.

He found a deep coiled-ware pot just inside the next room he checked. However, it was empty so he ran out of the cave and followed a well-worn path to the creek. At the edge of a pool in the creek, he stooped and filled the jug. He jogged up the carved set of steps, just as hundreds and hundreds of feet had done before him. When he knelt at her side, he felt foolish; he didn't know what to do for her and the crudely made jug filled with water seemed incredibly insufficient to tend her injuries.

Pulling a handkerchief from his back pocket, he soaked it and wiped the drying blood off of her face. She didn't move or make a sound. Dipping it in water and squeezing it almost dry, he left the compress on the knot on her forehead and began to look around for something to wrap around her ankle.

It was damned frustrating. In his apartment in the bottom drawer below the sink in his white-tiled bathroom was a selection of elastic bandages. Cam had a funny elbow. The doctor tried to tell him it was tennis elbow, but Cam had flushed and told the doctor that he didn't know what he was talking about, that Cam *didn't* play tennis, that it couldn't be tennis elbow. He didn't say that he thought himself much too *young,* too physically *fit* to have tennis elbow. It was a crushing blow to his self-esteem and Cam refused to do anything medically about the constant white-fire pain in his elbow. What he did do was try one type of bind after another, from good old Ace Bandage, to rubber girdles made especially for elbows that didn't want to bend without pain. At home he could have his choice, but here he had nothing.

Searching the rooms once again, he found woven mats and dragged them outside where he placed them on the rocks and gently moved her on top of them. In another room, one with a door shaped like a T, he found some weaving materials. There was a loom, some unfinished baskets, a pile of dried willow bark and another pile of green yucca leaves. He picked up some of the yucca leaves, also grabbing what looked like a spool of rough string.

Retreating from the room, his feet made a clomp-clopping as his cowboy boots hit the rocks of the plaza. He could hear his own footsteps echo off the ceiling of the cave. Because he was used to wall-to-wall carpeting which smothered the sound of footsteps, hearing his own footsteps bothered him, maybe even more than the silence in the canyon, the absence of a radio, absence of a phone, lack of any traffic sounds, a dog barking, a horn honking. The quiet was too loud and grated on his nerves.

While he wrapped yucca leaves tightly around her ankle, he wondered if she lived alone in the cave. By the looks of things, from the many rooms, the stone weapons and tools he had seen, from the number of woven mats in the various rooms, he had to guess that more than one person occupied the cave. He didn't like the thought, for if his guess was correct then another Indian, or perhaps *lots* of Indians, were going to come back to the cave, and they would find Cam. And they would find the Indian woman seriously hurt.

He wondered if the Indians were hostile. Did they roast their enemies over a bonfire? Did they make a captive run the gauntlet? Maybe these Indians had invented some ingenious slow, painful, torrid way to die. From the way she had been quick on the draw with her bone knife, and from the hate and venom emitted from her blazing eyes, he guessed he might be right. It was not a likable thought.

After he finished with her ankle, he used some of the yucca leaves to wrap his arm. The wound still oozed blood, but the pressure of the leaves closed the wound and the bleeding stopped. Sighing wearily, Cam rocked back on his heels and stared out at the canyon. He heard the far-off cry of a hawk. As if answering the cry of the hawk, a turkey jumped off a roosting post and scurried across the plaza strutting in front of Cam.

"Scat!" Cam cried.

The turkey squawked, flapped its wings and disappeared over the side of the plaza wall.

The silence heightened his anxiety. He felt as though he were waiting for something to happen and he considered leaving. The more he thought about it, the more panicked he became at the thought of remaining in the canyon where the rest of her tribe could find him. Nervously, he wiped perspiration from his brow. He had administered to her as best as he could, and told himself the smart thing to do would be to leave her and go.

Biting his lip, he stared at her. Ever so slightly her thin nostrils flared. Her color was better now than when he first found her, in fact, her cheeks were flushed and not ghost-white like before. Yeah, he thought she would be all right. Cam lifted her hand and placed it on her thigh. He moved the jug of water close to her so that if she awakened and was alone, she wouldn't have to move to take a drink. Now his eyes went back to her fingers. They had felt fragile to his touch just now, not rough and capable of handling a knife the way she had.

He shuddered, thinking of way she had crouched with the knife in her hand, waiting for the chance to plunge it in his chest. Swallowing hard, Cam pushed himself to his feet and sauntered to the edge of the plaza with every intention of going down the steps and disappearing down the trail. But guilt nagged at him. At the apex of the steps he stopped and looked at the ceiling of stone, unable to make up his mind whether or not to leave. Yes, he knew it would be a rotten thing to do to the woman, but he had his own hide to look out for. Certainly, he reasoned, someone would return to the cave soon, and certainly whomever it was, would know more about broken bones and bruises than Cam did. And certainly whoever returned, would not be happy to find Cam. Of that he was certain—he could feel it deep in his gut.

But he didn't leave. He wanted to, he really did, but a curious force held him back and he remained standing on the plaza. Craning his neck upward, then turning and following the arc of the cave until it came down in the rear where numerous pictographs gave the place a spookiness he hadn't noticed before, his whole body felt a chilled premonition of malevolence. Quickly, he looked away from the back wall and gazed out of the cave. The roof of the cave was a huge arc and below him the canyon valley spread out like a nature lover's patchwork quilt: aspen and cottonwood, raspberry bushes and willow, sage and pinion, pools of water and sandstone. Looking beyond the canyon to a flat desert floor, he squinted to see miles beyond where the two huge buttes reared up to catch the sky. His eyes flickered with longing. Then his forehead creased with a troubled frown.

He heard a low moan come the Indian woman.

As if defeated, his shoulders sagged. Cam tore his eyes off what he knew to be a sane world—even the backward town of Aguilar—and returned to the woman's side. No, he wouldn't leave her. He may be a rat where women were concerned, but he wouldn't leave her. Let them roast him, let them peel the skin from him. Cameron January might be self-centered, but he would not leave the Indian woman. He knelt beside her and gently touched her cheek. He wondered why she hated him so. When she had looked at him there had been nothing but abhorrence in the depth of her eyes. It angered him that she should dislike him so, because most women he met worshiped him, and it made him uncomfortable to know there was a female who would rather sink a knife in his heart rather than slinking into his bed.

All that the Indian woman had to do was stop and talk to him, he reasoned. She didn't have to run. He hadn't hurt her or her precious pile of rocks comprising her home. He grew angry thinking how stupid it was for her to be injured and him scared shitless in the middle of an anachronistic camp of stone.

She moaned again. This time Cam thought she aptly got just what she deserved, although his eye twitched as if to remind him he had caused it, that she really deserved to be left alone. While he watched the clouds darken and heard the thunder rattle the canyon, he decided he had made a poor judgment call by entering the valley. He should have kept away. He should have stayed away from her. She was too weird, too dangerous for him to be trifling with. Hadn't Woody told him not to do anything stupid? Hadn't Cam smugly waved his remark away? Yes, to both questions and it didn't make Cam feel so smug thinking about it.

While he sat by her side, he washed the dried blood off his arm and fingers. He poured water over the yucca leaves wrapped over the wound. The water stung like crazy. He swore and bit his lip until the pain subsided. Tilting his head back against a rock wall, he closed his eyes. His breathing became even, slow. Clouds covered the sun and the ensuing dark sky wrapped him in a soft cocoon. Before he drifted off into a light sleep, he placed his hand on the Indian woman's shoulder. Then he slept.

When the first bolt of lightning split the darkened sky, the flash of light caused Cam's eyes to flutter open. The thunder was a rumble, not enough to make him start, but it had awakened him. Now the sky was dark as murky lavender, a breeze making the cottonwoods sway. Dust whipped up and hit him in the face. A shaft of brilliant lightning hit the mesa top somewhere very close by and thunder cracked. It was loud and echoed inside the cave. With wings flapping, several turkeys appeared from nowhere, ran across the plaza and disappeared into rooms at the back of the cave.

A cool breeze brushed his cheek. He sniffed. A distinct acidic smell filled the air—almost a mixture of pine tar and vinegar. Thunder cracked loudly and rain fell in heavy metal-colored sheets.

At first he was mesmerized; he was inside looking out at the rain. It was like being in front of the largest plate glass window which overlooked the most lovely, most realistic garden. He moved closer to the Indian woman, not sure why, but feeling the need to be close to her, as if they were the last two people on earth and the forty day rains had just commenced.

Because of the roof of the cave, the rain missed the plaza, and Cam was amazed that the people who had built the village had known exactly where to place their outdoor work area so that they would be dry even when it rained. Getting up he walked to the edge of the plaza and glanced up at the overhanging lip of the cave. Drips of water cascaded over the side like bombs, splattering the rocks, making a very loud patty-pat. Then he heard a new sound and cocked his head to his left.

A thin tendril of water cascaded from the mesa top and landed in a circular formation of well-sealed rocks. Another waterfall appeared in front of him, then another to his immediate right. Suddenly, there were more than ten veils of water, becoming more capricious minute by minute, the circular wells filling with fresh rain water. A deafening sound of water hitting rock surrounded him, and a fresh sweet smell of rain cleansed the air and a wave of cool air danced across his cheek.

So as not to get wet, he backed inside the cave, then resettled himself at her side. A strange feeling came over him. He shivered and had to squint his eyes because they suddenly felt hot. He was surrounded by the remains of prehistoric culture of which he had no inkling, of which he hadn't known existed until now. He had been able to co-habitat with the outdoors just enough to get through his geological field work, although there were times he thought of going into some other form of work. The times his parents sent him to summer camp had been a dismal failure. He didn't like playing cowboys and Indians, he didn't like playing in sand or dirt, he didn't like fishing, hunting or hiking. In plain truth, he didn't like the outdoors. He had been raised in an apartment and did like playing with cars, modeling clay, watching television and collecting rocks. He *did not* hunt for the rocks, you understand, he bought them with his allowance money from a store down on Union Street.

He had attended college at Stanford University and was quite pleased to find an apartment with a pool on the ground floor, underground parking, microwave and automatic dishwasher. He drove exactly five asphalt-covered blocks to the campus, parked in a Cyclone-fenced lot and walked across cement walks to his classes in brick and glass buildings. Vacations were spent back in San Francisco or to some other place that he fancied, such as Switzerland or Sweden. He liked the clean countries, the ones where hotels were first-rate, the linens crisp and clean. After he graduated, he returned to San Francisco and on his salary he was able to afford a new apartment—in a development near the ship yards in South San Francisco.

The ships intrigued him, so he went on a singles cruise from Los Angeles to Mazatlan. On the ship, he went from basking in the sun during the day to drinking and bed-hopping at night. He met Sharon on the ship. She was not a vacationer, but a model, on board ship doing a job for Van Neyes Swimsuits. Tall and willowy with just the right amount of clavicle bones and hip bones sticking out, she was a knockout in the bright pastel suits she wore. Cam didn't get to first base with her on the boat, however, he did manage to wrangle her phone number from her, and called her a few weeks later. She agreed to a date, and he took her to Sausalito for a very fancy evening of drinks and dinner. From then on, he had dated her more seriously than all the other women he met.

Cam chuckled to himself, thinking back over the life he knew.

Now he was in the company of an Indian, sitting on the stone floor of a village that should be removed to the Smithsonian. He was staring in wonder at the rain and the cascading waterfalls and being lulled by the sound into a dopey sort of acceptance. Something inside him made him reach out and lift the woman by her shoulders. He resettled her in his lap, resting her head against his chest, holding her close. He could tell her breathing was shallow, because he could see just the slightest movement from her nostrils which were paper thin. With the back of his fingers, he caressed her cheek, then stopped, the action seeming to distract from the sounds of the water and the show presented before him by nature.

Sitting ramrod-still, Cameron January held the Indian in his arms and watched as rain and the night played out its majestic performance.

Chapter 9

Just as suddenly as it started, the rain stopped.

The silvery water spilling over the lip of the cave in veiled threads disappeared, and the pitter-patter of the waterfall on the rock plaza stopped. The sky cleared, and the clouds drifted away in an easterly course. Dark skies melted into the apricot color the sky turns before the sun dies. Long and dark shadows permeated the cave, while the last rays of sun bathed the top of the canyon in dying embers of magenta and orange.

Shaking his head as if to clear it, Cam wondered how long he had been watching the weather change while holding the Indian woman. It seemed like eternity, as if he had been transported to some other time in space where time really had no meaning whatsoever. A quick glance at his watch told him it had only been a little more than an hour. His stomach rumbled, however, which made him realize he was human and on planet earth, that he was made of flesh and blood, that he needed food.

The woman's face had more color than it had earlier, so he gently laid her down on the mat and began to rummage through the assorted clay pots to see what he could find to eat. His mouth watered for a bag of Lay's Potato Chips, or a bag of Oreos, maybe some Ball Park Wieners, or an instant Cup-O-Soup. Even half-burnt biscuits like Woody's would do. Ducking though a T-shaped door into a room near the back of the plaza, he found a tall basket with some strips of what looked like trampled beef jerky. He had to rub ashes off the piece he grabbed, and his nose wrinkled when he sniffed it. He put it back. He found a hardened half pumpkin shell filled with dried corn. *No good,* he decided. He found dried beans hard as rocks. *No way.*

Through the door, he eyed a turkey which roosted on a protruding log from one of the rock houses. *Nope.* In a refuse heap he found freshly gnawed bones. They were small bones, and he wondered to what type of animal they belonged. Then he thought of the rabbit he had seen the day before, and his stomach lurched from hunger and disgust.

Climbing up a wood ladder, he crawled through a smaller door formed like a T and entered a room, cool and dark and smelling of something like onion. When his eyes adjusted to the darkness, he found an intricately woven bowl filled with a pile of strange-shaped bulbs. They were long and skinny instead of round like onions or potatoes. He picked one up and sniffed it. It smelled yeasty. Frowning, he put it back. He wouldn't eat anything he couldn't name. Next he found many jars filled with dried corn and more beans.

Quickly leaving the room, he climbed down the ladder into the kiva. Inside the round room it, too, was dark, but warmer than the room in the back of the cave. It smelled musty, but not like old dust from an attic, but from the dirt floor and embers of a dead fire. The odor was right for the under-ground pit, and as his eyes adjusted to the dimness, he searched the stone bench which circled the radius of the room. In a shallow basket, he found a pile of fresh berries which were cool to his touch. Tentatively, he tasted one. Fresh raspberries! *Bingo!* Next to the berries were other things, bulbs and fresh beans, which had been placed in the kiva so as not to be spoiled by the broiling heat.

He squatted on the dirt floor and devoured the berries, his throat constricting with the sweet-tartness of the wild fruit. It didn't satisfy him. Searching the baskets, he found one filled with compact round things, again undefinable as to what they were. Sniffing them, he decided they didn't smell. He cast them aside. With a despondent look on his face, he went back to the tall basket filled with the rotten looking meat. This he ate, gingerly picking it up, chewing thoroughly, swallowing slowly, trying not to guess what it was, and hoping it wouldn't turn his stomach inside out.

Night came on fast. First long shadows stretched across the plaza, then disappeared entirely when the sun slipped below the horizon. The first stars blinked on in the East while the western sky remained deep purple. Before he knew it, and before he found dying embers of fire in a different kiva, it turned pitch black. Cam was used to blinking neon lights of a big city and handy switches in his apartment to turn on lights at the whim of his fingertips. Flashlights worked nicely, too, he mused as he groped around in the darkness, trying to determine where it was that he wanted to go.

Settling himself in the plaza next to the Indian, he watched the night sky begin to unfold. Suddenly, a wave of cold air drifted down from the top of the mesa. It disappeared as quickly as it came, but then another wave came after it, and another, until the air turned biting cold.

He swore, damning the hostile conditions: fiery hot, freezing cold, scorching sun, unrelenting rain, blinding sun, inky blackness.

Shivering, he grabbed the woman under her arms and inched backwards, away from the gaping mouth of the cave until his back hit the outside wall of one of the houses. He left her there and went back for the woven mats. He found one woven with feathers which was soft and this he gently placed over the Indian. Then he gathered her in his arms, pulled her close and stared out at the canopy of brilliant stars.

Somehow he slept.

The following day by the time the sun was overhead, Woody's mental exercise was on the verge of worry. Although this went against everything he believed, he knew something had happened to the city boy since he hadn't returned the night before and there was no sign of him this morning, either. Coupled with his absence was the fact that his horse hadn't shown up. Cam's mare was like a well-trained puppy and would hightail it home if it had shaken a rider from its back.

Woody hated his infirm body. If he were younger, he would saddle a horse and go lookin' for the city slicker. If his daughter and grandson would allow him, he would hop in a Jeep and drive out on the dirt roads for a look see. But they refused to let him drive, said he was too old, his reflexes too poor, his eyesight too bad.

What did they know?

Maybe he had failed his driving test and not scored so hot on the eye exam. Maybe he had put the Jeep into a ditch a time or too, but it was his life. It should be his decision to drive or not to drive, not theirs.

So he paced. From one end of the house to the front porch, down the steps, sit down, get up, back up the steps, back inside the house to the back bedroom and stop. Turn around. Back to the kitchen out to the front and down the steps. Sit down, get up. A hundred times. No, maybe two hundred. *What did it matter?*

That morning, when he was in his sitting-on-the-step phase of his pacing, he looked up and his eyes were sharp enough to see a tail of dust coming up off the desert just this side of the buttes, maybe half a mile or so away. He got up and started walking toward the dust.

Even though Cam thought Woody a cankerous old geezer, he couldn't have been happier to see the familiar face as he rode toward the ranch. The Indian woman was cradled on his lap, hunched forward, as limp as death, while his arm wrapped around her to hold her on the horse. It was no easy feat getting out of the canyon with her, either. The horse didn't like carrying two and tried as best it could to sideswipe its passengers at any obstacle.

When he had entered the canyon, he had walked the horse up the canyon because of the brush, but now he had to ride it to hold her in the saddle. Branches grabbed at his hat, thorns clawed at his pants, rock walls seared his leg as the horse pressed against them. While this was going on, Cam struggled with the limp Indian. She sagged this way and that while fresh blood dripped on his arm from the cut on her forehead.

He had uttered just about every epitaph he had ever heard by the time they passed the buttes. Now the horse realized it was in familiar territory and oats and sugar cubes were not far away, so the mare increased its tempo to a bone-jarring trot. With each prance of the horse, the Indian woman bobbed up and came down on his groin. There was no way he could move to stop the torturous pain, and Cam couldn't get a good hold on the reins to pull in the horse to make it slow down. He had to grab the Indian firmly beneath her breasts so she wouldn't flop around on him so hard and with each bounce, he could feel her breasts hit his arm. Thinking he couldn't endure the agony of her bobbing on top of him and thinking he didn't like the pleasurable feeling of her breasts on his arm, Cam sighed with relief when the mare came to a bone-jarring stop in front of Woody.

"What the hell you got there?" Woody asked.

Cam groaned. "An Indian…I think."

Staring at the blood coming from the Indian and the Cameron January's bloody shirtsleeve, Woody asked, "You scalp him?"

"Hell no!" Cam roared. "And it's a 'her', not a 'him'."

"Where'd you get her?"

"I think she got me," Cam dryly replied, anxious to get off the horse and her off his lap. "Damn-it all, Woody! Take the reins and lead the animal to the yard. One more bounce and I think my balls are going to explode."

Chuckling, Woody took the reins and started for the house, and as he shuffled across the desert, he nodded absently to himself, commending himself for his lack of worry.

Cam carried the Indian inside the house and gently laid her on his bed. He flopped in the chair beside the bed and hung his head. Wearily, he sighed.

"She needs a doctor," Cam said as he wiped his brow with the back of his shirt sleeve.

Woody stared at the Indian. She wasn't like anything he had ever seen before, and for a minute a flash of a defiant Indian high on a cliff sprang in front of his eyes. As he watched her, she rolled her head on the pillow. She moaned. It appeared to Woody she was beginning to regain consciousness. The gash on her forehead looked clean, the skull not concave—just a lot of dripping blood which was common for a head injury. Her ankle was wrapped in yucca leaves and he could tell it was swollen, but the way she moved her body back and forth on the bed led him to believe no bones were broken.

"She'll mend," Woody said.

"I think she's dying," Cam countered.

"Hardly. Little rest, some food and she'll be up and around and purring like a kitten in a few days."

Cam laughed. "Kitten! More like a wildcat. She nearly killed me with a knife." He pointed to his arm. "She went for my heart, but only managed to try and sever my arm from my body. I don't want to be anywhere around her when she's up and around. Let's take her to a hospital and let doctors deal with her. Maybe we should call the sheriff too. I think she's crazy. She lives in a cave all by herself—"

"Where?" Woody interrupted.

"In a cave up a canyon."

"Describe it to me," Woody impatiently said.

Cam sighed. "Okay. First of all, it was a hell of a long way from here. Way beyond the buttes. There was a creek coming out of a mesa. I figured it was a canyon, so I entered it through a gulch formed by breaking away of part of the limestone cliffs. There were shrubs hiding the entrance and the ceiling of the tunnel entrance was low—"

"How low?" Woody asked.

"Low enough I had to get off the horse."

Woody held his gaze. "Hmmm," he commented.

"At first I wasn't going to go into the canyon, but curiosity got a better hold of me and I went in. I was thoroughly shocked to find a broadening valley, a creek and at the head was the great cave and ruins. Only they weren't ruins. It was a lived-in city. Only she was the sole occupant. She fell down the cliff after she tried to kill me and I chased her."

Woody was gray around the lips. His knees felt like oatmeal, and he leaned against the wall to give him strength.

This is impossible! The same canyon. An Indian! The prophesy of my life has been fulfilled.

Without a doubt, he knew the Indian on the bed was an Anasazi. The realization paralyzed him for a moment.

"I think her leg is broken," Cam said. "And her head...I don't know. Maybe a concussion. She needs a hospital."

"I don't think this Indian would much like a hospital,"

Woody thought out loud. "Looks like you took care of her good enough."

Cam chuckled. "My first aid is archaic," he stated truthfully, obvious by the bandage on her ankle. "I didn't want to touch her, but I couldn't leave her there, alone and unconscious, so I wrapped those leaves around her ankle. I got her forehead to stop bleeding, but it started again as we rode into the ranch." He took off his dusty Stetson and ran his fingers though his hair. "Hell," he drawled, "I don't know if I did her more harm than good. She needs a doctor." Then he cast an inquisitive glance at Woody. "And why wouldn't she like the hospital?"

"Son, what you got there is a person from the past. She's an honest-to-goodness Anasazi Indian. She's never seen a hospital, a doctor, a needle, an ambulance, a car, asphalt, gasoline." He pointed at her. "She might as well have been in a time machine, coming from her world to ours. You pick her up and deposit her in a hospital and she'll die, sure as shootin'."

Cam frowned, not sure he understood what Woody said. "What the hell you talking about?" he blurted.

"I'm talking about what all the historians and archaeologists will do to her once they hear she stepped out one of the Anasazi ruins. She's the greatest thing to happen to the Department of the Interior. She's an archaeologist's dream come true. Why, they'll wire her and study her and poke and prod her until she'll quit eatin' and die. She's like a wild animal." He shook his head. "She don't belong in a hospital. In fact, she don't in our world, just as you didn't belong in hers. She is fragile, very fragile."

Woody's words made him laugh hard. "Fragile? Are you serious? Living in a cave? A knife-welding, shrieking maniac? You wouldn't believe what she eats. Fragile? No way."

"I didn't mean fragile like in soft and feminine sort of fragile. I mean fragile in exposure to the modern world. If you take her to a hospital, she'll take one look at all the people leering at her, the needles, the machinery and curl up into a ball and go into shock."

With the memory of her venomous eyes fresh in his find, his arm began to throb where she sliced him open with her knife. Cam touched his arm. "I don't think you know what she's like. She's tough as nails. She's wild. I think you should call the Humane Society. Tell them to bring a cage and a tranquilizer gun."

"Boy, you just don't understand this country, nor the feelin's of this Indian woman."

Cam wiped the dripping sweat off his brow with the back of his hand. "I understand there's something really weird about her, something I don't understand, something I don't want to try and understand. Everything is really wrong about her—"

Woody frowned, interrupting: "Nothing is all wrong, Sonny. Even a broken clock is right twice a day."

It was tough to argue with a man twice your age, Cam thought. "I just wish I hadn't found the canyon. I wish I hadn't seen her. I wish she hadn't fallen." He paused, took a deep breath and in a low voice added, "And I wish I hadn't brought her here, but I had no choice."

"Ain't no good to wish. It's just like spittin' into the wind." Woody cast a sidelong glance at Cam, eyeing the younger man with a pharisaic glint. "You *did* find the canyon," he stated, knowing full well there was some other dimension at work on Cameron January. "I'm an old man, boy. I've searched for the canyon myself for years and years and years. I seen it but once. I kept on lookin' for it, but where my tracks were the day before, weren't there the next day. There's places out on the mesa you see one time and can never find again, not in your lifetime. That's mean country out there, like I told you. Hot. Dry. Evil. Wild! Yes, wild country. Years ago I seen a man go in there and come back stark ravin' mad. People say the country is evil. People say ghosts dance on the buttes. People say you're a fool to want to see what's there.

"I say they're wrong. I say the roots of America lay out there. Why, you and me, boy, we ain't got the blood of true Americans in our veins. No sir. The Danes and the British weren't the first to set foot in America. Way back yonder, the Anasazi were the first—"

"You trying to tell me that *I* am descended from a race of extinct Indians?" Cam blurted.

"Hell, boy, I ain't trying to tell you nothin'. And whether you believe in the Bible or The Theory of Evolution, we all got one common ancestor, whether he is called Adam or Eve, the Big Bird in the Sky, or Ape, it don't make no difference."

Cam sighed. He was not one to argue philosophical thoughts, particularly on a hot day with a liver-spotted old man, especially when it was about a beautiful young Indian woman who had tried to place a knife in his heart. "I don't know what you're getting at, Woody, but I'm too hot and tired to argue with you. The fact is I don't know where she came from, I don't know who she is or what she was doing all alone on the mesa. I don't have any idea why *I* found her or the canyon. Nor do I care."

"You found the canyon because the gods wanted you to," Woody said flatly. "She *did* hurt herself, and you *did* bring her here. Them's the facts. Can't change what's done. Can only make do with what you did."

"Yeah? Well, if 'them's the facts', and you won't call the hospital or sheriff or Animal Control Officer, then *my facts* are that I wash my hands of her. I don't want to mess with an anachronistic relic from the past—"

"A what?"

"Anachronistic. Outdated. Old. Ancient."

Woody leaned forwards and stared at the Indian. Then he gave Cam a queer look. "You calling her old? I'm *old*. She's fresh from the womb. Pretty thing too. Ain't you got eyes?"

Refusing to remember the shock he felt when he first saw her face or the way she had felt in his arms when he held her through the night, Cam said insipidly, "I've got eyes, but not for her, and I didn't mean she was old, speaking in the amount of years. I meant socially speaking, as in fitting in with the way of life as we live it now, and you were the one, anyhow, who said she was that type of old, not me."

Woody waved a hand at Cam. "You youngsters don't know how to express yourselves. You're always in a hurry to go here or be there and don't know how to communicate any longer."

What did communication have to do with the Indian? "Hell," Cam began with a weary sigh, "I damn well can communicate to you that I don't want to have to worry about what's going to happen to that…that," Cam paused, not sure what he should call the woman who was sprawled on his bed, then pointed at her and finished, "savage! I've got enough to worry about without worrying about her. You understand?"

Woody retreated to the kitchen, grabbed a dishcloth, soaked it in water, wrung it out, shuffled back to the bedroom and placed the wet cloth on Ketl's forehead. Without looking at Cam, he replied, "I understand, city boy. Remind me to teach you how not to worry."

"You?" Cam said with a laugh, thinking Woody would be the last person in the world to teach anything to Cameron January.

"Yes, me." He pointed to Ketl. "And I betch'a that Indian could teach you more than you ever learned in school."

Cam threw his head back and roared with laughter. "Old man," he said between gulps of air, "you don't know what you're talking about."

&. &. &.

Ketl regained consciousness in the evening. Outside the

sky was a rosy-red and radiated a warm glow through the window, turning the cracked and peeling plaster walls of the room into what appeared to be the insides of a fire-ember. The strange surroundings and red-walled room made her heart thud inside her chest which in turn caused her head to begin a rhythmic pounding, each beat feeling like a stone axe was smashing against the insides of her skull. It was very quiet around her, but it was a different quiet than what she was used to; she could not hear the trees as they bowed to the evening breeze, nor could she hear the ripple of water over the rock dams, nor could she hear the soft voices of her ancestors when they spoke to her from the Fifth World. These were the things she heard when it was quiet and she was alone.

Now her ears perceived a strange hum. She had never heard the sound before, and it sent a spike of fear up her spine. Vaguely, she remembered the stranger who had invaded her canyon. Her heart beat faster. Her memory was hazy, but bits and pieces floated in and out of her mind and she remembered trying to kill her enemy and failing and running and falling. The last thing she remembered was her enemy holding her leg…then letting go, letting her fall to what she thought would certainly be her death.

Perhaps she was dead. Perhaps this was the Fifth World. Mockingbird did not describe it as such, however, and she expected to see her father, who had journeyed to the Fifth World long ago, and Pavi's wife and those of the Eagle Clan that she could remember from her childhood and who had gone on to the next world. Listening carefully, she wondered if the strange hum was the gods calling to her.

She knew she was not in Willow Canyon. This was not her home. The realization raised the level of panic in her veins, and her palms turned icy cold while her forehead burned as sweat broke out as the fear caused havoc within her body. Cocking her head, she centered all her attention on the peculiar sound and tried to determine if it was one of the other gods trying to communicate with her.

In the kitchen, his expression tight with strain, Cam listened to the same hum from the old refrigerator. Sitting opposite him at the table, Christopher ignored the hum from the appliance—he'd listened to it hum since he was a kid. Cam frowned as he watched the old man. Woody was getting on his nerves. Woody had paced and talked nonstop for the last hour, relating everything he knew about the Anasazi Indians. At least three times, he had told the same story to Cam and Christopher about finding the canyon as a boy and the Indian he had seen on the cliff.

Trying to remain indifferent, but feeling a growing level of discomfort, Cam listened while he eyed the bottle of Jack Daniels on top of the refrigerator. He didn't want to believe the things Woody was saying about a whole group of people who vanished from the face of the earth without leaving any written trace of why they came or why they left. Even the old ruins hadn't told the archaeologists very much, Woody explained.

Cam's arm began to throb in a constant rhythm which seemed to match Woody's steps. His pacing bothered Cam, and he pointed to the Jack Daniels, "Mind if I kill the ache in my arm with some of your whiskey?"

Woody only grunted.

Cam went to the humming refrigerator, grabbed the bottle of liquor and a glass and stomped outside to the front porch, eager to anesthetize both his arm and his brain.

Christopher got up and walked toward the back bedroom.

While Ketl listened to the humming, still trying to figure out where she was, she felt the side of the bed and realized she was not sleeping on a mat on the floor like she had done all of her life. The knowledge frightened her even more, because she knew she wasn't at the Hopi mesa, nor was she at any of the other ruins belonging to her people.

Suddenly she was aware that she was not alone in the strange room. Her skin prickled. Slowly, very slowly with perfect sang-froid, she turned her head in the direction she felt the presence of the other human.

Fascinated, Christopher watched from the doorway as the softest pair of green eyes turned to him. Woody had described the Indian and Christopher had peeked at her while she slept, but he was not prepared for the look on her face or the slight flaring of her nostrils when she saw him. She didn't flinch or jump, but sat rigidly still. She was like a creature in the wild: frightened, innocent, one feral creature meeting another for the first time. She was incredibly beautiful, even with a bruised forehead, and he felt as though he was gazing upon the Ninth Wonder of the World.

Smiling at her, his heart in his throat, Christopher approached the bed and knelt beside her. "Hello," he whispered.

Ketl was alert to the danger of facing her enemy, the white man. However, this man was not like the other white man. Anger didn't grow in his eyes, nor did her blood dash through her veins like a swollen creek when he came toward her. She didn't feel threatened by him and managed to return a frightened half-smile.

"*Namatacham*," she replied which was the polite way to greet a stranger in her own tongue.

Christopher thought her voice sounded like velvet. "Do you speak English?" he asked anxiously.

She knew what he asked. To the other man, the one who invaded her canyon, the one with the piercing eyes the color of dancing waters, she would have refused to answer, refused to let him know that she spoke the tongue of the white man, but this man was different.

"Small talk," she said, not wanting to let on how well she could speak his language.

"Small talk," Christopher repeated. "I think you mean that

you speak only a little English."

Ketl nodded.

"Who are you?" Christopher asked.

"Ketl," she replied after a long pause.

He wasn't sure if that meant she was from a band of Indians called 'Ketl' or it was her name. "Is that your name?" he gently asked.

She nodded and pointed at herself. "Ketl." Then she pointed at Christopher. "*Hakomi?*" she asked in her native tongue.

"Christopher. My name is Christopher."

"Chris…" she tried.

"Yes, you can call me Chris."

"Chris," she said again, thinking this man had some brains, for he had answered her simple question while the other man had looked at her as if she had diseased skin when she asked his name.

Pulling her legs up under her so she could situate herself better on the elevated mat, she winced as her ankle twisted and a spear of hot pain shot up through her leg. Grabbing her ankle, she bit her lip to hold tears at bay.

"It hurts you?" Christopher asked.

Ketl nodded.

"Gramps!" he hollered without taking his eyes off of her.

Woody came shuffling down the hall and peered over Christopher's shoulder at the Indian. "She awake?"

"Yes, and her leg hurts."

"If'n she's awake, it should hurt," Woody said.

"Well, do something for it," Christopher said, fuming at his Grandfather's dry remark.

"I ain't no doctor."

"No you ain't, but you fixed more bones and cuts than most doctors around these parts."

He pointed at her ankle. "Her leg ain't broke, just mussed

up a bit. It hurts her now because she's got it all cockeyed. It needs to be straight." Woody pushed Christopher aside and reached for Ketl.

No white man was going to touch her! Ketl screamed. She pushed herself against the outside wall while her eyes darted from the men to the door and back and her breath came in ragged gulps. Terrified, she glared at Woody's outstretched hands.

"I don't think she wants you to touch her," Christopher said.

"I got eyes," Woody spat.

"Her name is Ketl. Tell her what you want her to do. She understands a little English."

Woody rocked on his heels, studying his grandson, then glanced at the Indian girl who was trying to mold with the wall. He mumbled something to himself and then patted the end of the bed while turning his whiskered-face toward Ketl.

"Stretch out your leg," Woody told her. "I won't touch you. Promise. Scout's Honor."

His voice was gravely, his eyes old and yellowed, yet his tone was gentle and he reminded her of Pavi. Her fear melted. Ketl did as he bid and outstretched her curled leg. Immediately the throbbing in her ankle stopped. "*Hakomi?*" she questioned.

"That means 'Who are You?'" Christopher said to Woody.

"You think I can't hear?" Woody snapped.

"No Gramps, I just thought you might not understand her."

"I understand more than you think. Now you go. I want to talk to her alone for awhile."

A deep frown crawled up Christopher's brow. "She's the most interesting thing that will ever happen to this godforsaken place. She's history in the making! Now that something really exciting is happening around here, you're telling me to go! It ain't fair, Gramps!"

"Life in general ain't fair, and I ain't tellin' you to leave forever. I spent my whole life wonderin' about the Injun' I saw and before I die I want to set my mind at ease. I want to ask her about him, and I don't want you distracting her. Is that too much to ask?"

He Shrugged, "No, but what am I supposed to do?"

"Well, I'd suggest you join Mr. January out on the front steps where he's killing a bottle of Jack Daniels."

"Why's he gettin' drunk?" Christopher asked, knowing that Cam rarely drank more than one or two beers.

"Hell if I know," Woody replied.

Sighing with exasperation, Christopher shook his head. His eyes narrowed however, as he took one last look at Ketl, from the tip of her bare feet up her lanky thighs, to the points of her breasts through her cotton smock, to her lovely face. Smiling at her, he waved good-bye.

Ketl didn't respond.

Shrugging, Christopher left Woody with the Indian and grabbed a glass. Next he headed to the front porch to find Cameron January and the bottle of Jack Daniels.

Chapter 10

On Tuesday at four in the afternoon, Stanley arrived at the Farmington Archeology lab, which was the central clearing house for all artifacts discovered in the Four Corners area. By Thursday morning, preliminary results from the carbon-14 tests were complete; the bones of the skeleton removed from room 214 in Pueblo Bonito were no more than 100 years old, in fact, perhaps less. However, the clay vessel buried with the skeleton dated back to 1130, and the turquoise trinket, which was threaded through a hole with braided yucca fiber, dated close to 1250, give or take a few years.

The news left Stanley stunned.

This turned out to be a mystery even greater than the mystery of why the Anasazi Indians disappeared. Who was the woman? Was she white? Indian? And if she was white, where did she come from? Who buried her? And why a burial in the dark shallow floor of a room in a crumbling Indian ruin? Why were old Indian relics buried with her?

In his office, sitting at his nicked and scared walnut desk, the list of questions Stanley jotted in one column on his legal pad far outnumbered the adjoining column where he noted answers to the questions. He was getting nowhere fast.

He tried supposing: Suppose the woman had been a pioneer who died on the trail west? No. No trail existed through the harsh country of Chaco Canyon, only ancient roads the Indians themselves constructed, roads almost invisible to the human eye after hundreds of years of windstorms and rain. Suppose this woman had been lost and had wandered into the canyon where she died? Maybe. But wandered from where? And who buried her? Suppose the ring had been taken from a pioneer, traded a number of times and ended up on the finger of an Indian? Maybe. But again, who buried her in Pueblo Bonito? And where did the much older relics come from?

Although his mind ran wild with unscientific reasoning, he had no answers. Perhaps, through some time warp, this person stepped back in time, lived with the Anasazi, died, moved forward again in time, and was buried in Pueblo Bonito in the dark recesses of one of the stone rooms; perhaps this 'modern' person actually walked and talked with the Anasazi Indians of long ago.

That last thought made a jolt of excitement run up his spine, because he had studied the Anasazi for more than ten years and was no closer to determining who they were, what their beliefs were and why they left, than he was when he first heard the name Anasazi. To think that a person with modern thought process had walked among ancient Indians was mind-boggling.

The Hopi Indians claimed to be living in the Fourth World, having come from the more evil and wild Third World. Perhaps, Stanley rationalized, this person fell through a gap in the dimension we live in and arrived in the Hopi Third World. That was really far-out, and Stanley castigated himself for thinking it, being a man who recorded facts as he found them.

Yet it was impossible not to let his mind roam at will and invent ways a person who belonged to the 1800s could have been buried in a city occupied in the 1200s, with burial artifacts of the same time period, and in a city that was abandoned by 1350.

But for all of his mind rambling and scientific reasoning, he could not figure out the mystery of the ring and "Goldie" his skeleton. For the next week, Stanley spent his time writing up a report on his find. He applied every hypothesis he could think of to the mystery and documented the report with photos. When he was through, he found his report painfully incomplete with no answers to the most glaring of questions, and he decided to drive north and stop at the Hopi reservation to make polite inquiries to see if maybe, just maybe, some old medicine man or elder might be able to shed light on Goldie.

ن   ن   ن

In the evening, Woody spent a long time with Ketl. Talking gently to her, he found out things he wanted to know, although he had already accurately guessed many of them. He sat beside her bed until darkness had blanketed the desert and the North Star pulsed brilliantly in the sky.

Although her first spoken English words were limited, he understood everything she told him, and he shared her worry about her mother and grandfather who had both left Willow Canyon and begun the long walk to the Hopi Mesas. Toward the end of their conversation, she asked Woody where she was, because she didn't remember being carried from the base of the cliff to the stone city, nor did she remember Cam's protective arms around her while he brought her to the ranch on the back of his horse. Had she remembered, she would have been horrified.

Woody told her she was about ten miles west of Willow Canyon.

She couldn't comprehend the term 'miles'.

"It's 'bout a day's walk," he clarified.

Ketl's body stiffened. "My home. Go home," she said.

"You can't travel until your leg gets better."

"I want to go home!" she repeated indignantly and tried to get off the bed. Placing weight on her foot brought a new onslaught of pain from her ankle. Groaning, she fell back on the bed.

"I told you," Woody said, pointing at her ankle. "You can't go nowhere until your leg is feeling better."

"Take Ketl home," she pleaded.

"Soon…you can go home soon." Woody fussed over her, settling her back on the bed, then checking the wrap on her ankle.

Exhausted, her leg throbbing, miserable because of her circumstances and the gnawing fear of what was happening to her home, she inched backward until her back touched the wall. When she closed her eyes, her world turned black. She willed her mind void, shut out all sounds, forced her heart to beat at a slower pace, then prayed with all of her might to Mockingbird.

&a.　　&a.　　&a.

Cam was stinking drunk. Christopher was only slightly less so. One empty bottle of liquor lay in the dust at the bottom of the stairs and a fresh pint of whiskey sat on the step next to Cam, a bottle Christopher had retrieved from his car. Stars blinked on and off overhead. Far off in the distance, moonlight highlighted the buttes so they glowed like platinum.

Cam's arm didn't hurt, his brain was like mush and when he tried to speak his lips felt like he'd been sucking on a Popsicle for weeks. "She can't be real," Cam said, forcing his mouth to form words.

"Sheees too," Christopher slurred.

"Then…" Cam stammered, working to form the words, "she's…she's a living fossil."

"Yeah...I think I'm in love," Christopher announced with starry eyes.

Cam slapped his knee and howled with laughter. "All right, man! Love! For Christ sakes!" Waving his hands in the air, Cam laughed hard, thinking of Christopher having strong romantic thoughts about a woman who lived in a cave and fought like a savage. The hard laughter made his throat dry.

Unsteady fingers wrapped around the fresh bottle of whiskey and brought it to his lips. The whiskey burned his throat as it went down. Sucking in air, he exhaled and said, "In love with...a...freak!"

"Sheees not a *freak!*"

Cam punched Christopher in the shoulder. "Ah, shit, sheees too! She's from the stone age. I bet she can shoot a friggin' arrow straighter than Annie Oakley could shoot a gun. She...she smells like bear grease and keeps turkeys for pets. She's descended from Cave of Clan Bear, for Christsake—"

"It was Clan of Cave Bear," Christopher corrected with a hiccup.

"Yeah, that's what I said. Hey, I got it. She could go on tour and make millions as the greatest freak in the world!"

Christopher blinked. Something Cam said whirled around his cranium like loose marbles in a bowl. Breathing in deeply, he filled his lungs with the dry desert air. He blinked again, trying to figure out what was so important that Cameron January had said.

"Man," Cam said, taking a huge gulp of night air, "I knew I hated this part of the country." Cam pointed to the weird looking buttes in the distance. "I hate the desert...hate sagebrush...hate desert sand. I hate the heat. I damn well hate horses. Most of all, I hate Indians." He nodded and wiped the back of his sleeve over his whiskey-wet lips. "I knew I would regret coming here. Thank Goodness I'm almos' done." He placed his head on his hands and shut his eyes. "I can't wait to see San Francisco again. Freeways. Water. Boats. Clean sheets. Microwave. My BMW. Can't wait," he mumbled.

Then two and two connected in Christopher's head to become four, then eight, then eight hundred, then eight thousand, then eight million. Dollars, he was thinking dollars. He was thinking fancy cars and a nice home, linen suits and French wines.

That's it! The Indian! A way out! Ketl would be his ticket out of Aguilar, New Mexico!

Standing up, Christopher lifted his arms to the sky and emitted a blood curdling howl. Then he did a wobbly skipping dance with his cowboy boots. Staggering to his Bronco, he opened the passenger door and collapsed across the front seat. He didn't move again.

Cam thought Christopher deranged. He stood, tottered, then glanced out at the desert beyond the buttes to everything he declared he hated and to where he knew a silent canyon lay in the darkness. On rubbery legs he stared off into nothingness. The night air was warm, swarming around him like a cocoon. The quiet created a fullness in his ears which made him turn his head, squint his eyes and take a couple of unsteady steps farther away from the house. From out there, something beckoned to him. He took three more unsteady steps forward. The stars were chips of white light, the sky blacker than the blackest black imaginable. The air held that same strange sweetness he had found so pleasant before. Waving, the whiskey causing his sense of balance to be askew, he stumbled farther out into the desert, the lights of the house growing dimmer behind him.

He wanted something from the unknown of the desert. It wanted something from him. It called to him, pulling him out into the night, and he willingly answered, walking until the darkness engulfed him.

Alone, he stopped and listened to the voice that called him.

There was no answer and a heavy silence hung around him like a wet blanket. Cam placed his hands to his mouth. "Where in the hell is everybody?" he screamed at the top of his lungs.

The silence pushed in on him, making him cringe. Unsteady legs took one last step forward, then the legs paused and turned for the house. Once Cam looked over his shoulder to make sure no one was following him.

৵   ৵   ৵

Harboring a gigantic hangover, his head as thick as cement, his mouth tasting like dead vermin, having slept like the dead on the ratty couch in the kitchen after stumbling back to the house, Cam left the ranch early the next morning before Woody was up and before Christopher was aware he was alive. When Cam climbed in the saddle, he glanced at Christopher's car. Christopher's boots hung out of the car, still attached to his legs. It didn't look like he had moved.

He had better wake up before the sun bakes him, Cam thought as he guided the horse in a northwesterly direction.

He kicked the horse into a trot, eager to finish his work, go home to San Francisco and return to civilization.

Ketl was awake and heard the hoof beats of the horse as it trotted away from the ranch. Pulling herself to the window, she saw the retreating back of her enemy, the white man. To her dismay, she saw that he headed in the direction of Willow Canyon. Her nostrils flared and renewed hatred reared in her heart. Then she sat down, placed her hands on her lap, closed her eyes and pulled Mockingbird into her consciousness.

"She won't eat," Woody said to Christopher.

Nursing a swollen head, sipping his fifth cup of coffee, Christopher winced with pain as Woody's words registered in his brain. "Why not?" he asked slowly, testing the pain level of his speech this morning.

"I think she's fasting," Woody replied.

"Fasting?"

"Yep. It's an Indian custom. Sort of like taking drugs. They go into another dimension and talk to their gods."

Christopher cocked a dark brow. Even that hurt. "She tell you that?"

"No, I *know* it. Just 'cause I'm old, don't mean I ain't got any brains left."

Christopher rubbed his temples. "When my head feels better, I'll make her eat," Christopher said confidently. "I just can't move yet."

"Hmmm, I thought you'd be the one up and gone this morning, not that citified cowboy."

Color flushed Christopher's face. "Shit, he just didn't drink as much as me, that's all."

Woody didn't say anything, but knew it wasn't true. He left Christopher alone and went out to the front steps to have a look-see. Wearily he sat down and let his old eyes roam the desert.

Ketl refused food at noon, also, in mid-afternoon.

When his head was not so thick, after eating biscuits and more coffee and after taking a hot shower, Christopher swallowed three aspirins, followed by a short nap. When he woke, Christopher went to Ketl's bedroom. He found her sitting upright, eyes closed, hands clasped tightly on her lap. Her face had turned pasty-flour white, and her breathing was very shallow, hardly perceptible. Her deathlike appearance scared the hell out of him.

"Ketl?" he whispered.

No answer.

"Hello? Ketl?"

She didn't flinch.

A human body could not sit upright and be dead, he told himself, which made him feel only mildly better. For a long time, he stood and watched her, detecting just the slightest raise and fall of her chest, but no other indication she was conscious. Once more her beauty left him numbed. In the daylight, he could tell her hair wasn't totally black but streaked with bronze highlights. It was full and caressed her face. She seemed asleep, but not asleep, like in a trance, yet her face was very relaxed although white, her full lips moist, her straight nose pointed slightly downward. More than anything it was her serenity which impressed him; she was real, but seemed not real, like an apparition, like she really wasn't inside her skin. He couldn't help himself and found his eyes roaming the ceiling as if he would find her spirit floating up there. It was really weird.

Trying to shake off the odd feeling and pulling his eyes from the ceiling, he gazed at her exquisite face. "Ketl, I'm your friend," he tried. "Tell me what you want and I'll do it for you."

From her subconscious, where Mockingbird was guiding her though a maze of sandstone blocks, she heard his words, and thanked Mockingbird for bringing her the one who would guide her home. Slowly, she batted black lashes open. She inhaled deeply and a rosy tone flushed her cheeks.

"Home," she said in perfect English. "Ketl go home."

He sat on the edge of the bed next to her. For a second his head felt dizzy as he smelled her strong musky odor. It wasn't repulsive, not the way Cam had described it, but heady, like a woman ready for sex. It incensed Christopher and his loins began to swell painfully. There was no way he would take her home. No way in hell.

But he lied, saying, "You must eat to get strong. It will make your ankle better. Then I'll take you home."

"You will take Ketl home?"

"Yes," he said, his eyes riveted at her breasts which pointed out from the cotton material of her shift. "I'll do anything for you."

    ❧   ❧   ❧

Ketl ate. Woody talked to her, helped her with English. He

found she had been taught English while at the Hopi mesa, although she didn't speak it while living in Willow Canyon. She was only rusty, he decided, after encouraging her to use more of the words she had learned many years ago. He showed her how the water worked in the washroom and she managed to take a shower which she found strange, standing under water that fell from above her. With the aide of a stout walking stick, she made the trip the outhouse when she needed to. One day, while Christopher and Cam were both gone, Woody got her to change into some of his clothes while he washed her cotton smock, then hung it outside to dry. Stains of dried blood remained on her smock. When he showed her the stubborn blood stains, he suggested that she continue to wear Woody's clothes for the time being. She agreed, but thought the over-sized cotton T-shirt strange, the cotton khaki work pants even stranger, but she wore them. However, she was careful with her tunic and left it folded at the end of her bed.

A clean body and clean clothes caused Ketl to shyly smile with appreciation—cleanliness was dear to her, and made it easier to leave this world and communicate with Mocking-bird. At home in Willow Canyon, she would not have allowed herself to become so foul with dirt, sweat, and blood. Religiously she washed in the creek, using soap made from yucca roots. Although the white man was her enemy, she would never forget Woody's thoughtfulness for seeing that she was able to clean herself and remove smell of blood and the strong odor of the white man.

While Christopher was at the house, he didn't leave Ketl's side for long. Whereas Christopher was enamored with her, Cam refused to go into the bedroom and see her. He was a very stubborn man, childishly so, his mother used to tell him. He knew it to be true, but in this case it didn't change his refusal to speak to the Indian woman. After all, he had nothing to say to her. He couldn't forget the way she had lunged at him with a sharp bone knife. Her intent had been blatantly evident—she had meant to kill. As a reminder of her irascible nature, he had kept the weapon. He placed the knife in the center of the kitchen table and a day didn't go by that he didn't pick it up and feel the sharp blade, running his fingers down the bone of the handle.

Woody told Cam that he was mulish. It was nothing new to Cam, who continued to refuse to have anything to do with the Indian. Besides, he got a stomach full of Christopher telling him how beautiful she was, how graceful, how wonderful. Eventually, Christopher claimed her as 'his woman'. It was enough to make Cam's stomach roll.

Ten days passed. Her ankle healed. She grew strong. She could walk about the house, but refused to do so when she knew the 'other man' would be there. In her heart there was a great hatred for him, whereas the man, Chris, was kind and gentle and promised to take her home. Shamelessly he fawned over her, bringing her trays of strange food that she had never before tasted, bringing her a tall vessel she could see through that was filled with frozen chunks of ice and a sweet-tasting brown liquid he called *Coke*. One day he brought flowers. Another day he brought picture books called *Life Magazine*.

He sat with her the whole day, leafing through the marvelous pieces of paper, pointing out things to her, showing her how the rest of the world existed. Her head whirled with new ideas. Some things she couldn't fathom, and it took Christopher the longest time to try and explain them to her. She could not understand the theory of space flight; she didn't understand the ugliness of war, and it was very difficult to explain it to her. But Christopher persisted, managing to sit close to her and touch her fingers, even stroking her leg as he inspected her healing ankle. He couldn't wait to get her alone, out of sight of Woody with his infernal manner of popping into the room every few minutes.

She picked up speaking the white man's tongue very quickly. Memories of Stella Red-Feather, a young friend at the Hopi mesa, made Ketl smile, for Stella had been the one to prod Ketl into learning the English language. Ketl knew Pavi had disapproved of her use of English, so had Una, but Ketl, well, she wanted to know what the girls and the boys were saying and they didn't speak the twangy Anasazi language, so if she wanted to be accepted by them, play with them, listen to their stories about the world, then she had to learn to talk the way they did, and Stella was a patient teacher. Stella had given books to Ketl. She took Ketl to the Hopi school. She became Ketl's friend, just as Chris was becoming now.

Ketl began to trust Chris. His face was pleasing to her. She knew he would not have penetrated Willow Canyon like the other one had done. Chris would not have threatened her, he would not have chased her up the rock ladder, then captured her and finally dropped her, hoping to end her life. The Evil One, as she referred to Cam, should not have entered Willow Canyon in the first place, should not have touched her, nor attempted to harm her. Most of all, he should not have taken her from her home. Certainly by now Pavi and Una were back from the Hopi Mesa and must be frantically worried about her. For the worry The Evil One had caused Pavi and Una, she grew a festering distaste, and there wasn't a day that went by that Ketl wished she had plunged the knife to the hilt in The Evil One's heart.

Chris seemed not to like The Evil One, either. Chris told her The Evil One was from a faraway land, that he didn't belong to the desert. He told her Cam belonged to a place where cement and steel took the place of dirt and trees. People lived in boxes stacked high into the sky, Chris had told her, trying to describe high-raise apartments. Cam worked for a company that searched for a dark liquid which lay in deep pools beneath the surface of the earth, Chris further explained. His company took the liquid, put it in steel drums and sold it to other people. She didn't like the thought of The Evil One taking anything from *her* desert. It was very evident that The Evil One was not at all in harmony with nature, nor with other human beings. He would have been an outcast had he been one of the People. He would have been sent away, told to complete his migrations so he would come into harmony with the world. It gave Ketl a certain amount of satisfaction to think of the Evil One struggling along the ancient roads, trudging for days upon days to reach the great oceans to the North, South, East and West. He would never do it. He would die and she would be glad.

Woody had keen eyes; a lifetime of common sense had been drilled into his head, and he could see Christopher being attracted to Ketl. He could see Cam throwing up a wall of forced indifference to the Indian. He could see Ketl responding to Christopher, and it bothered him, because he knew Ketl had to go back where she came from. Once she healed, she must be taken back to Willow Canyon, left there and forgotten. It was the only way.

Woody knew what would happen to her if those bonepickers ever found her, and he could well imagine what would happen to her home. He planned to keep his mouth shut about the Indian woman, knowing he would go to his grave with knowledge that no other mortal possessed. It was enough and filled him with a special peace.

One afternoon when Christopher sauntered out of Ketl's room, Woody said, "Don't you go gettin' yourself too attached to that woman. She ain't for you. She ain't for any white man. She's goin' back where she came from."

Christopher was startled by the sincerity of his grandfather's voice. *What did he know? He was just an old geezer.* "I'm just being nice, Gramps," he replied, hoping to pacify Woody.

Woody grunted. "Don't go being too nice. She can't end up liking it here. She's got a grandfather and mother back at her home who will be missin' her. Besides, she don't belong to this century. She's gotta' go back!"

Christopher didn't believe a word Woody said. Ketl wasn't going to come into his life, offer him a chance to be somebody, be his ticket to a fat bank account and then disappear back into the desert. No way. But Woody couldn't know what Christopher was thinking. So he replied, "I know, Gramps. I'm just trying to be nice to her while she's recovering."

Woody pointed a shaky hand at his grandson. "And don't you go tellin' anybody about her. You hear? No one! Not one single soul. Not your mother, not your friends, no one. You hear?"

"I hear you, Gramps," Christopher replied, breathing hard, ready to silence his grandfather with a quick right uppercut, but holding back. He curled his fingers into tight fists, then stormed out of the house.

🐚   🐚   🐚

On the thirteenth morning of Ketl's recovery on the Hayes ranch, Christopher tore down the road with little regard to ruts, gullies or soft sand. A plume of dust rose a hundred feet behind the Bronco. In front of the house, he slammed on the brakes, fish-tailed to a stop, left the motor running and ran into the house.

"Gramps!" he hollered. "Gramps, it's Mom!"

Woody shuffled from his room. "What you screachin' about?"

Christopher was pale-faced. "It's Mom, Gramps. Bacon grease caught on fire on the stove this morning and spilled all over her. She's burned something terrible. I got her to the hospital, but I want you to come!"

Woody's throat went dry. "Let's go," he said.

Ketl appeared in the door. "Go home?"

Both Woody and Christopher threw her a worried glance. She couldn't come with them. She would have to stay put until one of them came back. Cam was already gone; he'd left the ranch at daybreak, as he had done most every day since he brought her to the ranch.

"Get in the car, Gramps," Christopher ordered. "I'll leave a note for Cam." Then to Ketl he said, "Stay here until I come back. Please, stay here."

"Is it time for me to go home?" Ketl said, not understanding what was happening.

"Yeah, you're gonna' go home," he said as he finished the note. Then he pointed at her. "Just stay here," he said, which was confusing to her.

Then Christopher bolted for the car.

Limping to the doorway of the ranch house, Ketl watched the machine roar away, leaving a cloud of dust which silently settled back to earth.

With the sun dying in the West, Cam returned to the Hayes ranch, dusty and tired. He was surprised not to see the Bronco parked in the yard, because he knew Christopher had not wanted to be separated from the Indian woman for long. He was further surprised not to see Woody sitting on the front steps as he usually was about that time of day.

Cam wouldn't have admitted it, but the early evening generated the most spectacular views of the buttes, the desert, the fading sun, the mesa tops and the vast empty world which surrounded all of the Hayes property. Cam could attest to the comfort of those steps and how naturally a body seemed to stay once deposited there, but now they were empty. Quickly checking the location of the sun, Cam decided Woody was going to miss an impressive sunset. Then he led the horse to the barn, removed the tack and rubbed the mare down.

Hot and very thirsty, Cam stomped into the house and

threw his Stetson on the couch. Only the hat wasn't new anymore, now a shade darker from the fine red dust with a ring of sweat, a permanent marker on the brim. "Woody?" he called.

Silence.

"Woody, where the hell are you?"

Silence.

Never before had Cam been bothered by being alone, in fact, Cameron January liked his own company, but Woody naturally went with the ranch house, and it seemed eerily void of comfort without the old geezer shuffling around. Cam grabbed a beer from the refrigerator, then found the note on the table. As he slowly read it, he swore under his breath, and the skin around his mouth turned pale gray.

The note explained why Woody and Christopher were gone and further instructed Cam to look after Ketl, including the instructions to fix her some dinner. "Over my dead body," he mumbled to himself, his eyes falling on her knife.

For a laconic moment, he stood in the middle of the kitchen and stared down the dark hall to the bedroom where he knew *she* was. *The living fossil. The Last Mohegan. The Indian Princess.*

In one gulp, Cam drained his beer. While the sun set the sky on fire, while the clouds put on a magnificent show, Cam closeted himself in the bathroom. While the shower cooled his body and soap removed the grime of the desert, he hoped the water would clear his mixed emotions. It would be much easier if he didn't dislike the Indian so, but he did, because she reminded him of everything he hated about the desert.

Cam opened his mouth and let cool water fill his mouth. Yeah, he knew he was being childish by feeling as he did about the damn Indian. Certainly Christopher found her desirable, even friendly. And Woody? Why he told Cam she was the most fascinating person alive today on the face of the earth. In her head she held the mysteries of the whole Anasazi people. She was more important than an alien from outer space. She was a true American and could shed invaluable light on man's past in the Americas.

So why was he acting like a stubborn jackass? He knew he was stubborn, but that was an immature emotion he thought he had conquered long ago. So why was he acting like he was? He didn't know. He was afraid to guess, and frowned when he remembered Woody pointing a finger at Cam and saying, "Some people love themselves so much they're afraid to *like* someone else for fear they may like that person more than himself."

Like the Indian woman more than himself? Forget it. Never.

All Cam knew was that she was like no other woman he had ever met, seen or held in his arms and the feeling rocked him to the core of his boot-weary feet. Cam didn't belong in New Mexico, on the desert or mingling with a beautiful Indian woman. He belonged in the city, with Sharon or someone equally as world-like, with a fine machine like a BMW beneath his weight instead of a horse and living in an air-conditioned apartment where at the touch of his phone he could order a pizza, place an ad in the paper or call a girl for a date. In his world, he could work out in a gym, take karate lessons, shop for fine wines and sip a cold Martini if he wanted to. People in his world were reasonable and spoke a language he understood. People could rattle off most of the United States Presidents, knew all the states, worshipped a god of their choice, voted to make lawmakers, bought original silk dresses and furs, could eat greasy hamburgers or French cuisine anytime they wanted to.

Ketl ate squirrel and groundhog. She dressed in yucca sandals and a handmade smock. She forged archaic weapons out of bone and would attack a much bigger man without flinching.

Yes, Cam was frightened of her and her ways; he didn't understand her, nor did he want to, in fact, the sooner he left the Hayes ranch the better, he reasoned. He didn't want to become involved with a woman who ground corn and lived in a cave. No, he didn't. No.

Yet he couldn't shake the feeling of her pressed against him that night in her cave of rock homes. The water was magical, cascading down the canyon walls. The smell of freshness, of pinion, of lingering smoke from the fire sure beat the hell out of the smell of smog. And her aggression, with her recalcitrant spirit, went way beyond the so-called aggression the business women back in San Francisco possessed. Those women wanted to work in a man's world, do a man's job, wear banker's wool suits—of course with skirts instead of pants. But then they wanted to have doors opened for them, have men fawn over them, have all the benefits of being thoroughly feminine. It became confusing and Cam wasn't sure if it was really aggression those women possessed or split personalities.

Ketl was so different from any women—or person—he had ever met that it frightened him, and he, therefore, decided to stay as far away from her as possible.

So far he had been successful. This turn of events changed the course of his plans, though. He really couldn't avoid her what with him being the only person in the house who knew how to prepare food in a kitchen that was as foreign to her as was camping to Cam. So as he dressed in clean jeans and a white T-shirt, he decided he could manage to fix her something to eat. He'd take it to her too, deciding that was a very big concession, but one he could handle.

With wet hair still hanging on his forehead, wearing clean Levi's and a white T-shirt, he walked barefooted down the hall and peeked into what used to be his room and now was hers.

She sat on the bed with her back like a pole, her nipples pointing at attention through the T-shirt, her legs draped over the edge of the bed. She stared at the door, eyes glaring at him as if expecting him to jump on her.

"Hi," Cam said, noticing her hair was shiny clean, her face pale but even more beautiful than he remembered. Her green eyes shimmered like emeralds, and Cam remembered Woody telling him Indians had black eyes. It was odd.

Ketl gave him a hostile glare.

"You hungry?"

"Where is Woody?" she asked in perfect English.

"Ah, so you talk. Last time you replied to me by trying to kill me."

"Where is Woody?"

"He and Christopher are gone for a while." He smiled and raised his brows. "How about that. It's just you and me," he said glibly.

This was her enemy. She remembered how his leg had flown through the air and hit her like a fist. He was dangerous. "How long?"

"I don't know. I hope they'll be back tonight. Now you and I are all alone. We were once before, too, if you remember. I guess you don't, or you don't understand what I'm saying to you. Anyhow, Woody said I should fix you something to eat. I'm not such a hot cook. How about eggs and bacon? Some toast and coffee?"

Blankly, she stared at him.

"Okay. Since you approve, I'll get on it." Swinging his towel over his shoulder, he eased out of the room, confident he had the situation under control.

Ketl watched him go, her eyes narrowing into angry slits. She had understood every word he said. Yes, she remembered being alone with him. She had tried to kill him. Then he chased her and dropped her from the cliff. She would like to kill him now, but she had no arrows or spear or knife, except for the one in the kitchen, the one in the same room with The Evil One. All the rest of her weapons were at Willow Canyon.

And it was where she should be too.

Quickly, Ketl tied her yucca sandals on her feet. Quietly, Ketl raised the window screen. Silently, she eased herself out the window and limped away across the desert, blending with the land. Pausing only once, she looked over her shoulder to see The Evil One through the kitchen window, busy making food for her to eat.

She would never eat the food anyhow, she told herself. Not if the Evil One had touched it. With a half-snarl at her enemy, she tossed her head, faced the desert and began to walk home.

Chapter 11

While he poked at bacon sizzling in a cast iron pan, Cam hummed an old Billy Joel tune. Nursing a cold beer, he found himself surprisingly happy, fiddling in the kitchen, doing the cooking that Woody generally did. Although a bachelor, Cam never had the inclination to fix himself anything more advanced than spreading peanut butter on crackers. It was much easier, living as he did in a city the size of San Francisco, to go out to eat than to cook, or to have his present girlfriend cook for him, although Sharon wasn't a gourmet chef. But she could mix a mean Caesar salad.

Bacon and eggs he could manage, and as he speared a crisp piece of bacon and dragged it to the waiting triple absorbent paper towel, he wondered if the Indian had ever tasted bacon. It looked better than that rawhide-looking stuff he had eaten at *her* place, yet he wondered if she would find it as odd and disgusting as he had found her food.

With the refrigerator humming back at him and knowing the Indian was only a few feet away, Cam didn't feel alone, although the Indian wouldn't have been his first choice for company. Cam would choose Woody over the Indian if given the choice.

If he didn't know better, he would say he was nervous about being in the house alone with the Indian. Hell, he'd never been the least bit tense around a woman in his entire life. He *thrived* on the presence of the female species. But he couldn't call *her* female. He didn't know what to call her— maybe a savage. Yet it wasn't her being so aggressive that bothered him. In fact, it was close to being the contrary, the shock of seeing her a few minutes ago—her gentle over- whelming beauty and the defiant way her shoulders were squared. And the look in her shimmering green eyes: inno- cence, fear, surly dislike. It had hit him in the pit of his stomach.

He remembered when he first saw her in the canyon, angry as all get out. Her eyes had darted with interesting flecks of gold. He remembered her blackish hair and pretty face, but today he wasn't prepared for the incredible fragile beauty who rested on his bed in the back room. Her eyes weren't angry but haunting, the wealth of dark hair caressing her face like a halo. Tonight her face was pale, the skin of her straight nose nearly translucent, and he could see her breathe because her nostrils flared ever so slightly. She seemed ethereal, haunting him in a strange way.

It seemed impossible to think she had attacked him with a knife. She didn't look like she was capable of holding a knife, much less lunging at him with lethal intentions. She looked vulnerable now, soft and innocent.

Working at the stove, blood pulsed in his temples. Despite his best intentions, he couldn't make his fingers do what he wanted them to do. Nerves, he knew. Perhaps his anxiety was because he had never before dined with an Anasazi Indian. Perhaps it was because he had never cooked for a woman—it should be the other way around, he told himself. Whatever, his nerves were shot and he resented her being the cause.

"I hope you like scrambled eggs, 'cause I don't know how to do them any other way," Cam yelled.

There was no answer, but then he didn't expect one.

He knew she understood English. Woody and Christopher both talked with her. Why she had only spoken those weird words to him while in her canyon he didn't know. It rankled him to think she did it because she didn't like him. Hell, he'd never known a woman who didn't *lust after him*, much less not like him. No, it couldn't be that, besides she didn't even know him, so how could she dislike him? It was something he meant to ask her over dinner.

Sighing deeply, Cam decided his days of stubborn avoidance of her were over. He was a mature person and could get beyond her first inclination to kill him. She was a savage, after all and didn't know any better than to attack an invader to her territory. Sort of like a wild beast, Cam thought.

Yeah, maybe this was the chance he needed to explain himself to her. Certainly, she could understand he had been just as surprised to find her, as she had been to see Cam in her cave. Yeah, he would spill his guts to her, and when he left the Hayes ranch, he would feel better. There would be no burden of guilt on his shoulders.

While he threw slices of toast under the broiler, he hummed a country tune he had heard at Rose's Cafe. The dark yellow eggs began to set, so he yanked the pan off the heat. Next he flipped the bread under the broiler. With no toaster, Woody's toast usually looked like charcoal. Cam watched the bread turn brown, then rescued it before it burned. Placing two plates on the table, he cut orange sections and arranged them artfully on the white plates. The eggs he seasoned carefully with pepper and minced dry scallions. The bacon was crisp, the coffee hot and steaming, the toast perfect. Satisfied everything was flawless, he found a tray and placed both plates on it.

"Here comes dinner," Cam shouted.

Carefully he carried the tray down the hall. Whether she liked it or not, Cam decided he would join her for dinner. They would share a meal and bury hostile feelings once and for all. Like a peace treaty. Yeah, he liked the thought. Long ago white men and Indians smoked peace pipes, but Cam and the Anasazi woman would eat bacon and eggs while they made peace. It would almost be a picnic, only not quite. It would be fun, he told himself as he padded down the hall to her bedroom.

Perhaps she would end up understanding him, and perhaps, she in her own way, could explain her actions to him. Perhaps they could be friends, after all.

Then he turned the corner to her room.

"Oh shit!" he said as he saw the vacant bed and open window. He dropped the tray. It landed with a crash. Hot coffee dripped down his pants.

"Ouch...damn!" Cam yelled.

Madly, he blotted the coffee with a towel.

"Shit," he swore again as he stepped in eggs with bare feet.

"Damn Indian. Damn. Damn!" Cam ran down the hall. Angry, he pushed the door open and leaped down the front steps. He ran twenty feet before stubbing his toe on a cactus. "Goddamn-it all!" he roared, holding one foot while standing on the other.

His eyes squinted against the dying sun. Shading his eyes with his palm, he scanned the desert, his lips thin with anger.

He saw nothing move.

Sage, rabbitbrush, sand, dried grass. That was all he could see. Nowhere did he see a limping Indian. "Shit," he swore. Hopping on one foot, he retreated to the house to find his boots.

 za   za   za

He was certain he could overtake her on foot. She was a

mere slip of a girl. Her ankle was injured. She was weak. He was strong, virile, fit and could cover eighteen holes on a golf course in less than four hours.

Angry at himself of thinking he had the situation under control, and more angered to think of how he had decided to make peace with the Indian, Cam ground his teeth together, while yanking on his boots. He ran out of the house, slamming the door behind him, determined to find the Indian and ring her neck.

With a three-quarter moon shining brightly on him, Cam had his first doubts. Although the stars were radiant overhead, like chips of diamonds, the sky velvety black, the moon created strange shadows on the ground from cactus, grass and sage, shadows that caused Cam's pulse to thud in his temples. The house had been long out of sight. He was alone and had neglected to bring water. Swallowing hard, Cam realized he made a mistake; he should have ridden the horse, should have brought water, should have let the damn Indian go.

The desert at night was an eerie, lonely place. Night creatures, those that hooted and howled, those that pointed their noses to the sky and emitted a blood-chilling scream, those that hid in dark deep holes during the day and slithered across the desert during the night, did nothing to ease his discomfort. With no more than a suggestion of a path to follow, he dodged sage and cactus while heading beyond the moon-frosted buttes.

Here and there he caught sight of human footprints. Female footprints, he knew. Ketl's yucca fiber sandals. He was no tracker, but he could tell she was limping; one footprint was very heavily imprinted in the sandy soil while the other was much lighter, hardly a print at all. Her ankle must hurt like hell, he thought, and winced, damning her for running from him, damning himself for assuming he had everything under control.

Wild shrubs tore his pants. He had neglected to put socks on and now his boots rubbed his feet. At least he had boots, he told himself. His boots were calf-high and made of tough leather, and it made him wonder how *she* could travel in sandals without ending up with bloody toes and shredded skin.

His stomach growled; he hadn't eaten. Thirst caused his tongue to swell, and he damned himself for leaving the ranch without a canteen of water, but then he never dreamed he would come so far or for so long. He had imagined he would find her a quarter mile from the ranch, no more. Glancing over his shoulder, he knew he was more than five miles from his starting point.

Suddenly off to his left, he saw something large dart through the shadows. It was so quick that he couldn't tell what it was, but it made his skin prickle. Picking up his pace, he veered away from the sagebrush where he had seen the blur. Ahead of him, this time just a little to his right, he caught sight of something else bound though the shadows.

Something was following him.

As his breathing increased in tempo, he told his heart to stop crashing inside his chest. Cold sweat broke on his brow and glistened in the moonlight. Breathing hard, he picked up his pace, watching and waiting for whatever was out there.

Behind him, he heard a twig snap. Glaring over his shoulder, he saw nothing. He swallowed hard. He didn't stop, but kept a constant watch, his body honed, ready to run, ready to react to whatever stalked him.

To come without a gun was foolish. *Idiot!* Maybe more hostile Indians waited for him. Perhaps alien beings lived in the desert at night. Maybe there were worse things. If the Indian woman was from prehistoric times, perhaps leftover animals also survived who breathed fire and ate humans like potato chips. Cam's imagination went wild—he concocted images of scaly-bodied monsters and evil spirits who inhabited the desert and fed on lost men from the city.

Ahead of him he caught a glimpse of a dark flash. He stopped. Squinting, he saw something dart from one large shrub to another, then disappear. The thing was quick and seemed to slink from shadow to shadow. Breathing hard, he waited. There! Another blur of movement. This time yellow eyes glowed in the dark, looking directly at him. Warning spasms of alarm shook his body. It was a dog, but not a dog, sort of like a mangy half-starved mutt.

Then he knew: coyotes. *Do they eat humans?*

He didn't know. He didn't want to speculate and picked up a piece of sagebrush to use as a club if he needed it, although he didn't think a club would have much effect against a whole pack of coyotes.

Tentatively he started to move through the brush. The animals stayed away, but he was acutely aware of their presence. Above him the sky was deep, black, endless, with only a slip of a moon hanging in the sky. A soft wind sporadically brushed his cheek and made him jump. It was odd too, because the night air smelled sweet, oddly sweet like ripe melons. It wasn't hot, either, not like during the day when a breath of air could scorch his lungs. No, the night air was actually pleasant, and should have been enjoyable, except for the damn mutts which were becoming bolder and more numerous. His pace made his heart beat rhythmically, yet he was tense, waiting for something to happen.

Sweating lightly, the air hit his face and automatically cooled him. No matter how sweet the air, no matter how sensuous the night breeze, no matter how wondrous the stars, no matter how his senses were honed, how alive he felt, he never would admit to liking the desert. It was still a foreign and unpleasant place for a man like Cameron January to be.

A dark shape bolted from a sage bush and brushed against his leg. Cam jumped and wildly swung the branch. "Get away, you damn mutt!" he screamed.

The coyote disappeared. With blood thundering in his temples, Cam watched mangy shapes with yellow eyes dart in the sagebrush from one bush to another with bolder abandon. The animals had definitely smelled his human odor and were interested in him.

Man's best friend. Ha!

He began to wonder why in the hell he was out in the middle of the desert, chasing after an Indian woman. He should have been thankful that she left Woody's place. Gone. Isn't that what he wanted in the first place? Didn't Woody say she had to be returned to her canyon?

Yes. So why am I making myself coyote bait?

A sense of responsibility? Perhaps, but very unnatural for him. For the adventure? No, definitely not. Adventure to him was a Friday night stroll down North Beach or undressing a striking blond. Curiosity? *Getting warmer,* he told himself. Ketl was different. He had discovered her. In a sense, she belonged to him, but only in the sense of claiming the actual *event* of finding something, but there was something else, something he had never felt before, something new and unnatural to him—a disturbing feeling of fear for her. He felt as though she were in danger. Of what he didn't know, but Cam felt he should protect her from whatever threatened her.

And so he walked on, sure the coyotes had found Ketl, too. He only hoped he would reach her before the pack decided she was more tender than he was and would make a better dinner.

શ   શ   શ

Ketl wasn't worried about the coyotes. At first they followed her, then for a while they led the way through the maze of cactus, sagebrush and thorny bushes, trotting through the darkness like faithful guardians. In the desert, she was in harmony with the creatures of the night and they with her. She knew the four-legged creatures were merely curious of the animal that walked on two legs. They sensed no fear, smelled no odors that let them know she was worried, injured or weak, in fact, she emitted a strong smell of friendly confidence, so they left her alone, moved stealthily though the darkness in search of prey that was not in harmony with nature.

Ketl thought about Cam. Greatly relieved to be separated from The Evil One, her concerns lay entirely with her ability to find her way back to Willow Canyon, and she prayed to Mockingbird to guide her in the right direction. She knew she must travel beyond the buttes, go across the great valley, then find the opening to Willow Canyon along the sandstone wall of the mesa. So many times she had traveled along the mesa top and overlooked the great valley where she now trudged on her way home. Distances were deceiving, however, and she knew she could walk aimlessly up one canyon after another before she came upon her home. She didn't want to cause Pavi and Una anymore undue worry than was necessary, and she was sure Pavi and Una would be waiting for her at home.

By blocking all thoughts from her mind except a vision of Mockingbird, the great god of the Fourth World, daughter of Spider Woman, and by breathing in a shallow manner and by staring straight ahead without error, she was able to block the painful ankle out of her mind. Close to being in a trance as she covered the miles across the desert, she felt no pain, no worry, nothing. She moved along in a hazy void, centering her attention straight ahead as if she were trotting down a long, narrow cone where the sides curved upward to keep her on the right path. Sometimes the sides spun slowly around, but only the sides, not the path she followed. Mockingbird waited at the end of the path, urging her on, smiling down on her, letting her know all was well. Mockingbird told Ketl she would not fail Ketl and dutifully lead her home to Willow Canyon.

❧ ❧ ❧

On the verge of being exhausted, Cam felt blisters forming

inside his boots on his heels and on the top of his toes. With each step he took, he would swear, damning himself, damning the desert, damning Ketl, damning anything that came to mind. The coyotes now were a constant blur of bodies moving from shadow to shadow. On occasion, he could hear one growl at another. It gave him the creeps.

He walked into the night, listening to the night sounds, feeling the darkness surround him. When he heard the sound of the running water, his tongue was stuck to the roof of his mouth, so he ran the rest of the way to the creek, forgetting how torturous each step was with blisters on his feet the size of jelly doughnuts. When he reached the creek, he jumped down the bank, walked into the water, falling to his knees, scooping water into his mouth.

Nothing had ever tasted better.

Rocking back on his heels, he looked up. The opening to the canyon was on his left. If he didn't know where to look for it, he would have missed it. In the first light of dawn, the opening was dark, hidden by brush and trees. Nothing moved. Cocking his head to listen, he heard the far-off yowl of a coyote and the closer trickling sound of water. He couldn't believe the Indian had covered the distance faster than he had. Yet he hadn't passed her, and he was damn sure she wasn't behind him—there was only a pack of coyotes behind him.

She wasn't human, he told himself.

Dripping water, he climbed out of the creek. Throwing a worried glance over his shoulder, he started for the opening in the mesa. Tentatively, he entered the canyon and left behind him hungry coyotes. He expected the coyotes to follow him, but once he passed through the narrow opening to the canyon, the mangy beasts seemed unwilling or afraid to follow and after hearing a disappointed yap, he didn't see or hear the coyotes again.

In the darkness, the canyon turned eerie. Long shadows

streaked across the canyon floor. Overbearing rock cliffs pushed in at him. The quiet of the night was broken only by the barking of a fox across the canyon. The sliver of the new moon disappeared behind an overhang of the western cliff, leaving fading low-hung stars overhead.

Cam shivered. Slowly, he walked deeper into the canyon. Whereas he had become used to the elements on the valley floor in the past few hours, now he faced a new set of conditions. The steep walls blocked the moon randomly. The cliffs looked ominous. The shadows were inky black, so very black he would jump every time a rock loomed out of a dark vortex. His heart beat so hard it sounded like drums in his ears. He wondered if someone in tune with nature could hear his heart. He didn't like the thought.

He had no idea how many Indians lived in the canyon, but he would bet tickets to a 49'ers game that the Indian woman wasn't the only one. Woody spoke about the woman's grandfather and her mother. Cam remembered Woody telling about being a teenager and seeing the Indian with blue eyes on the cliff. Yeah, Cam bet this was the same canyon and Woody's Indian was an Indian from her tribe. Cam imagined she came from a whole tribe of Indians as weird as she, and he worried about what they would do to him if they caught him.

Sanity should have made him turn on his heels and retrace his steps, but the look on the Indian woman's face continued to bleep in front of his eyes. She had a strange hold on him. It was as if a force inside him compelled him to lead him into danger, to force him to cross the desert at night, to sneak up the canyon to the cave like a common thief.

And when he found her, he expected she would attack him again, just as she had done before. No matter, Cam continued toward the cave, determined to see the Indian woman one last time.

He expected the Indian woman or one of her tribe to jump

out of a shadow with arm raised, knife in hand. With his nerves stretched to the limit, he crept up the canyon with his knees bent, his hands in front of him, primed, ready for anything. Turning, placing his back to the rock cliff so as to protect his back from attack, he squinted and listened hard, trying to listen to the night sounds. When he pushed a large shrub out of his way, he stepped on a dry branch. He heard a loud crack. Jumping, Cam lunged with a karate kick at a ghost of a shadow. His kick was so violent that it swept him off his feet. He landed on his butt with a grunt. Quickly, he rolled to his knees and sprang to his feet. Breathing hard, he pressed his back to the rock cliff and waited.

He heard an owl hoot. Hoo…hoo…hoo…echoed across the canyon. Taking a deep breath, Cam brushed dirt from his pants and chuckled to himself. Now he was jumping at his own shadow!

He reminded himself one more time that he didn't like the outdoors, definitely didn't like the desert, didn't like night animals and sounds, and didn't like this canyon at night. Making an agreement with himself never to come back, he started for the cave, and after pushing a large shrub out of his way, he saw the ruins.

The cliffs cut the moonshine in half so the cave looked neatly sliced in half; one half lay in blinding moonlight while the other half was blanketed in darkness. The half of the cave in the moonlight looked like it belonged in a fantasy book. The rock ruins looked like aluminum, the plaza appeared to have spotlights on it while deep, dark shadows hid the actors. The petroglyphs on the back wall were cast in the light and looked like they were about to jump off the wall and come parading out to greet Cam. It was too weird, seemingly from another time, another dimension. Surely Luke Skywalker and R2-D2 would feel at home the stone plaza. The whole scene was so dramatic he had to blink twice to make sure his eyes weren't playing tricks on him. No, the rocks, stick figures and homes were still there.

Go back, he told himself. At the same time that he ordered himself to turn around, he took another step closer to the ghostlike village. Drawing himself up to his full height, he took a deep breath and walked up to the base of the rock stairs. The same force he felt at the entrance to the canyon refused to let him leave the ruin. It seemed to pull him inward. It made his numbed feet take one step after another, his steps making a soft crunching sound on the ground. The magnetism was very strong. It pulled him up the set of carved stone steps, up into the great cave. He had no power to stop it. It wanted *him.*

ë   ë   ë

Ketl heard him coming. She'd heard him when he was more than three hundred yards away. Sniffing, she smelled something foreign to her canyon. She knew what it was, and it left her with a brewing anger. Usually she could control her anger, but for the white man she permitted the mounting rage to grow and fester. That he had followed her was bad enough, but once again a white man had invaded her canyon. His feet poisoned her kingdom. Mockingbird had told her the white man would mean a great change to her tranquil existence. Determined to defend her canyon against all invaders, Ketl bit her lip, silently telling her god that she would not allow *this* white man to curse her life. He would not be alive by morning, she further told Mockingbird. His evil ways, his attempt to kill her would be avenged.

Her mind was calm, her hands steady. Wrapped in the fingers of her right hand was a knife made of very sharp elk bone, similar to the one left at the Hayes ranch. In Ketl's hand it was a lethal weapon, and this time, she assured Mockingbird, there would be no mistakes, there would be no survivors.

This time he would die.

As she waited for him, crouched in the shadows of one of

the rooms, she knew he would walk right past her and would not sense her. He was not in harmony; he knew nothing of being in tune with nature. She knew it the first time she had seen him awkwardly walking in his tall boots among the rocks and water. He looked like a duck on land. He was not agile, nor observant. He would be easy prey. She would slit his throat from ear to ear and laugh when the red blood of life spilled on the great plaza which she considered the heart of her home.

Closing her eyes, Ketl breathed rhythmically in shallow gulps. She took herself to another dimension where there was nothing but blackness and her gods. Although she couldn't see her enemy, her ears were superbly keen, she knew exactly where he was at each second, and she followed his hesitant footsteps up the stairs.

A smile tipped the corners of her mouth as he came closer. Her whole body grew numb. She was close to being invisible. Mockingbird was still with her, guiding her actions.

As he came up the steps, his boots made a tap-tapping as his heel landed on hard stone. Each step rang in his ears. He wondered if his footsteps were as loud as he imagined them to be.

He is close. Yes, Mockingbird, here he comes.

She crouched deeper into the darkness, her muscles tense and ready. Her eyes were clear, her breathing deep, cleansing her lungs with each breath, and in her right hand the knife was firmly clasped.

His footsteps are coming closer.

Suddenly he came into view. With a shriek that split the deathly silence, Ketl flew through the air and landed squarely on Cam's back. She raised the knife to send it deeply into his throat.

Her scream scared the shit out of him. Every nerve, every pore was honed, on the verge of popping like a tightened rubber-band. Her scream was the last tension to snap it.

Reacting from fear, he grabbed her arms, unaware of the knife which dug into the skin beneath his chin. Anger and fear gave him a superhuman strength. Groaning, he bent forward and flipped her over his head. She landed with a thud, and he thought he heard a whoosh of air escape her lungs.

Stunned, Ketl shook her head. Glancing over her shoulder, she sniffed the air. She could smell the white man's fear. *The coward.* Her lips turned upward at the thought of his pending death. Like a lithe cat, Ketl stood, her eyes never leaving her prey. She waved the knife in the air in front of her.

Cam's eyes grew wide when he saw the knife. "Damn!" he spat as he brought up his fists crouched in the ready position. "Listen, lady, we've been through this…."

Ketl flew at him.

This time Cam met her head on, grabbed both her fists, flung his leg behind her heels and threw her to the ground. He heard her grunt when she hit. Cam jumped on her and held both arms above her head. Pressing his thumb into her wrist, he added pressure until she dropped the knife.

"Geronimo," he said with a gasp. "Got ya."

Ketl hissed at him. Then she spat at him and her spittle hit him on the cheek.

"You damn heathen!" he roared.

Ketl hissed at him again.

"Don't you dare spit at me again, you wildcat. I'm not going to hurt you." He shook her wrists. "Understand me? I'm not going to hurt you!"

Cam met her stare of hate and they locked eyes. The whites of her eyes were huge, her rapid breath causing her chest to heave against Cam's weight.

He gasped for breath, too. Angry and hurt that she rewarded his concern for her by a second attempt to kill him, he glared at her. She wiggled to free herself.

"Now listen you," he said harshly. "I can't let you go

because you keep trying to kill me." His mouth was no more than six inches from her face. As he spoke, he watched the thin skin of her nostrils move in and out. Her mouth was shut and her lips, perfectly shaped, seemed cemented together. "I don't know why you keep on trying to kill me. I didn't do anything to you."

"You are The Evil One—" Ketl said with a venomous voice.

Cam was shocked. "Evil One? Hell, you have to be kidding. I'm just a regular nice guy. You're the first Indian I've ever met." He adjusted his body on her so he had her hips pinned beneath his groin. "How in the hell did you decide I'm 'The Evil One'? Hmm? What about Woody? What about Christopher?"

"You invaded my home," she hissed angrily.

He bent closer to her so his nose was almost touching hers. "I didn't know it was *your* home," he said slowly and loudly.

He was too close. His body radiated warmth and his strange white-man male smell made her heart beat as erratically as a summer storm. With all of her might, she tried to throw him off by twisting and pulling her arms away.

"Oh, no you don't," Cam said, holding her tighter.

Still she wiggled and squirmed to free herself from his steely grip.

Her gyrations made her body press hard against him. He could feel her firm breasts beneath the thin material of Woody's T-shirt. Her legs were twined between his. The night was sultry warm, her body arched against him creating a maddening and different sort of heat. Moon-glow frosted her face, turning the devil of a woman into an angel. Forgetting everything sane and determined to quiet her spasmodic movements, he stopped her motion by planting his mouth on her lips.

He felt her shudder, then struggled against him. He held her tight and explored her lips. Then he felt her body grow limp. Her lips were warm, soft, sweet. He felt the peaks of her breasts graze his chest. He became lost, irretrievably lost, in her touch, her taste, the scents around him, the craziness of where he was and who lay beneath him. He lowered his chest until he covered her, then released her hands, gathering her face in his fingers. Groaning from her exquisite beauty, Cam found her lips again. He traced the outline of her lips with his tongue, gently urging them open.

Paralyzed, Ketl didn't know what was happening to her. The Evil One lay on top of her, touching his lips to hers. His lips felt like a whisper, then they became more of a scream and it surprised her to discover his mouth was both soft and hard at the same time. When she felt his hot tongue on her lips, she understood what he wanted and involuntarily opened her mouth. When his tongue invaded her mouth, her eyes grew wide with surprise, yet she found herself relaxing and slowly bringing her arms up and placing them limply behind his head. Something inside of her told her to meet his eagerness and to kiss him back, so she did.

The fear melted to her toes, and hate and anger slowly flowed from her body. Something else took the place of the fear and anger, something she had never felt before, something uncontrollable, something that frightened her much more than a coiled rattlesnake or a torrential rainstorm. Spikes of pleasure dotted her skin. All of her flesh began to burn in pleasurable pain. She wanted him even closer to her and arched against him.

Surprised at her response, incensed by the sensual smell of the outdoors, lying on rocks with a mad Indian beneath him, he felt as though his whole body burned with fire. He kissed her cheek, her nose, her eyelids then claimed her lips and explored the sweetness of her mouth. Touching, probing, caressing, his tongue ventured where no other man had ever before been.

Her dark world slipped away from her. Mockingbird had deserted her. She was painfully, fearfully alone, feeling things she had never felt before, finding that she actually liked the way the Evil One was touching her with his lips. She ran her fingers though his wavy hair and was surprised to find it thick and glossy much like her own. She touched his ear, trailed a finger down his throat and placed her hands in the opening of his shirt. She was both shocked and thrilled to feel a mat of fuzzy hair there inside his shirt which she repeatedly touched.

No man had ever been so familiar with her. No man had ever placed his lips upon hers. No man had turned her blood to liquid fire the way this man had done. She did not feel guilt, because it was an emotion totally foreign to her. She was curious more than anything else and found it strange that her hostility had melted like snow in the sun. He could have come to kill her; no, his lips were too gentle and warm to mean her harm. What was even stranger was that her lips wanted to kiss him harder, to do something to quell the aching throb which had begun to beat down in the pit of her stomach, so she arched her back and responded passionately to him.

Cam had only intended on kissing her to stop her from struggling. He knew it had been a stupid thing to do and at first was sorry he had attempted it. He did not expect her to be so damn inviting. One thing just sort of led to another and before he knew it, his hand was caressing her ribs, his thumb reaching around and finding the valley where her breasts joined her chest. His tongue was on an exploratory course all its own, and he felt his manhood swell as she met each thrust with a willingness that did not go hand in hand with a woman with murder on her mind. Sanity should have allowed him to stop, but where she was concerned there was nothing sane. He kissed her deeply, thoroughly. For the first time, *he* felt his head spin.

Then above him he heard a turkey flap its wings and scoot

across the plaza.

A lucid mind returned to Cameron January.

Pulling away from her, he gazed down at her, uncomprehending how he could have kissed her like that, how he could let the peck of a kiss he intended turn into such a passionate encounter. Embarrassed, he removed his hand from her body.

She breathed lightly between still-wet, parted lips, then ran fingers across her swollen lips. "Why did you do that?" she asked.

"I don't know," he replied honestly. He frowned, looking down at his hand as if it had a mind of its own. "I was tired of you fighting me and I thought it would stop you."

They both looked at the knife which lay on the ground just out of her reach. Then Ketl's gaze returned to Cam. She didn't tell him that although she thought his method of fighting not very fair, she found it had been very effective, and she would have to remember it.

"I'll get off you now," he said very slowly to make sure she understood him. "I'm going to trust that you won't try to put the knife in my heart. You and I are going to sit and talk like civilized people—"

"Civilized? I don't understand the word."

He laughed, then sat up and pulled her up to face him. "No, I suppose you wouldn't. It means a person like myself, not like you."

"Evil?"

Again he chuckled. "Something like that," he replied.

Chapter 12

With a long drive from the home of the Hopi mesa to Farmington ahead of him, Stanley drove hard, arriving in town about eight o'clock tired and disappointed. The Hopi Indians had told him nothing to help shed light on the skeleton. It didn't surprise him, however, but filled him with discouragement, plus odd discomfort.

The Indians always left him with a vacant, uneasy feeling. Oh, he had studied them for years, had dug up more Indian remains than most archaeologists, had written about them and had even dreamed about them, but still, when he came face-to-face with them, his skin went clammy-cold. It was the way an Indian looked at a white man. Hopi Indians didn't possess the word 'stare' in their vocabulary, nor did they consider it rude to gawk at a white man while in the Hopi's presence. It made Stanley nervous. Stanley felt a Hopi Indian could look right through him, right through his flesh and bones to whatever was behind him, and in so doing, the Indian knew what was in Stanley's mind. It was darn hard to talk to a person who looked through you, Stanley knew, darn hard.

So Stanley was tired and edgy when he drove into Farmington. He owned a small, two bedroom cottage-type house three blocks from the Archeology Laboratory and usually went right home after being on the road for a long trip, but he was tired and knew his refrigerator was empty, so he pulled his car into the parking lot of the Antelope Valley Inn which was across the street from the Farmington General Hospital.

Perched on a high stool at the bar, Stanley ordered a T-bone steak, fries and a tall, cool Tom Collins. A cowboy sat next to Stanley. One glance and Stanley decided the cowboy was permanently planted on the bar stool, elbows holding up his head, shoulders slumped, legs wrapped around the stool. The cowboy was drinking straight whiskey. While Stanley carved his steak into bite-size pieces, he watched the cowboy toss down a shot glass of whiskey, then place the empty glass next to five empty shot glasses lined up on the bar like members of a marching band. Obviously the cowboy was drunk; he made rude remarks to the waitress, and as he moved the empty shot glasses around in an effort to place them in a straight line, his movements were spasmodic and his straight line looked like a circle.

Stanley tried to ignore him, but found it difficult because the cowboy kept sagging off the bar stool and bumping into him. The cowboy bumped Stanley again, this time harder than before, and Stanley dropped a hunk of steak in his lap.

"Ss...sorry," Christopher Hayes slurred.

"It's okay," Stanley replied while wiping grease from his pants. "Maybe you should quit drinking."

Christopher blinked, hearing words come from the guy next to him, but not understanding what he said, "Man," he began slowly, thinking hard to make his tongue work, "I know I should stop. It's jus'...tha' it's been one-hell-of-a-week."

Stanley gave a perfunctory nod.

"Yeah," Christopher drawled, "my ma burned herself somethin' terrible. Stupid...plain stupid."

"Too bad," Stanley remarked.

Christopher stared at Stanley. Squinting hard to bring the man into focus, he took a long look at the man. There was something different about him. Maybe it was his wire-rimmed glasses, Christopher thought. Or maybe it was his closely cropped hair which was parted perfectly on one side and combed with some sort of ointment to make it stay plastered to the other side of his head. Maybe it was his long thin nose and strong chin. Maybe it was his scrupulously clean fingernails and long slender fingers which cut and severed chunks of meat like it was an operation.

But most of all, it was soulless eyes which made Christopher's back bristle: red eyelids, blue eyes—cold and chilly, nearly opaque. Contrasting sharply with his frigid pair of eyes, his face was tan. The eyes didn't go with the face, yet when he had looked at Christopher he didn't sneer or snarl like some people might who had the misfortune of sitting next to a drunken cowboy. Although Christopher thought there was something odd about him, he let it pass, unable to put his finger on what it was besides the strange eyes that made the man seem different. Besides he wanted to talk to someone and this surgical-perfect meat cutter would have to do.

"Say...you ever seen second degree burns?" Christopher asked.

No, Stanley hadn't and he didn't want to try and visualize them while chewing on rare meat. "No," he said. "I haven't, but I bet it's not pleasant."

"Sure ain't. She got them mostly on her hands. They blistered." Christopher paused and belched. "Peeled somethin' terrible. I can't believe she was so careless. Hot grease ain't meant to be any place but in a fryin' pan."

"I guess not. Sorry to hear about it." Stanley tried to turn himself on the stool so his back faced the cowboy.

"Yeah, it sure is." Swaying back and forth while staring straight ahead, Christopher paused as if thinking about something. "But tha's not the important thing compared to what else happened this week."

Stanley barely listened.

Christopher waved at the bartender to fill another shot glass. "Yeah, the mos' incredible thing happened jus' a few days ago. In fact, I think…no, I *know* it's the most important thing ever happened to New Mexico, maybe even in all the World."

Stanley's brows crawled up his forehead. Slowly, he turned his head toward the drunken cowboy. "What'd you do, discover gold? Oil?"

Bleary-eyed, Christopher turned toward Stanley. "Man, it's better than that! I found a goddamned living Anasazi Indian!"

Stanley dropped his fork. It clattered to the floor. Choking on a piece of steak, he coughed and sputtered, "What did you say?"

"An Indian," Christopher repeated. "Anasazi. One of the *Ancient Ones.*"

Stanley managed to swallow the chunk of meat. His throat was acridly dry and the words came out slowly, painfully. "What is he like?"

Christopher laughed, thinking of Ketl's beautiful face. "It's no *he,* it's a *she!*"

"A *she?*"

To and fro, the bottles of liquor waved in front of Christopher. He blinked to focus, but the bottles became more fuzzy and seemed to be tilting upside-down and sideways. His stomach rolled, then churned and he thought he was going to be sick. "Oh, man," he groaned and placed his head on the bar.

Stanley roughly shook Christopher's shoulder. "Hey, hey!

Don't pass out on me! You've got to tell me about the Indian!"

Promptly, Christopher went limp and slid off the stool, landing in a heap on the floor at Stanley's feet.

Half-finished with his dinner, Stanley stood, threw a twenty-dollar bill at the bartender, heaved Christopher off the floor and dragged him outside. Grunting, Stanley held Christopher under his arm and half-carried him to his Wagoneer.

After he shoved Christopher's legs inside the car, Stanley climbed in the driver's seat, brought the engine to life, ground the gears and sped away from the Antelope Valley Inn.

          ɚ   ɚ   ɚ

"My name is Cameron January," he informed her, still sitting cross-legged in front of her on the stone plaza.

"I know," she whispered.

Cam tried not to grin. "I mean you no harm. I come in peace." His voice echoed off the back walls of the cave. He realized he sounded like the first white man who discovered America.

"You tried to kill me," she said simply.

His body jerked at her words. Taking shallow breaths, he kept his anger in check, but it was difficult. She had things confused, he thought, remembering her crouched in front of him with a knife in her hand, remembering how she had cut him. Even now he could remember the sting of her knife and the feeling of warm blood trickling down his arm. However, he didn't want to get her riled and have her jump at him again, so he said, "I meant you no harm."

"You dropped me from the cliff."

"You were heavy," he explained. "I don't like heights. I was dizzy. My hand was covered with blood. You slipped from my grip."

Ketl remained silent, trying to comprehend if The Evil One was telling the truth. "You took me away from my home," she argued.

"I thought you were seriously hurt. I wanted to help you."

"You did not speak to me...where it was you took me."

"True," he said. "I apologize for that. I didn't understand you, who you are, what was happening. I thought it best if I left you alone. You seemed angry with me," he added, thinking he put it mildly.

"You did not think clearly, White Man."

He could feel his face grow hot. He wasn't sure how much of her tactless remarks he could handle without losing his temper. And she had a maddening way of staring at him, almost right through him. "My *name* is Cameron," he said sharply.

"Mockingbird says you are called The Evil One."

"Who in the hell is Mockingbird?"

Queerly, Ketl looked at Cam, angered he wasn't aware of her most important god. "She is *Alo,* in your language a spiritual guide. She is granddaughter of Spider Woman and the one who guides us through the Fourth World."

Cam would have laughed in her face if she weren't so deadly serious. *Who ever heard of Mockingbird, Spider Woman or the Fourth World?* She might have been speaking to him in a foreign language; he didn't have a clue what she was talking about, which only confirmed his beliefs that she was weird as hell.

Deciding to forego this topic of conversation and get onto some safer ground, he said, "Okay, so we know who I am. How about you? Woody says you are Anasazi."

Her fist rolled into tight balls. Angrily she spat on the floor which Cam decided was very disgusting. "I spit on what you say! We are called the People. We have called ourselves so since we settled here, long before the white man ever began his infestation. It is the Tavasuh who call us the Anasazi, and the Tavasuh are our enemy just as the white men are."

"Who are the Tavasuh?"

"You white men call them Navajo. Tavasuh means 'a person who pounds'. The Tavasuh come from far away, out of the North. They are wild barbarians, because they kill a captured enemy with a rock-club. They are hatred enemies of the People."

"Well, I mean no disrespect," Cam said dryly, "but there are millions and millions of people in the United States who recognize the Indians who lived in this area by the name Anasazi. They are not Tavasuh, nor Navajo and they are not wild barbarians. They aren't a threat to you or your people."

His remarks settled heavily on her mind. "All white people are a threat to my people," she stated.

She was very stubborn, very difficult to deal with. "I am no threat to you. Woody is no threat to you. Christopher is no threat to you."

Ketl stared through him. "Why should I believe you?"

That's a good question, he thought. He wondered why he was going through all of this to make her understand. All he was supposed to do was to bring her food, which he could easily deposit in her room, like feeding a dog, then leave.

He didn't have to explain himself to her, nor did he know how to convince her he really had been concerned about her well being. Then he thought of his following her across the desert, the coyotes, his fear and the painful blisters on his feet. He thought he knew how to convince her he wasn't lying.

Struggling with his boots, he pulled them off. "See the holes in my feet?" he asked.

Ketl looked at his red, swollen and blood-smeared feet. Huge blisters had broken. They were bloody and had to be extremely painful. She stared at Cameron January's pain-filled face. In a soft voice she said, "Evil One, you are not in harmony with nature."

❧   ❧   ❧

On a mat beneath the clear sky with so many stars blinking

at him that he wondered why he never knew the heavens possessed such an abundance, Cam slept better than he had in weeks. Beneath the ceiling of the cave, with the ancient petroglyphs of stick-men, horned animals and numerous swastikas on the wall over the rock buildings giving the place the eerie sensation of an occupied settlement, Cam awoke to the smell of smoke and the sound of turkeys bantering at one another. For a minute, as his eyes slowly adjusted to a new day, he wondered if he wasn't dreaming. Then he remembered where he was and stared at the ceiling of the great cave, the earth tones of soft reds, giving way to ambers, earth tones and sun-bleached tans as he sat up and looked at the sunlight on the canyon walls.

Inhaling the mixture of smoke, pinion and earth, his stomach growled. He had never smelled such heavenly air, and a soft blanket of contentment covered him. As the sun peeked over the cliffs and bathed the red-rock walls in a golden glow which highlighted the chalk drawings, he slowly turned around to stare at the art. The animals came alive, bounding across the desert while a spear-wielding Indian raced after them. He could well imagine the effort required to take down game with a spear, with no horse, no guns, no metal-tipped arrows. It left him shuttering in awe at the class of people who lived in these harsh elements.

Then Ketl stooped at his side, offering him a ceramic bowl filled with food. He smiled and took the bowl from her. He noticed her hair was still damp as though she had recently been in the shower. Her face was shiny clean and her green eyes were brilliantly bright. He noticed, too, she had changed from Woody's clothes back to a tan-colored tunic which suited her.

He pointed at the bowl of food. "Thanks," he said.

She nodded and went away.

Cam admired the bowl. It was shallow, but had black zigzag decorations running across the bottom of it. It was beautiful. It amazed him to hold it, knowing an ancient-class of Indian, probably Ketl herself, had made it. Inside the bowl was an assortment of edibles; there were corn pancakes rolled up to the size of cigars, inside of which was a filling of mashed beans—he guessed beans anyhow. Tentatively he picked up one of the pancakes and took a small bite. Surprisingly, it was tasty, having a distinctive taste of outdoor cooking; however, it was gritty, although he didn't know why.

Besides the pancakes he found a pile of fresh raspberries and chunks of an unidentifiable type of meat. He didn't want to know what type of meat it was, and this time, not like when he nibbled at the corn pancake, he threw a chunk of meat into his mouth. It tasted odd, not like beef or pork, the two basics he was accustomed to, but it was filling and that was the important thing. Ketl had also left him with a clay water vessel, and he drained the cool water from it.

When he finished, she padded next to him, retrieved the bowl and water vessel and replaced those items with a pair of yucca sandals. The sandals were large, with leather toes and thongs to tie around his ankles. He noticed black and white feathers dangled from the ends of the thongs.

"For you," she said. "For your walk back to *Aponivi*."

"*Aponivi*?"

"Yes, *Aponivi*: Where the wind blows down the gap. Where you took me. Where Woody and Chris sleep."

"It's called the Hayes Ranch."

"Yes, *Aponivi*."

There was no sense in arguing. "Thank you," he replied, touching the sandals and blowing at the delicate feathers.

"Eagle feathers," she said. "So when you walk, you will be closer to the clouds."

It makes perfect sense.

"Thank you," he said again. Then his brows cocked at her. "Are you inviting me to leave?"

"You must go back. You cannot stay here alone."

"Alone?" he asked, puzzled. "You're here."

"I must go. I must find my mother and grandfather. They went to the Hopi mesa and should have returned. I must go."

"How far is it?"

"A journey of six moons."

Damn! Did that mean ten miles, thirty miles, a hundred miles? "Farther than the walk back to *Aponivi*?" he asked, then realized he had used *her* term and he wondered if he was going crazy.

"Yes," she answered. "Many times. It is very far."

"And you will go alone?"

"I must go."

"I'm going with you." He said the words and then looked over his shoulder to see if someone else had spoken the words, because he had no intention of saying such a thing.

Ketl frowned. "It is a difficult walk."

"I don't care." There was the voice again. "You can't go alone."

Ketl thought for a laconic moment. She did not like the thought of going to the Hopi mesa alone. She was afraid her grandfather might be ill and need help getting home, or her mother might be having trouble negotiating for a husband. Ketl didn't know what the Hopi would do if she came to them alone. The white man would be an outside threat who might make the Hopi more reasonable with the negotiations. He had caused her undue harm by coming to her canyon, by chasing her, by dropping her from the cliff, and he owed her some compensation for the harm he had caused her.

Yes, she decided, the white man would accompany her. "You will come," she said firmly.

"When do we leave?" he asked through dry lips.

"This afternoon, when the sun is low in the sky."

"Why not now? Why not get a jump on it?"

Slowly, she shook her head. "You have no harmony with the earth, Evil One. We walk at night when it is cool and rest during the day when the earth is on fire."

A Boy Scout would have known that or a survival expert. However, Cameron January was as close to a neophyte to desert trekking as Ketl was to modern ways.

❧   ❧   ❧

Christopher Hayes woke in a strange room. As his eyelids slowly opened, the ceiling spun around, making his stomach rock and roll. By turning his head, he saw a strange man sitting in a chair at the end of the double bed. He didn't have a clue who the man was or where he was. All he knew was that his throat tasted like a rat's nest, his stomach felt like a washing machine and a set of brass cymbals clashed inside of his head.

"Where am I?" he asked between bangs of cymbals.

Stanley tried to remain calm. "You are in my home. My name is Stanley Cahill. You fell off the bar stool next to me last night at the Antelope Valley Inn."

Christopher vaguely remembered. As an especially large set of cymbals made a horrendous racquet with accompanying pounding inside his head, he groaned.

Stanley shook his head. "You were thoroughly drunk. Disgustingly drunk, I might add."

Christopher vaguely remembered.

"You began talking about Indians. One Indian, in particular. An Anasazi."

Christopher didn't remember anything about it. Yet he knew when he was drunk, he was not known to keep his mouth shut. He wondered how much he had said, and if this guy was more than mildly interested or just was being nice to a drunk. Somehow he didn't think it was the latter.

"I am an archeologist, Mr. Hayes," Stanley said.

"You know who I am?"

"I took the liberty of checking your wallet for some

identification. I also took the liberty of calling the Post Office in Aguilar and asking about you. I know your family recently sold a large portion of land which is known to contain Anasazi ruins. I am very interested in hearing more about the Indian you found."

Slowly, inch by painful inch, Christopher sat up, his head pounding painfully. "I was mistaken," he said.

"I don't think so," Stanley countered.

"There ain't no Anasazi woman."

"If there was, Mr. Hayes, she would be an invaluable credit to science. She would make history. And I can assure you, that if you were to lead me to such a woman, I would see to it that you received all the credits from her discovery. You would be as famous as she. You would earn a lot of money from film rights, among other things."

Suddenly, Christopher's head stopped thudding and was very clear. "Yeah? How much?"

"Millions," Stanley replied.

Christopher's eyes brightened. "Millions?" he repeated and grinned.

Chapter 13

It required the greater part of the day to get ready for the trek to the land of the Hopi Indians. Ketl insisted on going to the mesa top and taking water to the sacred water vessel. Proud of her garden, she invited Cam to accompany her. Cam declined, remembering with a shiver the horrible feeling of being half-suspended in air on rock and wooden steps up the side of vertical cliffs. Whatever the reason, he hated heights, and heights hated him.

So Ketl went alone, scampering along the rocks like she was a billy goat. From the plaza Cam watched her. He was amazed to see that she only slightly limped although he knew her ankle had turned nasty colors of blue and yellow. When she was out of sight, Cam sighed, suddenly feeling lonely.

To shake off the unwelcome feeling, Cam decided to explore Ketl's village of rock houses. Throughout its entire length the cave was full of houses—simple stone rooms with small, high doorways and few windows. At the south end of the structure stood a four-story structure that touched the cave roof. Ducking through a T-shaped window, Cam entered the tower. He climbed on perfectly positioned footholds to reach the second floor, then the third floor. In the third-story room he found a beautiful painting in red on pearl-white walls. The art work was exquisite, the masonry exemplary.

Cam touched red figures on the wall. He traced a man with an arrow, a dog, a strange circle. He tried to imagine the artist who had painted the wall in such darkness and cramped quarters.

The closeness, the artistic figures, the silence, all cast a spell over Cam. There was no sound except of muted clucking of turkeys and throbbing of his heart. With trembling fingers, he traced the outlines of the body of a frog with human hands. To reach the top hand, he had to go up on tiptoes. At last he developed a cramp in his leg and the spell was broken.

He climbed through the top of the tower and headed to the rear of the cave, crouching to duck through a rock passage, climbing a pole ladder to reach the highest and deepest rooms. He poked into every dark corner. Cool and dark in the deep recess of the great cave, in these small rooms Cam found baskets of corn cobs, tassels and shucks, dried brown beans, hard lumps of dried squash, tools set aside for another time. In several rooms he found human bones.

In the center of the cave was a graceful round tower. Every stone had been carefully rounded to fit the curve of the wall and the entire tower tapered uniformly toward the ceiling of the cave. Cam poked his head inside a small window. The inside had not been elaborately painted like the tower in the southernmost part of the cave. The use of the tower room puzzled Cam although when he looked through the highest window he found that he had a commanding view of the valley.

Cam climbed out the tower window and began to study designs which had been painted on the back wall of the cave. The designs meant nothing to him: circles, circles within circles, swastikas with arms not finished. Some swastikas were completed while some resembled more of a cross than a swastika. One was painted on the red-rock wall in black ink and was just above his head. By reaching up, he could trace the lines of the design with his fingertips. When he touched it, a weird feeling radiated down his fingertips to his toes. For a split second, with the silence bombarding him, the sun and shadows equally creating spirits around him, he thought of how it must have been to be an Indian hundreds of years ago standing beneath the great canopy of rock and painting on the wall what must have been something of great meaning. Moving to his right, careful of where he stepped lest he place his foot into a hole, he made his way along the roof tops of ancient houses, looking at drawings of animals: frogs, deer, beaver, squirrel, elk, bear, birds, fish. There were people, very stylized, crudely drawn, but nonetheless he knew they represented the people who inhabited the canyon, and seeing them, being able to grasp a feel for the souls of the men and women who had created memories in this village of stone, made him feel very insignificant.

By the time Cam had scrambled down from the back walls of the cave, Ketl had returned from her journey to the mesa top. She was satisfied that the gods wouldn't be without water while she was gone. Her next job was to make ready her bow, arrows and the stiff elk skin quiver which held her arrows. With that done, she retreated into a kiva and returned with a spear and atlatl. The atlatl was a prehistoric missile launcher her people had used for hundreds of years. It was an innocent-looking wooden handle with a hooked tip. It enabled Pavi to throw his spear hard enough to kill a moving animal without having to creep up on it.

A bow and an arrow was much preferred by Ketl, but she only owned the one bow and one set of arrows. The Evil One should have a weapon on their trek, so she handed him the atlatl and a spear. "You take this," she said.

He reluctantly took it. "What is it?" he asked while he studied the atlatl.

"To kill game," she answered, sure he was an idiot.

Cam dropped the weapon as if it were hot. "I'm not killing anything!"

Ketl looked surprised. "What happens when you are hungry?"

Cam thought of any number of fast food restaurants with greasy burgers made out of hamburger. "The food I eat is already dead," he explained.

Ketl shrugged. She thought the Evil One was very strange, eating meat he found which was already dead. Certainly it must be tough and strong. He was very strange indeed. Picking up her bow, she marched away from him, shaking her head, knowing she would not go without her bow; she would have fresh meat, even if he wouldn't.

Besides her bow and quiver of arrows, she brought a satchel filled with sweetish dried squash, dried pinion nuts and sunflower seeds, rolled corn cakes and toasted pumpkin. They would have to supplement their food supply with rabbit, ground squirrel or, if the gods favored them, a young deer.

Later in the afternoon, Ketl began the chore of fixing a meal for them to eat before they departed. Food preparation was a constant and tedious job, but one she was accustomed to. Bending over a row of bins made of stone, each with a grinding slab slanting down from one end, Ketl rubbed corn kernels with a rubbing stone. She chanted while she did this so she would maintain a certain rhythm.

Fascinated Cam watched her fix food, using the crudest of utensils while he placed the yucca sandals on his feet and figured out how to wind the leather thongs around his leg. When he was satisfied he had it right, he ended with the sandals secure on his feet with eagle feathers flickering alongside his calf. They tickled, he thought, but he didn't find it bothersome.

Cam watched Ketl scoop ground corn from the rock bin and moved it to a bowl. Then she returned to her singsong like chanting and grinding. He realized the grittiness he had found in the corn pancakes must have come from the soft sandstone on which the corn was ground. He swallowed hard, wondering what sand did to one's stomach.

It looked to Cam like she was going to be chanting and grinding away for a while, so he wandered to the creek. Beneath the shade of the cottonwood trees, he found a spongy patch of grass. It had been trampled recently, and he knew it must have been where Ketl had come to wash her hair. He imagined she washed her whole body, too, for there the creek was deep, having been stopped by a damn of red rocks which was obviously manmade but looked centuries old. There on the lee side of the damn, the water pooled. He saw skeeter bugs dance across the shady water, then a fat trout leaped out of the water and snatch one of the bugs.

The water looked refreshing and inviting. Crystal clear, in the shade of the trees little green ferns bowed and swayed over the water. It was an enchanting place, very friendly looking except for the big lunker trout he had seen coming from the shadowy bottom. He thought trout didn't attack humans, although the size of the fish he had seen looked capable.

He was hot and sweaty. The water reminded him of his swimming pool back at his apartment in San Francisco. His mind worked hard, plotting the pros and cons of going into the water. Ketl would never see him and he was out of sight of the plaza. The blisters on his bare feet hurt, and he imagined how the cool water would soothe his feet. He darted a nervous glance to the cave, then back to the water.

"Hell," he mumbled to himself and pulled his T-shirt over his head, then dropped his jeans to the grass. Lastly, he removed his sandals. Wearing only white jockey shorts, he waded into the water.

As he suspected, the water was incredibly soothing. The bottom was covered with red silt and was soft beneath his toes. Nowhere did he see a fish and soon he relaxed and ventured farther into the water until submerged to his waist. He lay back and floated. Above him in the trees birds chattered. Small brown birds, they hopped from branch to branch as if trying to find a position better than the last. Above the deep green of the leaves, the sky was turquoise, bluer than he had ever seen. Of course he generally looked at sky through smog, fog or storm windows. Generally he couldn't tell where the bay ended and the sky started because it all was the same color, and on foggy days, which was 30 percent of the time, the sky, the air, the earth all looked like what he imagined the space was between death and the afterlife—a big, giant gray mass. At home, he generally took a shower, generally swam in the pool in his apartment and had never before had he swam in a river or creek. It was an interesting experience.

Up on the plaza, Ketl had finished preparing the food and she looked for the white man. The fire had been covered with ashes, and Ketl was anxious to finish eating and put away the rest of the baskets and water vessels. She had seen the Evil One wander toward the creek. In sandal-covered feet, she skipped down the red stone stairs to see what was keeping him. Ketl knew how to move without making any noise, and as she followed Cam's footsteps to the edge of the creek, she did so without the slightest hint of her presence. She spotted his clothes, then scanned the water and was shocked to see him in the middle of the creek.

With his back to her, he stood thigh deep. Water ran down his muscular back in rivers. Black hair was plastered to his head, and she could make out the outline of thick, sinewy legs beneath the water. Never had she seen a virile man without clothes covering his body—only Pavi, but he was old and wrinkled. This man, The Evil One, was not anything like Pavi.

Staring, she watched the white man move to shallow water. His well-muscled body moved with easy grace. She had no idea his hips were so slim, his stomach so flat. He paused and spread his legs. His stance emphasized the force of his thighs and it made Ketl gasp. She thought the white man looked a lot better than most of the Hopi braves she'd seen during the Antelope Snake Ceremony dance which they all pranced about a crackling fire with only loin cloths for cover. His body was tawny brown, the muscle planes of his back glistening with rivulets of water. As he turned, she saw a broad chest covered with a fuzzy mat of hair which thinned to a V where it disappeared into a skin tight covering. No Hopi had hair on his body like the white man—not Pavi, not any of the Anasazi. Her fingers tingled as she fantasized touching the hair on his chest, then her fingers burned as did her cheeks for thinking such an impossible thought.

Cam played in the water like he was a kid. He splashed water with his palms, threw handfuls of it into the air and tried to catch it in his mouth. What water he caught, he spat out in a long arc. Then he heard someone laughing.

Quickly he dropped to his knees, knowing his soaked white jockey shorts were close to being transparent. Over his shoulder he spotted Ketl with a look of delight on her face. "How long have you been there?" he charged.

"Not long," she replied playfully with a spark of a smile.

From the tone of her voice, he guessed she had been there long enough to be thoroughly entertained. "Get the hell out of here," he said with an edge to his voice, "so I can come out and get dressed."

"I'm not stopping you."

She had an impudent way of staring at him, Cam decided. He glanced behind him, feeling her eyes bore through him.

Looking back at her, he found her impaling gaze unchanged. "You have a rude habit of staring at me," he told her.

Ketl shrugged. "You are interesting to look at," she replied.

Cam glanced down. He might as well have been wearing nothing. "Ah hell," he mumbled. When he moved toward her, his jockey shorts clung to his groin like Sani-Wrap.

Ketl didn't move. Engrossed in his physique, she continued to glare at him while he padded to shore and struggled to pull on his jeans, hopping on one foot and then the other. He left his jeans unzipped and yanked his T-shirt over his head. The flimsy material stuck to his back. Cam swore and spun in a circle as he tugged on his T-shirt.

Ketl laughed hard at his gyrations.

Cam shoved his T-shirt in his jeans, yanked the zipper up, then stomped to her and pointed his finger at her nose. "If you say one thing about my not being *in harmony* I'll turn you over my knee and spank you."

Wondering what the word 'spank' meant, Ketl frowned, then shrugged her shoulders. The corners of her lips lifted ever so slightly and she said, "The Evil One does a strange dance."

"It's not a dance," he ground the words out between clenched teeth.

"Very strange," Ketl said again, then started for the great cave.

In the protection of shade, they ate her food. Both sat cross-legged on the stone plaza. She served him the gritty corn cakes again, this time rolled and filled with raspberries which had been mashed and mixed with wild honey. A stew of beans and hominy was splendidly seasoned with mint bee balm and tiny wild onions. Cam requested more dried sweetened squash, and he noted she gave him much more than she served herself. He ate every bite of squash and wondered if he ever dare tell his mother that he ate squash, because he had hated it all of his life.

The food was washed down with a drink—sort of a lemonade made from sumac berries, sweetened with prickly pear juice and served in pottery mugs artfully painted with a black checkerboard design. While chewing one of the corn cakes, he paused and stared out of the cave, taking in the majestic setting: cottonwood trees, the creek darting into view here and there, the sandstone cliffs, the rock palaces surrounding him, the drawings on the walls. He sniffed and smelled the scent of pinion and smoke in the air. Suddenly, he was overwhelmed with amazement.

He wondered how long ago it was that he sat behind his desk in his office in the Bank America Building, sipping coffee made from an automatic coffee machine, talking on an IBM Telephone while reading a fax. How long since he sipped a martini at a rooftop restaurant with Sharon sitting across from him dressed in a slinky gown, her perfectly sculpted nails tapping on a crystal glass, looking at Cam with hungry eyes? How long since he sniffed Chanel #5 or the imported leather in his BMW?

Eons, he decided.

Then he bit down on his corn cake and hit a large piece of sand. Instantly, it brought him back to reality. He spat the offensive gritty substance aside, then poked at his corn cake with a finger. "This stuff is full of sand," he commented. "Why don't you eat something sensible like the fish in the creek?"

Ketl looked horrified. "We do not eat *fish*."

"Why not? Can't catch them?"

Indignantly, Ketl squared her shoulders. "If I wanted to, I could catch them, but fish are sacred. We would not catch them, let alone *eat them!* To do so would offend the rain and water spirits. The rain spirits bring the summer showers which feed our crops." Her eyes narrowed and her onionskin nostrils flared with quiet indignity. "The water spirits," she said in a soft whisper, "give us life."

How many times had he seen a beady-eyed trout staring up at him through Saran Wrap in the super market? He had never thought of water spirits or rain gods, yet her words made him feel ashamed. "Ketl," he began, "you must excuse me. I am not knowledgeable about your customs."

"I know," she responded, "that is why you are out of harmony."

ख ख ख

By the time the sun was at the precipice of the cliffs, they were ready to go. For the trek, Ketl had changed into an ivory-colored tunic. It hung to her knees and was sleeveless. Around her shoulder, she wore a brightly designed scarf which was hand woven from cotton Ketl had grown, then colored with dyes she had made from wild plants and roots. She would use it at night wrapped around her shoulders when it turned cold, and during the day as a mat when it was hot and they would seek shelter inside a cave. Around her neck hung a thick clay vessel in which she carried a cone of coal to start a new fire. Besides this she carried her quiver and a woven water jug. She handed a water jug to Cam, explaining to him to drink water only when necessary.

Cam placed the leather thong around his neck and put thirst out of his mind. His palms were sweaty and his heart thudded loudly in his chest. Already, Ketl had started for the stairs leading up the cliff to the mesa top, while he lagged behind, dreading the climb.

In his yucca sandals, carrying the atlatl and a spear, with the water jug around his neck, he reluctantly followed Ketl who carried her bow, plus the satchel of food. At the foot of the sheer wall, where the first set of stone pillars shot up against the canyon, he hesitated. His knees were weak as he squinted against the sun at the top of the canyon and fought off a building wave of nausea.

Scampering ahead of him, Ketl climbed from rock to rock to pinion ladder. Turning, she saw him at the bottom of the cliff, pale and unmoving. "Evil One, climb up," she said.

Cam stood rooted in his tracks.

"White man," Ketl mumbled and retraced her tracks. "You are scared," she said, standing in front of him.

"Of course not." He couldn't look at her.

"You do not tell the truth. I can see it in your eyes."

"Well...yeah—"

"White man, clear your mind. Believe you are in harmony with nature, even if you aren't."

Cam frowned.

"Believe," Ketl persisted. She pointed to her heart. "In here, this is where you must believe. Do not look down. Look straight ahead at my sandals." As if to offer more reassurance, she added, "Mockingbird is with us. She will see you safely out of the canyon if you believe...and show no fear."

Her words weren't comforting. He glanced around him and didn't see and bird or spirit. However, he was glad he was in 'harmony', although he wasn't sure he could walk up the side of a cliff and not show fear, but he knew he had no choice. Sighing deeply, he nodded at her. She smiled and turned her back on him. She climbed three steps, heard him swear and looked around to see his eyes riveted on his feet.

She went back to him and placed her fingers under his chin. Pulling his head up, she said, "Like this. Up. Keep your head up. Don't look down." Again she knocked her chest. "Believe. You must believe."

His chin felt like she had zapped him with an electric prod. She was deadly serious, though, and he felt himself nod and stare back at her emerald eyes. Then abruptly she dropped her hand, again turning away from him.

As though he walked on clouds, he climbed the stone and

wooden ladder steps to the top of the canyon. The three-hundred-foot drop never phased him, in fact, he made it without flinching, nor breathing. He went the entire distance in a trance-like condition. He felt himself outside his body, floating along on a mystic journey. It was like he was observing himself diligently placing one foot in front of the other while not looking down, but centering his eyes on the feet of the Indian in front of him. When he reached the top, his spiritual body gently floated down and merged with flesh, the two becoming one. It was only then that he looked at the sheer drop. For a second he felt dizzy, his stomach rolled and he felt his face pale.

Taking quick gasps, Ketl stood at the edge of the canyon to take one last look at her world. She couldn't resist letting her eyes gaze on the tranquil valley where the cottonwoods, aspen and pinion created varying depths of shadows. It was a startling contrast to the dying sun which bathed the cliffs in salmons and beautiful hues of pink. Beyond the valley as far as the eye could see stretched a desert with those two lone buttes rearing up like guardian sentinels.

Her eyes settled on the great cave. A heaviness squeezed her heart. The sudden sadness was odd, for she had left Willow Canyon on other occasions, but this time she had a premonition that her life was taking a path that had no end. Call it a preview of things to come, of life changing events, Ketl felt it and savored the look of the land, tasted the sweet scent of air, remembered each shadow and color. And then, with the sun dying in the West, she turned and walked away from Willow Canyon. She showed no emotion and said nothing, for the heaviness pressing down on her could not be placed into words.

Slowly, Ketl led Cam through thick pinion trees. Behind her, her world disappeared. The canyon was impossible to see. Sighing deeply, Ketl increased her pace, feeling the force of nature around her. Yes, she decided, things were in harmony. Casting a quick glance over her shoulder to make sure the White Man was following her tracks, Ketl looked ahead of her, to the pale lavender sky, to the drifting clouds, to her destiny.

In front of her, the vast emptiness beckoned, and as her yucca sandals crunched on the sandy earth, she answered the call.

Oblivious to anything except watching where he put his feet, Cameron January followed the Anasazi woman.

Chapter 14

As the sun dropped in the sky, they walked northwest. A faint road—just the outline of rocks on either side of a wide swatch of sandy land—stretched before them. For a minute Cam visualized Ketl's ancestors trudging across the path for more than 50 miles in search of trees. Then their return march, pulling heavy pine logs behind them. It was an incredible feat.

The desert was still, the air sultry. Lost in thought about the Anasazi, the desolate land and his situation, he lost all sensation of present time—what day of the week it was or what time it was. He chuckled, thinking how time had become unimportant; he hadn't glanced at his watch in days. Now the sun dropped low in the sky and hung on the horizon, a blazing ball of fire. Waves of heat radiated skyward and made squiggly lines in front of the sun. The sun was huge, brilliantly orange. He had never seen anything like it and mentioned it to Ketl.

"The Sun god is happy," she told him.

"Aha. What's it like when the Sun god is not happy?"

She frowned. "White clouds, then streaks of blackness cross the sky, and white light shoot from the clouds."

"And then a big boom?"

"Yes, he screams at us. But it does not rain."

"And that's the Sun god talking?"

Ketl nodded. "Taking in anger."

"Why is he angry?"

She shrugged. "It has taken the People many years to learn to be in harmony with the land, the sky. We don't always please the gods."

"How do you know all that stuff?"

"It was taught to me."

"Who taught you?"

"My grandfather, his father, my father. Only the men. They are teachers."

"You remember your great-grandfather?"

"Yes. He was very old when he left to continue his migration."

"Migration....I don't understand."

"You know nothing, do you?" she said tartly.

He hated her acrid tone of voice. "I know how to drive a car, program a VCR, order a French wine, run a computer and can read English," he answered sarcastically.

"Just as I thought, you know nothing."

Cam sighed, too tired to argue. "Since I know nothing, how about you teach me?"

"I am not a man, I cannot."

"I'm not Anasazi, so you can."

Ketl threw her shoulders back in defiance. "I am not a man, I cannot," she spat at him.

Boy, she angered him. He pointed a finger at her perfectly shaped nose. "Let me tell you something, Queen Princess, you may not be male, but you sure as hell are the last of your breed, and if you don't tell someone about your heritage, you're doing more disrespect to your gods than by catching and eating a goddamned fish!"

She was stunned by his words. "I am not the last!" she shouted at him. "My grandfather and mother are alive!"

He sensed she was wrong, yet the desperation in her eyes kept his pessimistic thoughts to himself. "I hope so," he said, wiping the back of his hand across his brow. "I really do."

Then he stepped ahead of her, letting her follow him.

They walked a long time in silence.

Coyotes joined them, but stayed a safe distance away. Tonight they didn't bother Cam like they had the previous night. He sensed no threat from them. He knew it was crazy, that man couldn't communicate with animals, but he definitely felt it, and he noticed that Ketl paid them no attention whatsoever.

When the moon had crested the western horizon, she spoke to him. Obviously she had given their earlier conversation much thought, because she said: "I suppose because you are not one of the People that it would be all right to tell you some things about us. But not all. Not those things that are highly sacred."

"I'm not interested in sacred shit anyhow," he replied gruffly, maddened she wouldn't trust him completely.

"So? What is it you want to know?"

He thought for a moment. "Okay," he began, "let's start with the connection between you and the Hopi. How come you live in Willow Canyon, yet go to the Hopi mesa? How come you don't live with them?"

Ketl felt blood pool in her cheeks. "The Hopi are the Hopi. I am one of the People. They are not one and the same. Among the People there are many clans. At one time, the Hopi were a clan belonging to the People—The Bear Clan. They are no longer. They succumbed to the comfort and luxury given them by the white man. No longer do they rely upon the Creator. No, they are Hopi and I am a True Person.

"My village is that of the Eagle Clan. We have lived in

Willow Canyon since before the coming day of the white man. Now only my grandfather, my mother and I remain of our clan." Here she paused, and fell farther behind him so he had to slow his pace to be able to hear her. "My mother went to the Hopi to find me a husband," she said in a voice barely audible.

A quick shake of his head ended his laconic state of mute immobility. "A husband?" he croaked. "Your mother was going to find you a husband? Like go and shop for one?"

She didn't know what he meant. "The Hopi chief would choose my husband," she explained.

"You've gotta be kidding! That's not going to upset the gods?" he asked glibly. Then he grew more serious. "How about you? Doesn't that upset *you*? Wouldn't you like *to know* the man before you marry him?"

She considered it her duty to marry. What made her happy hadn't entered her mind. Yet now that he said it, and the way he said it, made her begin to wonder what life would be like with a male whom she might not like. It didn't matter.

Ketl lifted her chin. "The Hopi chief will chose my husband, but the chosen one will ask for my hand in marriage. My father picked my mother while she was still a girl by asking her for a drink of water at the creek. That is usually the way a young brave would seek to marry a maiden. This is the way my husband will ask for me."

His eyes grew wide. "By asking you...for...a drink of water?"

"Yes," she said. She thought nothing strange about it. "A brave of the Eagle Clan would ask for me so, but there are no young men left. They have all gone. There is no other way than to go to the Hopi and have them choose a brave for me."

Cam shook his head. His attention centered on her statement about asking for a drink of water being a marriage proposal. He was stunned. He couldn't believe what he heard. He could picture a preppie accountant hanging around the water cooler at the Bank America Building, waiting for a good-looking secretary to come down the hall in her spiked heels and styled hair. Then he would turn on the water and ask her if she wanted a drink.

She would swoon, fall into his arms and say, "Oh, yes. I'll marry you!"

This is too much, Cam decided. "All right," he said, mopping his brow with the back of his hand, "let's forget marriage customs for a while. You said all the young men are gone. What do you mean? Where did they go?"

"They have been gone for a long, long time. They went with the other people of the Eagle Clan who continued their migrations. My mother is a Hopi. My great-grandfather married a white woman who was a captive of the Apache's. The Apaches traded her to my great-grandfather for three baskets of corn, two turkeys, and a bow with eagle feather arrows."

Slowly Cam shook his head. Her response didn't answer his question and made things more cloudy by the minute; now a white captive was involved; now other Indians were affected by the presence of the Anasazi clan. It was more than he could absorb all at one time, he decided, leaving the last bit of information about a white woman for a more thorough discussion at a later date.

"Where did they go?" he asked again. "What is a migration?"

"It is a long story," she said with a sigh.

Cam looked around him, at the endless miles of nothingness stretched in front of him. "I've got plenty of time."

As the stars began to pulse above them, Ketl began to tell Cam the laws of the Four Migrations. "Masaw, who was the father of Spider Woman, the one who charted our destiny on Earth, told Spider Woman that each clan must make four directional migrations before they all arrived at a permanent home, one common to all. You see there are many clans of the

People. As I said before, I am of the Eagle Clan, but there are many other clans: Side Corn Clan, Pumpkin Clan, Parrot Clan, Blue Jay Clan, Arrow Shaft Clan, Snake Clan, just to mention a few."

Cam's head spun. He wondered how she could remember all of the clans. "Okay," he said, nodding, "there were a lot of clans."

"Yes," she said, "all different, but all the same, all the People."

He nodded.

She continued, "All the clans were told to go on their migrations. They must travel to the end of land—West, South, East and North. They must meet the great water at each end of—"

"The oceans?"

"We call it *paso*. It means where land meets the water."

"Okay," he said, trying the word, *"paso."*

"Yes," she said. She grinned at his pronunciation of her language. "Each clan must complete their migration before finding the Center of the Earth where the Creator chose for us to live forever. Some clans started their migrations to the south, some to the north, some retraced their routes and headed east and west." She drew a cross in the air with her fingers. "All of these routes form a great cross, the center of which is the land we call home."

"The Four Corners area?"

"The what?"

"Never mind," he said, because he knew she had never heard the term. "The desert around Willow Canyon."

"Yes. But you see it is not just one tiny little spot. It is a general area. The Parrot Clan settled north of the Hopi mesas. They built huge cities beneath the cliffs. The Bow Clan settled to the South, in a great valley where they built a large village. My grandfather told me this and it is documented on the walls of our cave."

"How? I didn't see writing—"

"Not writing like white man's pen. Writing like Anasazi. We write in pictures. The circles and the crosses and the crosses with the arms tell us which clan went in which direction. It is very simple. You just do not have the harmony to know what the pictures mean."

He felt his pulse speed up as she told him again how he lacked harmony. It was galling to be continuously told you had no harmony by a petite woman who obviously possessed enough harmony for the two of them. Trying not to show his anger, he asked, "Did they finish their migrations?"

"Only the Bear Clan did," she said with a sigh. "They are now the Hopi. Remember? I told you how it was. They finished their migrations, but since have fallen from grace with Masaw. No longer do they rely upon the Creator. They have lost their power, in fact, it is said some have returned to the Third World where all is Evil, that they must emerge again into the Fourth World and start their migrations all over again."

This was getting a little far out for Cam. "Okay," he said, mentally straightening out what she told him. "Let me get this straight. Each clan made a migration to the ends of the earth, to where land met the oceans. Then they returned to this area to settle." It was incredible, for he realized the Indians would have passed through thousands of miles of fertile, less hostile land, and they didn't stay, but returned to the desert. "The Hopi completed their migrations, but lost grace from god. Is that it?"

"Yes," she said.

"Okay, that's clear." *Clear as mud,* he thought. "What about your clan. What did you call them, the Eagle Clan? Did they fulfill their migrations?"

"Not exactly," she said, her voice full of shame.

"What do you mean 'not exactly'? Either they did or they didn't."

"Because we are the Eagle Clan, long ago one of our leaders, Qualetaga, told our clan that the Bird that Soars, the *Kawavo,* for which our clan is called, could fulfill our migrations."

Cam's eyes widened. "Now a bird is trekking across the continent for you?" He couldn't help but laugh.

Ketl felt the hairs on the back of her neck straighten. "You make fun of me!"

"I'm sorry, but it's hard for me to believe."

She shook her head and steeled her back. "Perhaps if you did believe, your life would have harmony."

He was tired of her talking about harmony, and he snipped back at her, "Honey, I usually make sweet music." Then he wished he could sever his tongue. He sounded like a cad who was trying to pick up a one-night-stand in a sleazy joint.

Angry Ketl walked in front of him and didn't say anymore. They went down a steep traverse along a rocky outcropping, then along a sandy-bottomed ravine. Cam could imagine what it must be like when a flash flood hit the ravine, and he looked up, thanking god—which god he wasn't sure—that the sky was clear.

For a long while he watched her back, her firm buttocks and shapely legs as she led the way. He found it hard to accept that she was making this arduous trek to find out what had become of her mother who was shopping for a husband. It seemed archaic. It was archaic.

And Ketl seemed not to tire. She kept an even pace, up inclines, down knee-wrenching declines, across smooth slabs of sandstone, through ankle-deep sand. She did all this while he suffered sore hamstring muscles, tired feet, and the perpetual fear of the unknown. As the hours passed, he his anger passed and he gained a deep admiration for her physical and mental persistence. He cursed himself for being so surly with her. She had tried to explain her beliefs to him, even if they were impossible to believe. He shouldn't have laughed. He should have been more respectful. He should have possessed a little more *harmony!*

Feeling sheepish, he jogged around a thicket of sagebrush, caught up with her and lightly touched her arm. "Hey," he said.

She flinched, stopped and shot daggers at him. "What, Evil One?"

Moonlight bathed her face, turning it pale, almost milky quartz in color. Shadows fell at her sides, outlining her figure beneath the tunic. Swallowing convulsively, Cam fought off an unrestrainable urge to pull her into his arms and kiss her passionately. By practicing self-control, Cam fought off the urge, but couldn't resist reaching out and feather-touching her cheek with the back of his fingers. He found it difficult not to slide his hand down along the creamy smoothness of her throat, farther on down to the shadows between the swell of her breasts. A mere tug would rip her smock off her delectable body and leave her naked, facing him in the moonlight. The thought was severely tempting.

Blank innocent eyes stared up at him. Abruptly his thinking of possessing a naked Indian came a halt when he realized how guilelessly she stared at him. Her eyes were wide but unseeing, full of pure innocence, and he immediately felt like a criminal for thinking such lustful thoughts.

"You're very beautiful," he said, feeling the contour where her cheek blended into her neck.

"When a man touches a woman so, it means he intends to make her his woman," Ketl whispered, mesmerized by his look and heated touch.

Cam would like to make her his woman, right here, right now, on the desert floor, except that he knew what he meant by 'his woman' differed from what she meant by 'his woman'. "I thought a man made a woman his by asking her for drink of water."

She could smell his musky male smell. It made her head light, and she was no longer able to think clearly. Leaning against his fingers, she closed her eyes, her heart wildly thudding inside her chest. "By touching a maiden, a brave shows his intentions of asking her for a drink of water," she whispered.

The hot air of her words scorched the skin beneath his shirt. All his self-control evaporated in the desert air. Tilting her head up to him, he said, "What happens when a man does this?" Then he lightly kissed her.

His lips were hot and strangely soft at the same time. For only a few quizzical seconds, she resisted the pressure of his mouth, then found that the sensation ignited a fire deep within her. She yielded to the fire and returned his kiss, lifting up on her tiptoes to arch closer to him. Cam parted her lips and explored the sweet recess of her mouth, pleased by the eager response of her darting tongue. His kiss became deeper, stronger, giving her more of him. Ketl's legs grew weak and she leaned against him. He groaned at the feel of her body pressed against his.

Her bones were collapsing, her pulse racing, her breath caught in her throat, along with a terrified gasp—a terror created not by the meeting of lips, but of her own reaction to his hot desire and wild promise. Lost in this new sensation, Ketl melted against him, and her heart leaped when she heard a primal groan of hunger escape his lips.

Even his growl of desire surprised him. Slipping his hands down to her tiny waist, he held her away from him, curious to see her expression. He wished he would have seen a smile, but it was no surprise to find a confused blankness on her face.

Damn! He knew she'd never been with a man, much less

stolen embraces and passionate kisses. Although he was an expert womanizer, he had never made love in the desert and had never taken a woman's virginity. However, it was difficult to restrain his mounting desire and not to admit to the attraction that existed between them. He had to go slowly, not frighten her, because he knew she was so naive she didn't recognize the physical charge between them for the magic that it was. Dipping his head, he kissed her again.

Ketl knew she should not let the white man touch her as he had done, nor should she mold against him as if to become one with him, but she felt separated from herself as if a spirit had taken over her body, and she pressed herself against his chest, welcoming his kiss. The night was sultry, the yellow moon bathing them in a sensuous milky blanket. Kissing her deeply, he found himself highly aroused by the night, the feel of her body and by his crazy desire to possess her. He thought her a savage, but now a delicate, heart-searing savage, one he wanted to tame by consuming her totally. Parting her lips with the thrust of his tongue, he sank deeper into the sweet recess of her mouth.

As their tongues met, she felt her body buffeted by the hot winds of a strange savage harmony. She felt transported on a soft and wispy cloud. She felt her body leaving earth, soaring like the eagles, dipping lower, climbing higher, crossing in front of the blazing sun. She felt like a wanton She-Tiger, a woman who belonged to the Third World, but who slipped into the Fourth World to entice men to do sinful things. Only those who were truly in harmony with nature and who had found the Center of the Earth could be free of her lustful ways.

Close by a coyote howled. It shattered his cocoon of craziness and rocked Cam to his very core. All at once he opened his eyes and glared down at her long lashes which were delicately closed.

You fool, he told himself. *She's an Indian!*

Recoiling from her as if she was vermin infested, Cam dug his thumbs into her waist and pushed her away. He wiped his hand over his lips and looked away from her. "Sorry," he said coolly, "I shouldn't have kissed you."

The cold air separating them sent a chill through her body. His coarse abandonment left her more confused. Her heart suddenly felt squeezed together so she had trouble taking a breath of air, and the call of the animal she took as a sharp warning from Mockingbird that what she had done was wrong. Ashamed, not sure why her body felt so strange—all tingly like fire—Ketl staunchly resolved not to let the She-Tiger into her body.

Squaring her shoulders, she said, "Evil One, you must not touch me like that again."

As if in a trance, Cam nodded in agreement. Her lips had been soft, warm, and so very sweet. She felt damn good in his arms, and that alone set alarm bells ringing. He knew he was asking for trouble to become romantically involved with her. Admonishing himself for so foolishly thinking he could steel a quick kiss, he turned his back to her and brushed his pants as if he could remove the luster of sexual arousal. He knew must never kiss her again, not if he wanted to keep his sanity.

"Don't worry," he told her. "I won't touch you again."

Ketl expected him to argue. She didn't expect him to agree with her. Offended, yet relieved, she gathered her arrows from where she dropped them. "Come, we must go," she said and melted into the darkness.

Thinking it a mistake to have accompanied her, Cam glanced over his shoulder, questioning whether he should try and find his way back to her canyon and to Woody's place. Everything looked the same. He'd never find his way back. Kicking the dust with his sandal, he caught sight of her head disappearing into a gully. "Shit," he swore as he started out after her.

They walked a long time in silence. An irreparable gap had come between them which neither know how to bridge. It was very immature, Cam told himself as he watched her hair bob up and down with each of her steps. He wished he could see her face. Moreover, he wished he could get into her pretty little head and find out what she was thinking.

But didn't Woody say it was no good to wish? That it was like spitting into the wind? Yeah, he vividly remembered the old coot's words.

Filled with resolve to sort this out, Cam picked up his pace and fell in stride with her. "Look," he said. "I'm sorry about what happened back there. I shouldn't have touched you. I shouldn't have kissed you." He wanted to add she damn well shouldn't have pressed her firm breasts against him and matched his desire like she had, but he kept silent about it. "Where I come from, it's acceptable for a man to kiss a woman," he tried explaining.

"You are in my territory now, White Man, not yours."

She used that snotty tone of voice which drove him crazy and refused to turn her head to look at him. He'd like to throttle her. "I realize that," he said with a tired sigh. "I can't do anymore than apologize to you and promise it won't happen again. I am appealing to your sense of harmony."

She remained silent.

"Are you purposely being rude or do you lack harmony about my apology?"

She stopped and glared at him, narrowing her eyes until they were mere slits. "I have learned my harmony in many years of lessons. You do not have the right to question my harmony, White Man. However, you are right that I am most rude not to accept your humble apology. It is a sign of a strong man who can admit his weaknesses."

Cam wanted to blurt that he wasn't weak, that he was doing the very thing most women found to be his greatest strength, but he decided she wouldn't understand and would only harp about his lack of harmony or melody. "Can we forget it?"

"Yes, it is gone from my memory."

"Good," he said, sighing, wondering if he could really forget her lips. "Now would you mind finish telling me about the migrations?"

"I have told you all," she said, turning her back, hiding the confusion running rampant through her mind; for she was positive she would never forget the way the white man had marked her lips and body.

Far behind them she heard a coyote call to its mate. Glancing in the direction of the coyote, she expected to see Mockingbird. However, the desert was empty. Ashamed of herself for letting the white man confuse her emotions so, she began to walk toward the Hopi mesa.

She was shutting him out. Damn, it pissed him off, and he started after her. "If you don't want to tell me anymore, at least you could be civil to me," he yelled after her.

"I will be whatever you want me to be, White Man."

The tart reply was worse than being shut out. "Great," he spat at her, "then finish telling me about the migrations."

She turned hostile eyes on him. "Only if you remain civil and do not laugh."

He placed his palms up in mock surrender. "I will be on my best behavior. Promise. Scouts honor."

She seemed satisfied, lightly tossing her head. "What more do you want to know?"

Cam relaxed a little. He stepped in stride with her and asked, "You were telling me about your clan's migrations."

"Yes, I was, and I said Qualetaga told us the great bird would fulfill them."

She stopped talking, and Cam thought she was finished, as if she didn't intend to tell him anymore, or perhaps she was waiting to see if he would laugh at her again.

"Yes?" he prodded, careful to keep a serious tone of voice. "What happened?"

Ketl's lips lifted slightly and she threw Cam a quick glance of acceptance. She sighed wearily and pushed hair off her cheek. "I believe Qualetaga wanted us to fail, so we would return to the Third World where he was The Great One. Many of the elders argued this point. Some trusted him while others doubted him. Those that doubted him left Willow Canyon and continued their migrations. My father left, so did my grandmother and great-grandmother and great-grandfather.

"Recently, I have doubted the wisdom of Qualetaga. Our clan does not prosper. We have failed. I believe we *must* complete our migrations ourselves and not leave it to *Kawavo*."

He could just imagine her, setting out on foot with her bow and arrows, her water vessel and dried squash, attempting to reach the East and West coasts, North and South poles. She'd last one month and be gobbled up my modern America.

"I wish you luck," he said, a hint of sarcasm in his voice.

"Thank you," she replied confidently.

He rolled his eyes. He thought over what she had told him, then asked, "Woody said all the Anasazi people vanished. Do you know what happened to them? He said it was from oppressors and because a long drought forced them to leave."

"Haven't you been listening to me?" she shrieked. "They didn't vanish! No enemy of the People was fierce enough to penetrate our villages. The People are still of this world...somewhere. They are busy with their migrations—"

"Whoa! Whoa! Do you mean all the ruins in this area were occupied by people who left to continue their migrations?"

"Yes, that is exactly what I just said. There was no long period without rain. The sacred water vessel assured us rain in the summer. We always had ample. Our crops flourished. We were able to protect ourselves from the Athabascans. That was not a problem. But completing the migrations caused the clans to leave. Others, migrating from far away, might arrive and live in the dwellings constructed by another clan. Then they too would leave again. Many clans would settle somewhere for years, maybe even generations. They were tired from migrating. Then they would start out again on another quest of reaching the end of land. In so doing, they purified themselves of all the remaining evil from the Third World. It was especially true for old people who wanted to die while on their migration, for it was known that they would pass into the Fifth World if they died seeking their destiny."

A huge bell rang in his head! *Bong!* The pieces of the puzzle were falling into place. These people didn't vanish, they simply wandered away on their migration quest. It made perfect, perfect sense, and he wondered why others hadn't realized what he knew. Then he realized no one else had the opportunity to speak to the last Anasazi.

Ketl still talked: "The People knew they were led to this land as their chosen place on earth because here they have to depend upon little rainfall for survival. To bring rain they must obey the laws of Masaw, using their powers and prayers, and so preserve forever the almighty power of The Creator."

"It sounds confusing."

She outstretched her arms like a huge bird, lifting her arms to the sky. "No, White Man, it is very simple," she said. "That is the way it was."

Chapter 15

Deep inside a kiva in a long-abandoned ruin, it was dark and cool, while outside the desert temperature soared past a hundred. In the kiva, Cam and Ketl slept peacefully.

While Ketl and Cam slept, Christopher Hayes bounced down the dirt road to the Hayes ranch in his Ford Bronco. He glanced in his rear-view mirror to make sure Stanley was following him.

He was.

After they pulled into the driveway, Christopher ran into the house, yelling, "Cameron? Where the hell are you?"

Christopher was horrified to find the house empty, no sign of Cameron January, nor of the Anasazi Indian. With Stanley on his heels, Christopher stomped through the house, out to the barn and back to the house. He noticed a plate full of uneaten bacon on the stove and broken dishes and a mess of scrambled eggs and dried toast on the floor inside Ketl's room. Flies hovered on the food. Inside Ketl's room, he saw the open window.

Behind Christopher, Stanley said, "I don't see an Indian."

Christopher fumed, filled with consummate rage. Kicking a coffee cup along the floor, Christopher kneeled on Ketl's bed and looked out the window. Yeah, he could see her footprints in the soft dirt.

"Damnation," Christopher swore. "She's gone."

"Who…the Indian?"

"Yes, the Indian—"

"Sure you weren't drunk when you—"

"No!" Christopher roared. He picked up Ketl's smock which had been neatly folded and placed at the foot of her bed. He shoved it at Stanley. "Look at this. It belongs to the Indian. She bled all over it. Gramps washed it for her. Come here." Christopher brushed past Stanley.

Looking at the hand-loomed cotton smock, Stanley followed Christopher to the kitchen. Christopher handed Stanley Ketl's elk-bone knife. "This is hers," Christopher said.

Amazed at the perfect balance of the knife, Stanley held it in his hand and fingered the rings of flint around the handle. "This has to be 800 years old," Stanley mumbled.

"Yeah, and it's sharp as shit. She cut January with it like a hot knife through butter."

"January?"

"Cameron January…the geologist who was here. He thought she was weird as hell and didn't want to have anything to do with her. When my ma burned herself, we left her with Cam. He probably spooked her. She's gone, Cameron January too, but I know where."

Wide-eyed, Stanley studied the things Christopher had given him. He had never seen anything like the knife. And the tunic. Obviously made from hand-loomed cotton, it was crude, but beautiful from an archeological point of view. Stanley fingered the fabric, then sniffed it.

"Amazing," he mumbled. Blood stained the tunic, collaborating Christopher's words that the Indian woman had suffered an injury. "Where did she go?"

"She called it 'Willow Canyon.' I think I know…no, I do know where it is. There hasn't been rain for days and her tracks will be easy to follow."

"Lead the way," Stanley said.

Christopher nodded and headed for the door.

By mid-afternoon, Stanley and Christopher were leading horses to the narrow mouth of the canyon. They paused at the shallow creek, drank their thirst away and watered the animals. Red-faced, his armpits wet, with sweat dripping down his temples, Stanley stood awestruck at the almost hidden entrance to the canyon. He had been to hundreds of ruins and was well aware of the physical force necessary to visit many of the ruins, but this place—the ride across scorching hot desert, then the wall of the mesa in front of them—was an athletic feat he didn't want to repeat. Yet he shivered with anticipation. In front of him was an immense cliff with scattered rocks and thick brush before a hidden entrance to a canyon. In wonder, he shook his head.

To think that a group of people with no horses or motorized vehicles ventured this far into the arid desert, then found the canyon and remained hidden in it for hundreds of years was mind boggling. But now, seeing the hidden cut in the mesa, he understood. Yes, he could understand how a tribe of Indians remained hidden from mankind for hundreds of years.

However, it still seemed difficult to think humans had willingly come to this spot and the forbearance to go around the rocks and into the canyon. It was *incredible!* And to think beyond the narrow gap lay a thriving Anasazi village, plus a living prehistoric person. A human fossil! His mind swooned, thinking of the ramifications of such a find, and he paced anxiously at the edge of the creek, eager to enter the canyon.

When their horses were well watered, they squeezed between the low-hanging rocks and led their mounts between the narrow cliffs. Before them, quietly waiting, was Willow Canyon. Both men were stunned by the beauty and serene quietness of the place. As they walked the horses along the narrow trail, the great cave came into view, hanging suspended in the cliff like a mirage. The solemn grandeur of the sight took the wind out of Stanley's lungs. His legs grew weak. His mind wanted to jump ahead and run to the cave, but he was tired and his legs refused to cooperate. Breathing deeply, holding tightly to the reins to keep his hands from shaking, Stanley willed his body to act. Slowly he took one step, and then another toward the village of stone, knowing what a great and wonderful thing of archaeological value he was approaching.

Less impressed by the importance of the discovery, Christopher felt a strange and eerie feeling pass through him. It was though unseen eyes watched him, eyes that wondered what aliens had invaded their sanctuary. His heart thudded wildly. He darted a nervous glance left and right while an unhealthy layer of sweat beaded his brow. From every direction, he felt eyes watching him and a threatening presence encircle him, one he couldn't see, but one that seemed to squeeze his heart to a standstill. Above all else, he wished he could turn and run, never to set foot in the canyon again.

But Stanley was hurrying to the cave ahead of him.

And Christopher knew Ketl would be there, and he desperately wanted to see her again.

But to his dismay, they found Ketl gone.

Stanley ran around the village of rocks like a mad man. He scampered in and out of every room and kiva, ranting and mumbling. He picked up things, examined them closely, put them down then furiously wrote in his notebook. Christopher noticed Stanley's face became pale, and his cold blue eyes seemed to burn with an intensity that could have melted ice. It gave Christopher the creeps, and he grew more anxious to leave the canyon.

While Stanley touched baskets, bowls, tools, tasting this and that, Christopher lightly walked across the plaza. He felt like an intruder. Ill at ease, he wanted to leave everything in its place. He took his time, noting a recently burned fire, baskets of food carefully tucked away, a stone axe, a basket with a bone needle and cotton thread, an unfinished pair of yucca sandals.

Then he found Cam's cowboy boots. Holding the boots, a mean scowl covered his face, and his eyes turned to knife-sized slits. He knew Cam was with Ketl. Somewhere he had taken her, or she had taken him, he wasn't sure which. It angered him to think of Cam with her when it should have been him, and he grew even more uncomfortable being in the cave without her being there. He could sense her presence. She was supposed to be there.

Damn her!

The rest of the afternoon, Christopher fought off the conflicting emotions inside him while Stanley ignored him. Guilt lurked inside of his brain like a disease, while anger at Cam and Ketl kept the guilt from consuming him, because he reasoned that they would get what they deserved for spoiling his plans. He sat in the shade of the great cave, leaning back against the rock side of a room, letting his imagination take him away from the desert, from the canyon to a place where Christopher was lavished in only the finest clothes, best wines, newest house, most expensive car and surrounded by gorgeous women. Closing his eyes, he slipped away to a fantasy world which was purchased by the money Ketl would bring him.

When it was dusky gray, with the first fading light casting weird shadows in the cave, Christopher woke with a start. Blinking hard, his pulse pounding in his temples. Sleep had not removed the unearthly feeling he had in Ketl's canyon.

He found Stanley in a kiva. "Stanley, it's getting late. We better go."

"Oh?" Stanley questioned, at a loss for a sense of time.

"It'll be dark soon."

Disappointment covered Stanley's face. He knew Christopher was telling the truth about the Indian woman. The ruin was not a ruin, but an occupied village. Sure, he was disappointed to find the Indian gone, but every sign pointed to the fact that she was coming back, and Stanley knew he wasn't presently equipped to handle a person who had stepped out of the past. No, there was much to do back at the laboratory before they took her there, and as his mind centered on the job ahead of him, his face lighted.

"All right," Stanley said, snapping his notebook shut. "I'll be coming back in a few days to set up a permanent camp. It'll take years to document all of this," he said, thinking out loud. "I'll have to have the President proclaim this a National Historic Sight. This canyon will become the most important place in the United States. Millions of people will come to see it."

Glassy-eyed, Stanley continued to mumble to himself as he climbed out of the kiva, crossed the plaza and walked down the sandstone steps away from Christopher.

Christopher's jaw sagged open. Willow Canyon and the cave was unspoiled, exquisite as it was now. *Millions of people!* Stanley's words echoed in his ears. The cave would be sanitized and dehumanized. Although Christopher knew it was inevitable, that the cave was a fantastic scientific find, he cringed with the thought of Stanley and his people being in control of the canyon. In fact, Christopher thought it would be the beginning of the end.

༂ᩮ   ༂ᩮ   ༂ᩮ

Ketl's thoughts ran along the same lines, only for a different reason. It was dark. After walking for an hour, they climbed up a seemingly gently rise, but which turned into a long hard pull up a sandstone incline scattered with rocks, and when they reached the top and looked out at a huge expanse of flat terrain, off in the distance they saw buzzards take flight from a dark lump.

Suddenly a rock fell into the pit of her stomach.

She guessed what the lump was.

And she was right.

Blinded by stinging eyes, running as fast as she could, then coming to an abrupt stop with Cam on her heels, at her feet lay her dearly beloved Pavi. Bloated, grossly swollen from the heat, Pavi's body hardly looked anything like the grandfather she remembered. The buzzards had attacked his face and torn chunks of flesh from his legs. The stench was unbelievable.

The sight and smell made Cam turn away and bile rise in his throat. He couldn't help himself and vomited.

Ketl dropped to her knees and stroked the old Indian's hair. "Grandfather," she whispered.

Tenderness and years of memories oozed from her soul.

Her chin trembled when she bit her lip to stop the ache in her throat. Biting down harder, attempting to take the pain in her heart away by the pain of biting her lip, Ketl tasted blood, then she opened her mouth and sucked in a lungful of air. A huge sob escaped her lips.

After wiping his mouth with the back of his hand, Cam heard her gasp painfully. Managing to control the nausea, he turned back to her although he refused to look at the dead man on the ground, and he tried to breathe through his mouth. He had only seen a dead person in a coffin with makeup, embalming fluid in the veins and dressed in appropriate clothes. He had never seen a body which had been dead for days and which had been picked on by scavengers and smelled like death ten times over.

He wrapped his fingers around her slender upper arm and

pulled her to him, not only to give her comfort, but to give himself the strength he required to help her.

Desperately needing someone, Ketl collapsed against him, and let his arms envelop her. With her chest heaving, she took strength he offered. The Magic Waters came and tears spilled down her cheeks.

Gently, Cam stroked her hair, neck and back. He planted his chin on her head and smelled her hair which carried the fragrance of wild sage. "I'm sorry," he said sincerely.

She cried harder. At long last her sorrow abated, even though he could feel her body shiver, so he pulled her closer as if to protect her from the hurt in her heart. Her head fit perfectly in the crook of his neck, and he found himself tenderly kissing the top of her head.

Ketl pushed away from Cam, taking a deep lungful of air. She wiped her cheeks with the back of her hand and licked her bloody lip. "We must bury him," Ketl said.

Cam sighed wearily. The ground was rock hard. They had no shovel, nothing. "There is nowhere to bury him," he told her. As an afterthought, he added, "I'm sure his spirit will be fine."

"I'm not concerned about his spirit," Ketl replied in a tired voice. "He has already made the long and happy journey to the Fifth World, but we must not let the birds take his flesh to many parts of the desert. He must remain whole, to please the gods."

Cam wiped his brow with his shirt sleeve. "Okay," he conceded, "but how do we bury him?"

"With rocks," Ketl said. "We bury him with rocks." She moved toward Pavi. Beneath a heaven of stars, with the moon bathing the ground in light, she began to gather rocks, gently placing them around the body of her grandfather.

Cam helped her, careful to block out the smell by breathing though his mouth.

When they were nearly finished with only his shoulder and left arm exposed, Ketl paused and her eyes grew large and liquid. Her chin quivered.

"I show my grandfather no respect," she moaned.

"Why?" Cam asked, pained to see her cry again.

"I have no turquoise, no decorated water vessels, no adornments to bury with him. It is disrespectful."

That same unknown power which had put words into his mouth and agreed to accompany her on this trek, took over Cameron January. Without realizing what he was doing, he removed his gold Seiko watch and handed it to her. "Here," he said. "Will this do?"

She smiled at him, her emerald eyes sparking with thanks. She took the watch from him, bent down and smashed the edge of it on a sharp rock.

Cam groaned. *An eight-hundred-dollar watch, demolished.*

Glancing at him, she showed him the smashed watch. She saw the mute disbelief written on his face. "It must be so. The edge of your time maker must be broken to release the spirit so that it can accompany grandfather to the spirit land."

Cam wasn't going to argue with her, but he could imagine the oddity of an old Indian wandering though the next world with a broken Seiko watch.

Removing a rock close to his head, Ketl placed the watch in the hole and replaced the rock. Then she placed the last rocks in position on what was now a big lump of rocks in the middle of the desert.

Stepping back, she said, "It is done."

"Yes," he said, "it is."

He thought of the loss of the expensive watch, the one Sharon had bought for him, and wondered if he wasn't crazy, giving his watch to Ketl to bury with a dead Indian. Then the soft desert breeze brushed his cheek. Breathing deeply, he took in the sweet desert air and held it. A million stars blinked their approval. Releasing the air, he glanced at Ketl, watching the way she tenderly made sure all the rocks were properly placed around her grandfather. He felt good. It made him feel damn good. He had made her happy and helped the old man on a new journey. *Why the hell not?*

Without saying anything, Ketl took a handful of sand, sprinkled it over the grave, then stood and walked off into the desert. Cam followed her. A second sense told him to stay behind her, not to attempt to speak to her, to leave her alone until she was ready to talk to him. So he walked behind her and watched her, a slim figure bathed in moonlight. When they had walked about a mile from the grave of her grandfather, Ketl paused and let him come abreast of her.

Without looking at him, she said, "White Man, I am beginning to hear your harmony."

Cam smiled.

Then she walked ahead of him, her head held high, her gait sure and strong.

❦   ❦   ❦

At ten o'clock the next morning, a long string of four-wheel-drive vehicles crossed the desert, creating a giant rooster plume of dust in the sky. It looked like an army of men. However, it was an army of archaeologists, with Stanley in the lead, taking his men into battle against the last Anasazi. They made their own roads. They tore across the old roads made by 'the Ancient Ones'. When one vehicle became mired in sand, another pulled it out. When one radiator exploded, they abandoned the car, transferring all the materials into the other vehicles. In all Stanley brought with him twenty men and women, with more government officials, state officers and the like due to convene on the place in the next few days. The President had been notified of the find, and he promised any help Stanley needed.

Stanley was in his element.

Christopher was a little lost. People paid the cowboy no attention, or asked rudely who he was, as if he were an outsider who was elbowing his way into something that was none of his business.

When they arrived at the mouth of the canyon, they had to transfer all their supplies and tools up the canyon by foot. It was too narrow for the cars and the supplies too cumbersome to tie to the back of horses. When they made endless trips back and forth, they trampled the raspberry bushes, stomping through the creek and keeping the trout terrified, hidden in the shadows. Stanley's first order of command was to send three men up the cliff to the mesa top, where they were to set up a stakeout, turn their walkie-talkies to channel twelve and wait, because Stanley was convinced Ketl and Cameron January were coming back, and he intended on greeting them when they did so.

By nightfall the camp was set up on the flats under the cottonwood trees. They had gas camping stoves, gas lanterns, tents, mosquito netting, coolers, bottled water since they didn't trust the water in the creek, sleeping bags, insect spray, instant trail food and a ghetto-blaster, plus plenty of batteries. Someone had prudently remembered to bring the marshmallows, Hershey Chocolate Bars and graham crackers to make s'mores.

They were definitely not in harmony with nature.

The next day they began in earnest their assault on the village. Turkeys squawked in protest as they were chased, caught and examined. Water vessels and baskets were removed, tagged and crated, then removed from the cave to the vehicles for transportation to the lab in Farmington for further study. Ketl's food was placed in plastic baggies for examination. A helicopter buzzed overhead as the government officials arrived. The ghetto-blaster boomed a Country and Western song, *Feed Jake.*

The trout remained hidden in the shadows.

Men climbed all over the rock houses. They ran tape measurers up and down, across and back, while other men scooped solid material into more plastic baggies, then tagged them. Ketl's sleeping mat was rolled up and carted away. Three men spent their time taking pictures of every nook and cranny. To better photograph it for all time, a roof of one of the kivas was removed, the logs and clay mortar cast aside in a pile. Her new pair of sandals, the ones she was making for Pavi, also went into a large plastic bag, was closed and placed in a box to be removed from the canyon. Ketl's pride and joy, a sash made of dog hair and turkey feathers, was tagged and thrown aside into a crate. Rock clubs, bone scrapers, bone awls, arrows, tools of all sorts were methodically placed into boxes and marched down the canyon to the awaiting cars. Then they were driven away from Willow Canyon, forever.

A new form of headquarters was being set up at the house on the Hayes ranch. Stanley had given orders for the inside furniture to be removed and desks and office supplies to be brought in. A team of recorders, both female, were entrenched there. A gas generator was brought in from Farmington to provide better electrical voltage for the computers on which the women stored the incoming information.

It was a busy place and as Christopher observed all that was happening, he felt a gnawing start in his stomach, as if a school of sharks had taken up residence.

ᴈ৯   ᴈ৯   ᴈ৯

With the unpleasant event of finding her dead grandfather well behind them, Cam and Ketl talked softly. "Tell me about your white great-grandmother," Cam asked as they fell into an easy gait

"Her skin was white. Her eyes were green, but her soul was pure Anasazi."

"What was her name?"

"She was called Chatakl. It means Flower of the Spring. The Apache had treated her miserably. They had broken her spirit, so she could not talk, and her eyes did not carry life. This I am told. The Apache are brutal. They have no harmony whatsoever, and it took many years of peaceful life with our clan before my great-grandmother came to see the beauty of our ways."

"So she willingly stayed with your great-grandfather?"

Ketl laughed. "Where would she go? The canyon is our world. She belonged there. She was an Anasazi."

"I thought you said she left—"

"She was still one of the People. She went with her husband and my father because Mockingbird had told them to continue their migrations. She was very, very old, Pavi told me."

Cam thought about this for a while. "Did she know she would never return to your canyon?" he asked quietly.

"Of course. It pleased her to know she would die while attempting to complete her migration. That way she was assured entrance into the Fifth World."

"We call it heaven," Cam told her.

She looked shocked. "I am surprised you white people believe the same truths as us."

"We believe in our gods, just as you do yours. We have a heaven, and a hell. We believe in good and bad. We praise honorable acts, punish dishonorable ones. We have very similar beliefs, Ketl."

Raising her head a little higher, she replied, "It surprises me."

"It surprises me, too," Cam added and smiled at her.

Ketl found herself smiling back.

      ৰ   ৰ   ৰ

It was only at night that they saw anything of the coyotes.

During the twilight hours, just before dawn and just after the sun fell below the horizon, the coyotes were nowhere to be seen. To Cam, it was really spooky how they weren't there one minute and then appeared, trotting though the low-lying sage. He'd never seen a more mangy animal. They ranged from black to near-white, tan and orange in color. All of them had yellow eyes, which came close to glowing in the dark. Their tails were bushy—different from the short hair on their body—and they didn't prance like a dog did with his head held high, his tail cocked. No, those varmints slunk around like determined pickpockets. In the moonlight, their eyes were weird; the whites were nearly neon, the yellow iris close to glowing. One came close enough once so he could see its face was all scarred like it'd been through ferocious battles.

After a while he didn't think about the coyotes. Something happened, though, that evening which gave him a whole new set of worries.

Cameron January did not like snakes. It wasn't even a case of mild dislike. It was a passionate, skin-crawling, pulse-stopping sort of mortal fear. He couldn't even look at a snake on television, in a magazine or in a museum without the cold sweats taking over his usual suave demeanor.

It is well known that snakes inhabit the desert and Cam was not fool enough to think that he might not encounter one during his time on the Hayes Ranch. He just planned to run in the opposite direction if he saw one, not leaving any human footprints as he went.

One evening Ketl had pointed out the slithering tracks of a snake which had crawled off to prey on some innocent rodent. He told her, "I hate snakes. They hate me. Don't show me tracks, skin or the *living* thing! Please!"

Ketl pointed to the tracks in the sand. "They move about at night hunting. Have no fear. They do not coil and wait for you like during the day."

No comfort was gained by her observations, yet he was relieved to know he wouldn't be out under the sun, in yucca sandals, coming round a rabbitbrush and meeting a ten-foot rattlesnake in its coiled attack position.

It didn't happen that way, as things went. No, nothing so dramatic. It happened this way: After burying Ketl's grandfather and walking until the sun broke the blackness of nighttime, they took refuge in a small ruin that Ketl explained was built exactly for the purpose they used it for—shelter from the sun while trekking between Willow Canyon and the Hopi mesa. They slept soundly though the scorching daytime hours and awoke at twilight refreshed.

The early stars were just beginning to pulse. The sky was still softly gray in the West. The ground was damp; it had obviously rained while they slept and the air held a heady, honey-sweetness to it. It was a lovely time of the day—even on the desert. Cam stretched as he awoke and wandered away from the ruin to find a place to relieve himself. He'd gone maybe a hundred yards from the kiva thinking how soft the night air.

In front of him grew a large sage bush. Stepping around it, he spread his legs and unzipped his fly. He felt something soft under his foot as if he had stepped on a bough of the sage bush. Then he heard a strange sound, sort of a sudden sucking sound. For a second he thought he had stepped on a frog. As quickly as he heard it, he looked down while beginning to urinate.

"Ah, shit," he moaned and urine trickled down his pants.

His right foot lay smack across a big rattlesnake. The snake's head and thicker neck, if he could describe a snake as having a neck, were under his foot. Its mouth was open, and the noise he heard must have been when the snake opened its mouth and gasped for air.

This snake was not coiled like the ones he had seen in books. By cocking his neck and looking over his shoulder,

Cam spotted the snake's tail under the sage bush and coming out the other side. This snake was a big sucker.

And Cam had it pinned.

Now he heard a rattling sound. His eyes grew wide when he saw the snake's tail curl up and begin to shake. He didn't count the rattles on the tail. He couldn't, because his eyesight was mixed with flashes of red and yellow, fear reacting in him like the lights on a pinball machine.

He didn't know what to do. Besides being frozen to the spot, his blood had turned to ice, his muscles ready to set like cement. The dark patch of urine on his pants was unsettling, too. Hearing the subtle rattle pause, he looked over his shoulder to see the tip of the snake limply flopping from side to side. The sight made his heart stop for a nanosecond. Bile rose up in his throat, and he thought he was going to be sick.

He didn't know how long it was that he stood there, for time became suspended. His whole world spun out of control. The sky looked like the ground, the desert became the sky. All he knew was that he was going to be sick, then pass out and the snake would bite him and he would die.

His life was going to end like his most horrible nightmare.

Suddenly he saw Ketl standing in front of him. She seemed to be standing, but actually she was waving to and fro like a flag in a stiff breeze. Her lips were moving and she was pointing at him and then down at his foot.

He couldn't hear anything.

Then she stepped in front of him. He wanted to tell her to get away from him, because he was about to vomit all over her, but his lips were paralyzed and he remained silent. She moved closer to him. Looking back on it, Cam knew she had to be directly in front of the snake's nose. She stared up into his eyes, that no-nonsense, assertive look of hers gaining his attention.

"Look into my eyes," she said.

He heard her but nothing registered.

"Evil One, pay attention," she said with firm resolve. "Look at me."

He managed to focus on her eyes as she requested.

"White Man, you have invaded the space of the snake. You do not make it happy."

Numbly, Cam nodded. He wasn't so sure he was going to throw up anymore, and it was a great relief.

"The snake wishes you no harm. It wants to journey into the night. But it can't. You are stepping on it."

Again, he nodded, although her bringing back to his attention the situation he was in didn't help his arrhythmic heart functions.

"Now," Ketl said, her voice gentle and soothing, "if you would kindly step off the snake, it would go on its way."

"Just like that?" he mumbled though a dry throat.

Ketl held a forked stick. Calmly she placed the fork next to Cam's foot, imprisoning the snake. "Just like that. Because the snake is angry, I will hold it until you move away."

"That's very gracious of you." His head was clearing, his heart crashing inside his chest, but beating with a normal rhythm. His stomach settled, and was no longer trying to climb into his throat. "Now?" he asked, praying he *could* move.

"Now," she replied.

Cameron January willed his foot to move. Although his whole leg felt as though it weighed a ton, with a Herculean effort he moved it off the snake and stiffly moved away.

He couldn't look back.

Ketl was at his side. The stick hung limply in her hand, but, thank god, the forked end of it was empty. She didn't look at him, but followed his gaze, as if trying to join his thoughts.

What was a guy supposed to say? He'd had the living shit scared out of him. He was supposed to be big and strong. He could snap three boards with the swift chop of his hand. He could make a woman beg while under the masterful influence of his hands. Yet he had just demonstrated the utmost cowardice. He couldn't even move, for Christsakes! And he had urinated on himself. He wouldn't blame Ketl if she laughed in his face.

She didn't touch him or look at him. Simply, she said, "I do not like snakes, either." Then she threw the stick away.

For the first time since he felt that lump under his sandal, Cam was able to breathe easily.

ba   ba   ba

While Stanley and his men worked in Willow Canyon, and Ketl and Cam continued their journey to the Hopi mesa, Woody was miserable. His daughter had been released from the hospital, but the burns on her hands precluded her from being able to cook or clean, so Woody took over those chores. His daughter, Marybeth, didn't order him around so much, now that she was dependent on him, but he missed Cam. He missed Ketl, and worried about her. Christopher had been strangely absent. He felt an ill wind brewing, yet was confined to the house by the sheer bars of his age. Marybeth couldn't drive and wouldn't allow Woody behind the wheel of a car.

The worst was that Marybeth wouldn't let Woody sit on the front steps of the house. Every time he did, she would swing out the door and say, "Father, honestly, what are you doing out here in the heat?"

"Sittin'," he'd reply.

"It's too hot. You'll have a stroke." She shook her bandaged hand at him. "I've fixed up the front room with an air conditioner and a new recliner just for you. Come on, you can sit in there and see everything you see out here. Now, come on. I want you inside."

Groaning, knowing an air-conditioned room and soft recliner was not the same as the front step of the house, but tired of her incessant harping, he grumbled, then pushed his old bones off the steps, and shuffled into the house.

When he was settled in the recliner, thinking it was damn *chilly* in the room, he swore he would get away ...somehow...someday.

The thought made him smile.

Chapter 16

On the mesa, Ketl and Cam slept, huddled together beneath a low-hanging outcropping of sandstone. A shadow of a beard gave him a rugged look. His jeans were filthy, his T-shirt more brown than white, his feet permanently dyed red—the color of the desert sand. Snuggled against him in the narrow swipe of shade, Ketl slept peacefully,

Sensing the dying sun, her eyes batted open. The white man's arm protectively lay across her ribs. Although it was not an unpleasant sensation, she removed his wrist from her stomach and placed it on his thigh. Moving silently, she inched away from him, sensing the cold on her back where only minutes ago his body heat had warmed her.

Taking her bow and arrows, she wiggled out of the rock cave, sniffed the air, then studied the ground around her. Smiling, she headed for a thicket of saltbrush. She chose her quarry carefully. A fat Black-tailed jack rabbit munched innocently on purple verbena flowers. With a steady bead, Ketl drew her bow. The arrow went straight and true, rupturing the rabbit's heart so that it fell dead instantly.

She collected dry twigs and drier grass. From around her neck, she retrieved a small clay pot which held a cone of charcoal. This she put beneath the dried grass and blew on it. Soon the charcoal glowed red and the grass smoked. Adding pinion roots to the fire, it began to crackle as flames leaped skyward. Methodically, she skinned and gutted the rabbit without leaving any blood on her hands. Then she fashioned a small pyramid of green Tamarisk tree sticks over the fire and from this she hung the rabbit.

Cam wakened to the aromatic scent of meat grilling.

With his lips turned upward at the ends, he propped his head on one hand watched Ketl turn the rabbit. Behind her the sky was salmon, the clouds pearl-white and deep purple. As she worked her breasts strained against her tunic, and Cam watched her, his eyes hungry, a dull twisting in his chest.

He remembered her sleeping next to him, her body pressed to his. He'd spent an unsettled day of sleep, made endless by the scent of her hair, the feel of her lithe body pressed against him. He was tormented with visions of supple legs twined around him, strong fingers wound into the hair at the nape of his neck, low groans of pleasure slipping from her lips when he made her his, drawing her deeper to him.

Cam swallowed hard watching Ketl stretch a leg out to poke a burning ember with a stick. Why did he watch her whenever she wasn't looking? Why was he fascinated by her innocence? Why did a gnawing sense of emptiness, of need grow inside of him as the hours, the days passed in her company? Even now he longed to stride across the few yards that separated them and bury himself in the dreamy-naive world in her eyes.

But of course he wouldn't. They came from two different worlds. He would have to be satisfied with looking and thinking and fantasies. Smiling, he watched Ketl remove the rabbit from the fire, place it on a flat rock and remove the yucca thread she had used to hang the rabbit. He caught her pick a bit of well-done flesh and pop it in her mouth. She seemed as natural preparing a wild rabbit as Cam did working on his computer.

After licking her fingers, she glanced over her shoulder. "So," she said, "you are awake."

"Yeah," he drawled, "and I'm damn hungry."

"Come, I have food for you."

His stomach growled.

When the sky lost its salmon color and turned pale lavender with the first diamond chips of stars blinking on, Cam sat across from Ketl. It seemed perfectly natural to be sitting on the ground, tearing meat from the bones of a rabbit, savoring each bite, wiping greasy fingers on his pants and quietly chatting with an Anasazi Indian woman. A few grains of sand were now easily chewed and swallowed with little afterthought. In the fading twilight they devoured the rabbit along with pinion and sunflower nuts. As the North Star came out and began to pulse, they buried the rabbit bones, smothered the fire and began to walk toward the Hopi mesas.

While Stanley and his men ravaged Willow Canyon during the day, during the night Ketl and Cam kept a steady pace. Cam now felt tireless. His muscles didn't ache, and he thrived on the challenge of the rough country. That last night together they walked longer and harder, pushing themselves until long after the sun had crested the horizon. Cam watched the earth began to heat, sending up mesmerizing waves of hot air. Shiny-wet with sweat, they rounded a bend of an arroyo and saw in front of them the first of the three Hopi mesas called Kiakochomovi.

"It means Place of the Hills of Ruins," Ketl told Cam.

"Yeah," Cam replied as he studied the Hopi villages perched on the top of the high mesa. The villages looked parched and bleak, baked under the midmorning sun. "Who named it?" he asked as he rubbed his fingers over the stubble on his chin, then wiped his hand across his brow.

"The People." Ketl pointed to a village in the middle of the mesa. "They first settled there at Oraibi. It means 'Place of the Rock Called Orai.' Come. We must find Una."

They approached the knob of land, the most Western mesa belonging to the Hopi clans. They climbed a rutted road to the top of the mesa and there one of the young men of the clan greeted Ketl warmly, while casting an arrogant beady eye at Cam. The Hopi braves then ushered Ketl and Cameron January to Qommatu, who ruled the Hopis. Qommatu met them inside of his pueblo where it was dark and cool.

A large-muscled, black-eyed, dark-skinned Indian with a wide flat nose and thick lips, Qommatu was an impressive Indian. All around him was an air of expectancy as other Indians waited for their chief to say something. With his silvery-gray hair, his arms folded over his chest, he commanded a great deal of respect. Just like the younger Indian, the chief appraised Cam with cold black eyes.

Although the chief was not as tall as Cam, he was thick with huge arms and a broad chest, pushing the confines of a blue denim shirt. Cam decided he would not like to meet the son-of-a-bitch in a dark alley. Cam also noted the chief looked right though him with haughty arrogance while he greeted Ketl with open fondness.

Qommatu's eyes examined Ketl carefully. "Your mother spoke highly of you, but did not do you justice."

Mumbled remarks from the crowd of young Hopi men caused Ketl's cheeks to turn rosy. "Where is Una?" Ketl blurted.

"She left many days ago," Qommatu replied.

Shocked, Ketl mumbled, "She left?"

"Yes," he said with a nod. "She bargained well for the right to have you and Tommy Bright Eagle marry. She left to take you the news. Did she not return to Willow Canyon?"

All color drained from her face. A suffocating sensation closed her throat and for a minute she was rendered mute. In a strangled voice she managed, "No, she didn't return."

Cam moved next to Ketl, sure she was going to collapse in a new set of tears. He almost felt like crying himself; after all they had been through, after all the endless miles they had walked, after finding her grandfather dead and half eaten by scavenger birds, after the coyotes, after the snake, after walking for four straight days, it was a bitter ending not to have her mother here to greet them.

As Cam inched closer to Ketl, Qommatu moved between them and stared at Cam, the chief's features hard and chiseled. His eyes were eerily penetrating, cold and disapproving. It gave Cam the creeps, yet he didn't give up his position next to Ketl.

Then the Indian chief spoke directly to Cam, his lips so close, Cam could feel air on his face. The chief's words were carefully chosen, spoken slowly so there could be no mistaking what he said: "You do not belong, White Man. Ketl belongs to Tommy Bright Eagle. You will go."

Cam wanted to take the old fart down with a karate kick to the groin, but with a dozen Hopi Indians surrounding him, he decided he was outnumbered just like Custer had been and it would a foolhardy thing to try. Just then a young man pushed through the crowd of Indians, creating a loud disturbance when he entered the pueblo. Although ugly, he was huge. His face was broad, his eyes too wide apart, his lips too thin to go with such a huge face. Bare-chested, muscles the sizes of grapefruits on his arms, his thighs the size of thick tree trunks, his total appearance was that of a grotesque land mass. His hungry eyes claimed Ketl.

"Bright Eagle," Qommatu said, "your bride has come."

Cam's stomach climbed into his throat.

Ketl was unsure what to do. She was concerned about her mother, not at all caring one way or another about her chosen husband although one look at Tommy Bright Eagle told her that her mother must not have thought a handsome husband held much importance.

Determined not to hurt her eyes by resting them on Tommy Bright Eagle, she went over in her mind the various different routes between Willow Canyon and the Hopi mesa. She wondered which her mother had chosen and which one Ketl would take back to search for her mother.

Cam tried to move closer to Ketl so he could talk to her. Both Bright Eagle and Qommatu stood in his way, and with Ketl's intended groom standing in front of him, it was like looking at a wall of flesh.

"Listen," Cam said, trying to remain polite, but finding his patience strained, "I want to talk to her. Is it all right if I just talk to her?"

Bright Eagle puffed his gargantuan chest and he stared right through Cam. "No, you may not speak to her," he said through narrow lips. "You must go. You are a white man. You do not belong."

Cam's control snapped; his politeness disappeared. He would like to push Tommy Bright Eagle's already flat nose through his small cranium. He definitely felt no harmony. Balling his fist, he took back his arm and released a powerful right jab to Bright Eagle's gut. The punch never connected.

Although Bright Eagle didn't move—his reflexes being poor—the punch was cut off when Qommatu seized Cam's arm in an ironclad grip. Cam had never seen anyone move so fast. In fact, he never saw the Indian's arm move! He also thought the odds, two to one, unfair and would have pointed this out to Bright Eagle, but his vocal cords were severed by the pain in his arm.

Bright Eagle replaced Qommatu's steely grip with his

own which Cam further decided was very unsportsmanlike. He thought Indians believed in fair play, but then Cam didn't read factual tales about Indians, or he would have known better.

Sport to Tommy Bright Eagle would be to snap the white man's wrist just to see him scream with pain. Grinding his teeth together, Bright Eagle twisted tighter, but stopped before the bone broke, then he threw the limp wrist aside, only partly satisfied by the ashen paleness of the white man's face.

"Ketl will tell you to go," Bright Eagle announced. "Then you will leave." His lips clamped into a hard line, while his piercing eyes shot daggers though Cam.

Ketl was in a quandary. The Evil One had proven his good intentions. His harmony, once nonexistent, was now weak but growing, yet he was not one of the People. Although this was not her home, it belonged to the Hopi and she could not refute what had already been decided.

A quick glance at Tommy Bright Eagle left her stomach uneasy; for his face was not one born to please the gods. Certainly, the man was strong. He must be trustworthy, and certainly he would make a good husband and take her back to Willow Canyon. Surely he would help her find her mother, she reasoned. Squaring her shoulders, proud of her Indian heritage, she stepped in front of Bright Eagle and looked Cameron January squarely in the eyes.

"White Man, you must go," she said with firm resolve.

Her words cut him to the quick. Her face was like stone, and for the first time since he had met her, when she spoke to him she didn't look through him. Instead, she looked into him and stayed there, her emerald eyes locking with his blue ones. Her soul seemed to leave her and invade his body. He felt a warm rush radiate up his spine and his mouth go painfully dry. It made those coyotes come in from the dark and begin circling in his stomach.

Just as suddenly as he felt her take a firm hold of his physical body, he felt her let him go. Poof! Just like that. He was a balloon that popped, a bridge that collapsed, a plane that crashed. He felt weak. Limply, he raised his arm to her.

Without changing expression, Ketl turned her back on him and walked out of the hogan. Bright Eagle was on her tail like an oversized puppy while Qommatu waited for the white man to leave the Hopi Mesa.

Breathing raggedly, Cam stomped through the crowd of people, pushing Indians aside as he left the pueblo and emerged in dazzling sunlight. For a second he was blinded. Squinting, he searched the village for Ketl. The last he saw of her was as she ducked to enter another pueblo with Bright Eagle right behind her.

         ஐ   ஐ   ஐ

When he stomped down the dusty road from the Hopi mesa, Cameron January was in a rage. He was filled with consummate anger when he thumbed a ride on the dusty dirt road. He could hardly talk civilly to the Indian who drove him to the nearest town. The Indian's car was a broken down Ford Fairlane with nonexistent shocks. The inside of the car was hotter than a pizza oven. The Indian talked in unintelligible grunts. It was just as well, because Cam's gut festered with an illogical hatred for all male red-skinned, black-haired, brown-eyed Native Americans.

It was a dusty, bumpy ride into Hanksville which was the Indian's destination. Cam swore he would never return to the desert when he arrived in the small, no-place sort of town.

Once in town, he thought of calling Woody, then decided against it; he wanted to erase the past few weeks from his life forever. Patting his rear pocket, he thanked his lucky stars that one bit of civilized habits had not escaped him completely, for there in his pocket was his wallet. It was filled with desert sand, but was also filled with money and credit cards.

The money bought him a cold Coke Classic and a greasy hamburger in a no-place sort of diner. The credit cards bought him the use of a sorry-looking Buick station wagon to drive to Grand Junction, Colorado. It cost him thirty bucks, and Cam decided that was a royal rip-off, because the whiskered owner of Jake's Garage and Car Rentals told Cam not to drive the car at night because the lights didn't work.

Cam's body was rank, his clothes covered with grease and fine desert sand. The car smelled of stale cigars and old whiskey. The stink of the car made Cam even more angry, and he floored the rental car, grinding his teeth, seething with unbridled irritation as he drove to Grand Junction.

Padding through the airport at Grand Junction in his yucca sandals, he told himself that Ketl had not gotten under skin, told himself to forget her, that the experience had been an impossible nightmare. So then why did he remember the touch of her lips? Why, when he took a lungful of air, did he smell the desert and an Indian's hair washed with yucca soap? Why was he unable to wipe her beautiful face, innocent green eyes, black hair framing her face, and sun bronzed skin, from his vision? Why did the way Tommy Bright Eagle look at Ketl set up attack sharks in his stomach?

The air-conditioned airport didn't chill his overheated blood. Nor did the perfectly manicured woman who was seated next to him in the plane and who looked at Cam like he was the slime monster from the sewer; he did smell like year-old gym clothes, wore funny sandals with feathers hanging from them, sported a ragged, five-day beard, was filthy, and he didn't answer her when she asked him if he had recently been on vacation.

When the plane lifted off the ground, forever leaving behind the desert and the Last Anasazi woman, he thought surely he could forget her although he kept his nose pressed to the window of the plane when it took off, hoping just by chance to get a glimpse of three mesas, for he knew that was where *she* would be. He couldn't find the mesas, and frantically searched the land for one last look at a mesa cut by a deep canyon. However, he saw only desert, cactus, and rabbit brush and the lazy Colorado River winding through parched country.

Then he told himself: That is the way it was.

ॐ ॐ ॐ

When Cam arrived in the *real world* that Saturday, the San Francisco airport swarmed with smartly dressed travelers. He paid them no attention, ignored their rude stares and walked through the airport to the hop the shuttle to the outlying parking spot where he had left his car. He waited half an hour for the shuttle and told his nerves to relax as he finally boarded the van along with the other tired, red-eyed people. Traffic on the frontage road which flanked the Bayshore Freeway was light. A stiff westerly breeze turned the sea air crystal clear, the bay vibrantly blue, and white sails dotting the water should have made him cheery.

They didn't.

He grew in a more foul mood, too, when he went to his car, which he had parked beneath an overhead light. He had locked it when he left and placed a car cover over it. Now he found the cover tossed aside, the passenger window broken, his Fuzz-Buster removed. Shredded glass covered the seat and exposed wires from his Fuzz-Buster dangled out the broken window.

My harmony is being severely tested, he thought as he stared at the window, then kicked the tire of the car and swore a long breath of epitaphs. Moisture-laden air poured into the open window as he drove home. His chest felt heavy. He coughed and wondered if his lungs weren't drowning. On the coastal hills, a wall of fog lay there, black, thick and menacing, waiting for darkness when it would creep down and absorb the city in its blanket of gray. Craning his head out the window,

Cam quickly looked up at the sky as if to remind himself there were stars up there which he wouldn't be able to see once the fog took over. Then he hit the steering wheel with his palm, swearing and telling himself he was a stupid-son-of-a-bitch.

He made it home to his apartment in South San Francisco, a Cape Cod looking walk-up in the outskirts of Naval Bay. He was surrounded by the rigs of tall ships, by swarms of swooping sea gulls, the smell of sea water. He was also surrounded by fog—the complete opposite from Willow Canyon.

Showered and shaved, in the quietude of the apartment without having turned on the stereo which was his custom, Cam collapsed on his bed. He thought of Sharon and picked up the phone to call her, but replaced the receiver on the cradle. Although bone-tired, he couldn't relax. He was hungry, but couldn't eat, and he wanted a woman, but not Sharon. He felt empty and angry, but he couldn't pinpoint why.

Rubbing the cool cotton sheets, he closed his eyes and imagined the material between his fingers to be yucca mat. Sighing deeply, he pretended to smell desert sand and sage. Ketl's face danced in front of him, then was gone.

Sometime later he dozed.

 za   za   za

The next morning, Cam ate the 'Breakfast Special' at a Lyon's Restaurant. He ordered an extra sweet roll and consumed four cups of coffee. He stared at cars passing by outside, wondering why people didn't walk more often. His ears seemed offended by the constant clanking of plates and music from a jute box.

Finished with his breakfast, he still couldn't shake the empty feeling in his stomach. When he returned home he vowed to shake the lingering effects of the desert and the Anasazi woman. He decided to call Sharon and punched the numbers on his phone as if he had a hatred for the machine.

"Hello," a drowsy voice answered.

"Hello, babe," he drawled, listening to her sleepy voice.

"Cam!" she gushed. "Darling! When did you get home?"

"Early this morning," he lied.

"Why didn't you let me know? I would have met you with some champagne."

"It was way too early."

"Well," she said, "how was it? Did you survive?" She didn't wait for him to answer. "Did you miss me terribly?"

"Yes," he lied again.

"I missed you too," she purred into the phone.

He could read her tone of voice like a phone book. He knew what she had missed although he wondered if she really did *without* while he was gone. "What have you got going today?"

"Nothing until early afternoon, except for doing my nails. Then I have to be at Enrico's in Sausalito for a cocktail showing of Dove Van Damme's new fall line." Sharon sighed heavily. "Oh, Cam, you'll love Dove's designs. There so, well, so *me!* "

Cam could give a shit about how clothes looked on Sharon. Right now he wanted her without clothes. "Can you come over?"

There was a pause. "Ah…yeah, but first I've got to do my nails. Deep purple, I think," she replied as if talking to herself. "Then I'll come over, but I insist you come with me to Enrico's."

"Okay, babe, anything you say."

ﻉ   ﻉ   ﻉ

He had hoped Sharon wouldn't notice, but she did immediately. When he let her into the apartment and she threw her arms around his neck, then grasped his hands and stepped back to take a good look at him, Sharon noticed his watch was gone.

A frown marred her lovely brow. "Cam, what happened to

your watch?"

Visions of a dead Indian floated into his mind. He knew Sharon would *never* understand. "It's all right, babe. It got sand in it and I had to leave it with a jeweler in New Mexico. They're going to send it to me."

Relieved, she smiled. "Thank goodness. The watch means a lot to me. I bought it for you on the third month anniversary of our…hmmm…relationship." She clasped his hand and intimately sucked on his middle finger.

His other hand reached out and grabbed her tight ass. "Don't worry about the watch, baby," he said as he found her lips. "It couldn't be safer."

⁞   ⁞   ⁞

Sharon's nails were long, shiny and very, very purple. One had a gold half-moon cemented to the tip. That nail trailed up and down Cam's muscled back like a harp player. Cam lay on top of her, his head turned to the side, positioned between her breasts. His eyes were open and staring at the blank wall.

He had taken her savagely, nearly ripping the clothes off her. Crushing her lips, he fell on top of her on the bed, grinding his pelvis against her, digging his fingers into the flesh behind her neck. She groaned, his lustful need being on the verge of painful. Cam had never been so forceful, nor so aggressive, usually engaging in many minutes of foreplay and stroking which Sharon could do without. Her hands on his skin had seemed detached, her lips too wet, too hot, too accomplished. And her eyes had been hard and empty, eager to take from Cam what he had to give.

Quick. Hard. Lustful. He assuaged the needs of his body, using Sharon to empty himself of empty passion as expediently as possible. With his eyes squeezed shut, Cam felt her hands on his body. And damn, if he didn't imagine what it would be like to have the innocent Anasazi Indian's hands on him. With each of Sharon's pleasure-filled groans, Cam's mind reeled with the whispers—soft, yet surprised gasps as he envisioned initiating her to the magic passion she had never known.

Now their lovemaking was over. Cam was far from satisfied, in fact, he felt a chill stirring in the pit of his stomach that was close to pain, close to fear. Cam's heart beat wildly.

Purring like a satisfied cat, Sharon pushed him off of her, and she smiled wickedly at him. "The desert has made a changed man out of you, my darling."

"It just made me horny," he replied.

Sharon trailed purple nails down his chest. "Hmmm, I like that."

Trying to wipe away the emptiness that gnawed at his insides, Cam attacked her lips once again, determined to ease the ache in his body. After he had exploded inside of her, Cam left her dozing in the crumbled mass of sheets and walked naked to the bay window in the living room. Peeling back the sheer curtains, he gazed outside at the parking lot, the cars, the perfectly planted grounds, the outlines of big ships through shrouded mist of fog.

He thought he was going to be sick.

🐸   🐸   🐸

There was no way out of this event at Enrico's. Cam had attended dozens of fashion shows in which Sharon modeled. White-jacketed parking attendants parked expensive cars. Snooty, jewelry-bedecked people attended, flaunting designer gowns. Champagne was always served, along with caviar and silly little crusts of bread.

The outfits were ridiculous. Every woman, swaggering down the elevated stage, wore an original which was usually so impossible for a woman to gain entrance to, or so inappropriate for any normal social event, that the owner would have to create a happening just to wear the garment, and then she would need assistance to dress for the event. Dove Van

Damme's fall review was more of the same: A woolen shirt, balloon in shape, cinched tight above the knees, obviously expanded by some invisible force of nature: a pure white cape with a trail three feet beyond the model, (obviously not designed for chasing children around a house): mini-shirts and ankle length sweaters: all horrible, all very, very expensive.

And the models. Cam shook his head as a friend of Sharon's walked down the isle with her hair swept up off her face, lacquered into three spiked points, each trying to reach the ceiling. And Sharon herself: her hair ratted, standing out a good foot from her head in every direction. But what really got him was her puffed lips. He knew Sharon and her modeling friends all injected their lips with some god-awful substance that made their lips swell. Swollen, full lips were really *in*, man.

Cam was having a hard time with the whole shindig. The champagne was bitter to his tongue. Caviar looked like trout eyes and made his stomach do flip-flops. Idle chatter grated on his nerves. The smell of expensive perfume was disgusting. His Brooks Brothers herringbone suit and striped silk tie he wore felt constricting, and he tugged at his tie so he could breathe easier. His palms turned clammy. His vision grew fuzzy. A cold sweat, like dew, sprang out on his face, and in the middle of the show, he had to get up and leave.

The restaurant was perched on a cliff, overlooking Richardson Bay. Hurrying, as if he couldn't get away fast enough, Cam ran down the flight of cement steps from Enrico's, down to the street-front flock of shops, across the street to the grassy park, and beyond that to the edge of the bay where the water lap-lapped at the rocky shoreline. He collapsed on a bench, gasping for breath, yanking at his tie, trying to tell his heart to stop racing, while he stared out at nothingness of gray water and dismal fog.

Sometime later, it must have been much later, because

Sharon had removed most of the god-awful makeup and wore her khaki trench coat, she sat down next to him and placed purple nails on his shoulder. "You all right? What is it, Cam?"

"I don't know," he answered truthfully.

⁊⁀   ⁊⁀   ⁊⁀

Before going to work the next day, he had to leave his BMW at a garage to have the smashed window replaced. After he left it, hoofing it the five blocks to the Bank America Building, he paused in front of a book store. Impulsively he went in, spoke with the clerk, went to a specific section which was up the stairs and to the left, glanced quickly at the racks, grabbed three books, came down the stairs, paid for the books and was out the door in less than four minutes.

When he entered the elevator in the Bank America Building that morning, carrying his bag of books plus another brown bag, the surge of people getting on the elevator suddenly gave him an acute sense of claustrophobia. It came over him suddenly like a heavy blanket, but was so intense his throat closed, the cold sweats came back again and his heart went on the warpath. Faces around him all appeared distorted. Strange people stared at him, but didn't look at him, staring through him. He began to panic. He had to get out! Before the doors closed, he screamed to keep the doors open and bashed his way through the elbow-thick people. He fell through the crowd, tripped and sprawled on the floor in front of the elevator.

One woman, aghast at his actions, looked down at him on the marble floor and asked, "Are you all right?" Then the elevator doors closed.

It was a long walk up eighteen flights of stairs.

Andy Patk was surprised to see Cam back in the office. "I didn't expect you," he said. "I thought you would let me know when the work was completed."

"It was a snap," Cam hastily replied, placing the sixth-grade book, *Anasazi Indians*, on his desk.

Something was different about Cam, Andy thought. He couldn't put his finger on it. Maybe it was his hair; it needed a cut. Maybe it was his face, all tanned and healthy looking. Maybe he was just tired. Whatever it was, Andy was inwardly glad Cam showed some ill effects of the job which he called 'a snap' and which Andy knew to be a blatant lie.

"How long before you'll have the final reports on my desk?" Andy asked.

Cam twiddled one thumb over the other. "Not long."

"You all right?" Andy asked, narrowing his eyes at the younger man.

Cam slammed his fist on the table. "Christ! That's all people have been saying to me! Yes, I'm all right! Just leave me alone!"

Andy picked up the book from Cam's desk. The front cover was a beautiful winter shot of Spruce Tree House in Mesa Verde. He noted the title, the large type and easy words, then replaced on the desk. "Not losing control are you, January?"

More than a year ago, at a company party, Cam had taken home a woman Andy had escorted to the party. Cam had ended up spending the weekend in the woman's bed. Andy had never forgiven Cam, and Cam knew Andy would love to see the junior partner rattled. It would make his day. "I am in perfect control," Cam hissed through clenched teeth.

"Yeah? Doing a little juvenile history reading? Huh?" Then Andy tipped the other brown bag upside-down. Out fell Cam's yucca sandals. Between two fingers, Andy picked up a sandal, twirled the eagle feather against his cheek and laughed. "Feathers? On your sandals? Isn't that a little far out even for you?"

Cam never changed expression, but stared right through Andy. "The eagle feathers are there so when I walk, I'll be closer to the clouds, you dumb-ass."

Thinking Cameron January had suffered sun stroke on the desert or was losing his mind, Andy swallowed a dry lump into his stomach and strolled out of Cameron January's office.

Chapter 17

"If you won't come with me, I'll go by myself," Ketl said to Tommy Bright Eagle as she stood defiantly in front of him with her feet spread, her arms crossed over her chest.

His expression consisted of a bland mask of indifference. "Willow Canyon is a dead city. You will not live there."

"I've lived there all my life!" Ketl replied hotly.

"Your life is not your own to do as you please," Bright Eagle told her, enunciating each word slowly. "As my wife, you will do as *I* decide."

"Willow Canyon is my home," she steadfastly argued.

Bright Eagle's nostrils expanded. "Your home is here."

She wasn't afraid of him although his massive size cried for respect. She moved closer to him. "Are you sure you want to marry me?" she asked. "Are you sure my mother bargained for you?"

He didn't hear the second question. "You are mine forever." He stepped closer to her, his black beady eyes bored into her. "Forever," he repeated, his breath hot on her face.

"Please, Bright Eagle," Ketl pleaded, "I'm willing to be

your wife, and I promise I'll make you a good wife, but I must return to Willow Canyon and see if my mother has returned home. I must go by another road and see if she is hurt and waiting for me to bring help. Please, do this for me, and I'll do whatever you want. Can't you understand? I must go."

Rigidly she stood plated to the dirt floor of the Indian hogan. He didn't move or make any indication he would answer her.

Boldly, Ketl placed her hand on his huge forearm which was crossed over his chest, resting on his other arm. "Please come with me," she begged. It really galled her to have to grovel to this insensitive flesh mound. After all, he was going to be her husband; he should willingly agree to go with her. All of Willow Canyon, all that was left there, belonged to Ketl, therefore it would become the property of their union and would be passed to their daughters. He *should* want to protect those vested interests, shouldn't he?

Looking up at him that day, with her hand touching his skin, she wondered how his lips would feel on hers. Would he grab her and passionately kiss her the way the white man had? Would he make her skin catch on fire, her knees turn weak, her bones melt, and that strange hunger gnaw in her loins? Although he wasn't pleasing to look at, she hoped his heart would be warm and she would grow to love him. She longed to feel the way she had when The Evil One held her in his arms, and it excited her to think of Bright Eagle setting her skin on fire with his touch. Inching closer to him, ever so slightly arching her back so her breasts pointed from her smock to tempt him, she hoped he would find her pretty enough to claim her lips like the other man had done.

Maybe if I tease him a little, she thought, letting her breast brush against his elbow.

They were alone in the hogan. Bright Eagle felt the feather touch of Ketl's breast on his arm. Dropping his hands, he reached out and grabbed her, closing her upper arms in a viselike grip that made her yelp in pain. He yanked her to him and punished her lips with an assaulting kiss. He ground his mouth against her soft skin and tried to force open her mouth.

Ketl reeled with shock. Her mind screamed with rage! This was not like before—Bright Eagle's mouth was sour, his lips hard, and her stomach rolled in revolt instead of the pleasurable yearnings she felt when Cameron January had placed his mouth over her lips. When she felt Bright Eagle's tongue invade her mouth, she recoiled and bit down on it as hard as she could.

Bright Eagle hollered in pain and threw her away from him. With a frown turning his forehead into a mass of stacked worms, he stepped away from Ketl, an angry fire in his eyes mentally finishing the job his slobbery lips had not been able to do. "I will take you to Willow Canyon," he spat. "We will leave this evening. It is only to seek out your mother, so she can return with us to be at our marriage. It is the only reason," he emphasized. "Willow Canyon is dead. You must put it in your mind as a lost memory. When you marry Tommy Bright Eagle, you will be a Hopi. The Anasazi are no more."

He nodded, stepped around her and stomped from the cramped two-room adobe house he called home.

ð&   ð&   ð&

Ketl spent the rest of the day in misery. She had no friends, no one with whom she could talk. The women avoided her like she was lice-infested, while the other Hopi men, those who knew she was pledged to Tommy Bright Eagle, kept a safe distance from her. Even the children, noisy and playful as any group of children, stayed away from her. She was an outcast in her new home. She wondered if it was because she had arrived at the mesa with a white man, or whether it was because she was not actually wed to Bright Eagle. Maybe that was it, she reasoned. Or maybe it was because she was

Anasazi. The last reason saddened her, because it was something she couldn't change, something she was proud of being and would let no man shame her for it.

It was puzzling, because the other times she had been at the Hopi mesas, she had been treated as one of them or at least treated with politeness like a visitor should be treated. This time was different, however, and that day when she went down the mesa road to sit by herself to talk to Mockingbird, she met Stella Red-Feather. Stella was a young woman Ketl's age who Ketl had developed a friendship with the winter Pavi had broken his leg.

"Stella!" Ketl called in greeting.

"Hello, Ketl," her friend replied stiffly.

Even Stella acted strange. "Aren't you glad to see me?" she asked with an air of expectancy.

"My eyes are pleased you are at the Hopi mesa, but my ears have told me you displease the elders."

"What?"

Stella brushed back her waist length black hair. "The white man. He should have not come with you. He crossed sacred grounds of our forefathers."

"In the desert, you mean?"

"Yes."

"He did not foul it. He was very respectful."

"They say he laid claim to you with his eyes."

Ketl grew red-faced. She thought how The Evil One *had* claimed her with his mouth, but she didn't remember him looking different or strange in the hogan when they talked to Qommatu, and she certainly knew The Evil One had not wanted to come with her to the Hopi mesa. "Nobody claims me," she said defiantly.

"I say to you, Ketl of the Anasazi, the sooner you marry Tommy Bright Eagle the better. The longer you wait the longer the vicious tongues will wag and the harder it will be to prove you are pure and the rightful receiver of Bright Eagle's offer of marriage."

Ketl would like to spit on Stella, on those who had evil in their hearts. No Indian was purer in spirit than Ketl. Her harmony was stronger than most of the Hopi women who had accepted many of the white man's ways. To say Ketl was unworthy was an obscene insult. "Goody-bye, Stella," Ketl said and stormed away from Stella Red-Feather.

"Remember," Stella called after her, "there are many who would be only too happy to take your place and marry Bright Eagle. Be careful."

The last was said *almost* as a friend, but not quite—more as a warning from a jealous hag. However, the audacity of her words left her shaking with rage which did nothing to help her clear her mind of all clutter, slip into a trance and speak with Mockingbird.

The rest of the day she spent trying to release her pent-up frustrations and allow her mind to be as tranquil as a pool of water, but she couldn't do it. There was no place she could find that was truly quiet. The sound of cars on the road bothered her, the faraway sound of music from the small black boxes the Hopi called 'radios' were bothersome, the constant yips and yells of the children bothered her that day when they had never done so before. Squinting her eyes together tighter, she clenched her fingers and willed all the noises to be free of her inner being. It didn't help. Biting her lips, she tried harder, now holding her breath, actually growing angry at Mockingbird for not being there when Ketl wanted her.

Suddenly, she opened her eyes and saw herself as Mockingbird must be seeing her. The sight made her turn red and her shoulders sag. She had momentarily gone crazy! Her harmony was not with her! Her gods were not ones to call in a whim, nor scold like a naughty child when they didn't do what was her pleasure. No! The Anasazi gods were to be held in great reverence. They were to be loved and honored, to be shown the greatest respect, and if they were shown gratitude then they would lead the way and comfort the lost in case of adversity.

Ashamed of her loss of respect, Ketl rose and walked away from the road, farther off the beaten path and into the dry, grassless sand of the desert. Stopping, she sat on the ground next to a clump of flowering wild potato and crossed her legs. The sun had dropped low in the sky. With her back to the sun, she centered her gaze in front of her, just above the shadow her head created on the sand. She tried to clear her mind, but it was very difficult with all the happenings which had transpired since Una had left to go to bargain for a husband for Ketl. She didn't call to Mockingbird, because Ketl knew her god would come when it was time.

A long time passed. She could get herself into a trance, but Mockingbird did not come to her.

Instead, in her vision was a tall, dark-haired man with gray eyes.

❦   ❦   ❦

Sitting behind his desk with an autobiography of Alfred Wetherill in front of him, Cam strummed the desk top with his fingers. The book was fascinating. The Wetherills were the people who discovered the first and grandest cliff dwellings in Mancos Canyon. They did this in 1893. Albert was an accomplished writer and kept complete dairies of those discoveries. What made the book so interesting was the descriptions of what Albert had found. He and his brothers were the first people to view the ruins, to step among the rock houses, to see the trash heaps, the baskets, the abandoned looms, weapons and piles of yucca sandals.

Cam could have made a couple of corrections about assumptions made in the book, but on a whole, he read every page, and was thankful Albert Wetherill had written it all down. His bookmark had a big note written on it, "Call

Woody." When Cam finished the last page, he slowly closed the book, pulled at his tie and picked up the phone.

In a gravely voice from the house in Aguilar, Woody answered. "Yup...hello?"

"Woody! This is Cameron January—"

"Who?"

"Cam. The city cowboy."

"Hey, fella, how you doin'?"

"Fair," he replied. "How about yourself?"

"I'm breathin', that's about all I can say."

"Sorry I didn't get to say good-bye."

"You young pups are all in such a hurry."

Cam grinned. He liked being called a 'young pup'. But only by Woody. "I wasn't really in a hurry. It was the Indian. She bolted when you two left. You know she wasn't very fond of me. I chased her and ended up going with her to the Hopi mesa. She's got a husband all lined up who looks strong enough to carry the world on his shoulders. I think she'll be just fine."

Woody was silent.

"You there?"

"Yeah, I'm here. Wish I weren't, though."

"You miss the desert?"

"Son, I'm just missin' the livin'. I feel half dead."

Cam thought he could agree with him. "I sort of miss the ranch myself," he admitted. "Kind of grows on you."

"Like moss. It sticks."

Cam smiled and laughed. He hadn't felt so good in days. The old duffer had a way about him. "Say, Woody, I've got a favor to ask you."

Woody blinked. "Whatcha you got in mind?"

"I left rather abruptly, you know, after the Indian ran away. All my survey reports are back at the ranch. They're in a green folder. I think it should be on top of the refrigerator. Could you get Christopher to take you out to the ranch and get them for me?"

"I ain't seen Christopher in a week."

Visions of Christopher leering at Ketl jumped to mind. "Where is he?"

"Out at the ranch—"

"Why?"

"He don't tell me nothin'. He's probably mopin' around 'cause the Indian is gone. I just bet he's scoutin' every canyon he can find to look for her."

It didn't surprise Cam. It didn't worry him much, either, thinking that Bright Eagle only had to sit on Christopher and the kid would be mincemeat. "Probably," Cam said. "Can you get me my reports? I'll give you the address so you can send them to me. Hire a cab if you have to, but I need those reports. My boss is wondering what in the hell I did out there, you know?"

"I can imagine," Woody said with a grin.

"Get a pencil. I'll give you my office address. Send the stuff to me there."

Woody poked around the counter top, shuffling magazines, salt shaker, dirty lunch plates and spilling a box of crackers, making a big mess out of what was once order. He found a pen, but couldn't locate a blank piece of paper. He wanted a nice big sheet of paper, too, so he could see his own writing and wouldn't lose the damn thing. His daughter had one of those nice little note pads with two-inch square pieces of paper that couldn't fit two letters much less two words.

"You ready?" Cam asked.

He still hadn't found anything. Rolling up the sleeve of his flannel shirt and holding the pen tightly, he said, "Yeah, I got it now."

Cam rattled off the address of the Bank America Building and Woody wrote it on his arm in nice sized black letters.

"Got it all?" Cam asked.

"Yep." Woody rolled down his shirt sleeve. "I got it. Say, you want your clothes and stuff sent to you, too?"

"No," Cam replied. "I don't think I'll need any of that stuff. Just junk it."

"Okay. Maybe I'll just save it for you. Maybe you'll be coming back this way."

"No, I don't think so."

"You were just gettin' the hang of the desert, Son," Woody said as tried to button his shirt sleeve. "I think you might have even liked that Indian woman."

There was a laconic pause. "Say, Woody," Cam said, "what would you say if I told you I know what happened to the Anasazi. I *know* why they left the desert. I really *know!*"

"Boy," Woody drawled, "I'd say you had too much sun."

❦   ❦   ❦

Christopher didn't return to the house. All day Woody sat in his recliner with Cam's address on his arm, covered by his shirt. He rocked and waited. He needed Christopher to drive him to the ranch; Marybeth couldn't, and a cab in Aguilar was an unheard of commodity. No, he needed Christopher to come home and give him a ride to the ranch, and Woody was not a good rocker, nor was he a good at waiting for people. Even a cold beer didn't make the time pass any more quickly. He began to mumble to himself, then he took up the fine practice of pacing. He paced long into the night, but Christopher didn't come home.

The next day, although not worried, because Woody didn't worry, but mildly disconcerted, Woody began to pace the entire length of the outside porch again, back and forth, hitting the tenth board from the end every time which emitted a spine-curling squeak. The board was directly outside Marybeth's bedroom and she could time it perfectly, exactly 45 seconds between squeaks. It was driving her crazy.

Finally Marybeth could stand it no longer. She appeared on the porch and stood in Woody's way. "Will you stop that infernal marching back and forth? You did it all day yesterday too. It gets on my nerves."

"Well, terminal sitting gets on my nerves."

"Then do *something!*"

"What you got in mind? Knitting?"

"How about cleaning the garage? How about puttering around and fixing things or painting the outdoor furniture?"

He waved at her and his brows arched together. "That's work. My working days are over."

Marybeth sniffed, a foul odor assaulting her nostrils. "How about taking a shower?"

"I ain't dirty."

"How about watching television? Most people your age spend the afternoon watching soap operas."

"I'm not most people."

"Don't you have any friends who'll come over and visit you?" she said almost in a shriek.

"Yep, I sure do, and they all love to pace."

She sighed, totally exasperated. "Well, do something."

"I'd like to sit on the front steps, but you won't let me."

"That's not *doing* anything."

"You and I, we got different perspectives of the term *doing.*"

"I'm tired, dad," she said, giving up trying to reason with him. "How about being an angel and keeping busy and out of my hair while I lay down for an hour. And that means no *pacing.* I can hear every footstep you make and every rusty nail you hit."

Woody grunted. Banished from pacing, banished from the front steps, hateful of the recliner, Woody padded out the back door to the yard where he faced a messy garage. Inside the garage, he found an old milk crate to sit on in the backyard.

Dragging it from the garage, he placed it under a cottonwood tree in the shade. Sitting on the box, he scooted it sideways, adjusting his position so that he had a clear view of the driveway. That way he would know when Christopher came home. And as the summer sun arched across the sky, and the afternoon clouds put on a spectacular show for him, he was beginning to think the spot wasn't half bad.

When his neck grew tired of gazing upward, he spied the old Jeep. It was parked behind the garage with just the front end visible. It was nearly vintage; no top, split leather seats, rusted exterior, missing windshield. Woody could remember many fond outings in the car. Chuckling to himself, he remembered when they were stuck in Old Salt Wash, the car hopelessly mired up to the hubs in cement-like mud. They had to hoof it back to the ranch, then drive to town, rent a chain-pull and retrace their steps. It took more than two days to get the Jeep out of the muck. He remembered that Christopher had learned to drive in the Jeep, and it was Christopher who lost the keys while skinny dipping over at Hoosier Lake. Marybeth had been furious. Woody found it humorous, especially when he heard the keys were lost when some girls stole the boys' clothes and left them jay-bird naked and they had to walk to a neighboring rancher's house to get clothes and a jump for the car. They never did get the keys back, so since the Hoosier Lake episode they had to hot-wire the Jeep to get it started. Woody smiled. It gave a great spark when the wires touched. He wondered if it still ran.

Pushing himself to his feet, he ambled over to the Jeep. Two wires dangled down from under the dash like they were begging to be held in his fingers. As Woody stared at the wires, a fresh gleam of life sparked in the depths of his eyes. Driving the Jeep was *something to do*, wasn't it? *Uh huh,* he told himself. Groaning as he pulled himself into the driver's seat, he smiled as he brought the two wires together and pumped the gas pedal three times.

Marybeth never heard the engine of the old Jeep roar to life, nor did she see it weave out from the back yard, lurching as Woody got a feel for the gas pedal. In a deep sleep, she never heard the bang-crash as Woody sideswiped the trash cans as the Jeep careened out of the driveway.

ȝ⚓   ȝ⚓   ȝ⚓

Bright Eagle kept a heart-wrenching pace. The man was inhuman, Ketl decided as she trailed far behind him on the desert. He was not much fun, either. He didn't like to talk, not like the Evil One had liked to converse. He wasn't much interested in her ancestors, either. He didn't allow her to hunt along the way, so they subsided on jerky, water and something Bright Eagle called Granola Bars. He brought a whole sack of them.

When they slept during the day, Bright Eagle was very careful to stay away from Ketl, no matter how close the quarters, no matter how uncomfortable he might be. At that she was relieved, because she didn't want him close to her. She didn't want him to kiss her, and she began to worry about her promise to marry him and be a good wife to him. She supposed she would have to kiss him then, and the thought made her want to gag. Looking at his massive frame across the small kiva, she decided he acted just like a fat pig when it came time to sleep. She noted he fell asleep immediately—lie down, groan once, shut eyes, asleep. He snorted, too, as he slept, she realized with a great deal of aversion.

Lying in the dusty confines of the ancient home of one of her ancestors, she remembered how The Evil One had needed to talk before he fell asleep. He did so almost in a whisper. It was a comforting thing to listen to, and Ketl realized she missed him more than she would have liked to admit. Lifting her finger to her mouth, she traced the outline of her lips, remembering how they felt when he had held her so fiercely and passionately kissed her. She closed her eyes. Into the dark void she invited Cameron January. He came and stood in front of her, so handsome, so tall, so very odd in the clothes of the white man. He smiled at her, and as she slipped away into the world of sleep, she smiled back.

They had taken a more northerly route between the Hopi mesa and Willow Canyon. The roads of her ancestors were many, but only a few were still well enough defined to follow. This route, more difficult than the one she and the Evil One had traveled, was shorter. It was physically a challenge: cliffs, sand banks, huge rocks to climb up and down. Drinkable water was less frequent and shelter was a problem, so it was a route not generally traveled by her clan unless time was of the essence, and this is why they took the route. Una might have wanted to return to Willow Canyon quickly. Ketl had to check, whether the way would be hard or gentle, hot or cold, good or bad.

Because the daytime shelter against the heat was less inviting, they covered more territory during the long night walk. In fact, they began walking before the sun went down and continued until it was well overhead.

It was the last night of their trek. They had been walking for some hours, the country getting rougher and rougher as they approached the mesa where Willow Canyon was quietly tucked. Ketl's knees were scraped from climbing down a steep arroyo and up the other side. She was dirty. She was tired and sweat-soaked, and Bright Eagle didn't offer her any assistance, just plodded on in front of her, his greater strength making the trek easy for him.

In front of them was a series of arroyos to cross. Ketl steeled herself for the effort needed for the first one, which was about a hundred feet ahead of her. As usual, Bright Eagle reached the lip of the arroyo first. Watching his back, she expected to see him slip over the side, out of sight as he had done before, but he stopped and looked down into the gorge. He didn't move. He had spotted something.

Puzzled, she increased her steps, her heart beginning to wildly thud inside her chest. She was running now, the fear of what she would find making her stomach roll. She nearly ran into Bright Eagle as she reached him at the edge of the precipice.

She looked down.

Horrified, she threw the back of her hand to her mouth and released a pitiful wail.

Chapter 18

Tommy Bright Eagle pointed to the dead person at the bottom of the arroyo. "It is Una. Your mother is dead, your search finished."

As a nauseating weight sank into her stomach, tears stung her eyes. *How could he be so heartless?* He spoke as if Una were nothing, as if Ketl should turn around, go back to the Hopi mesa and forget her mother ever existed. A sob escaped her lips. Bending over, she had to hold her stomach which was going to return the three Granola Bars she had eaten an hour earlier.

She remembered how the white man had held her in his arms when they had found her grandfather. He had given her his strength. Desperately she wanted someone to give her strength now, and her watery eyes looked up hopefully to Bright Eagle.

Crossing his arms over his chest, he pressed his lips sternly together and glared down at her as if she had insulted him. "You are weak!" he bellowed.

"I'm not," Ketl gasped.

"You are! My wife will not shed tears!"

Ketl tried to stop her pending tears, but her throat burned and her lower lip quivered so she had to bite down hard to keep it still. Feeling as though she were carrying the weight of the world on her shoulders, her legs suddenly grew weak, her knees melted beneath her weight, and she sank to the ground. Despite her intentions of holding back her tears, a solitary tear slipped down her cheek. Her whole body shook with shame while inside her, a raw emptiness yearned to be comforted. With pleading eyes, she again looked to Bright Eagle.

Standing above her like a powerful god, he scowled at her and began to climb down to the bottom of the rocky ravine.

Ketl followed, dragging herself to her feet and forcing her body to make the descent into the arroyo. It was difficult. Grief and despair tore at her heart. She didn't want to be the last Anasazi. She wanted her mother, her grandfather, yet she had neither. A flash of loneliness stabbed at her. Oh, how she longed for someone to share her pain. Lost in self-misery, wondering why her gods were putting her though such an odious test of her faith, she felt the bottom of the ravine with her feet, then turned to see Bright Eagle using a large stick to move Una under a rock outcropping.

Her distress ended immediately. "What are you doing?" she screamed at him.

"I am removing the body from sight of the gods."

Her eyes blazing, her nostrils flaring in anger, Ketl attempted to shove him aside. "She must be buried properly!" she shrieked.

Her attempt to move the huge hunk of flesh was a failure. "She needs no burial," Bright Eagle said, shoving aside Una's leg with his foot. "Her spirit has been gone for a long time now. Do not waste the time to bother with her."

His insensitivity turned her back straight and Ketl faced him with steely resolve in her eyes. "I am Ketl, the Last

Anasazi. I will do as I please. I will bury my mother. And I will return to Willow Canyon to claim my belongings."

Bright Eagle had never been spoken to in such a recalcitrant manner by a woman. "You show me no respect," he said gruffly.

Staring him in the eyes, seething with hate, she retorted, "You gave me no respect to start with."

Then she began the chore of burying her mother.

&. &. &.

Tommy Bright Eagle and Ketl approached the mesa top above Willow Canyon very early in the morning. Ketl was thoroughly worn out. Bright Eagle marched along, strong as an ox, still determined to gather her things and return quickly to his mesa to make Ketl his wife. His loins ached to have her beneath him, and he knew he could break her will and make her bow to his every whim. Because it was a husband's right to beat an obstinate wife, he intended on doing so to make her obey him. But for now, he stayed behind her the rest of the way which was a sure sign of acrimony for her ill-tempered behavior.

Bright Eagle refused to walk abreast of her, or ahead of her which was where he should be. With his large skull, but a brain inside his skull the size of bat guano, Bright Eagle didn't have an original thought in his head, and he didn't consider treating the Anasazi woman any differently than other Hopis treated their women—that she was pretty, that she had suffered a great shock, didn't phase him, and he smiled, thinking himself a good Hopi to treat her shabbily. Let her think she could do or say what she wanted; it would only last until Qommatu sprinkled the holy water over them which would forever bind her flesh and soul to him. Then he would walk in front, then he would make her obey, then he would take her savagely and wipe all thoughts of the white man from her pretty head. He could hardly wait.

It is just as well, Ketl thought miserably as she turned and caught a glance of Bright Eagle marching behind her. Their harmony was not on the same plane, she decided as she came along the rim of the mesa which overlooked Willow Canyon.

Upset by the discovery of Una, further disgruntled by Bright Eagle's growing dissatisfaction with her, Ketl was not paying close attention to what nature was telling her. Her censorious perception was off kilter, because she didn't sense the intrusion of white men who were camped nearby in the scrub pinion. The loud stillness should have warned her, but she didn't hear it, nor did she see the one sentinel who had stayed up all night, sitting in a folding camp chair out of sight of the trail which led to the bottom of the canyon.

She didn't hear him come rigidly awake and nearly topple out of the chair when she came into his view, nor did she hear the man pull out a radio and whisper, "Come in Willow Canyon Camp. This is Mesa top. Come in."

Down below the radio crackled. Stanley's sleepy voice squawked back at the mesa top guard. "What's up?"

"She's here!" He paused to take a better look with field glasses at the male Indian who followed her. "Yeah, she's here and she's got a blimp-sized male Indian with her."

Stanley's heart flew to his throat and his lips grew pale. He knew the greatest moment of his life was upon him. "All right," he said calmly. "Don't panic. Wake the other men. *Gently*! Don't let them make a whole lot of racquet. Follow them to the edge of the cliff, but don't start down after them. They'll see you."

"They'll see the camp before they get all the way down," the guard commented. "Why don't we just capture them up here? I've got a tranquilizing gun all charged."

"I don't care!" Stanley wanted see her. He wanted to watch her come down the cliff of stone. He couldn't stand the thought of going to the top and finding her already unconscious without him first seeing her. "We'll do this my way," he said in a heated voice. "The camp is still in the shadows, perhaps we'll be lucky and she won't see it until all the way down. You start down and cut off any retreat when they are almost to the bottom. If you have to, use the gun on the man."

"Roger," he replied, because he always wanted to say that. "Where are they now?"

"About fifty feet from the edge."

She's coming! She's actually coming! Stanley thought as a bead of sweat broke out on his brow.

ஃ   ஃ   ஃ

In San Francisco, Cameron tossed and turned in his bed. The mattress was too hard, so he punched it. No, he decided, it was too soft, and punched it again. Oh hell, he didn't know what it was, it just wasn't right. Punching his pillows and kicking at the twisted sheets, he flopped over on his back and stared at the ceiling, sighing deeply. He checked his new watch. It was after two o'clock, and he hadn't been able to get to sleep since he turned off his light at eleven. The *Wetherill* book was on the floor next to his bed, next to *Penthouse Magazine.* Neither books helped him get to sleep, nor had hot milk which was disgusting, nor had watching a late night movie on television until his eyes were bleary.

That evening Sharon had invited him to have dinner with her at her apartment, but he had lied to her and said he had to attend a karate club meeting. Why he lied to her, he wasn't sure, except Sharon was getting on his nerves. When they made love, he almost became angry, and when it was over, he found himself still not satisfied. He couldn't explain it.

It had something to do with *harmony.*

Sharon didn't have any. He didn't have it.

What harmony he had gained on the desert, he'd lost.

He dreamed scary dreams of snakes, hot deserts and being chased by Indians.

He wanted to dream of Ketl. He wanted to see her happy, in her sun-drenched canyon. He wanted to see turkeys, rock clubs, smoke escaping from a kiva, long shadows on rock houses, and her beautiful face smiling.

However, what Cameron January saw that night as he fitfully tried to sleep was the same vivid dream he had most nights. As he closed his eyes, he forced himself to see Ketl at Willow Canyon, slipping gracefully among the rock homes, but as he fell asleep the dream changed and he envisioned Ketl in danger—a life-threatening danger. A giant man threatened her, running after her with his hands outstretched. Wide-eyed and frightened, she ran from the man, but not fast enough, because he was about to place his giant hand on her shoulder and stop her. Before this happened, though, she successfully dodged out of reach and seemingly was on her way to safety, but then, to Cam's horror, others emerged from shadows and started after her, not as big as the first man, but with Uzi guns in their hands, and it seemed as if a whole army was determined to run her down. She was a mere a slip of a girl, unarmed, so vulnerable, with a god-awful look on her face, and Cam knew she didn't have a chance of escape.

That's when Cam would wake up. He was always in a sweat and breathing very unnaturally for someone who is supposed to be sleeping.

That was why he couldn't sleep, because he knew once he fell asleep, the dream would come to him and he dreaded the thought.

❧　　❧　　❧

Ketl went over the side of the cliff, searching and finding the footholds chiseled into the face of the cliff. She was home. Good. It felt good, even if it was for the last time. Well, no, she told herself; it would not be the *last* time, because one day she would bring her daughters here. But that was a long way in the future, so her heart was heavy, her feet dragging her body down the trail of stone and wood to the refuge of her home. Hot and dirty, she longed to immerse her body in the cool creek, and she hungered for some dried squash and rabbit stew. Most of all, though, she ached for someone to hold her.

Suddenly she tensed and shivered. *Something is wrong!*

The sure knowledge hit her as if a rock-axe had fallen from the sky and knocked her on the side of the head. Tensing, she lifted her head and sniffed the air. She could smell danger. Her whole body sensed that something terrible was about to happen.

Her eyes told her things in her home had been removed, changed, violated. The birds didn't sing, in fact, she sensed all the birds had taken flight in fear. The trees didn't speak to her.

Then she saw movement down below. Someone was hidden in the cottonwoods! Terror rocketed through her veins.

From the shadows a whole pack of white men charged her.

Spinning on her heels, she attempted to run back to Bright Eagle. He was far behind her on the rock trail, fear turning him as stiff as the stone beneath his feet. Bright Eagle watched as the men reached Ketl, two of them bringing her down by grabbing a leg. He heard her terrified screams.

She was not giving up: fighting, scratching, clawing, kicking, spitting. "Bright Eagle!" she screamed at the top of her lungs.

He heard her call. Quickly he turned and ran back up the cliff trail. He didn't go to her, nor did he try and help her. He met three men at the top of the cliff, who took one look at the size of the Hopi and the anger in his eyes, and gingerly stepped back, placing their hands up in the air in mock surrender. Even the man with the tranquilizer gun didn't have the courage to point the thing at the massive frame of flesh.

Because the three men still blocked his path, Bright Eagle growled, a low throaty sound. They nodded at him and stepped back to let him pass. Bright Eagle stomped by them and disappeared into the brush.

Ketl was losing ground with her captors. They were everywhere. She had no weapon. From out of nowhere, ropes were thrown around her arms.

"More! Hurry, bring more ropes!" she heard someone shout.

She kicked harder, connecting with bony flesh.

Someone yelped in pain. Then in angry retribution, a fist struck her against the side of her head. Her world became a dark tunnel of blinding fire. The ropes cut into her skin, she was being dragged down the rocks, and her skin tore. She knew her life was coming to an end. Again she screamed and caught a glimpse of the trail where she had last seen Bright Eagle. Now the man whom she was to marry was gone from sight. In desperation, a pain so great in her heart that she thought it might burst, she tilted her head back, fighting the gag someone tried to force inside her mouth.

"Camer-o-nn," she emitted in a high-pitched scream.

Then her world went black.

              🌢   🌢   🌢

Entangled in his bed sheets, still struggling with his dreams and with his sleepless night, Cameron January suddenly sat upright in bed, his eyes fully open. A cold sweaty sheen covered his body, and he was breathing very hard.

From some faraway place, he thought he had heard Ketl call his name. Her cry wasn't faint, but clear and loud—so loud his ears echoed with the tail end of his name. It was a terrified scream, one that sent a chill down Cam's spine.

It was strange. She had only called him The Evil One or White Man, never Cameron, but in his dream, she did. It was a frightened, desperate call for help, and it had scared the hell out of him.

              🌢   🌢   🌢

With his white hair flying in the breeze, the tires of the Jeep on the road then off the road, then back on the road again, Woody fought the uncontrollable steering wheel. He was on top of the yellow line, on the wrong side of it, wherever, he didn't care. He was having the time of his life. At first he went only 15 miles per hour, then 30 as he gained the confidence only an old man can have, pushing the rickety speedometer up to 45 when he got on the outskirts of town.

The dirt road to the ranch was the place that had always given him the most trouble even in his good days of driving. The danged road had shoulders as soft as quicksand, gutters on either side deep enough to swallow a car, and potholes just where he wanted to steer the wheels. It was hard enough to see the middle of a road when there wasn't a white line down it, and even harder when the car had no windshield so the air hit him in the square in the eyes, forcing him to squint to see, and he was constantly wiping a bug from his eyes or off his face.

Downshifting, grinding the gears something fierce, Woody took a particularly sharp turn too early and too sharp. After he went down into the gully-deep shoulder, straddled the sage-covered embankment and came out the other side of the turn, all four wheels leaving the ground when he came up from the deep shoulder, he shook his head at the infernal man who had built a road such as this. Woody was so busy trying to keep the car on the road while avoiding the potholes so his teeth wouldn't chatter that he didn't notice the huge tail of dust coming in his direction from across the desert.

Three vehicles headed into the ranch from Willow Canyon. Stanley was in the lead car. He was not driving, however, Christopher was. No, Stanley was in the back of the car with a very upset Anasazi Indian woman. She had given them nothing but trouble all day since they had first apprehended her. Shaking his head, he admitted to himself that he had never met such a small body with such an abundance of energy. If he could capture a tornado, that's how he would have described the Anasazi woman. She wouldn't speak and spat at Stanley every time he removed her gag. He had tried to calm her down by talking calmly to her, offering her food and drink, telling her he would untie her and remove the gag if she wouldn't fight, but nothing did any good, and her green eyes continuously clawed at him like talons.

After leaving her alone for a while—tied in ropes and gagged, he went back to her and tried talking to her again. Her eyes were closed and he thought she was asleep. Gently he bent over her and plucked the gag from her mouth. She came to life like a bucking bronco. Although her eyes conveyed the fury within her, it was her deadly aim with a mouthful of spit which let him know she had not changed her mind whatsoever.

With his patience sapped, Stanley wiped the glob of saliva off his cheek and called to his workers, "Get over here, boys, and help me load her into my car. She's going in just the way she is."

Five men slowly came over to Ketl's side. None of them wanted to haul her into the car like some discarded baggage, but Stanley was in charge and they did as he directed, and before they left Willow Canyon he radioed ahead to a doctor friend of his to meet them at the ranch with a sedative ready to inject into the rebellious Indian. Stanley expected the doctor was already waiting for them at the ranch.

Ketl was more frightened than she had ever been in her life. On the ground, tied and gagged, her thrashing had opened cuts on her legs and forehead. She was bleeding, yet still fought the ropes and men who stared at her like she was an oddity from the Third World. Once she looked up to see Chris standing over her. Her expression begged him to do something to stop these men from taking her, from destroying her home, but he only tilted his hat back off his face and then walked away.

They dumped in her into something hard. She landed on

her side and her ribs hurt. She couldn't sit up or see where she was or where they were taking her. She knew it was an automobile when the engine roared to life and sped away across the bumpy desert with her in the back. It was her first ride in a car, and it was not a pleasant experience.

Woody was shocked to see all the cars parked in the front yard of the ranch, so shocked in fact, that he ended up not watching what he was doing, and he parked the car in the middle of a fence post. Because the Jeep's fender was tougher than any old fence post, the post crunched, then the top half slowly fell over, as if it had been neatly lopped in half. As he stiffly got out of the car, many strange eyes landed on him. A man with a black bag stood in between two women. They all wondered who in the hell this old coot was who had rammed his car into the fence. Woody was equally as confused about who they were and what in the hell they were doing on *his* ranch.

First off Woody stomped past them and went into the house. Nothing looked right—his furniture had been thrown out and tables with computers installed in their place. Indian relics had been tagged and neatly set on the tables. Ketl's things, he knew: bowls, weapons, clothes, beautiful baskets, feather cloaks.

Red lines running across his cheeks stood out like roads on a map. On the refrigerator was Cam's green folder. He grabbed it and stomped back outside.

"What the hell is goin' on around here?" he said as the fleet of cars arrived at the ranch.

Woody's question was left unanswered.

The doctor and women converged on the car where Stanley was working with a kicking, twisting, hog-tied savage.

"Get over here quick, Jack," Stanley called to the doctor. "I've had all I can take of her! Jesus, she kicks hard."

The doctor wasted no time. From his bag, he extracted a hypodermic needle and a small bottle of clear fluid. Turning the bottle upside-down, he drew a syringe full of the liquid, then removed it and squirted some into the air. Opening and removing an alcohol swab, he went after Ketl.

Terror, stark and vivid, registered in her eyes. With her last bit of strength, she kicked at the white man who was coming at her with a vicious looking weapon. She caught him in the groin. He grunted, swearing under his breath. He threw the sterile cotton to the ground and grabbed her leg with his free hand. He pulled her roughly out of the back of the car, close enough to him so he could plunge the needle into the soft flesh of her upper arm. He was not gentle. He did not slowly inject the medication, either.

It stung like fire and Ketl moaned.

When Woody saw what was going on in the back of the car, he had no color left in his face. Shocked and bewildered, he watched helplessly as Ketl collapsed into a heap in the back of the Toyota. Gleaming with the pride of the possessed, Stanley pushed her dangling legs back into the car and slammed the door.

"Let's go," he said to Christopher.

With a forlorn look on his face, Christopher peered through the car window at Ketl. He couldn't even tell if she was breathing or not. "Jesus," he swore. "What did you do to her?"

"Nothing that wasn't for her own good," Stanley said with all the confidence in the world.

Christopher looked in the car at Ketl and back to Stanley as if trying to determine if Stanley was right.

Woody knew it was Christopher who had told these people about her. No one else knew. Limping to his grandson, he pulled Christopher around to face him. "What in tarnation did *you* do?"

Christopher wasn't sure what he had done.

Woody thought the world must be crazy. They had treated Ketl like she was a prisoner, or worse yet a wild animal. *Ropes! A gag! Drugs!* These men were violating every right she had as a human being, not to mention the sensitivity he knew she possessed as the Last Anasazi. He couldn't let this happen!

Woody hobbled from Christopher and accosted Stanley who was giving final instructions to his fleet of helpers. "Hey, you bloodsucker," Woody began, having that certain way of gaining a person's immediate attention, "that ain't no way to treat a lady!"

Stanley felt his skin crawl. Nobody called him a 'bloodsucker' and got away with it. "Who in the hell are you, old man?"

"You're standing on my property, you liver-bellied, flesh monger."

"This property belongs to Allied Oil. I know. And I've filed a request with the Department of Interior for it to be declared a National Historic Sight. I'm in charge here! Now, who *are* you?"

"I'm Woodhue Hayes. And I demand you remove the ropes on that Indian, ungag her and let her go!"

Stanley roared with laughter. "Are you crazy, old man? She's mine. She's going to the lab."

"You'll kill her—"

"You fool," he said, dismissing Woody with a wave of his hand. "I'm not going to kill her. I'll have every means known to science available to me to make sure she stays alive. She couldn't be safer. She'll be watched constantly." Stanley turned his back on Woody.

Woody was shut out. Having none of it, Woody stepped in front of Stanley. "That's what I'm sayin', you pup! You'll kill her. She don't belong in no laboratory. She don't belong hog-tied and unconscious in the back of a hot car, neither."

Stanley waved to Christopher, paying no attention to

Woody. Christopher joined the two men, sheepishly refusing to look at his grandfather, with his head bowed and kicking at the dirt with his foot. "Get this geriatric mental case out of here," Stanley ordered.

"I ain't goin' nowhere," Woody hollered.

"He's your grandfather, isn't he, Christopher?" Stanley asked.

"Yes, I'm afraid so."

"Then be responsible for him and get him out of here! Now! I don't want some old geezer getting in my way."

Christopher took Woody by the arm and started to lead him away from Stanley and the Toyota. Woody shook of the grip. "Let go of me, you hypocritical two-faced lout!"

"Gramps, come on. Don't be so ornery."

"Don't tell me how to be. I ain't ashamed of my life."

Cold sweat appeared on Chris' brow. "I'm not either, Gramps."

"You should be. Your life may not be much, but it's all you got, and you've screwed it up somethin' bad."

"I don't have to listen to you," he replied hotly.

"You sure as hell don't. Didn't listen to me when I told you not to tell anyone about her, did you? Didn't listen to that Indian girl, either. No, sir. She wanted to go home. That's all she wanted. You said you'd take her. I *heard* you say that. You never did do it, did you? No, instead Cameron January did what you should have done. And instead what did you do for her? Hmm? Instead you took the whole bleepin' world to her sanctuary. You took her home, all right. Right into the hands of the bone-pickers."

Christopher had had all he could take of his grandfather even if he was telling the truth. "You don't know nothing, old man. Nothing!"

Stanley had the Toyota ready to go. Leaning out the door, he called, "Christopher, you coming?"

Woody was glaring at him. The Toyota began to roll. "Christ," Christopher said, then ran to the car and jumped in.

All three vehicles left the Hayes Ranch, roaring down the dirt road, leaving Woody standing in a cloud of dust.

When the billow of dust settled, Woody was seated in the Jeep, jamming the wires together. "There's more than one way to skin a cat," Woody mumbled to himself. "Even if the varmint is a *polecat!*"

ș   ș   ș

Lillian MacNeish was just about ready to cash out her drawer. As head teller at the Farmington Savings and Trust Bank, she usually tallied her drawer first and then tended to problems that the other tellers might have encountered during the day. Brushing back the few errant gray hairs that had escaped her chignon, she placed her bifocals on her head so she could read the numerals of her adding machine accurately. That afternoon the bank was quiet. Air-conditioning pumped in brisk air and the deep purple rug on the floor added just the right amount of cool ambiance so a person inside didn't have any inkling the outside temperatures soared past 90 degrees. Lillian had placed her rubber finger guard on her thumb, had settled her glasses on her nose, adjusted her forever sagging panty hose one more time, and was about ready to start the tally on her cash out slips, when a man hobbled in the front door. Lillian frowned. He looked like a derelict—dusty, dirty, his hair looked like it had spent time in a hurricane, he hadn't shaved in days, and as he stepped up to her window, she sniffed and realized the man reeked of sweat.

And is that a fly in the corner of his eye? My goodness, yes it is!

With casual snootiness, Lillian raised her chin, refusing to look at Woody. "May I help you?"

In one hand he had a newly purchased blue nylon duffel bag. It was not large. In his other hand, Woody had his withdrawal slip ready. He shoved it across the marble-topped counter to Lillian.

Matter-of-factly, Lillian picked it up, glanced at it and her bifocals fell off her nose.

Chapter 19

Woody's eyes were weary by the time he pulled the old Jeep into the parking lot of the Farmington Airport. Country driving was much easier than city driving, he realized after he neatly removed a flowering daisy bush from its bed, then scrapped the hell out of the side of a long, fancy station wagon as he attempted to park the Jeep in what seemed an impossibly narrow parking space.

Limping, his hip bones sore from jostling in the Jeep, and clutching the stuffed duffel bag to his chest, Woody entered the airport and deposited himself at the ticket counter. "You got a plane going to San Francisco?" he asked, squinting at the ticket agent.

"Yes, sir," the ticket agent replied. He looked at his computer monitor and punched in some letters. "One leaves this evening at seven. You arrive at nine-oh-five."

"You got room for me?"

"Let me check." Again, fingers pushed buttons. "Smoking?" he asked.

Woody thought for a moment. Shaking his head, he

replied, "No, if the plane is smokin', find me another one."

Chuckling, the agent found Woody a nonsmoking seat. "That will be one hundred sixty-nine dollars."

"Fine," Woody replied. Opening his duffel bag, he peeled two hundred dollar bills off of a banded stack of money.

The ticket agent's eyes bulged.

        ða   ða   ða

The San Francisco Airport was a far cry from the one in Farmington. Hundreds of people were rushing in one direction, then the next. The loud speaker blared a long list of names which Woody couldn't understand. Black people and Oriental people mingled together, people with white robes and black ashes in the middle of their foreheads, people in military suits, people in shorts, people in overcoats. It was a potpourri of people. Signs pointed every which way. It confused Woody. Miles and miles of corridors went every which way with no discernible exit from the place.

Clutching his duffel bag to his chest, Woody finally escaped by riding up an escalator, going down an elevator, along a moving walkway, across a bridge to a parking lot, then down another elevator and finally out through a set of automated doors. He thought it a long way to go just to get outside the terminal.

At first he had planned on renting a car, since he had been so successful driving the Jeep, but after seeing the ocean of moving vehicles, his common sense told him not to attempt it. However, he spied an army of cabs, and he hailed a yellow one. The driver stopped, got out to open the back door for Woody while Woody opened the passenger door and slid into the front seat of the cab.

The cabby shrugged and hopped back into the cab. "Where to?" the cabby asked, eyeing Woody with a pharisaic grin on his lips. The old coot looked as if he just come from ten years of hard labor on a manure farm.

Woody rolled up his sleeve and placed his arm under the cabby's nose. "I gotta' go there," he announced.

Thinking his passenger weird as hell, the cabby noted the address, nodded and shoved his cab into gear. *In this business you get all kinds*, the cabby was thinking to himself.

&a &a &a

The effects of the hypodermic had worn off. Stiff and sore, Ketl awoke in a strange place. She was not bound by the ropes and not gagged, but her body ached, her wrists hurt from rope burns, and her mouth tasted strange—gritty like dirt and bitter like poisonous berries. She lay on a hard bed. A strange light hung down from what looked like a rope in the middle of the room. The light didn't glow or fade like a fire, and it was shiny round. She saw a window in the room, but it wasn't a window. When she looked at it, she saw herself in it, like a refection pool. High on the wall in one corner of the room was an odd-looking black box. It seemed to have one large eye and was looking down at her. Cocking her head, she could hear the machine make a faint buzzing sound. She shivered and decided it must be evil.

Outside the room, Stanley watched Ketl through the one-way mirror while an assistant in another room watched Ketl on the television screen from the remote camera. Garbed in a white lab smock with a clipboard in his hand, Stanley jotted down her every move. Behind him on his desk lay a pile of unanswered letters, order forms, books, notes, a very old skull and a plastic box with the wedding band he had taken from the skeleton in Pueblo Bonito.

Christopher dozed on a couch across the room.

"She's awake," Stanley excitedly announced.

Christopher jerked awake when he heard Stanley and joined Stanley at the window.

"I'm going inside," Stanley said.

"Why don't you let me speak to her?" Christopher suggested. "She knows me. She won't be so frightened."

Stanley's eyes were cold and hard. Handing Christopher the clipboard with his notes, he stiffly replied, "No, I want to note her reaction to me."

Grinding his teeth, Christopher took the board while Stanley continued to stare at Ketl with cool unreadable eyes. Licking his palm, he smoothed back his hair, straightened his white lab smock, then slipped into the room with the Anasazi Indian.

Wide-eyed, Ketl inched backward on the bed, her legs drawn up tightly behind her, fear radiating through her like a bolt of lightning had struck her. She recognized the man as the one who had captured her. She breathed in short quick gasps as the man approached the cot. Clenching her fingers together so hard that her nails dug into the flesh of her palm, she wished she had her knife so she could plunge it into his heart and slowly twist until all of his life had spilled on the floor. He deserved no less.

"Hello," Stanley said, forcing a smile, his icy eyes impaling her.

He stopped in front of the bed two feet away from her. Ketl had worked up a mouthful of saliva and sent if full force into Stanley's face.

"Oh, Jesus," he muttered, totally disgusted. "Stupid Indian."

Every muscle was honed in her body. She would fight this man to her death rather than let the white man have control of her. She would never do as he asked, and she would attempt to rip his heart out, even if she had to do it with her fingers. The spit in the face was just to let him know she considered him a vile human being and her enemy.

With a clean handkerchief, Stanley wiped the spit off his cheek. "I know you speak English," he said, trying to contain the anger from his voice. "Christopher told me."

"Chris?" The name startled her.

"Yes, Christopher. You remember him? Your friend?"

He was no friend of Ketl's. He had betrayed her. "I spit on Chris," she said, breathing harder now, waiting for the right moment to spring on him.

Stanley's calm demeanor grew thin. Patience was not a virtue with which he had been blessed. He was desperate to make her understand how important she was to America, to all Indians all over the globe, to archaeologists in particular and to the human race. He had tried to tell her. Lord knows, he had tried. To Stanley it was so simple.

"Please try and understand," he began again. "I only want you to talk to me. Tell me about your people. Tell me about you. Let me write it down so future generations will know about the Anasazi. You are a very proud people. Don't you want the world to know how proud you are?"

Ketl thought of being captured and tied and gagged. She thought of all the things she had seen taken from her home and she wondered how he thought she could have any pride left. "I spit on you, White Man," she said viciously.

Stanley sighed. Running his fingers through his hair, he bent over and pointed a finger close to her nose, although for a second he wondered if he wasn't trusting her a little too much with the safety of his finger. One bite of her teeth and he would possess only three fingers.

"Listen you, I've just about had it with your antics," he said. "You scratched me, kicked me, nearly put my eye out with your thrashing around." Slowly, Stanley recoiled his finger and stood straight as a sentinel. "Now, I don't want to hurt you, but you're going to have to settle down and do things my way if you don't want me to get rough."

She was seeing red, flashes of yellow and black, all mixed together.

Stanley continued: "You're a scientific oddity and I intend

on finding out everything about you and your people."

She remained silent, her heart crashing inside her chest. Never would she cooperate with this white man.

"I'll find out, too, whether you choose to tell me or not. I have drugs I can inject into you which will put you to sleep and you will start talking and never stop."

Furious, Ketl again spat at him.

With his sangfroid shattered, Stanley slapped her hard across the face. That was all Ketl needed. She sprang at Stanley as if she were a wildcat, raking her fingers along his cheek and pounding on him, while the two of them went over backward on the floor. Just as she intended to do, she went for his chest, trying to rip and claw her way to his heart, but her fingers were no match for the tough resiliency of his cotton lab jacket, and she didn't get very far.

She was incredibly strong. Stanley had a hard time catching her wrists which flailed around like writhing snakes. All at once her right hand got inside his shirt and she pulled as hard as she could. Buttons popped and went flying across the room. Those incredibly fast fingers attacked his chest, and he yelped in pain as she raked her nails down his pectoral muscles, making a groove in his flesh. He thought he was crazy, but he guessed she was attempting to tear out his heart.

The little savage hellcat! Stanley felt blood trickle down his chest. "Stop!" he ordered.

Ketl clawed at his chest. She felt skin come away under her nails.

He glanced sharply around toward the one-way mirror, his eyes blazing. The sight of himself in a blood-spattered lab coat shocked him. He couldn't stop her fingers, and with horror, he realized her fingers were ready to tear his chest again. Yelling at her to stop, Stanley pulled his right fist back and plowed it into her stomach.

All the wind whooshed out of her, her fingers grew limp,

and she crumpled into a ball on the floor.

The next time she woke, a mortal hatred for all white men brewed inside of her. Licking dry lips, Ketl moved off the floor and sat on the cot, crossed her legs, placed her open palms on her knees, steeled her back and closed her eyes. She willed her heart to slow to a near standstill. Her breathing became very shallow, almost nil. Her face turned pale as she shut out the white man's world, prayed to her gods, and called Mockingbird to her. This time Mockingbird arrived immediately.

꙳ ꙳ ꙳

Cameron usually arrived at the office a little after eight-thirty to avoid bumper to bumper, stress inducing commuter traffic. Andy Patk chose the early method of avoiding commuter traffic and arrived around seven-thirty. However, this morning the Bay Bridge had been a snarl of cars even at seven. A flatbed truck had lost a tire smack dab in the center lane and all cars had to snake around it, creating a nightmare for the police officer whose job it was to try and keep the cars moving. So Andy was later than usual, but it still was Andy who arrived at the office first and who found Woody sleeping on the floor in front of the office door with his head on a duffel bag. The street people slept over hot air vents, not in the corridor of the Bank America Building, Andy told himself as he poked the sleeping man in the ribs with his Italian shoe.

Smacking dry lips, Woody grunted and wrapped his arms tighter around his chest.

Irritated, Andy kicked Woody again. "Hey," he shouted. "Old man, wake up and get the hell out of the building! You don't belong here!"

"What?" Woody said, blinking, coming awake.

"I said to get your ass off my floor and get the hell out of here before I call the police."

With a myopic stare, Woody looked up at the impolite man. "Who are you, Sonny?"

"None of your business." Again he kicked at Woody. "Get going. You hear me?"

Woody sat up and pulled his duffel bag close to him. Straining, he pushed himself up along the wall, swearing at his creaking bones. "I ain't goin' nowhere," he told Andy.

"Obstinate, huh?" Andy opened the door of Allied Oil offices and let himself inside. "We'll just see how stubborn you feel when the police arrive." Brusquely, Andy marched to the phone.

When Andy had finished dialing 911, standing with the receiver in his hand with an imperious grin on his lips, Woody said, "Cameron January sent for me."

Andy looked at Woody as if he had recently arrived from outer space. "What did you say?"

"I said I have an appointment with Cameron January."

Raking his eyes over Woody's disheveled appearance, he said, "I find that hard to believe."

Woody was used to people calling him "old man," "old geezer" and having little respect for his age, but the floor had been drafty cold and hard as cement, and Woody had hardly slept. Now Woody was dog-tired. This man showed him no hospitality and Woody's patience snapped.

Stepping up to Andy Patk, Woody gazed from the perfectly knotted striped tie into Andy's irate face. "Cameron said his boss is a fine man. I'm lookin' forward to the pleasure of his company, since I ain't enjoyed it yet."

Andy's face turned red.

That was when Cam turned the corner into his office and found Woody and Andy in a hate-staring face off. "Woody!" he cried.

Woody smiled, turned his head to Cam and said, "Aha, at last, a member of the human race."

"Cam, do you know this derelict?" Andy rudely asked.

If harmony could be defined as peaceable or friendly

relations, it was definitely not in the office that morning, Cam decided as he looked from one man to the other.

Andy was showered, perfectly groomed, no hint of being ruffled, while Woody looked like he had stepped out of one of Cam's more vivid nightmares. "Yeah, I know him," Cam said as he stood next to Woody.

Woody beamed.

"Well, get the old fart out of my office. He was sleeping on the floor, he stinks…and he's probably half loaded, too. Damn old geezer."

The hair on the back of Cam's neck stood at attention. As the snobbishness of his boss loosened the bridled anger in his voice, he pointed a finger at Andy and said, "Don't ever call Woody names again!"

"You threatening me, Cam?"

"No, I'm telling you. You treat Woody Hayes like you'd treat your best friend, because he deserves it. He's not crazy, either." Cam stepped back, looked at Woody's rumpled looks and said, "Right now I suspect Woody needs coffee and something to eat. Right?"

"Well, son, any other time I'd be obliged, but we have a bit of a problem back at the ranch," he said, knowing his words were an understatement.

Cam's smile faded. "What happened?" His heart beat erratically. His mind flashed with bits and pieces of his dream where Ketl was running from armed gunmen. "Is it Ketl?"

Woody thought Cameron would ask about the Indian woman. "Yep." He frowned, shook his head, his lips pale, quivering slightly. "They came and got her, son. Took her away. It was horrible. I never seen anything like it. They had her in ropes. The look in her eyes was somethin'."

"Oh, Christ," Cam said, his throat painfully constricted.

"Who is Ketl?" Andy asked. "What's going on?"

Cam paid no attention to Andy. "We got to get her back,"

he thought out loud.

"I'm thinkin' the same thing," Woody said, then wiped his finger under his nose. "That's why I came."

"Who? What are you talking about?" It was Andy again.

Lost in thought, Cam gently put his arm around Woody and began to lead the old man out of the office. "Let's go."

Over his shoulder, Woody threw a forced smile at Andy, then stopped. "Oh, I...I got your reports," he said and retrieved them from the duffel bag.

Cam took the green folder from Woody and threw it on the receptionist's desk. Papers went everywhere.

Andy grabbed one and realized what it was. Dumfounded, he looked after Cameron January and Woody Hayes as they left his office.

❦   ❦   ❦

The next plane leaving for Farmington, via Phoenix wasn't until close to noon. There was nothing they could do about it. Jumping up and down, screaming, begging, nothing could get them back to Farmington and the laboratory faster than that flight, so with grim resolve, Woody and Cam found a seat in the airport and stared at the walls.

Woody wrinkled his nose. He sniffed deeply twice. A frown crept up his brow. "Holy cheesecake! Do I *smell!* I guess I been doing too much worrying. I only sweat when I worry, ya' know, and when I sweat, I stink."

"It doesn't bother me," Cam said, lost in thought.

"Well, I ain't livin' with a body that smells like skunk cabbage." Woody got up. "Come on, we got to do somethin' about it."

Since they had ample time, Cam suggested they drive back to his apartment and let Woody shower. It was better than sitting in the airport and worrying anyhow, and was better than watching Woody take his clothes off in the men's room at the airport to wash his body in the sink.

Woody agreed. The left the airport, drove to South San Francisco, stopping along the way at a JC Penny's so Woody could buy new clothes. With the mission accomplished, they went to Cam's apartment where Woody disappeared into the bathroom with his new purchases and his duffel bag. A little later, freshly dressed, having used Cam's shaver, Woody appeared looking clean, even handsome.

Cam waited for Woody, having changed from his three-piece gray suit into khaki pants, a pale blue Izod shirt, tennis shoes and a cable-knit pullover sweater to ward off the last fog of the morning. Pacing his living room, he held the yucca sandals Ketl had made for him. He loved to feel the silken texture of the eagle feathers.

Woody noticed the sandals. "Work of art, ain't they?"

"Practical, very practical. See the feathers?"

"Yep."

"Eagle feathers. She put them there so when I walked, I'd be closer to the clouds." His voice held a catch to it.

Woody nodded with understanding; he was in harmony. "She won't live long, ya' know," Woody told Cam with a weary sigh. "They'll scare the daylights out of her, and she'll go into a trance and quit eatin'. She'll starve herself."

Cam squeezed the sandals hard. "Shit! Why did this have to happen?"

"I guess Christopher couldn't keep quiet—"

"Chris? Christopher?" he roared. "He told them where to find her?"

"He was with them when they caught her."

"That bastard! He led them to her. I can't believe it. He loved her."

"Son, Christopher's life story has no morals. He loved the thought of fame and fortune more than he loved anything or anyone, including Ketl or himself."

"I'll kill the bastard!"

"He ain't worth it. Even Ketl will tell ya' that."

Harmony. Where is my harmony? His mind wheeling with anger and worry, Cam pounded the table with his fist. The sandals jumped. He'd like to feel Christopher's neck between his fingers, squeezing the life out of him, but he knew Woody was right, that it wouldn't change the course of events, nor would it improve his *harmony,* and having harmony had become important to him. Cam glanced at the kitchen clock. It was time to go.

Cam grabbed Woody by the elbow and headed for the door. "We just better be able to get her back, that's all."

"Son, I'm gonna' tell you somethin'." Cam stopped and looked at Woody's deadly serious expression. "It ain't never gonna' be the same for her. They know about Willow Canyon. They've torn it apart. She can never go back there. It ain't the same for me, neither. I can't go back. I'm dyin' there."

Cam looked around him: leather couches, a large screen television with full stereo, wool carpets, original art work on the walls, pictures in brass frames of him and beautiful women. He had it all, yet he had nothing.

Who is he kidding?

Things had changed for him, too. Nightmares took the place of peaceful slumber, an emptiness gnawed at his stomach after each meal, the dank foggy air seemed to be suffocating him, even Sharon couldn't make him happy. He knew he couldn't come back here. He knew he didn't belong anymore.

With a firm grip, Cameron January led Woody through the door of his apartment, shutting the door behind him with a loud click. "Well, Woody, if it's any consolation, I'm dying here, so between you and me, we had better go and find where the living is happening."

"Boy," Woody said with a grin, "I like the way you think."

☙   ☙   ☙

When the airplane reached a cruising altitude of 33,000

feet, the fasten-seat-belts sign blinked off. Cameron didn't notice. When the stewardess began to serve drinks, passing by Cam and eyeing the unpardonably handsome man with interest, Cam was oblivious to the attention, because he was deeply engrossed in listening to Woody tell Cam about Ketl. Already Cam disliked Stanley, and he was having a hard time keeping calm while being forced to sit still and wait until the plane made the flight to the Four Corners area.

"May I get you something to drink?" a red-haired stewardess with a honey-sweet voice asked Cam.

"What'll it be, Woody?" Cam asked.

"Beer. Good an' cold."

"Same for me," Cam said, turning to see a boldly pretty face smiling down at him. "How much?"

"Five dollars," the stewardess replied.

Cam went for his wallet. Then Woody placed his hand out and pushed Cam's wallet aside. "This is my trip. I'm payin'." Pulling his duffel bag into his lap, Woody opened it and reached inside. Woody pulled a banded stack of hundred dollar bills from the bag. Peeling one off the stack, he handed it to the stewardess while Cam's eyes turned into saucers as he craned his neck over Woody to see into the duffel bag.

"Woody," Cam whispered, darting a nervous glance around him, "what in the hell do you have in that bag?"

"My whole life, Boy."

The stewardess handed Woody a handful of change and plunked down two beers. With a smile at Cam that could melt ice, she said, "Thank you, gentlemen."

Cam forced a grin, then turned and stared at Woody. When the Stewardess was out of sight, Cam grabbed Woody's bag and pulled it wide open. Inside it looked like The San Francisco Mint.

"What do you mean 'Your whole life'?" Cam asked, his voice shaky.

Woody picked up one of the stacks of hundreds. "The Hayes Ranch. Right here in my lap. Hell, the money your company paid me wasn't doin' me any good sittin' in that bank. Tarnation, my daughter wouldn't let me use my own money to live the way I want to live, and my grandson ain't got no brains left inside his head. So I says to myself, 'Woody, you old coot, why don't you just mosey down to that bank and get your money. Use it to have a little fun. Use it to go see Cameron January. Use it to see if you can't save the Indian woman.' So I did. Feels pretty damn good, too." Woody sat back and sipped his beer.

Shaking his head with disbelief, Cam zipped the bag and stared at it. "How much?" He pointed at the bag. "How much is in there?"

"Oh, I spent a little gettin'—"

"How much?"

"Oh, a little less than a million bucks, give or take a few hundred. Well no, actually not that much, because it all wouldn't fit into the duffel, so I put the rest of it in a locker at the airport."

Cam reached for his beer and took a long pull. The beer did nothing to cool the heat in his head. He thought of Woody getting to San Francisco on his own, of sleeping in the Bank America Building—alone, with a million bucks for a pillow. Shaking his head, then chuckling, Cam knew the saying, 'god looks after old men, small children and drunks,' had to be true.

Cam admired Woody more than he could say and as he settled back in his chair, he said, "Woody, tell me about your life."

"Me?" he questioned. "Why would a young pup like you want to know about an old coot like me?"

"I guess it has to do with harmony. I'm finding mine, and knowing how you found yours is going to help me."

Woody grinned from ear to ear and began to tell Cameron

January about seventy years of his life.

❧ ❧ ❧

Flight 607 touched down in Farmington a little after 2:12PM. This time when Cam emerged from the airplane, the heat didn't affect him, in fact, he welcomed the blast of hot air like an old friend. With no luggage to collect, Woody and Cam made a beeline through the air-conditioned airport and to the parking lot.

"I brought the Jeep," Woody said, hobbling along next to Cam whose long stride outpaced Woody's one step to his two.

"You drove?"

Woody nodded. "Somethin', ain't it?"

"I thought you couldn't drive."

"Heh heh, proves them all wrong, don't it?"

"Yeah, I guess it does, although you never had to prove anything to me."

The car was in sight. Staring at the rusted, dented, rickety vehicle, Woody wondered how he had managed to drive it as far as he had. "You drive," he said to Cam. "My eyes don't feel so good today."

Cam looked at the Jeep and wondered if *he* could drive it; he was used to his sleek, late model sports car. This tank-shaped, rusty car looked like he might have to pedal to make it go. "Okay, but you'll have to coach me."

They eased into the Jeep, taking a minute for the seats to cool from broil to simmer before they could sit comfortably in the car. When Woody saw that Cam could hold the wheel and his legs were pressed to the seat, he said, "Just pump the gas and touch together those two wires hangin' down."

Cam found two wires under the steering wheel. He picked up the wires and stared at them. He wondered how it felt to be shocked by a car battery. He guessed he would have to find out, so he pumped the gas and touched the wires together. A huge spark made a loud crack without his body being whacked by a shock. At the same time he saw the spark, the engine roared to life. Cam jumped in surprise. Woody laughed.

"We can go now," Woody told Cam.

"Yeah," Cam replied dryly. Easing the clutch to the floor, Cam decided it felt like mush. He pumped the clutch a couple of times, then tried to get the gearshift into reverse. The gears ground something awful. "Is that normal?" Cam asked Woody.

"Yep. Just don't listen to it. It don't mean nothin'."

"Right." Cam worked the clutch and finally jammed the gear into reverse.

"Like I always said, if you can't find it, grind it," Woody said with a grin.

Shaking his head, Cam eased the car from the parking lot and drove away from the airport, the wind and dust hitting him in the face.

The New Mexico Antiquities Laboratory at Farmington was located south of town about ten miles. It was situated on 25 acres of land, donated to the state by the owners because remains of a very old settlement of people had been found at the sight. These remains were Anasazi ruins, but some of the earliest, belonging to the Basket Maker Period. The ruins were not tucked under protective cliffs, so the ravages of rain and snow and wind wore down what the Indians had built although even older ruins had been found under the first layer of debris. Although not all of the ruins had been excavated, little of scientific value had been found for these ruins were too easily accessible to foraging Indians and later to the pot-hunters, but it had proved to be an excellent sight to erect a permanent home for tedious work of documenting all the artifacts and information coming from the excavations at the hundreds of ruins throughout the Southwest. It was also a teaching location where students of archaeology came to learn the techniques.

The ruins included a very large "C"-shaped pueblo, 200 feet by 100 feet and containing some 120 rooms. Most of the rooms were semi-subterranean pithouses, and these had to be slowly excavated. At this sight the archaeologists were recovering some fine examples of baskets plus some of the first examples of pottery, both in plain gray and gray with black designs on it. A large kiva in the courtyard had been perfectly restored. It was very eerie to climb into the kiva, look around and see what it must have been like for the 'Ancient Ones' to do whatever it was they did down in those underground rooms.

The laboratory was the sight of the original house of Ralph Blackhouse and the ruins had been named The Blackhouse Ruins. With the Salmon Ruins nearby, with Aztec Ruin National Monument not far away, and with Chaco Canyon only forty miles south, it was centrally located to all the locals where excavations were being conducted. Inside the center was a reception area and museum, the walls of which were lined with glass cases. In the cases were artifacts—all Anasazi. Store rooms held more artifacts, bones, and the like while other store rooms were used for expedition supplies.

The lab itself, where the carbon-14 dating tests were done, looked like a hospital lab stainless steel counters lined with jars and test tubes. Down the hall was a large lecture room and a couple of class rooms. Across from the lab was the area where Ketl was kept.

This area—a small kitchen, bathroom, and bedroom—was at first supposed to be living quarters for someone to stay at the lab, but no one ever did that. The small bedroom in which Ketl had been placed had been used as an office, the outer room as a worker's lounge—a coffee machine, couch, magazines, the like. Stanley had taken his office furniture out of the office, and hastily had the room prepared for Ketl, complete with the remote camera and one-way mirror window. There was no window to the outside of Ketl's room, and the only windows giving light inside were in the bathroom and kitchen areas. The bathroom was behind Ketl's room and faced the desert with a couple of saguaro cactus growing directly outside the window.

As they pulled into the parking lot, Cam and Woody took note of the army Jeeps parked in the lot. They were further alarmed by the sight of a fire-plug shaped National Guardsman standing at attention outside the entrance of the center. The guard kept his feet spread, his eyes forward, his red neck perfectly still. In his right hand he held a rifle. As Woody and Cam passed by him, letting themselves inside the building, Cam threw the young man a nasty glance, and Cam noticed the guard didn't even flinch.

To their right was the museum and reception area. To their left was a set of swinging doors which were closed and outside of which stood another elephant-necked armed guard. Cam headed toward the swinging doors, intending to march through them.

Stepping in front of Cam, the guard blocked his way. His body tense, his lips a firm line, the guard emitted trained hostility. "Sorry, buster, no one goes back there."

"Why not?" Cam asked.

The guard's mouth tightened a fraction more. "Because those are the rules."

Cam and the recruit were nose to nose. "I want to talk to the rule maker," Cam growled.

The guard was trained to acknowledge aggressive behavior. When he peered into the steely black pupils of Cam's eyes and noted the way the veins of Cam's neck stuck out, the guard was prepared for trouble. "I'm the rule maker, good buddy, and nobody goes beyond these doors."

"Yeah?" Cam said, as he kneed the guard in the groin and dropped him to the ground with a karate chop to the back of his neck. "Rules are only made to be broken, good buddy," Cam added. Then he stepped over the guard and went through the doors with Woody on his heels.

Strumming his fingers on the desk top, Stanley sat rigidly at the window, staring at the Indian woman. He didn't hear the commotion at the doors, and was surprised to see Cam barge through the doors. Cam saw Stanley. Then his eyes went beyond Stanley through the window to Ketl who was sitting straight like young birch pole, her eyes closed, her face pale. With her face so pale, the ugly scratches and bruises on her face stuck out like lines on a map, and when Cam's gaze centered on the marks to her lovely skin, rage seethed inside him.

Frustrated by the intruders, Stanley stood. "What are you doing in here?" he charged.

As Cam stared at Ketl, his anger became a scalding fury. "I came to see Ketl," he said, the words nearly choking him.

"You have no right to be in here!" Stanley flared.

"You talk about rights?" Cam hollered, his anger close to consuming him. He pointed through the window. "You had no right to touch her! If you so much as hurt a hair on her head, I'll break every bone in your body!" Cam ran to window and pressed himself against it. Her deathlike trance scared the hell out of him. "You have no right keeping her like that in there," he said, his voice dropping as his heart twisted.

"Get away from there," Stanley said, wedging himself between Cam and the window.

Cam looked at Stanley as if he were the underside of a snake. "You had no right taking her, you jackass. You have no right breathing, you squeaky-faced turd!"

Appalled, Stanley blustered and stepped back from Cameron. "Who *are* you?"

"I'm Cameron January, and I was the first one to find the Anasazi woman. *I* found her and *I* put her back where she belonged. *You* had no right to take her! And who are you?"

He really didn't need to ask, because he was sure he was the person Woody had told him about, but Cam wanted to hear with his own ears the words from the man who studied fossils who thought he had a right to imprison a person for study.

"Stanley Cahill, archaeologist and administrator of this laboratory." Stanley grasped his jacket lapels. "Which gives me every right to contain for examination a relic of unidentified origin. I have the right of a scientist exploring the realms of the unknown. The Bureau of Land Management has given me the right, also," he added smugly.

"No man has the right to…to do this to another human being. It's ludicrous."

Stanley looked through the window at Ketl. He sighed. She hadn't eaten in two days. She also had refused any liquids. She just sat there with her eyes closed; she didn't seem to hear him when he spoke to her and her skin color looked like it belonged to a dead person rather than a young woman who could fight like a wildcat. Her pulse was steady, but weak. He did not want to have to start an IV to force feed her, yet he would have to if she wouldn't cooperate. Christopher had tried to speak to her, but all she did was spit at him and then go back into her deathlike trance. Hopefully Stanley asked Cam, "Could you talk to her?"

Astounded at the man's audacity, Cam replied, "I want her out of here!"

"I can't do that."

Just then the burly guard charged through the double doors and centered the bead of his rifle on Cam's head. The recruit was obviously angry. His quarter-inch hair appeared to be full of a hundred watts of electricity, his face hot with anger. "Slow and easy now, Mister. I'm placing you under arrest."

Cam looked over his shoulder. "What for, being nosy?"

The guard didn't answer, Stanley did. "Look, I'll tell the guard to lay off. I'll even let you talk to the Indian woman. But then you must go away. I don't want any trouble, and I guarantee you I can have five truck loads of National Guardsmen here within a quarter of an hour if you choose to make trouble."

Above all else Cam wanted to see Ketl. It was obvious he wasn't going to be able to talk any sense into Stanley Cahill and it was further obvious the irate Guardsman wasn't going to let Cam mosey around the building by himself. Moving around the desk, Cam pressed his palms to the window as his heart ached for what Ketl must be feeling. "All right," he agreed. "I'll talk to her."

Stanley used a key to open the door to the room. He held it for Cam. "This room is monitored by camera and hearing devices. Don't do anything stupid," Stanley warned. "And if you don't convince her to cooperate with me, I'll have the guardsmen place you under arrest, have a court order summoned to ban you from stepping foot in this place again, and I'll arrange to have the woman sedated and force-fed." Stanley glared at Cam. "Do we understand one another?"

"Perfectly," Cam replied.

"Good," Stanley said with a smile and stepped aside so Cam could enter the room.

Cam bolted past Stanley and fell to his knees in front of the bed. She looked half-dead. Her skin was deathly white. There was no indication she was breathing, only the slightest raise and fall of her chest. Her lips held only the slightest gray color. He knew she was in a self-induced trance; it didn't surprise him, in fact, he felt a profound sense of relief, knowing she could will herself away from the situation she found herself, but how deep a trance she was in, he didn't know, because he was not an expert on an Anasazi self-induced abstraction, and he hoped she would come out of it when she heard his voice.

Taking her clenched hands into his, he kneaded her hands with his thumbs. Her hands were cold and clammy. Softly he called her name. There was no response. He massaged the back of her hands, stroking each finger, trying to give his warmth to her. He tried to reach her again, repeating her name over and over very softly, praying his voice had enough harmony to reach the depths of her soul.

From a faraway place, Ketl heard her name being called.

It was very hard to open her mind to the outside world, but the voice was one which she wanted to hear, and she wanted to see the eyes that went with the voice. Struggling to fend off the black vortex of her non-world, she let her ears come alive and she heard him call her name again. The voice made her heart dance. Fluttering her lashes, she opened her eyes. The pleasurable shock of seeing Cameron was so great she gasped and her heart skipped a beat. "Mockingbird said you would come," she whispered though pale lips.

He kissed her fingertips. "What else did Mockingbird say?"

"She said you carry no more evil. I must not fear you, she said to me." Breathing deeply, faint color returned to her cheeks. "I do not like it here. Evil surrounds this place. Will you take me away?"

His heart sank, hearing the ring of hope in her voice. "The men outside this room don't understand your harmony. They know you are the last Anasazi. The want to watch you, to learn from you."

"I don't want to be here!" she repeated, her eyes growing wild and frightened.

Cam looked around him at the camera, at the mirror which was a window. He knew there was a microphone hidden someplace. "Ketl," he began slowly, calmly, "you have to trust me. You must do exactly as I say."

She once had trusted Chris, but he had not been strong. She had trusted Tommy Bright Eagle, and he had failed her. To each man she had given a bit of herself, and in return they had neglected their obligation to return tutelary actions toward her. Panic strummed in her veins. She was beginning to wonder if Cameron would fail her and abandon her too. Her heart couldn't stand it if he did. She threw her arms around his neck and clasped him to her.

"Don't leave me," she cried into his ear in one long, hot breath.

Cam groaned and squeezed her tighter. "Oh, baby, I'll never leave you again."

"Take me with you."

Whispering into her ear, pretending to be nuzzling her, he said, "The white man watches you from the reflection window. They have ears inside this room. We must fool them. Trust me. You are my woman, Ketl."

"And you are my man," she whispered back.

It felt good to have *one thing* settled anyhow, Cam thought as he peeled her fingers from around his neck and held her questioning gaze. "This is what I want you to do. I want you to eat and drink. You must be strong." She nodded. "I want you to tell them everything they want to know."

Her back stiffened.

"You must trust me." He kissed her cheek. "Do this for me."

From behind him, he heard the door open. As Stanley's footsteps thudded on the cement, he appeared at Cameron's side. "I see you've been able to talk some sense into her," Stanley said in a haughty tone of voice. "This is the first time she's been communicative."

Cam stood, grinding his teeth together. "You won't have any more trouble from her." He saw the guard at the door with the rifle point aimed at him. "There's one condition," he added as he reached down to take Ketl's hand in his.

"What's that?"

"You let me see her as often as I want. You do that and she'll tell you everything you want to know…agreeably."

Stanley didn't want to be indebted to any man. He really

didn't want any anyone but himself getting close to the woman, but until he gained her trust, he had no choice. "All right," he agreed be grudgingly.

"I want to get her out of this room," Cam said. "I want to let her walk outside, breath fresh air."

"Absolutely not!" Stanley boomed. He wasn't stupid. He knew Cameron January would use that chance to take Ketl. "You see her in this room or not at all."

Cam glanced from the rifle in the guardsman's hands back to Stanley. They weren't going to make this very easy, he decided. Wishing he could implant Stanley's nose in the back of his cranium, wishing he could shove the rifle down the guard's throat, Cam ground his teeth.

"Okay. I visit her in here," he stated firmly. "In this room. I'll be back tomorrow."

Over his shoulder he caressed her worried face with a confident smile. Their fingers slipped apart as he left the cubicle. Without looking back, he grabbed Woody by the elbow and hurried outside to the Jeep.

"You're leavin' her in there?" Woody asked.

"I'm not stupid enough to argue with a trigger-happy, lame brain National Guardsman." Cam jumped into the Jeep and jammed the wires together. "Come on," he waved to Woody, "we have work to do."

"Work?"

"Yes," he said. "Fooling Stanley Cahill will be more work than fun."

Grunting, Woody hauled himself into the Jeep, holding tightly to his duffel bag. Cam found first gear, floored the gas pedal and the Jeep roared from the compound, leaving a huge balloon of dust.

Chapter 20

First stop was a hardware store, second stop a music shop. Third stop was a department store, and last stop was a Jeep dealer who installed a windshield on the old Jeep because both Cam and Woody were sick of bugs hitting them in the face. Next they registered at the Farmington Holiday Inn where they ate steaks, drank cold beer and waited for night.

In their room over the double bed hung a reproduction of Remington's depiction of a white man greeting a plains Indian. It must have one of the first encounters between white man and Indian, because neither the Indian, nor the white man, had an expression of hate on their faces, only a look of mild curiosity. The painting bothered Cam and he refused to look at it.

Woody dozed while Cam tinkered with his things from the hardware and music shops. It pained Cam to think about Ketl in the little room; she'd never been closed inside a room without a window or door or open ceiling in all of her life. In Willow Canyon, her ceiling had been the sky or the great cave, her walls the desert air and sandstone cliffs of her canyon. To do this to her was a travesty of benevolence. To take her away from her home was sinful, and Cam guessed if he had the time he could hire a lawyer and find that it was against the law, but he didn't have the time, nor did he have the patience to watch Stanley gloat over the 'ancient' find he had made. No, Cam had to take the matter into his own hands and do things his way.

Sometime after midnight, Cam shook Woody awake. "Come on, it's time."

Blinking awake, Woody rolled off the bed and followed Cam outside where the night air was inky black. They climbed into the Jeep, jump started it, then drove out of town, passing the laboratory, turning down a dirt road and bumping along it until the road ended.

Cam separated the wires and the car died. Silence surrounded them. Sighing deeply, Cam looked up. Millions of stars dotted the sky. Narrowing his eyes to slits, he looked in the direction of the laboratory. To blend with the night, he wore dark jeans, shirt and his yucca sandals which he preferred to his tennis shoes for desert walking.

Adjusting a backpack on his shoulders, he told Woody, "I should be back in an hour or so."

"I'll be here. Ain't goin' nowhere. Sittin' is my specialty."

"Yeah...well, breaking into buildings isn't mine, but I've to know what the layout is in there."

"Bring her back with you."

"I will if I can. I'm just not sure what I'll find, and I don't want all those National Guardsmen coming after us."

"Right," Woody said. "You do what you gotta' do."

Cam gave Woody a thumbs up and crept away in the blackness.

   ❧ ❧ ❧

Strange how the desert night didn't bother him. In fact, he felt at home jogging along in his yucca sandals, dodging cactus and sagebrush like they were old friends. He noticed he didn't see any coyotes darting in the shadows, and he almost missed them. When he was about a mile from the building, he zigged and zagged his way though a series of Anasazi ruins. The ruins were spooky beneath the moonlight, and he hurried along, leaving the ghostly shadows of ancient people behind him.

Approaching the back of the building, he spied two three-armed cacti in front of one window. The window was small, high on the wall. Carefully maneuvering around the cactus, he went to the window. On tip toes he could see inside. It was a bathroom. The dusty window was cracked slightly with a screen covering the window.

Crunching on rocky soil, Cam crept around the building. No other windows were visible on the north facing end of the building. He peeked around the corner of the building, and by the front door was not one but two men both with rifles. He jumped back.

"Shit," he swore, knowing Stanley had doubled the guards.

Approaching the front of the building was out, he decided, and gaining entrance by the front door was impossible, so he crept back to the rear of the lab and stopped beneath the bathroom window in the shadows of the eight-foot-tall cactus. By stretching on tip toes, he could reach the hinges of the screen at the top of the window. With his arms burning, Cam removed a screw driver from his pack and used it to remove the hinges on the screen. When this was done, he placed the screen on the ground, then gently pushed the window all the way up. Next he curled his fingers over the ledge of the window and pulled himself upward. Grunting, he pushed against the spiny cactus to crawl through the window. As smooth as a snake, Cam slipped through the window and slithered down the wall, his head on a dead aim for the toilet.

Cursing, he pushed off the wall, rolled and landed in a

heap, his feet making a thud on the floor. Breathing deeply, listening for an indication that his entrance had been detected, Cam sat on the floor of the bathroom. He heard muffled voices from somewhere down the hall, but heard no change of pitch of voices, no panic, no evidence he had been heard.

Although a light sheen of perspiration coated his body, Cam began to breathe easier. He wasn't squinting so hard either as his eyes adjusted to the dim light. He was under the window, facing the toilet with a sink to the right, a shower to his left. The floor felt sticky to his touch, and he sniffed. Strong Pine-sol, he told himself.

He grabbed the toilet and pulled himself to his feet. Carefully, he stuck his head out from the bathroom and looked right and left. It was pitch black to his right, bright lights glowing down the hall to his left. So he went to his right, tip-toeing down the hall, silently opening doors, pointing his flashlight into two different rooms. Each room contained tables laden with bones, skulls, baskets, pottery and hundreds of other items. In the second room one whole wall was covered with shelving which held innumerable skulls. As his flashlight beamed on the sightless, seemingly grinning heads, Cam felt a cold shiver of fear race up and down his spine. The skulls gave him the creeps, and he shut the door quickly and retraced his steps to the bathroom.

He could hear voices coming from down the hall. He guessed the voices were guards, stationed outside of Ketl's room, but he wasn't sure. He *had* to go down the hall and peek around the corner and see who and how many were there. He didn't want to go, but he had to.

Swallowing, Cam inched down the wall, sliding his fingers along the cool, cement wall.

The voices grew louder.

Cam paused. He could make out the voices of two men. One was telling the other about his girlfriend. Cam's forehead wrinkled as one voice told the other that his girlfriend liked to cover him with Cool Whip and slowly lick every dollop off him.

The other voice groaned. "Man," he said, "my girl won't even have sex with the lights on."

"She fat or something?" Voice number one asked.

"No, but she's part Navajo and she has a lot of body hair."

"Help her shave it, using Cool Whip as shaving cream."

"Hey, that's a great idea," voice number two replied.

Cam chanced a glance around the corner. One quick look told him everything; the voices belonged to a new set of red-necked, rifle-totting National Guardsmen. And he guessed right. The pair sat at Stanley's desk, one in front of the desk in a metal chair with his feet up on the desk, the other behind the desk, shuffling a deck of cards. They were in front of the door leading into Ketl's room.

Dumb realization made him turn and stare at the wall he was holding up; Ketl was behind the wall. *So close.* She was no more than ten feet away from him, but separated by thick plaster and wood.

Cam could think of no way to divert the guards long enough to get inside Ketl's room, grab her and retreat down the hall to the bathroom window. Cam again risked a peek around the corner.

"You ever had Cool Whip mixed with Oreo cookies, then frozen?" Guard two asked guard one.

"Naw, my ma was a horrible cook. I joined the Guard to get away from her poison."

"Try it. Any idiot can make it. Come on, deal the cards, you've shuffled the hell out of them."

"That's 'cause I've had lousy hands all night."

"Just deal the cards."

"Okay, here we go."

Cam heard the slight flick as cards left the deck. He could

jump them, but no, they looked like farm-bred tractor-backs. It was damn frustrating.

"Duces wild this time," voice one said.

"I gotta' take a leak," voice two announced. "Back in a minute."

Cam heard the sound of metal chair screeching against the floor. "Oh shit," he mumbled.

Then he heard the voice say something else although he didn't catch it, because Cam was already three long strides down the hall, making a bee-line for the window over the toilet, and because his yucca sandals were not designed for the high polish of linoleum, his feet went out from under him as he rounded the dark corner into the bathroom.

"Oh shit," he mumbled again through pale lips.

He wondered if they would shoot him in the head or in the stomach when the caught him, or maybe just pound on him awhile until his face resembled hamburger. And he wondered, if they did kill him, how long before his skin would shrivel up and rot away from his skull until he resembled one of those unseeing skulls.

Still splayed on the floor, he heard the footsteps coming down the hall. *Thump. Thump. Thump.* There was no mistaking the sound of fatigue boots in a quiet hall.

He knew he'd never have time to get off the floor and climb out the window. He knew he was a dead duck.

Twenty-year-old Private Rocky Velasco hoofed it down the hall, pulling down the zipper on his pants. His bladder was painfully full from all the coffee he had consumed since he started his watch. Combined with the tales of the girl who was addicted to Cool Whip smeared on a male body, Rocky really had to relieve himself. However, Rocky had beaten his buddy in poker, he was five bucks ahead now, and he didn't want to waste time taking a whiz, so he wheeled into the john, and sent a steady stream of urine into the toilet, all without turning on the light. He shook off, turned on his heel and zipped back up while clopping back down the hall.

That was why Cameron January didn't get his brains blown out that night. White-faced, clammy-skinned, Cam squeezed from behind the bathroom door. He knew a good part of his arm must have stuck out, because you can't stuff a 200-pound man into a space made for bath towels. He looked up and said a silent prayer of thanks, and yes, he thought he might be praying to Mockingbird, for certainly someone was looking out for Cameron January that night.

With a leap, he was half in, half outside the window with his stomach balancing on the window frame. He dropped to the ground hard, flopping against the cactus. Catching a scream of pain in his throat, he jumped away from the cactus. His thigh felt as though it were on fire. Grabbing the pain, he jumped to his feet and limped though the moonlight.

ररर   ररर   ररर

Cam arrived at the laboratory alone the next day about noon. He carried a blanket, a box of tacks, a roll of tape, Ketl's bone knife and a small cassette player with a Cuban conga tape ready to play.

Cam faced the same guard at the double doors as the day before, and the guard looked as if his balls still hadn't recovered from Cam's knee to his groin.

"You again!" the guard, Freddy, said.

"Yeah, me," Cam said with a giant smile. "So how goes it? Love your job? Have you had any guerrillas try and get past you?"

Freddy would love to flatten the smart-ass preppie, re-membering with shame how Cam had taken him down with one fast kick. Freddy didn't get leveled without remembering the face behind the fist, and he would like nothing better than to make mush out of that face. Gripping his rifle tightly, Freddy stepped up to Cam. "You so much as touch me again, sucker, and I'm going to compress you into onion skin."

"Is that so?" Cam challenged. "Well, instead of finding out who'll end up flat on the floor today, why don't you go find Stanley Cahill and tell him Cameron January wants to see him. I'll think he'll tell you to let me in."

Freddy would have preferred a fist fight, but it didn't look like things were going to go that way. "Stay here," he said gruffly. "I'll go find Mr. Cahill."

He was back in less than minute, red in the face. "Go on in," he said, refusing to look Cam in the eye.

"Told you, sucker." Cam couldn't help but having the last word and brushed by Freddy.

He found Stanley sitting at his desk, strumming his legal pad with what appeared to be a gold ring. Though the window he could see Ketl sitting on the bed, eating something which had been brought to her on a tray.

Like a prisoner, Cam thought.

"Incredible, simply incredible," Stanley was saying.

"What's so surprising, Stanley?" Cam asked.

Stanley held out the ring. "Did you know about this?"

"What?"

"That her great-grandmother was a white woman. That she was abducted by the Apaches and sold to the Anasazi for a couple of sacks of corn?"

"Stanley," Cam chided, "you don't do her justice. Besides sacks of corn, she was traded for a hand-crafted bow and quiver of arrows. A sizable sum."

Cam's sarcasm went over Stanley's head. "I just can't believe it. I couldn't figure out how this ring got on the finger of the skeleton in Pueblo Bonito. I just couldn't figure it. Now I know. And to think the Anasazi clan was wandering around these parts no less than a hundred years ago. It's incredible."

"They're still here," Cam said. "Ketl is an Anasazi."

"Ah, but not full-blooded. Even her blood type is not O as

it should be if she were a full-blooded Indian."

Cam cringed, thinking of Stanley poking Ketl with a syringe and pulling blood from her. He'd like to take Stanley's neck in his hands and squeeze until purple indentations appeared on his throat, and it took all the determination Cam could muster to remain calm. "Technically she may not be physically 100% Indian," Cam argued, "but socially she is."

"Oh, I know," Stanley said with an annoyed sigh. "I know. She could have just as easily lived five hundred years ago or a thousand years ago in that blasted canyon and her life would be just the same. I don't doubt the veracity of her condition for a minute. It's just the ramifications of this ring and the skeleton in Pueblo Bonito. Don't you see? I know people would have called her an impostor, an improbable farce, but this ring is proof that she is who she claims she is.

"I know we'll be able to trace the woman, Maude, to whom the ring belonged. Most likely we'll find she came West, was abducted by the Apaches and then all trace of her vanished. Now a living Anasazi woman tells us the rest of her story. It's incredible. It's the most extraordinary *solved* archeological puzzle to happen in centuries.

"Ketl knows about the ring," Stanley continued while he played with the ring. "She can *remember* minute details about the woman who wore it. Those things were passed down to her from her Grandfather. Also, she knew about the inscription inside the ring. It sounds like the woman, Maude, transformed into one of the Anasazi clan. She left the canyon with a small band of Indians on something called a migration. She was very old, obviously. She didn't get far, although Pueblo Bonito is no easy jaunt. She died there.

"The other Indians buried her as they would have buried one of their own, back inside of one of the storage rooms. Perhaps at that time Pueblo Bonito was in better shape than it stands today." Stanley placed the ring in the plastic box and gently set it inside his desk drawer. "Anyhow, there will be no shred of doubt that I have discovered the last living Anasazi on earth. It will take years and years to gather all the information she will be able to tell me." He shook his head, disbelieving his good fortune. "She'll be famous. She'll make *me* famous!"

Cam hated Stanley with a seething, festering rage. He was conceited, pig-headed, insensitive and a whole list of other things that Cameron didn't bother thinking about. He claimed to be a professional at what he did, but he was no better than a kidnapper who tortured his victim. It made Cam sick.

Disgusted, Cam went around the desk. "I'm going in to see her now."

For the first time Stanley paid attention to Cam. "What have you got there?"

Cam held up the blanket. "Just a blanket," he explained with a forced smile. "She was cold when I visited with her yesterday."

"Okay," Stanley replied, then went back to the notes he was jotting on his legal pad.

Cam entered the room. Ketl's eyes beamed although her face was deathly pale, and Cam noticed dark circles under her eyes. Shutting the door, Cam got busy. He jammed a rubber stop under the door. Pulling black tape from his pocket, he peeled off a piece and neatly placed it over the eye of the camera. While Ketl watched, he grabbed a pack of thumbtacks and began to hang the blanket over the window. Four tacks did it. The cassette recorder, which had been hidden by the blanket, he placed on the floor near the bed and started the Cuban conga music reverberating though the room.

Satisfied that no eyes or ears would intrude on their privacy and ignoring Stanley's pounding on the outside door, Cam took Ketl by the hand and pulled her into his arms.

His gaze caressed her face as he examined each curve of her exquisite beauty. When he laid his hand on her cheek tenderly tracing a bluish bruise, she closed her lids to savor the moment. Cam traced the regal bones of her cheek, then the translucent skin of her narrow nose. The tender touch of his fingertip along her full bottom lip bred a lava-hot warmth in her center which flowed to the tips of her limbs. Her knees became weak. She was in awe of the power Cameron had over her.

In her trance, Mockingbird said it would be so, yet she was stunned at the power of his touch, his breath, his very nearness. Her knees sagged and she leaned against him.

The prolonged anticipation was almost unbearable. He held her fiercely since her legs refused to hold her weight. Ketl buried her face against his throat and wrapped her arms around his neck. Not able to contain himself any longer, Cam circled her cheek with his finger one more time, then trailed it under her chin and gently lifted her doe eyes up to meet his.

His hands roved up and down her back, over the firm curve of her buttocks, his touch impatient to touch every inch of her. He covered her with kisses—on her lips, her cheek, her chin, down her throat where a blue vein pulsed. He was starving for the taste of her, yet terrified of her innocence, her vulnerability, afraid he would frighten her with the depth of his passion.

Instead of recoiling from his touch, Ketl murmured a soul-piercing moan when his lips left hers to nibble on a delectable neck.

Slowly Cam found her eyes, searching for words to express how he felt, how lovely she was, how good she felt in his arms. He'd always been good at garnishing compliments on women, but where Ketl was concerned, he found himself speechless. There was only one way to tell her how he felt and that was by covering her quivering lips with a kiss that left no doubt he claimed her as his woman from now until the end of time.

Groaning with pleasure, Cam found her lips, his mouth

covering hers hungrily. She returned his kiss with reckless abandon and met his thrusting tongue with an eagerness that matched his unbridled passion. It was strange, their lips meeting, their bodies touching; all around them was the sound of beating drums, near hysterical screams and yells that went with the conga music, and above that Stanley was outside the door, pounding, hitting, slamming his fist against it. It didn't matter.

Cam had found Ketl and claimed her as his woman.

This is how it was.

      ào   ào   ào

When their kiss either had to stop or be consummated, Cam let his lips trail away from hers. It was difficult, but he did it nonetheless.

Ketl stood away from him, her chest heaving, her lips swollen and shiny wet, her nostrils flaring ever so slightly. He watched her eyes flutter open, loving her so much he burned with the intensity. More than anything he wanted to hold her in his arms and talk quietly to her, but with the loud conga music and Stanley beating on the door, it was impossible.

After squeezing Ketl's fingers, then bringing them to his lips and tenderly kissing them, Cam went to the door and yelled at Stanley, "You're going to break the damn door! Stop beating on it."

"What are you doing in there?" Stanley screamed while he continued to pound on the door.

"I wanted to visit her without the feeling of being in a zoo," Cam explained.

The loud thuds on the door stopped. "Ten minutes," Stanley said. "Out in ten minutes or I'll have the guards shoot their way inside."

Very effective people management, Cam thought. "Okay, ten minutes."

He went back to Ketl and handed her the bone knife he had

taped against his leg. "Don't let him see it," Cam told her.

Ketl's ran her finger along the sharp blade. "Shall I place it in his heart?"

Cam grinned. "That's an interesting thought, but no, save it until it's time for you to leave."

"Now? Am I not going with you now? I must get back to the canyon."

His heart sank. He didn't know how to tell her. "Ketl," he began, as gently as possible, "the white men are crawling all over Willow Canyon. They'll catch you again if you return. You must not go back there...not now."

Her face turned pasty white. "But it's my home. I am the last Anasazi."

"I know, babe, I know," he said and tenderly kissed her forehead.

She shivered, her wide eyes looking up to him full of curiosity. "What will happen to me?"

"You know the ring Stanley showed you? Your great-grandmother's ring?"

"Yes?"

"You are an Anasazi. You are the last. But you are something more than that. You are a true American, because you have mixed blood in your veins." She gasped as if he had told her a lie. "You know it's true."

"But my great-grandmother was Anasazi, even though she had white skin. Pavi told me this."

"Your grandfather told you that to ease your mind. You can't change the fact that your great-grandmother was white, and it isn't bad, in fact, in light of this situation, I think it's very good, and very important for you to understand its importance."

"I understand nothing," she said firmly, not liking the thought of having a *real* white person in her lineage.

The Cuban drums kept a heated beat, and Cam wished he

could turn the dam thing off, but he couldn't, because Stanley would hear everything he said. Yet trying to explain something as serious as her heritage to her was difficult. "Ketl," he began again, staring down into her green eyes with the utmost seriousness in his face, "the first white men came to this land many years ago because they couldn't stay in their homeland any longer, just like you. They were very brave men. They were frightened of what they would find, but nonetheless they came. They were a little more rebellious, a little more adventuresome than other people. They were like you, Ketl. Your great-grandmother must have traveled through this part of America long before there were real roads, before there were towns or settlements. She must have been very brave, very resilient."

"She was one of the People," Ketl said proudly.

"Yes, she became one, but she wasn't one of the People at first. And you have her blood in you. This is why I say you can leave here and not go back to Willow Canyon. You will always carry your heritage with you wherever you are, wherever you go. You can't change what you are. In fact, you can spend your life telling others about the Anasazi, in your own time, in your own way. What this man, Stanley, is doing to you is wrong, but his intent is right. You are the last Anasazi forever and ever. When it is time for you to go to the Fifth World there will be no knowledge of you and your people left on earth. It's important you tell the world, Ketl. Not like this, though…like you're a prisoner." He cupped her face in his hands and feather-touched her lips. "You and Woody and I, we'll tell the world. We'll write it down so others can read about your people. The world will know the truth, because it will come from your lips…the way you want to tell it."

Ketl frowned. "But where will we be? Where will I do this?"

He could tell she was still frightened, and he couldn't

blame her for her whole life had been spent in the canyon. "I don't know right now," he said truthfully.

"Perhaps it is time to continue my migration," she said softly, which was hard to hear above the beating drums.

"Yes, perhaps it is, and perhaps Qualetaga's instructions may prove correct after all, because with me you could complete the migrations by airplane."

Like a brilliant light had been ignited in her head, Ketl thought of the many times she had watched the silver bird streak across the sky. She remembered telling Pavi how she would like to see one, and suddenly she realized there were many, many things she wanted to see, if she were only brave enough to venture beyond her own world and take a look.

Her great-grandmother had the courage, she told herself, a half-smile tipping the corners of her lips. *Yes! She could do it!* She was brave, as brave as Pavi, as brave as Una, as brave as those of her clan who had left to finish their migrations.

The excitement of her new realizations nearly made her heart sing with delight and the shadows which had been with her for days lifted, a warm glow filling her completely. She reached up and wrapped her arms around Cam's neck. "Oh, yes," she cried, "yes, I can see now see what Mockingbird has been trying to tell me!"

He kissed her, the drums matching the rhythm of his heart, while Stanley began to beat his own rhythm on the door. "Listen to me, Ketl," Cam breathed into her ear. "This his how you are going to escape from here."

There was not much time; Stanley was threatening to have the door blown apart.

So quickly he told her.

When Cam kicked the door stop away from the door, Stanley charged through the door, red-faced with livid anger. "That's the last time you come in here alone," he boomed, pointing a shaking finger at Cam. He went to the window and pulled the blanket down, then picked up the tape recorder and roughly handed it to Cam. "No more tricks, January, or I'll have a court order restraining you from any contact with her."

Cam placed his hands up in the air in mock surrender. "No more tricks, Stanley," he said, feigning sincerity. "I promise."

"Good," Stanley replied, throwing Ketl a reproving glance. "Now get out of here, I have many questions to ask her."

Like an interrogation, Cam thought. "Right. I'll be back tomorrow."

"You won't see her alone!" Stanley reminded him.

"Your company is always a pleasure," Cam retorted, then left the room.

When he breezed through the swinging doors, he stopped just long enough to give Freddy a disdainful cursory look.

"Hey, geek," Cam jeered with a half twist to his lips, "shot any cockroaches today?"

Freddy tensed. "I'm looking at one, Slime-ball."

Cam glanced over his shoulder, then shrugged. "You must have let it get away."

Freddy's lips snarled. The veins in his stubby neck stuck out like worms. "I'm gonna' kill you, buddy!"

Cam pointed his finger at his nose. "You couldn't kill a fly...."

It was nearly more than Freddy could stand, but as he was about to reach out and grab Cam by the neck, his relief came marching down the hall, saw the hostility in Freddy's face and stepped between him and Cam. "Easy, good buddy," he said.

"This little piss-pants is gonna' get it!" Freddy growled.

"Yeah? On our time, Freddy. Cool it for now."

Cam smiled graciously, nodded and strolled out of the building, happy things were progressing as planned.

Chapter 21

For Cameron January, sleep was an elusive state. Lying awake in a Holiday Inn in Farmington, New Mexico, staring at the ceiling, listening to Woody snore, Cam was wondering how his life had come to this ridiculous condition.

Really, he told himself with recrimination, *just last month you were sipping champagne, feeling Sharon's lanky body next to yours, depositing a healthy paycheck into your bank account and wondering if the Giants or Angels would be in the playoffs.*

Life seemed so simple back then.

He was not used to this sort of shit he was involved with now. Saving an Indian maiden, plotting an escape, sneaking around in the dark and entering buildings where he could get his ass shot off if he were found, all that sort of stuff happened on television, not to people like Cameron January.

Woody's wind intake was very long and sounded like the rooting of a pig. Then Woody paused. Each time there was a long interval between intake and exhale, and Cam wondered if Woody would retract his lungs and push the air out which sounded like a plastic whistle with a hole in it. A suspenseful few seconds spaced Woody'd noises, yet every time Cam thought he'd taken his last breath, Woody would comply, blowing air, making enough cacophony to wake the dead. With no variation to the pattern, Cam had become used to it, actually finding the clamor comforting like the buzz of a hair dryer or the hum of a television when the channels have gone off the air and the black and white zigzags come on for the rest of the night.

A month ago, Cam couldn't imagine sharing a room with an old man, or thinking about being responsible for Woody. A month ago, thinking about running off with a virginal Indian, who he had called a living fossil, would have been the last thought dancing though his brain.

Now it seemed very natural, and he wondered if the world were crazy or if this was a premid-life crisis.

ﺑﻪ   ﺑﻪ   ﺑﻪ

The next day Cam rented a car: a small compact job that smelled of overheated bodies and stale cigarettes. He really preferred the Jeep, but needed another car. After Woody and Cam stuffed down a huge breakfast of pancakes, Cam checked out of the Holiday Inn. He synchronized watches with Woody, then shook hands with him. The two men parted company, each going their own way, knowing each had a job to do.

Woody got into the Jeep and started it to life with a spark and a roar. Grinding gears, he lurched out of the parking lot and was gone from sight. Cam eased his rental Chevy away from the Holiday Inn and headed for the lab.

As expected, Freddy was stationed at the double doors. Cam ignored the guard. Clutching his rifle to his chest so hard his knuckles turned white, Freddy watched Cam breeze by him, passing through the doors.

Relaxing a little, Freddy let out a deep breath, then stiffened when the door opened a crack and Cam said to him:

"You had a brain transplant yet today?"

Freddy jumped. He was ready to pounce on Cam, but the door swung shut and Freddy faced a metal door. Breathing hard, Freddy swore and watched a circle of moisture form on the door. Freddy had no idea why Cameron January was on his case like he was, but he decided, job or no job, uniform or no uniform, he was going to teach Cameron January which end of the set of knuckles did the talking.

Inside the room, Stanley sat on a metal chair, talking with Ketl while he jotted notes on his clipboard. Cam watched for a few moments as she waved her hands around in the air, obviously very engrossed with what she was relating to Stanley.

Ketl possessed a slim, wild beauty and Cam found himself staring at her. He'd only seen her in Woody's old clothes and a handmade tunic of rough cotton. Silks and tailored suits could do nothing to enhance what he saw through the one-way window. A belt around her waist delineated its smallness. Breasts, full and pointy, strained at the material as she made circles in the air over her head. Her complexion was a blend of Indian and white genes, ending up glowing with pale gold undertones. Dark, dusty black lashes needed no makeup to enhance their beauty, and he could remember all too well the feel and texture of her lips. Today, under the neon lights, her hair was black, like shining glass which highlighted the strange greenness of her eyes.

Cam's mouth suddenly went dry as he imagined some other male person having Ketl. He imagined her lying in bed with her arms draped over a hairy chest. There could be no other male, Cam told himself, a self-understanding entering his pores and radiating out to all ends of his flesh. Only one man would possess her...ever.

While he watched Stanley furiously write down the things Ketl was telling him, Cam stepped back and leaned against

Stanley's desk. Behind his back, his fingertips found the knob of the desk drawer and he slowly opened it a crack and felt around the inside of the drawer until he found the square object. Quickly, Cam cracked opened the plastic container, pulled out the gold ring and replaced it with a new one he had purposely made to look old by using sand paper and by good old-fashioned banging around. It only took seconds and after the exchange was made, the gold ring belonging to Ketl's great-grandmother, was safely tucked away in Cam's pant pocket.

With that chore done, Cam strolled into Ketl's room and said, "Hope I'm not interrupting anything."

Stanley frowned. "Yes, you are interrupting. I told you not to come back until late this afternoon."

"I was in the neighborhood." Cam looked at Ketl and gave her a subtle nod. "I thought I would just drop in and see how things were going."

Ketl rose from the bed, stretched and started for the door.

"Things are going fine," Stanley said. He threw a worried glance at Ketl. "Where are you going?"

Over her shoulder, she nonchalantly replied, "Down the hall to the wash room."

Stanley nodded approval, placed his notes on the bed and stood, arching his back with his hands on his hips. "I guess it has been a long time sitting," he said. "I'll get some tea for us."

Politely, Ketl smiled and padded down the hall.

Cam watched her go. His pulse began to beat faster, much like the conga drums.

Stanley headed for the kitchen where the hot water was steaming on the stove.

Strumming his fingers on Stanley's desk, Cam gave him a few minutes to fix the tea. Anxiously he glanced at his watch. Three minutes. Stanley hadn't returned. Good. Just as he heard the archeologist's footsteps coming from the kitchen,

Cam turned and headed for the swinging doors. This was the part of the plan he liked the least, but the most important part. He pushed hard on the doors, bursting though them, his eyes wild, his whole face flushed with pent-up anger.

Freddy glared at Cam.

"That asshole won't let me in to see the Indian!" Cam roared, his anger so great, the chords stood out on his neck.

"Serves you right, you preppie son-of-a-bitch—"

Cam sneered at Freddy. "Ah, what do you know? Your head is like coffee—vacuum packed."

Every muscle in Freddy's body stiffened. Overwhelmed with fury, he dropped his rifle and launched himself at Cam. Cam went to the floor with a whomp. Taking a blow to his ribs, Cam hollered. He kicked his feet and made as much noise as he could. Freddy was thick and strong and connected with a jaw-wrenching right uppercut.

Cam could have kneed him in the balls, but it would end the fracas too soon, so he managed a few not-so-great punches to Freddy's belly. They rolled through the set of swinging doors, throwing punches, swearing at one another. Cam's nose was bleeding, and he left a nice red trail of blood as they rolled on the floor.

Now Stanley rushed from the kitchen and stood over the two men, waving his arms and yelling at them to stop.

Cam twisted and broke free of Freddy's grip. He jumped to his feet, snorting and puffing. Blood streamed out of his nose. "Come on!" he hollered at Freddy. "Get on your feet, you little shit!"

Freddy did as he was told. He came up to Cam's chin, but outweighed him by 25 pounds. Confident from boxing instruction, he threw a combination at Cam, connecting with a left jab. Cam went backwards and sprawled over Stanley's desk, scattering everything. Tea mugs went to the floor with a crash. Stanley's papers fluttered to a stop in the middle of spilled tea.

"Will you two stop it!" Stanley screamed.

They didn't stop.

Freddy and Cam duked it out until the entire room was a shambles of papers, broken cups and glasses and blood. Finally Stanley went outside and brought the other guard to the fight and ordered the man to place both Cam and Freddy under arrest. The guard stood above the two struggling men and pointed his shiny rifle between them. He ordered them to stop.

Neither man wanted to argue with the end of a gun.

Gasping for breath, groaning from aching muscles, Cam pushed himself to his feet and managed a quick glance at his watch.

Ten minutes. Good.

Stanley gave both men a lecture. Blotting his nose with the back of his sleeve, Cam stood with his shoulders bent, his head hung and took the word lashing Stanley handed out. It took all he could muster not to laugh at his moral views on how men should settle their differences with their brains instead of their fists. Cam thought it particularly funny because he thought Stanley the most lacking person where morals were concerned.

Stanley pointed to the guard with the rifle. "I want you to take these men to the police station and let them cool off in jail overnight. Maybe the atmosphere of steel bars will make sense to them."

Cam did make a good effort of arguing with Stanley, but Stanley wouldn't relent and both Cam and Freddy were led away to an awaiting car to be transported to the Farmington Police Department. When they were going out the front door, Christopher Hayes was coming in it, and seeing Cameron January's condition, he decided he had better go along with Cam to the police station. It left Stanley the huge task of picking up his papers and trying to make order out of chaos in his office.

When the National Guard car drove away from the laboratory, Cam kept his eyes centered out the front window. He didn't look back, way back behind the lab building to see if he could catch sight of an Indian woman who would have been running across the desert in a southwesterly direction.

And Stanley? Well, since order was next to godliness to Stanley, it was some time later when he had things put back the way they should be and he realized Ketl was still in the bathroom. It was some time after that when he managed to break down the bathroom door and found it empty with the window open. And it was some time after that when he called back all his aides and helpers to start searching the desert for Ketl...the last Anasazi.

She was long gone by the time Stanley's helpers started fanning out and searching the ruins, the desert, behind each scrub pinion, anywhere they thought she might have gone.

Woody was laughing, having the time of his life, driving the Jeep along dirt roads while Ketl sat next to him, smiling, her hair flying in the breeze.

     ≥▲   ≥▲   ≥▲

Freddy and Cameron January were invited to spend time cooling off in the Farmington jail. It was a two-celled, mid-thirties looking jail. Nothing of much interest happened in Farmington to keep the building occupied except the weekend DUI's. The cells were not air-conditioned, either, and were tropical-forest hot.

The cot in Cam's cell was attached to the cement wall and faced the cot in the adjoining cell where Freddy sat and stared with beady eyes at Cam. Cam's jaw was sore. His side throbbed where Freddy had pounded him repeatedly. His whole body felt like it had been through a food processor, minced nicely, then spat back out into a warming oven. His nose occasionally dripped a solitary drop of blood onto his shirt which was no longer blue, but an awful looking purple-magenta mass of dried blood.

He was a wreck. He didn't care. He could stare back at Freddy without any anger; Freddy had served his purpose. He only hoped that in his lifetime, Cam never ran into the redneck war-horse again.

A reporter from the Farmington Gazette sat on the edge of the deputy's desk, asking questions about the charges brought against the two men. He'd heard it had something to do with the archeological lab; he thought there might be a story here, something more interesting than the usually hum-de-hum events occurring in Farmington. The deputy really couldn't tell him too much, just names and that the two men, one a National Guardsman had been arrested for disorderly conduct and willful destruction of public property.

"Why was the National Guard at the Antiquities Laboratory?" the reporter asked.

"I don't know," the young mustachioed deputy replied.

"Does the sheriff know?"

"You'll have to ask him."

"Where is he?"

"Out at the lab, I guess," came the reply.

"Aha, this is very interesting. Maybe I'll just mosey out to the lab and have a look around there."

"You do that," the deputy said.

It was at that moment when Stanley came barging into the jail. With his face crimson, his white lab coat open and trailing behind him, he looked like a choleric dove.

He bolted past the deputy and charged to Cam's cell. The sheriff was right behind Stanley, so were a number of tired, dusty people who had spent the last hour tramping all over the desert surrounding the laboratory.

Stanley grabbed the bars, rattled them furiously and

shouted, "Where in the hell is she?"

The deputy was on his feet, nervously wondering what he should do. The sheriff joined Stanley while Freddy jumped to attention.

Coolly Cam replied, "Who are you talking about?"

"You know damn well who I'm talking about," Stanley screeched.

"Who?" Cam whispered.

"Ketl," Stanley yelled. "The...Indian...the last Anasazi."

Cam clasped his fingers together and began to rotate his thumbs one over another. He looked at Freddy and innocently asked, "Do you know who he's talking about?"

Freddy didn't answer, but glared at Cam as if he had lost his marbles.

Sheriff Earl Castleton, a fat, roly-poly sort of man with a perfectly round face, bald head and glasses, patted Stanley on the shoulder. "I think you should calm down."

Seething with rage, Stanley gripped the bars tighter. "I am *not* going to calm down! I have a very big problem. That...that...idiot in there stole my Indian!"

"What Indian are you referring to?" the sheriff asked.

A heavy silence filled the room. A pin dropping would have sounded like the shattering of glass. Nobody but Stanley, his assistants and a few others knew about Ketl. He purposely had kept it that way. Now the room was full of ears who would tell the whole world of his remarkable discovery before he was ready to announce his find. Things were not going the way he had planned, and he glared harder at Cameron January, knowing he had something to do with the Indian being gone.

Stanley pointed at Cameron, his finger shaking with rage. "He knows what Indian." Then with his eyes, he found Christopher, who prudently remained in the shadows. Stanley turned his finger on Christopher. "He knows what Indian."

Christopher's face remained blank.

"Tell them, for Christ sakes!" Stanley ordered.

Christopher shrugged. "What Indian?"

Stanley grew redder and redder, the veins in his temples bulging and pulsing hard. "Where is she!" he screeched, rattling the bars and throwing poison arrows at Cam with his eyes.

With total placidity, Cam touched his thumbs together. "I don't have the foggiest notion what he's talking about," Cam said to the sheriff.

"He does too!" Stanley screeched.

Behind him, the reporter wrote furiously, catching every inflection between Stanley and Cameron.

"Calm down, Stanley." Earl said firmly. "There seems to be a difference of opinion. Suppose *you* tell me what Indian you are referring to, and maybe I can figure out if there's a missing Indian and if Mr. January is responsible for the Indian being missing."

"She is an Anasazi," Stanley declared between thin lips. Glaring at Cam, Stanley pointed through the jail bars. "He's a geologist. He found her by mistake. Then Christopher Hayes found her, then I found her and she's mine! Now she's gone! Cameron January stole her!"

Frowning, the sheriff tried to make heads or tails from Stanley's words, and it was more confusing than clarifying. "Anasazi," Earl mumbled. "That don't make sense."

"I don't care," Stanley said indignantly. "She lived in a canyon no one had ever found. She is untouched by modern man, untouched by civilization."

Earl studied Cam. He appeared well groomed, wearing khaki pants and blood-stained Izod shirt, and strange fiber sandals. He pointed at Cam. "You know about the Indian?"

"No. I don't know what he's talking about. I am a geologist. I came out here to survey the Hayes ranch. I went to the Farmington Museum to see the artifacts just like any other visitor to the area might do. That's when Freddy jumped me."

Shaking his head, the sheriff turned to Christopher Hayes. "You know anything about the Indian he's talking about?"

Christopher darted a glance from Stanley to Cameron. He knew what Cam was doing, and he would continue to do it anyhow, no matter what Christopher said he knew or didn't know, because Cam was that type of person—a stand up sort of guy. Ketl came into his mind, and Stanley's obsession with her came and went too. Suddenly Christopher felt as though he grew up in five seconds.

Christopher moved in front of Stanley. "I've never seen any Anasazi Indian. I think you've had too much sun."

Cameron January smiled broadly.

Stanley grabbed the lapels of his jacket. "I have proof," he said, cocking his head with triumph. "I have a wedding ring which belonged to a white woman who was buried in Pueblo Bonito. I have written documents on the find, made hundreds of photos, sent papers to the Smithsonian about it. The Anasazi woman knew about the ring. It belonged to her great-grandmother. It is the one link between prehistoric Anasazi existence and modern times." He turned and stared at Cam. "Just yesterday I received confirmation of the existence of a Maude Sapp from the archives in St. Louis. She left St. Joe on a wagon train headed for California in 1850. The wagon train took the Santa Fe tail. It was attacked by Apaches in the Arizona Territory and Maude and three others were taken captive. She was never heard from again." Stanley crossed his hands across his chest. "I have Maude's ring. She was buried in an Anasazi grave with mementos hundreds of years old. It proves there was a remaining clan of Anasazi. It proves I'm right! It proves there was an Indian, and it damn well proves," he pointed at Cam, "that that man stole her from me!"

The sheriff was thoroughly confused. The reporter was white-faced, writing so fast his fingers were beginning to cramp. Cam remained placid. It was the one thing he could do well. His existence in the city full of stress related living conditions made him a champ at remaining cool under pressure.

"Go get the ring," Earl said to Stanley. "I want to see it."

"Fine," Stanley replied, full of triumph.

It was a little later when Stanley returned to the jail. This time he did not charge in like a white knight. He shuffled in, much like Woody walked, his shoulders bent, the determined gleam in his eyes now a hazy, confused countenance.

The sheriff was sitting at the desk. The reporter was still there, nervously chewing on the end of his pencil.

"Well?" Earl asked.

"The ring is gone," Stanley announced. He threw the plastic case on the table. "It was in there. Now it's not."

The sheriff looked at the plastic case. Inside was an old looking gold ring. He really was sure Stanley had Corn Flakes between his ears instead of brains. "Are my eyes deceiving me, Stanley, or is that a gold ring I see in the case."

"Yes, but it's a fake. There's no inscription in it. Someone switched rings." Then his eyes grew wide. "I'd bet anything January has the ring!"

Earl asked the deputy, "Did you search them when you brought them in?"

"No."

"Well, do it now."

The deputy shrugged and headed for Cameron's cell.

Chapter 22

"Take everything off," Earl ordered.

On weak knees, Cam stood, frowning. He hadn't planned on Stanley discovering the switch of rings. "I want to call my lawyer," he said.

"After you take off your clothes," Earl replied.

"I want to call him now," Cam argued. "Aren't I allowed one phone call? Isn't that how it works?"

"In my jail, sonny, you ain't allowed nothin' I don't say you're allowed, and right now the only thing you're going to be allowed to do is to peel your britches off."

Cam swallowed hard. His throat was dry. Warily, he eyed Freddy. "Right here? In the middle of the room?"

He heard Freddy chuckle.

"Right here, Sonny. We don't have no separate stripping room."

Slowly Cam unbuttoned his shirt. After he slipped it over his head, he let it drop the floor, and a female lab assistant took a quick intake of breath at the sight of Cameron's muscular chest.

Earl sent the woman a scathing glare. "All you females get outta' here," Earl ordered.

Three women reluctantly left the room. Next Cam removed his belt, then dropped his pants. Each item was handed to Earl who pawed all the garments, checking every pocket and seam. Cam waited, standing buck-naked except for purple hip-hugging jockey shorts.

Tossing the pants aside, Earl said, "Now the shorts, Sonny."

Cam did as he was told, paring off his bikini briefs like the skin of a banana. He looked ridiculous standing naked as a jay bird in the middle of a bunch of fully clothed people. His yucca sandals, the eagle feathers brushing against his leg, made him look even more odd.

After Earl searched Cam's clothes, Stanley went over each garment, whispering swear words as his fingers went over flat pockets and seams.

Nowhere did Earl nor Stanley find a ring.

Stanley stood in front of Cam and ran his fingers through his usually well groomed hair. Locking eyes with Cam, Stanley tried to read his innermost thoughts, but found himself staring at eyes devoid of emotion. "Damn, he must have swallowed it," Stanley said, his lips turned upward in a near growl.

The sheriff contemplated Stanley's remark. It could be true. A small ring would be easy to swallow. Yet Stanley was talking about a ring that belonged to a dead person who was supposedly the great-grandmother of a non-existent Anasazi woman. It was farfetched. This was out of Earl's ball park. Earl rubbed his chin with chubby fingers. Or someone was lying, he thought. Someone was definitely crazy, anyhow, Earl decided—either the geologist had had his brain fried by the sun or Stanley had spent too much time by himself with skulls and pottery fragments.

Earl's eyes swerved from Stanley to the naked geologist, then back again. Who to believe?

Earl handed Cam his clothes.

"I want an X-ray of his stomach," Stanley said.

Earl hesitated. "I don't know. I'll have to write a report for the cost of the procedure, and it won't sound too reasonable."

"Goddamn it!" Stanley shouted, turning from Cam. "I'll pay for the X-ray. I *know* he took the ring. He didn't have time to hide it. He had to put it someplace!"

Earl threw his hands in the air. "Okay. You pay for any expenses incurred for X-rays. We'll take him over to the hospital, but if there's no ring, I'm lettin' him go. I want him out of my county by nightfall. I don't need a pain-in-the-ass mental case in my territory."

"Yes," Stanley replied in a sardonic tone of voice which made Cam's skin crawl. "But we'll find he has the ring in his stomach." Stanley ground his teeth together. "And I hope when he passes it, it causes him great pain."

Hand cuffed, they drove Cam to the hospital in a police car with Stanley sitting beside him, watching every move he made. The X-ray technician was a pretty little thing who seemed to all thumbs while adjusting Cam on the steel table.

She took three pictures of him: one of his lower stomach, one of his upper digestive track, and one of his chest, for whatever reason, Cam wasn't sure, because if he had swallowed the ring and it was stuck in his throat, he sure as hell would have been gagging up a storm.

Sheriff Earl Castleton, Stanley Cahill and Christopher Hayes all stood by anxiously by while the radiologist placed the dripping wet X-rays on the light box.

No ring was found.

ஐ   ஐ   ஐ

Christopher Hayes drove Cam away from the jail in Farmington. As they pulled onto the road, Cam looked over his shoulder to see Stanley standing in front of the Sheriff's office with his hands at his sides, his fingers curled into tight balls. Sighing, Cam adjusted his Stetson on his head and let out a long breath of air.

"Earl will talk about you for years to come," Christopher told Cam. "Nothing so exciting has ever happened here."

"I hope Stanley has a nervous breakdown over it."

"Not likely. He'll grow old and gray, documenting everything in the canyon. He'll probably get rich from his reports, probably become famous."

"At least his fame won't come from exploiting Ketl."

"Yeah. You pulled a good one on them."

"You helped, Chris. Thanks."

A stagnant paused filled the car. Both knew Christopher told Stanley about Ketl in the first place, and both knew what had been done couldn't be changed. "I didn't understand—"

"You don't have to say anymore," Cam broke in.

"I just want to say I'm sorry. My priorities were screwed up."

"So were mine to begin with."

Christopher pushed down on the gas pedal and breathed deeply. "People change, don't we?"

"Hell, yes, even if you try not to."

Christopher thought of Woody. "My grandfather has been gone for a few days. My mother's understandably worried. They argued just before he disappeared. She's worried that he's lost. You wouldn't happen to know where he is, would you?"

Cam grinned, thinking of Woody traveling to San Francisco with a bag of money in his lap. "Yeah, I know where he is. Don't worry about him, and you won't have to worry about him coming home again, because he's dead set against it."

"My sister will throw a fit."

"Cut the bullshit, Chris. Woody's been nothing but an

inconvenience to both you and your sister. Woody doesn't have a lot of time left...let it be quality time."

"He—"

"There's no sense arguing. Woody's made up his mind, and you should know that when he decides something, it's final."

Christopher threw a speculative glance at Cam. "You're going to watch out for him?"

"Yeah, me and some Indian gods...."

Christopher slapped the steering wheel. "Damn, the old man has a way of making things work for him."

"I think its called harmony," Cam mumbled.

"What?"

"Nothing." Cam pushed up the leg of his pants and felt for the bunch of eagle feathers attached to the thong of his sandal. The small feathers were white and fuzzy. In the middle of the fuzz he felt a hard, round ring. He untied it and held the ring in front of his eyes. "Pretty little thing, wouldn't you say?"

Christopher took a quick look and laughed.

Cam rubbed the ring between his fingers. "You know when she gave me the sandals I have on, she told me the feathers were there so that when I walked I'd be closer to the clouds. Never did she imagine they would save her skin and mine."

"Maybe her gods are stronger than we'd like to believe."

"There's some sort of power at work here that I can't explain." Cam looked out the window at building thunder-heads. Was Mockingbird watching him? Were ancient gods leading him on a path of their choice? Would his life ever be the same?

Christopher broke his thoughts. "You know I didn't like you when I first met you. I thought you were soft and went around with your nose in the air."

"I was and I did," Cam admitted.

"You ain't the same man."

"No, I suppose not." He threw a cursory glance at Christopher and remembered him backing up his claim of ignorance of Ketl in the jail. "Nor are you," he said. "We all changed, didn't we?"

"Yeah, she has a way about her of doing that, changing people."

They were quiet for a time, each remembering the events of the past month.

Hot hair blasted him in the face. Christopher chuckled. "By the way where am I taking you."

"I had planned on using my rental car to get to the Hopi mesa. It's parked at the laboratory."

"I'll take you to the Hopi mesa. It's the least I can do."

"Yeah, that's maybe a better idea than going to the lab and seeing Stanley again. Besides you can see Woody. He's waiting for me at the mesa."

"My grandfather?" He asked incredulously. "He drove all the way to the Hopi mesa?"

"In the Jeep."

"The Jeep? The battery has been dead in that thing for years."

"It started right up when I drove it."

"But that's impossible."

Cam shrugged. "Nothing is impossible since Ketl came into our lives. The Jeep gives a hell of a spark when it starts."

Christopher's jaw sagged. "And Woody is driving it? I can't believe it."

"I've got my fingers crossed he made it all the way to the Hopi mesa. That's the one place Ketl would be safe from Stanley. I told him he could make the drive. I told him to look straight ahead and not stop until the mesas came into sight, and Ketl is with him. She won't let anything happen to him. She has a god called Mockingbird who has a way of making people do things they think they can't."

"Man, I hope you're right," Chris said and took the car up to 60 miles per hour.

ᔥ   ᔥ   ᔥ

It was nearly dark by the time they reached the three mesas of the Hopi clan. They had stopped in Gallup for gas and some junk food to eat, and Cam made a point of buying a six pack of beer and a bottle of mineral water.

The plan had been for Woody and Ketl to wait for him where the road to the middle mesa branched off from the highway. He wasn't sure how long he would be held in Farmington, and he told them that if he didn't come by nightfall to go to the mesa, tell Qommatu and Tommy Bright Eagle what had happened. He knew they would be safe there—Ketl anyhow—and Cam bet Woody could talk his way into a bed for the night. Although he wasn't too thrilled about facing Tommy Bright Eagle again, it was the best place for Ketl. He'd like to see Stanley facing the Hopi clan and asking for his Indian back.

As it was, Christopher and Cam pulled up to the road at the base of the mesa, alongside Woody's Jeep. Woody and Ketl stood beside the Jeep, surrounded by numerous Hopis including Tommy Bright Eagle, Qommatu, Stella Red-Feather and young children. There seemed to be a heated discussion going on; Stella yelled at Ketl; Woody looked rather dazed; Bright Eagle looked mean and angry as usual. His whole tribe was bunched behind him. It didn't look good. Out of the pan and into the fire, as they say.

Ketl saw Cam and flew into his arms. He was her man. He had not let her down, and she knew the ache in her heart, the tingle in her womb, was the beginning of a long and glorious love.

As Cam pulled Ketl to him and encased her in his arms, Bright Eagle scowled and started toward them.

Protectively, Ketl pushed Cam away from her and spat venomous words at Bright Eagle. "I will never be your wife!" Now she clung onto Cam and gazed at him with trusty eyes. "He is my man!"

"He has not claimed you, I have!" the huge Indian charged.

Cam broke from Ketl, ran to the car, returned to her with the bottle of mineral water in his hand, snapped off the lid and held it to Ketl. "Would you care for a drink of water?" he asked.

"Yes," she replied, her long, slender fingers reaching out, crossing the span of centuries and accepting the water, thus welcoming his offer of marriage. She took the water, put it to her lips and drank every drop.

From his pocket, Cam found the golden ring. For a long, ardent moment he searched her eyes. Then in front of all the watching eyes, he slipped the ring on her finger. With his fingers, he lifted her chin and lowered his mouth to hers. At the moment of contact he felt a zap pass between them. He felt her jerk too and knew she felt it. Pressing her to him, he deepened the kiss by parting her lips. He sensed her pleasure, the awe building in her, the passion yet to be tapped, the innocence awakened, the promise of long nights of pleasure.

Gently he lifted his head, sorry to end the kiss, but content to know she was his woman. "Ketl of Willow Canyon," he said in a whisper so only she could hear, "you and all that belongs to you, are mine and you are free to do with my love what you want."

Tears formed in the corners of her eyes. "And you, Cameron January, are welcome to me and all I have, to guard it until it is given to our daughters."

Although he knew their words held no tangible meaning, for Stanley and his men had confiscated all in her canyon, the words felt right. Tenderly he kissed her lips one more time. Holding her hand in his, he turned and faced Tommy Bright

Eagle, Qommatu and the others.

Clearing his throat, he stared at Bright Eagle. "She has been offered marriage, accepted, and married to me. You have no claim on her whatsoever."

In a rage Bright Eagle flew at Cameron January. To Cam it was as if looking at a cement wall coming at him. Cam pushed Ketl to Woody, dodged the assault, spread his legs and placed his hands in front of him in the ready position. Qommatu stepped forward, but Christopher stepped in front of him.

He pulled a revolver from the waist of his pants. "I shoot snakes with this," Christopher said to Qommatu. "Don't make me do it now."

Qommatu frowned, then backed away.

Cam circled the Hopi Indian. "It's a little more even this time, Bright Eagle. Just you and me. No guardian to do your dirty work."

Bright Eagle grunted and charged again. Cam stepped aside, spun and kicked his right leg into the Indian's stomach. Bright Eagle groaned. Staggering, his face red, he turned and charged Cam again.

Cam bounced on light feet. With yucca sandals on his feet, with eagle feathers to make him as light as the clouds, he bobbed and skipped in front of Bright Eagle while the Indian swung a fat fist at Cam's head. Cam dodged the fist, bobbed forward and delivered two quick chops to Bright Eagle's chest. Again Cam bounced. Again the Indian swung. This time Cam dodged it, went behind him, kicked him in the stomach so hard he heard all the air whoosh out of his lungs, then stuck a leg out and tripped the Indian. Bright Eagle went to the ground with a thud. His face was in the dust. Cam stepped across his back, then bent over and with a grunt, rolled Bright Eagle onto his back.

Dropping to his knees, he sat on the Indian's chest and brought back his hand. Bright Eagle's neck was exposed and there was no mistaking the fatal danger of Cam's raised hand. Tommy Bright Eagle's body shook violently as he waited for the lethal blow.

For a second Cam's hand shook, then Cam brought it down and pushed himself off the Indian. "You're not worth killing, you fat ape." Cam pointed a finger at Bright Eagle's nose. "I suggest you go back to your ancient ways and find your *harmony*, because, buster, you don't have any."

Cam brushed dirt off his pants as if to remove the memory of Bright Eagle. He went to Ketl and held her fiercely to him, while Bright Eagle's friends hauled him off the ground.

Woody stood next to his grandson, blinking to clear his eyes of an old man's tears of satisfaction. Christopher looked at Woody and saw him like he had never seen him before. He wasn't old; Christopher was just young, and not so smart after all. And Christopher watched the two of them, Ketl and Cam. Christopher smiled contentedly, knowing the city boy belonged with the Indian.

She had taught them all about life. This fantastical creature from another time, another dimension had shown them how to love, to respect, to see into one's self and find what was really there.

"What now?" Christopher asked.

Cam hugged Ketl. "We have some traveling to do. We have some writing to do, too. Woody's going to help with that." Cam studied Christopher for a moment. "Ah, what the hell," he said, patting Christopher on the shoulder, "you want to come along?"

Christopher sighed, smiling. "No, thanks, I have some of my own traveling to do. I think we'll be going in different directions."

"Where you goin'?" Woody asked Christopher.

"Me?" Christopher asked. "I'm headed to the city. I'm going to find what it is Cameron is giving up."

"It's 'bout time," Woody commented dryly.

"I've got an apartment in San Francisco," Cam told Christopher. He reached into his pockets and threw Christopher the keys. "You're welcome to it. I won't be coming back."

"Thanks, I'll give it a try. And you? Where are you going?"

"We have migrations to finish," Cam replied, looking at Woody and Ketl for some help in answering the question. Then he shrugged. "North, South, East, West? What's it going to be?"

Woody began to shuffle to the Jeep. "It's dam well going to be east. We're goin' to Flagstaff." He reached into the Jeep and pulled out his duffel bag. From it he extracted a handful of money. "I ain't spending the rest of my days bouncing around in no damn Jeep. My bones are nearly ground to smithereens. No sir. We're headed to the first car dealer in Flagstaff and I'm buying us a big, fancy motor home. From there I say we just keep on truckin' east. I've never seen the East." He was talking more to himself than anybody else. "I think I'd like to see the Cape and maple leaves in the fall. I hear tell lobster meat is sweeter than elk. I say that's pure bunk, but I think I should find out."

North, South, East or West, it didn't matter to Cam. He was in harmony with nature. He was in harmony with himself. He had Ketl, the last Anasazi, so what else mattered?

And to Ketl? There was a whole world to experience. Mockingbird was smiling down at her. Her migrations would be fulfilled. She would do what was expected of her since she was an Anasazi. Yet she had a new understanding of her true heritage, because she knew white blood ran in her veins, and she understood that wherever she went, she was and would always be the Last Anasazi.

Yes, Willow Canyon was lost to her, but Mockingbird had

assured her it wasn't important. To her people, new homes were discovered during migrations. East, south, west, north, somewhere there would be a new home, a new way of life. And with Cameron, she was headed on a new journey. This was the beginning of forever.

Slipping her hand into Cam's, her lips twisted into a wiry smile when she glanced at Cam. If she had her way, her heritage would be passed on to her offspring—she would teach the females and Cam would teach the males—and maybe, just maybe she would not be the last Anasazi after all.

For this is the way it was.